Advance F

"*Friends to Lovers* left me feeling desperately romantic. Prepare for a book hangover—I loved it."
—Annabel Monaghan, bestselling author of *Summer Romance*

"A spectacular debut, *Friends to Lovers* has everything that I love in a romance. You'll want to savor every moment of this stunningly romantic love story."
—Betty Cayouette, author of *One Last Shot* and creator of Betty's Book List

"Your heart will explode when you read this book. I defy you not to fall in love with Joni and Ren, and if ever you needed a message on not giving up—whether that's on love, life, or your hopes and dreams—this is it."
—Tessa Bickers, *USA TODAY* bestselling author of *The Book Swap*

"With stunning prose and sun-soaked vibes, Sally Blakely perfectly captures the magic of finding love in the person who knows you best. Joni and Ren will steal your heart."
—Ali Brady, *USA TODAY* bestselling author of *Until Next Summer*

FRIENDS TO LOVERS

A Novel

SALLY BLAKELY

CANARY STREET PRESS

**CANARY
STREET
PRESS™**

Recycling programs
for this product may
not exist in your area.

ISBN-13: 978-1-335-01424-5

Friends to Lovers

Copyright © 2025 by Sally McHugh

For questions and comments about the quality of this book, please contact us
at CustomerService@Harlequin.com.

TM is a trademark of Harlequin Enterprises ULC.

Canary Street Press
22 Adelaide St. West, 41st Floor
Toronto, Ontario M5H 4E3, Canada
CanaryStPress.com

Printed in Lithuania

MIX
Paper | Supporting
responsible forestry
FSC® C021394

For Levi, of course.

SEVEN YEARS AGO

I thought I knew how our story would go, two parallel lines stretching into forever. But in retrospect, our lives were never destined to take that shape.

If I had to pinpoint the moment they started to veer toward each other, it would be a Saturday afternoon in college. Ren and I were at our favorite arcade bar, defending our Ms. Pac-Man high score, and I had asked him to be my plus-one for an old friend's wedding the following week.

"You don't already have a date?" he said, chasing down an orange at one corner of the screen.

I watched as he barely avoided a ghost in a tunnel. "I just remembered it was even happening." I had RSVP'd months ago but forgot all about it until this morning, when I discovered the invitation buried under take-out menus, doodles, and Polaroids on my refrigerator.

"Ah," Ren said dryly. He let the game sound out his death and turned to me. "So I'm a last resort."

It was true that I hadn't had time to find a date, but Ren Webster was my best friend, a part of all my favorite moments, and there was no one I'd rather go with anyway. I widened my eyes innocently, trying to emulate one of his many noteworthy expressions. I used to say I hated his big brown eyes, that they had a way of doing me in, but in the end, it was just another thing I had misread.

After a minute, he relented. "If you can beat our high score," he said, smirking as he nodded me toward the game, "I'll go with you."

His reaction didn't seem important or all that surprising at the time. Just a joke between friends, another way to add *RAJ*—Ren and Joni—to the game's top standings.

And the wedding was yet another item to add to the list of all the dumb things we'd done together. I didn't think it would balloon, turn into anything beyond that one weekend. I didn't pause to think about the fact that he didn't hesitate long, and his yes was as good as certain. That I so easily forgot the wedding, that I didn't even try to find a real date.

I didn't pause to think about it at all until everything was already ruined.

But like any good story, life has its twists and turns, and sometimes, just when you think things are going to end up one way, those two lines head straight for each other.

SUNDAY

chapter one

I pull up to the salt-weathered house late Sunday afternoon, seagulls announcing themselves above and the ocean crashing in far below. As I step out of the car, I suck in the Pacific Northwest air, like it's the first breath I've taken in two and a half years. It's briny out here on the coast, where the sky stretches endless and blue over water that sparkles in tiny fractals, and where one week from now, my little sister will be married under the red-roofed lighthouse that juts out from the green headland a short walk away.

The trunk of the rental car heaves open with a groan, a stark contrast to the perfect Oregon day. It's fitting that my return to the West Coast would not only be on the heels of losing my job, but involve a dented Mazda that sounded like a freight train running off the tracks the entire way from PDX. Coming back here was never going to be easy, but the journey could have been a little kinder.

Inside, the house is largely the same. The kitchen sits at the front, the long oak table that we can all fit around under the windows. Through a small mudroom opposite are French doors leading to the screen porch that runs along one side of the house. When everyone else arrives the day after tomorrow, there will be laughter rolling in from the yard, conversation in the kitchen, music playing.

For now, there's only silence.

I drop my car keys on the granite island and walk my bags into the living room, where the sun streams in through the floor-to-ceiling windows. I should go upstairs and unpack, start the week on a responsible note, settle myself in before the others arrive. But a wave of all the memories this place holds suddenly washes over me, and I find myself unable to move another step. This house has seen me through so many versions of myself, and this newest one feels like a stranger here, an intruder.

I brace myself. If I'm going to survive this week, I need to pretend that I haven't intentionally been staying away these past few years. I take another deep breath, pour a glass of wine, and fold my legs under me on the couch. It was this view of the ocean that sold my parents and the Websters on the place when they purchased it together twenty years ago. And now, with the familiar feel of the sun warming my shoulders, the sight of the waves shimmering before me, that same view quiets my mind for the first time in days.

MONDAY

chapter two

I wake up the next morning sprawled face down on top of the comforter, a dull throb behind my right eye. What started as one glass of wine turned into three on the back deck as I watched the sun go down over the ocean, curled under a well-loved Pendleton throw in one of the Adirondack chairs out there.

I close my eyes again for a minute, listening to the waves rolling in, enjoying the cool breeze drifting through the window as it brushes across my neck.

And that's when I hear the front door.

My eyes fly open. I sit up and scramble for my phone, checking to see if Stevie has texted that she and her fiancé, Leo, decided to head up early, but I don't have any new messages. Still, it wouldn't be *that* unlike my sister to show up unannounced. I stand with far too much confidence for a hungover woman alone in a coastal house, and shuffle downstairs.

Just in case, in the living room, I pick up a heavy geode from a sideboard and raise it above my head as I approach the kitchen, ready to—what? Pummel someone at short range?

At the sound of keys being tossed onto the counter, I lower

the rock, my heart slowing. "Hello?" I call. "Stevie?" I poke my head through the door, catch sight of the person turning at my voice.

It is not my sister.

At first, I think I might be making him up, as if despite the energy I've spent repressing him since the second I stepped foot inside this house, some memory managed to spring free and wander around like a reminder of everything I've been missing. But this person is flesh and blood, fully corporeal.

I take him in like there's a curtain slowly rising up to reveal him. Here are the long legs that used to bike around town with me when we were kids, here are the forearms that used to lean against the bar across from me, here are strong shoulders and here is a head of messy, dark hair.

"Joni," Ren says, my name familiar on his lips. "Hi."

I stare back at him. Dust particles catch in the bands of light filtering in through the kitchen windows behind him like he's a particularly well-lit figure in an indie film. His gray T-shirt sits against the tan of his arms, Wayfarers tucked into the front pocket.

I had one more day to get ready for this, one more day to live in delusion that this moment might never come, that I would never have to face him. The person who knows—knew—me better than anyone in the world. The reason I've avoided Oregon for so long. I was going to be cool, casual, act like nothing had changed between us while our families were around and ignore him the rest of the time. I wasn't going to be alone with him.

If the vague nausea I was feeling before was because of the wine I drank last night, now it is firmly due to the fact that not only do I have to face him alone, but I have to do it pantsless, in only a Portland Mavericks T-shirt that hangs partway down my thighs. As luck or fate or the laughably unfair universe would have it, he's here a day early, wrecking my plans.

"Hi, Ren," I croak. I clear my throat. "I didn't know you'd be here." Obviously.

My eyes snag on the barely there lines that frame the corners of his mouth, twin parentheses serving as proof of how much joy I know can fill up his body. They deepen even when there's just a hint of a smile on his face. I used to chase them like I did his laugh. But Ren isn't smiling now.

"I'm sorry," he says, in what might be the most quintessentially Ren answer possible. He's apologizing, like he really did break into my personal vacation home. "I didn't mean to startle you. I would have called if—"

"No, it's okay." I hadn't told anyone I'd be here early, hadn't wanted to alert them to the reason—the sudden and dramatic end of a job I loved—behind my last-minute schedule change. There's no way Ren could have known I would be here. "What are you doing here?" I ask him.

It takes Ren a beat to answer. He reaches up to either tug at his hair or rub at his neck, but he releases his arm at the last second, settles his gaze on me. "I thought I'd head up before everyone arrives tomorrow to get some things out of the way," he says. "You know, mow the lawn, clear the path down to the lighthouse, that sort of thing."

Right. Ren *would* be here out of selfless reasons. As Stevie's maid of honor, I have a list of all the things I'll need to prepare for starting tomorrow, but Ren, helper that he is, is diving in well before anyone even asks him to.

"Of course," I say. "Same."

"Your hair—" Ren says, and I glance up in time to see him nodding toward me.

"Shorter," I say, smoothing the back of my hair, which just clears my shoulders, the only vestige of its former self my bangs. I cut it a year ago, after Stevie told me hair holds memory or emotion or something along those lines. I was willing to try anything to fill the hole that had taken up residence in my life.

"You're still—" I gesture at him, coming up short, nerves climbing up my neck. His hair looks like it's been trimmed recently, but it's still his usual style. His shoulders seem like they might be broader under his T-shirt, but he's always been in good shape, so maybe it's just a trick of the light. The ways he's different are too minute to mention: a face and body two and a half years older in ways only someone intimately familiar with them would notice.

"—tall," I finally finish, wincing a little.

"Yeah," Ren says. "Been trying my hardest to knock off a few inches, but..." He shrugs, and I realize too late he's trying to make a joke, so my laugh comes out stilted.

"Well," I say. "I'm in my old room, but I'll stay out of your way."

Ren raises a fist to his forehead. For a moment, the mask falls, his eyes honing in on me again. Ren's always had a way of seeing through me, and suddenly I'm sixteen again, crying against his shoulder because I just failed a math test, or eighteen, anxiously poring over a dog-eared welcome packet as we drive north to Portland as college freshmen, or twenty-seven, standing on a cold sidewalk on New Year's Eve, the last time I saw him.

"Right," Ren says, eyes still on mine, then, "Actually, I should probably mention—" He stops short when he sees the small flinch on my face, like I'm bracing for what he's going to say next. His fist drops to his side. "We're on the screen porch again this year."

I clamp my lips together. "Hmm?" I say.

"You and I," Ren says, nodding between us like *that* is the part of his sentence he needs to clarify. "They put us on the screened-in porch again this year."

"Who is *they*?" I ask, though there's only one possible answer. *Our families. The* other *people you've been avoiding.*

"Well," Ren says. "The last couple years—" He pauses.

I paste as placid a look on my face as possible, like it's normal that I haven't been here for the last two summers, like it's normal that he and I are no longer a *we*, bound together by something that I used to think was profound, and now just feels like time, proximity, all those things that can tie people together.

"Stevie and Leo have been in the room you two used to share, and Thad's in the one I usually take."

"No worries," I say, smile tight, already angling my way out of the kitchen. What did I expect? That they'd walk by my room in hushed reverence all this time, maintaining it like a shrine when there's hardly enough space for all of us as is? That Stevie and Leo wouldn't use it as their own? "Let me know if you need any help. Otherwise, I'll meet you on the screened-in porch tomorrow."

His brows bend toward each other and his eyes go dark. "Right. I won't get in your way, then."

I, a nearly thirty-year-old woman, salute him on my way out.

chapter three

There was a time I would have been thrilled if Ren and I had a whole day here to ourselves, but the idea of being alone with him now has me hurrying away as fast as I can. I speed-walk back down the hall, fly up the stairs two at a time, close my door quietly behind me before leaning against it and letting out the breath I've been holding.

It takes me a minute to clear my head, to sort through the conversation I half blacked out downstairs, catalog each item so I can proceed accordingly.

Ren. Ren is *here*. Not just here, but off doing something, existing like I've been doing a mediocre job pretending he doesn't these past years.

And after tonight, we'll be sharing a room for the rest of the week.

The thought makes me claustrophobic, like this house isn't big enough for us and all of our history.

I need to get out of here.

I stuff a tote bag with enough supplies to last me months and lug a camp chair down to the beach. It's one of the rare days when the temperature will climb into the eighties, the sun already beating down intensely, the sand scorching my feet. I slather my shoulders in sunscreen and settle in with a book, ready to escape into the tale of a woman who falls in love with a guy five hundred years her senior, but it's okay because he's magic and heir to some throne.

But after a while, I realize I've read the same paragraph four times. The words are blurring in front of me, and the corners of the book keep digging into my legs.

I toss the book aside and trade it for my phone.

"Leo wants to play capture the flag," Stevie says by way of an answer.

"He— Now?" I drag my sunglasses back down my face now that I've abandoned the romantasy.

"No, on Wednesday." She's rummaging around on the other end of the line, a series of clinks and thumps.

"Stevie, you're going to have to provide a little more clarity than that," I say, pressing my toes into the sand.

She sighs. The rummaging stops. "It's some big tradition," she says. "He and his brother organized a whole crosstown event when they were kids. It's his singular request."

"Fair enough." I pull my phone away from my ear when there's a sound like an entire shelf of books has caved in. "What are you doing?"

"I'm in our office." Stevie huffs. "It was *someone's* bright idea to store all the band's extra shit in our suitcases to save space, but now I actually need to use them."

"Ah," I say. "The tour." Immediately following their honeymoon, Stevie will be joining Leo on his band's North American tour for the first three months of their marriage.

"Hey," Stevie says. "Where are you?"

"Just at home." The lie comes surprisingly quickly. I'd decided to wait to tell anyone about being fired until after Stevie's wedding. Coming here early to regroup had seemed like the perfect way to prepare myself for a week of lying to my family. That is, until the person I most dreaded seeing showed up early too.

"Last I checked, you couldn't hear the ocean in your apartment."

I grip the arms of the chair, curl my toes in the sand. Down the beach, a family is rapidly approaching, sand pails in the hands of a pair of shrieking kids, the father's booming voice telling them to slow down.

"Oh, it's a playlist," I say.

"What?"

"I listen to it when I'm trying to sleep. You know, rain sounds, ocean sounds."

"Huh," Stevie mutters. "Were you trying to sleep?"

"No. Just…" I scramble, trying to lie better. "Couldn't wait a second longer to hear those seagulls!" It comes out like a carnival worker trying to sell a wailing kid on a ride.

"What's going on?" she asks.

I squeeze my eyes shut, readying myself for this week to implode before it's even started.

"Is it because of Ren?" she asks. "Seeing him tomorrow."

Stevie is the only person in my family who knows Ren and I haven't spoken in the last two and a half years. She's confirmed no one else is the wiser on the Webster side of things either, so at the very least, Ren and I implicitly agree that our families should be spared our drama. But Stevie doesn't know what happened between us, the line we crossed. Something else Ren and I implicitly agree on, I guess.

"I'm a little stressed," I admit. A breeze moves through the beach grass behind me, teasing my neck. "But we'll be fine, Stevie. We're two people who used to be friends, and now we're not, and that's it."

Stevie snorts. "Yeah. That's *it*."

"Let's talk about the schedule for the week," I say, the sun catching my eye as it bounces off a dory fishing boat bobbing by. I squint out at it, then at where the waves come to tiny points of light. "You don't need to worry about Ren and me."

Stevie sighs again, but relents. "You'll probably get there before us tomorrow. Sorry we can't pick you up at the airport."

"It's fine." I don't mention that it's also the perfect cover for why I will have arrived before they do. Stevie and Leo are stopping at our parents' house on the way to the coast tomorrow morning so they can pack up all the wedding things they've been storing there: bins filled with favors, decorations, enough napkins for every wedding guest to douse theirs and their neighbors' in gasoline and still have extra.

"I think Ren will be there early tomorrow too," Stevie says.

"Will he," I say.

"Will you be okay?"

"Stevie," I warn.

"Fine, fine. Never mind."

We go over the order of things: everyone's arrival tomorrow, Leo's capture-the-flag tradition on Wednesday, the combined bachelor and bachelorette Thursday night, wedding setup before the rehearsal dinner on Friday.

"Can't believe I'm getting married," Stevie says.

I pick at a piece of vinyl peeling off the arm of my chair. "Couldn't be anyone but Leo," I say.

"I know. I hate it so much." The speed at which Stevie, former queen of no-commitment, fell for sunny, golden-retriever Leo surprised everyone. But she still has to be Stevie about it.

"Sure you do." I bring my knees up to my chest and gaze back out at the white-capped, endless Pacific that's been the backdrop to so much of our lives.

"Are you really going to be okay this week?" she asks.

I glance over my shoulder toward the house, where I can hear the sound of the mower running in the distance. "This week isn't about me, Stevie," I say, determined not to give her anything to run with. Ren is the A&R manager for Leo's band, Bearcat, and Stevie and Leo spend a fair amount of time with him in Portland, a fact that caused a lot of sleepless nights when I first realized it. Ren isn't just some person I can write out. His life will always be irrevocably intertwined with mine.

"It is if I want it to be. I'm the bride, and I don't like that much attention."

"Says the person who invited almost two hundred people to her wedding."

"Only half of them are coming. And I didn't invite them. My fiancé has never met a person he didn't like."

By the time we hang up, the sun is shifting toward afternoon in the sky, burning off the last of the mist hanging over the dense, coastal Oregon forest on either side of the house. The family from earlier is fading back the direction they came.

I stretch my arms over my head, twist back toward the house. I can just glimpse Ren at the far side of the yard, pushing the ancient mower in clean lines back and forth, avoiding the rocky patch where it slopes at the bottom and making sharp, careful turns at each end. He pauses, the sound of the mower dying as he peels his sweat-damp shirt over his head, his skin glistening in the August sun and—

I wrench my eyes away, but not before they've caught on him pulling the starter once, twice, the muscles in his back working.

I turn back around and wade into the freezing water.

That night, after trying and failing to distract myself, scrolling and not responding to a string of texts from my former coworkers "just checking in," repacking my suitcase for when I move into what's beginning to feel like the jail cell Ren and I will be sharing tomorrow, I turn off the lamp above my bed—Stevie and Leo's bed, more accurately—and roll over to get some sleep for what will probably be the last time this week. I close my eyes and count my breaths, do that thing where you clench every muscle in your body then relax five times in a row, tell myself a particularly boring story.

But after what feels like hours, I'm still awake. I check the time on my phone—twenty-eight minutes have passed—and flop back onto my pillows. My brilliant plan to come up here early has already failed, and tomorrow feels more daunting than ever. It's an unnerving combination, being in this place that's supposed to bring me so much solace while feeling so on edge.

Ren and I managed to stay out of each other's way today. When I walked into the kitchen to make myself dinner, I noticed his car was gone and wondered again, for a minute, if I made him up. If I'd been so worried about seeing him that I crafted some narrative that he showed up early.

But now I can *feel* him in the house, like I used to be able to feel him across town, across campus, across Portland, across the country, some point at the other end of a line that tethered us.

I kick the blankets off, stare at the ceiling. This nudge at my center that shifts with him, like every time he turns over in bed, he tugs a little—it used to be a comfort. Now it just feels like something else I can't control.

SIX YEARS AGO

Claudia and Clark

Portland, Oregon

chapter four

Ren knocks on my door at exactly the time he promised. I weave through the maze of boxes stacked in my living room and whip it open.

"Why are you always so punctual?" I ask, hurrying back to my bathroom and leaving the door for Ren to close. Tonight is my cousin's wedding, and I'm still in a baggy T-shirt, my hair half-done.

"Why did you tell me you lost that shirt?" he calls after me. The shirt—one of my favorites, perfectly soft, hitting the exact right spot on my thighs—is technically his, the logo of the music venue/record label where he works emblazoned on the front.

"Because I plotted for months to make this shirt my own!" I pick up my curling iron from the counter, try one last time to get my bangs to sit right. In the mirror, I catch Ren fiddling with my phone in the living room. I know exactly what he, the music aficionado, is up to. "Don't change this song!"

Ren sets my phone back on a box and holds up his hands. "Don't You (Forget About Me)" plays on undisturbed.

"You like that song," I say as he comes over and rests a shoulder against the bathroom door frame.

"As a person, of course I do." He runs a hand through his hair. "But you still have a week left in Portland. Save something morbid like this for the plane."

"Ren," I say, patting his cheek. "I'll *never forget about you.*"

He rolls his eyes and ducks his head away.

A month ago, when I'd announced I'd be moving across the country, Ren was, understandably, shocked. I could still barely believe it myself. I'd been interning at Novo, a stop-motion studio, since graduation, hoping for something permanent to come along, but it never crossed any of our minds that my dream job would open up in the company's new New York office. Leaving Portland, the life I'd established here, wouldn't be easy, but after a year of despairing as one by one my peers secured grown-up roles, as my mom warned me about "putting all my eggs in one basket," a not-small part of me was so relieved that I pounced on the opportunity like a cat on a mouse.

When I told him the news, Ren had stared at me in silence for a good minute. But then his face broke into a huge smile, and he wrapped me up in a breath-stealing, congratulatory hug, and my own shock dissipated a little along with his.

"I'll miss you too, Joni," he says now, resettling against the door frame. "But at least we have the weddings, right?"

"Weddings?" I ask, meeting his eye in the mirror as I prop myself against the counter, mascara wand in hand.

"There's *always* a wedding, Joni."

"Ah, right." I slam a fist to my forehead. "The plight of your twenties."

"And we'll *always* need plus-ones," he says suggestively.

After my old summer camp friend's wedding last summer, I went with Ren to his coworker's in the spring. We'd both decided that it was simpler just to take each other as dates rather than have a wedding be a first date with a stranger. But as fun as it's been, plus-oneing is easier when you live on the same coast.

"I don't know," I say, amused by Ren's optimism, skeptical that this won't end in disappointment. It assumes schedules align, time off is approved, we're invited to weddings. It means promising to drop everything to be each other's plus-ones from now until some unidentified end date. And then there's the obvious flaw. "We always get plus-ones? And we're always single?" I ask him.

Ren shrugs a shoulder in a *who the hell cares* motion. "It's tradition now. We're each other's plus-ones." He leans toward me, brown eyes never leaving mine. "It's a way for us to make sure we still see each other sometimes."

Sometimes. The word hits me square in the chest. "Ren, I'll still come home for holidays," I say. "There's still the beach house. We'll be fine." This is what I've been telling myself over the last couple weeks, as the move has become more real, and it's true. We don't need this tradition to ensure we'll keep in touch. Ren and I are fixed, a constant, best friends since age three, and no amount of distance will change that. We'll still be *us*.

His eyes trace over my face, something falling in his gaze. A muscle moves in his jaw as he frowns, almost imperceptibly, then notices me watching him in the mirror. "Of course," he says, with a small smile, nodding. He pushes off the door and walks down the hall.

I adjust a final piece of my hair, then head into my room to get dressed. Ren is lying on my bed, knees bent over the end and feet planted on the floor. His eyes are closed, arms crossed over his chest. He looks defeated.

"You all good down there?" I ask, sinking onto the bed next to him.

"Mmm," Ren mumbles, the sound low and rough at the edges. I can feel it reverberate through me. "Just tired. Show ended late last night."

"What's going on with a new position?" Ren is ever politely trying to climb the ladder at Sublimity, where he's been bartending for the last two years and is now their lead sound tech during the week. Music is what he loves, what he's good at, and he works so hard. No one deserves it more.

"Nothing new," he says. "It's fine."

He uncrosses his arms, absentmindedly rubs the hem of my T-shirt between his fingers. Our gazes both drop to the spot, but when I look back up at his face, it hits me. His suggestion that we make our plus-one arrangement a tradition, his expression when I all but dismissed it... Ren is worried, *really* worried, about what this move will mean for our friendship. And all these weeks I've been throwing it in his face, showing him pictures of the apartment I'll be sharing with my sister, who will be attending graduate school at NYU, asking him to help me with packing.

"Hey," I say, leaning over him, propping my arm next to his shoulder to hold myself up. Ren is good at hiding his emotions, and all these weeks I should have remembered that, and stopped for one second, among all the chaos, to tell him how much I'm going to miss him, to reassure him that I could *never* forget him. "We'll do it," I tell him, my hip pressed against his. "We're each other's plus-ones."

"Joni, it's stupid," he says, head starting to roll to the side, but I grab his chin.

"It's not stupid," I say. "It's a good idea." He's right. A plan wouldn't hurt. We'll make it work.

He doesn't respond, and suddenly I feel nervous he'll say no. That my initial reaction made him change his mind. That there's nothing I can say to reassure him. I bring my face over his, like the proximity might prove I'm serious. "I *want* to."

We stay like that for a while before he slowly smiles, an exhale of a laugh coming out of him. He pulls me into his chest, my head just under his chin. "Okay," he murmurs against my hair.

I close my eyes, let the familiar scent of him envelop me, until I'm reminded of the time, and I spring up from my bed, grab my dress from where it's hanging over my closet door. "Close your eyes," I say, and he does, pressing a hand over them for good measure. I tug my shirt over my head and toss it on the bed next to him before slipping on my dress.

"Done," I tell him. I lift my hair off my neck. "Zip?"

Ren pushes himself up and walks over to where I'm standing in front of my mirror. I watch as he zips my dress—green, wrestled off a rack in a vintage shop down the street. His eyes meet mine in the reflection. "You clean up nice, Miller," he says, fingers going still.

I straighten a strap of my dress. "You don't look so bad yourself, Webster."

Ren nods toward the door. "Should we get going?"

"Two minutes," I say.

In the bathroom, I put on a pair of tiny gold hoops and spritz perfume onto my wrists. As I'm inspecting myself one last time, my eyes find Ren waiting for me in the living room, a skyscraper in the middle of the low-lying buildings that are my packed-up belongings.

"Joni?" he calls.

"Coming!" I say, then, cringing, "Wait, I need ChapStick, just—thirty more seconds." I rush back to my bedroom and root around one of the boxes there until I find a tube of Burt's Bees.

When I turn to go, a flash of white catches my eye. The Sublimity T-shirt, carefully folded on my pillow.

chapter five

When my mom informed me I would be the one to represent the family tonight while she and my dad are out of town and my sister is at orientation, I almost said no. Historically, I have not been the biggest fan of my cousin Claudia. But her wedding might have me forgiving some of her past transgressions.

"The *vibes*," I say to Ren as we enter the romantically lit room, its long walls broken up by high, arched windows and doors that lead out to a greenery-lined rooftop. Everything inside is done up in golds and deep greens, tiny touches of blush in the centerpieces.

We head straight to the bar. The venue is above a cidery in downtown Portland, and we clink tiny glasses of what a sign says is Whiskey Pear, pale and sparkling and aged in bourbon barrels.

"You can count the number of hangovers in the works in this room," Ren says, wincing as he sets his glass back on the bar.

We order something lighter and meander out to the terrace. It's the kind of late-summer evening that makes everything feel happily slow. Sleeves are pushed above elbows, heads tilted toward the waning sun.

We stop at the balcony railing, Ren twisting to lean his back against it, his arm stretching along it.

Ren is one of those people who seems like he might have been made for formal wear: tall, long, lean lines, and an ability to coolly adjust a cuff, a collar. He's a different version of my best friend when he puts on a tie. Ren's always been handsome, in a way that began to attract attention sometime around tenth grade and followed us all the way to college in Portland, where the usual cast of girls obsessed with him got even bigger. It's not that I don't get it. I too tend to notice good arms and hair that looks like a tortured hand has just been run through it, teeth that should be in a Colgate ad. But there's also a picture of Ren wearing my Minnie Mouse swimsuit at my fifth birthday party sitting on the mantel at my parents' house, so at a certain point, his vague Peter Parker charm lost some of its impact.

The crowd shifts around us as the cocktail hour winds down and people begin to find their seats. Ren grabs my hand and guides us to a row near the back, where we can carry on our own quiet commentary without being too noticeable.

The music starts up, a string arrangement of a song that sounds familiar but I can't totally place. Claudia floats down the aisle in a dress with a train so long the photographer nearly trips trying to tiptoe around it. Once she reaches Clark, their Australian shepherd escapes with the rings attached to his collar tags. Ren presses a finger to my lips, trying to shush my laughter, but his shoulders shake too as Clark's best man lurches after the dog, sprawling across the front row as he tries and fails to catch him before Claudia's train slows him down long enough for one of her bridesmaids to nab him.

After dinner (wood-fired pizza bar: good, the receiving line: disorganized and short-lived, the DJ: late), we make our way to the dessert bar and wander back to our table with cake and coupes. My uncle gives a speech that raises the question of whether he even likes Clark, and Claudia's maid of honor hiccups her way through a toast about friendship, and then the DJ has arrived, and people are dancing, and the room is loud, and the bourbon-barrel cider this place is advertising as "shots" is flowing freely.

Ren spins me to "Dancing in the Moonlight" before I loop my arms around his neck for Ray LaMontagne's "Hold You in My Arms." Claudia and Clark sway gently nearby, guests milling around between the bar and the dance floor.

"Add this song to my wedding playlist," I say to Ren, who nods as if that playlist actually exists. It's one of the songs that would play through Ren's laptop speakers while we studied in his dorm room in college, soothing and slow no matter the context.

He turns me, palm sliding across my back. "I'm happy we'll have the weddings," he says, voice low. "I'm really going to miss you."

"I'm really going to miss you too," I tell him, swallowing against a sudden ache in my throat.

I've never had to say goodbye to Ren before. He, our friendship, is my anchor, has held me for as long as I can remember, and I've spent most of my life with the certainty that on any given day, if I want to see him, I can. Sure, there was the month he spent in Indonesia when his family went to meet his brother's husband's family, the semester I spent in Edinburgh. But I was always coming back to him, or him to me, and it strikes me now that while I've said goodbye to plenty of other people—friends, coworkers who opted to accept severance packages instead of relocating—actually saying goodbye to Ren hasn't ever felt real.

I tuck my face against his chest, hang on to him a little tighter. Ren has a habit of holding steady when he suspects I'm struggling, and the truth is I still haven't been able to shake the look in his eyes from earlier, the one I can tell he's been fighting to keep in all night. Maybe he was right to be nervous. Maybe

I've worked too hard to convince myself that I don't need to be. *Will* we still be us if we're not in the same city? If I have a bad day here, I can go over to Ren's place. If I need to talk to him, I can stop in at Sublimity. There's never more than half an hour between us. Once I move, though, going over will become a phone call, one he might miss. We'll have the weddings, but we won't have Wednesday night dinners.

Sometimes Ren knows how I'm feeling before I do.

After a few more songs, Ren pulls us over to the line for the photo booth. I try to push aside the thought of leaving him, pay attention to the time we do have left instead. We rifle through the table of props, feather boas and oversize sunglasses, tiaras, and cutouts glued to the end of flimsy dowels, things like *Congrats, Clark and Claudia!* and *I do!*

"Here," I say, stretching up to plonk a captain's hat on his head. I adjust it so it sits at an angle, framing him with my fingers. "You're missing something."

"A boat?" he asks as I comb through a box of scarves until I find a striped blue one, tiny lobsters dancing along the edge. "The ability to sail?"

"You could sail if you wanted to," I say, tucking the silky fabric under his collar, knotting it above his tie. "You certainly *look* like you could sail."

"Do you want me to learn how to sail, Joni?" Ren asks, head dipped toward me.

I link my elbow in his, lean my cheek against his arm. "I'll be your first mate."

"What, are we attempting to complete the first circumnavigation of the globe?"

"Boats still have crews," I point out. "First mate is still a station on a ship."

"Who knew you were so up on your nautical trivia," Ren says as laughter bursts from the photo booth and it expels no fewer than seven people, like a clown car unloading.

It's a tight fit inside, which makes the fact of the party before us even more impressive. After a minute of trying to arrange ourselves, Ren tugs me onto his lap, his arm wrapping around my waist to keep me from slipping off. He draws the curtain closed, the lights around the camera pinging on.

"Okay, what's our plan?" I ask, shifting so I can sling my arm around his shoulders.

"We have to have a plan?"

I make a face at him. If this strip of photos is going to serve as a reminder of our last hurrah in Portland together, it needs to fully encompass our friendship.

"We've been in photo booths before. We didn't have a plan then."

"One. One photo booth," I say. "And we were drunk, so it doesn't count. I look like a mole rat in those pictures."

"Two," Ren says while I fix my hair in the warped mirror affixed to the wall.

"What?"

"Two photo booths," he says. "The one you're talking about, at that bar in college, and the one at the fair when we were sixteen."

I look down at him. "The phantom photo booth." We'd stumbled upon it, cotton candy in hand, just sitting in between the livestock pavilions like it was off-limits. We'd ducked inside, taken one strip of photos before it stopped accepting our money. When we'd tried to find it again later, to see if we could get any more pictures out of it, it was gone.

Someone bangs on the side of the present photo booth. "Are you done?" a voice slurs.

Ren leans forward and presses the button to trigger the countdown. "Just—look happy," he says. He grins at the camera.

I reach up to remove an errant feather from my mouth as a series of beeps lets us know the first picture is impending.

"I *am* happy," I say. "But this has to be perf—" The flash goes off, and I scramble to rearrange myself, sitting up straighter. Ren shifts underneath me, resting his other hand on my thigh to steady me, something unfamiliar vibrating through me at the contact.

"Just make a funny face," he says.

"What funny face?"

"I don't know. The funny face you make when you have two seconds until the flash goes off," he says as fast as he can, so the words all blur together. I go with the most obvious option: holding up two fingers behind Ren's head while he crosses his eyes at the camera.

"Okay, now look at me like you love me," I say as the countdown begins again. I set a hand on either side of Ren's face, shake my hair back from my shoulders. When I look down at him, he's staring up at me, brown eyes gone as soft as I've ever seen them.

"I *do* love you," he says.

His cheeks are warm under my palms, and I'm suddenly mesmerized by the shape of his jaw, my finger grazing along it. I'm so used to looking up at Ren that this perspective feels strange, like I can study him from a different angle. I feel his hand flex against my waist as his eyes move to my lips, slowly work their way back up my face. When his gaze locks onto mine again, the molecules in the air between us seem to go still, time halting, our breaths hitching. There are vague beeps in the background, the countdown about to end, but they don't fully register. I tilt closer, his hand tightening on my thigh as my eyes start to close—

The flash goes off.

We spring apart, Ren's elbow whacking against the wall behind him as my head bounces against the opposite one.

"What do we do for the last picture?" I say, pulse hammering in my ears. Ren's hands are still on me, and I am still on his lap, and his face isn't that much farther from mine than it was three seconds ago because this photo booth is simply *not that big.*

"Just—look happy," Ren says again, his voice rough.

The camera clicks for a final time, and I yank the curtain open and all but fall out, gasping like I'm breaching the surface of a lake. Ren stumbles out behind me.

"I think I need some air. Want to get us drinks?" I force out as he grabs the strip of photos from the slot at the bottom of the machine.

Ren barely has time to reply before I'm winding through the crowd, shoving through a door on the far wall and bursting out into the cool night air.

I amble over to the terrace railing. Something is itching at the corners of my brain, energy racing up and down my arms. I fold them in front of me, press my fingers into the creases of my elbows, count my breaths, try to will away the images of what almost just happened. If I'd leaned a little closer, let my lips brush against his, if his hand had climbed into my hair—

When Ren joins me again, I accept the glass he hands me and take a long drink.

"Here," he says as he digs into his pocket and produces the strip of photos. "You keep these."

"Thanks." I jam them into my purse without looking.

Ren leans his arms on the railing next to me and we stare out at the lights of Portland. He sips his drink, casually checks the time on his phone. "Predictions?" he suddenly asks, sliding his elbow over to lightly tap against mine. It's a game we play where we guess at what will happen during our vacation with our families, like the one that begins tomorrow, both a tradition and this year a marker of my last week in Oregon. Six days at the house we've been going to since we were kids, the one our parents bought together in a fit of youthful hope: visions of us growing up there, vacations on the coast, a second home.

I finally look at him. Ren's acting so unaffected, his shoulders relaxed, breathing even. I can't decide if he's doing this to be nice, if he noticed the way my hands shook slightly when I took the drink, or if I imagined that moment in the photo booth altogether, that my emotions are just on high alert because I'm leaving, because I'm going to miss him. ·

"Stevie and Sasha get wine drunk the first night," I predict about our sisters, playing along.

"Our moms scold them," Ren says, his lips tugging upward. "But they've had more wine than them by the end of the night."

The images of life at the house start to slow my breathing as we settle into a familiar routine. "Thad and Sasha get into it about her shower schedule," I say. Ren's siblings are always fighting over the shower, so his sister has constructed a detailed plan for all of us to avoid any major blowups. "Thad and Gemi slow dance around the living room by...night two?"

"You move back onto the screen porch because Stevie won't stop snoring," Ren says.

"Only to discover you've already moved back out there too."

"So my sleep talking keeps you up anyway."

"I'm already up," I say. "And I so prefer your sleep talking to Stevie's snoring."

Ren laughs. We go on and on, trading predictions until they become utterly ridiculous. By the time we've finished our drinks, the photo booth seems like a distant memory for Ren, and so it becomes one for me too.

On Monday, we drive to the coast, the playlist Ren made for the car ride on. He drums out the rhythms against the steering wheel. The house has always been a special place, where the outside world—and all its worries—seem to fall away. We spend the week wading as far into the frigid, crashing Pacific as our bravery will let us, sprawling on the beach and shaking sand out from the pages of our vacation books. We drink chilled reds from the natural winery a few miles down the road and coordinate meals. We walk on the beach, nap in the afternoons, laugh our way through old movies, sit up late huddled in a blanket on the sand with Thad, Sasha, and Stevie, the soft din of our parents' voices floating down from the back patio, start and end every day together. It's the perfect send-off, which is what I say when we're all hugging each other outside the house on our last day, what I remind Ren of when he picks me up to drive me to the airport the next morning.

But on the ride there a knot begins to form in my chest, my anxiety about leaving growing as the minutes until departure tick down. When it's time to say goodbye at the security line, I'm having trouble breathing around it. "Can you imagine a better way to say goodbye to Oregon than a week at the house?" I choke out because I have to say something. I'd planned to worry my way through security alone, but Ren is Ren and insisted on paying for parking, walking me in, carrying my bags.

He shakes his head wordlessly and hugs me tight against him. I lock my hands together behind his back like I might never let go, wrap myself around this person so fundamental to me.

"New York's lucky to have you," he says into my hair.

I lean my head back to look up at him, chin against his chest. His arms are slightly freckled from all the time we spent in the sun this week, the back of his neck tan from his morning runs.

"I'll call you every day," I say.

He chuckles. "You'll be too busy to call me every day."

He starts to pull away and I tighten my grip because I don't want that Ren right now, the one who tries to hide behind levity, who never asks for anything. "We'll talk every day. Promise?"

He brushes a thumb under my right eye where a tear has escaped, lets it linger as he scans my face. "I promise," he finally says. He loosens an arm to reach into his pocket and withdraw his phone, taps on the screen before he pockets it again. "I made you a playlist."

I reach for my own phone, but Ren stops me.

"Look at it once you're through security." His fingers slip through mine and he squeezes, once, before he lets go. "Let me know when you land, okay?"

It feels unceremonious, like I should say something profound, but all I can manage is a nod.

When I'm next in the security line, I turn back, hopeful he might still be there, that he might give me one last boost of confidence. He's standing right where I left him, watching me. He smiles reassuringly, lifts a hand, and I wave back, big and exaggerated, because our last moment can't be a sad one. Ren and I will be fine, but I still hate the burn at the back of my nose, the way my stomach sinks. I keep waving until he laughs, mirrors me.

On the plane, I add the playlist to my library. It's long, as Ren's playlists tend to be. I take off to Death Cab for Cutie's "Marching Bands of Manhattan," observing Portland and all the greenery surrounding it shrink below me.

I smile to myself when "Don't You (Forget About Me)" comes on next, the image of Ren in his suit in my bathroom doorway flashing across my mind. He was right: the song feels more appropriate now.

The mood picks up from there, numbers that we loved in college, in high school, ones we've listened to in his car with the windows down and bands we've seen live together.

Then halfway through the flight, it changes again. "Where'd All the Time Go?", Langhorne Slim's "Changes," and "The Only Living Boy in New York"—Ren seems to have intuited the melancholy I would feel spreading down to my toes as the distance between my old life and my new one began to grow.

I sift through all the ways things are about to change. Learning a new city, new job, my whole routine shifting, of course, but also things like a new neighborhood coffee shop, time zones, not knowing that Sublimity is where I'll be going on a

Friday night. That there's a boy waiting for me there behind the bar.

By the time we're an hour out, the songs are upbeat again, and I spend the rest of the flight vibrating in my seat, reading through the emails my boss has sent about our first month in the new space once, then again, then scroll through the pictures Stevie sent me of our new place.

We land, and I rush out of the airport with my two giant suitcases and an unfounded air of someone who's actually been to New York before. I get in the back of a car and watch through the window as my new city flies by.

I call Ren and tell him all about it.

TUESDAY

chapter six

Ren is nowhere to be found when I move my things to the screen porch after a fitful night of sleep.

He's taken his usual bed, which is closer to the doors into the house. It's flawlessly made, also as usual, and I make a mental note not to let mine turn into the tangle of blankets it normally would be this week. Things like that were fine when we were close. Now I feel a sudden need to behave around Ren like I'm sharing a room with a colleague.

The same small dresser stands against the opposite wall, a row of hooks beside it where we would dry swimsuits and towels when we were kids. A black hoodie hangs on the farthest hook, the rest of them empty.

As my hands hover over the dresser, wondering if Ren left the top two for me like he used to, the door to the front yard clatters and I jump, letting out a small yelp.

"Sorry," Ren says as he removes his earbuds. He's just back from a run in a pair of exercise shorts and a T-shirt. He nods at the dresser. "I left you your usual drawers."

"Thanks."

"Did you sleep well?" he asks politely, inserting his earbuds into their case.

I stare at the middle of his chest, the rise and fall of it. "Sort of. You?"

He shrugs, casually grabs his water bottle from the windowsill above his bed, then sits on the edge, dangles it between his knees. Maybe I should do the same thing. Sit down, let him set the pace.

I opt to pick at the flaking paint on the corner of the dresser. "How's—" I begin, but Ren says something at the same time, and I wave him forward only for him to do the same.

"Were—" he says, gesturing toward me.

"No," I say. "Were you going to say something?"

Ren shakes his head.

The silence between us lasts for what feels like a lifetime.

"Well," Ren says, standing. It puts us that much closer in this narrow room, my spine pressed against the dresser, the backs of his legs touching his bed like he's trying to keep as much space between us as possible. Still, if we wanted to, we could reach out and brush our fingertips together. The sudden image has me clearing my throat, shifting on my feet. Ren seems to notice my discomfort and moves toward the door. "I'm going to shower. Sasha just texted that they should be here in an hour or so."

"Thanks," I say. I don't know why I'm thanking him.

After quickly unpacking, I make my way to the front porch and watch the spot where the road breaks through the trees, willing a car to appear through it, other people to join us.

Stevie's been texting me from the road too, noting every landmark they pass and sending me blurry, terrible photos of each. The fruit stand where we used to stop when we were kids to load up on cherries and peaches and plums. The gas station that hasn't ever actually been in service and we're convinced was built to be used as a movie set. The tunnel we used to hold our breath through. Things I hardly saw as I drove here on

Sunday in something of a fugue state, half-obsessed with dissecting the details of my firing and half in emotional free fall over being in Oregon again, both of which I very much didn't want to feel and was trying desperately to reconcile with the celebratory week ahead.

Ren comes out a half hour later and sits next to me. He drums his fingers against the arm of his chair, but doesn't attempt to make conversation. I try not to peek over at him, but can't seem to help it, my eyes landing on the tattoo below his elbow, the same one that I have, then traveling up to his hair, damp from the shower, one familiarly stubborn lock falling across his forehead. I look down at where our knees are angled slightly toward each other, only a few inches separating them, the tan of his skin against his olive green shorts a stark contrast to my paler, shut-in-a-studio-for-months-on-end legs. We've sat out here together countless times, in these chairs or against the balusters on either side of the front steps, talking about nothing and everything.

I twist in my seat toward him, his gaze jerking up when my knee just bumps his, some pointless question about the weather on the tip of my tongue, but at that moment the crunch of gravel sounds and "going to the chapel" floats toward us from Stevie's little blue car.

Ren and I glance that way, then back at each other, like we're both just remembering we have to pretend to be best friends, and then my parents' car is coming down the road too, and I can't remember what I was going to ask him anyway.

As Leo pulls into the spot behind mine, Ren and I stand robotically, march down the three steps to the driveway in lockstep. We must look like two servants outside a Regency home, positioned a measured distance apart, hands behind our rigid backs.

Stevie leans across Leo, turning the music up even louder. "Someone laugh! It's supposed to be funny!" she shouts, and suddenly I'm rushing up to the car, throwing open the door, and folding her in a tight hug. I've never been so grateful to see my sister.

The music cuts out as Leo shuts off the car, hopping out and wrapping his arms around us too.

"Boss man! Get over here!" he yells to Ren, who's still standing by the porch, hovering like he's not a part of this. Arguably, he's more a part of this than I am, given how much time he spends with the two of them.

He walks over, one thumb working at his opposite palm in front of him, feet crunching over the gravel. Our eyes meet briefly as Leo waves him into the hug, Ren hesitating before he slides his hand over my shoulders, a branding iron against my skin.

"Look at us," Leo says into our huddle. "Everyone together again."

At that, Ren's hand twitches against me, lifting off my shoulder then resettling like he remembered others are watching.

I force a smile for Leo. By virtue of being engaged to Stevie, he knows that Ren and I aren't friends anymore, but it's hard to be irritated with him. He wants everyone to be friends, all the time, and wouldn't that be nice if it were at all possible?

We're about to pull apart when my mom climbs out of my parents' car and hurries over, bags hanging from her wrists. "Wait, wait!" she calls. "Let me get a picture!"

We open our circle into a line and smile, Ren's arm still around my shoulders. When my mom prompts us to scoot closer together, the space we've left between our bodies disappears, his warm side pressing into mine. I smile wider, all bared teeth and pleading eyes. *Take the picture, take the picture.*

As soon as she's satisfied, my mom, angel that she is, yanks me into a hug of her own. "I can't believe I haven't seen you since April!" she says, my head hitting her chest. While I've been avoiding Oregon since Ren and I had our falling-out, I made sure to be at my aunt Charlene's in Madison for Thanksgiving and convinced my parents to take a trip to New York in the spring. "I know you're working so hard, though," she adds.

"Are the Websters on their way?" I ask her, desperate to change the subject.

"Just a few minutes behind— Hi, sweetheart!" She releases me, a smile breaking out on her face as she sidesteps me and reaches for Ren, who has to drop the bag he's carrying to return her hug. My mom has always adored Ren, but now I feel a little passed over.

My dad strolls up the driveway. "What a welcome committee!" he announces.

"Hi, Dad," I say, smiling at the sight of him. A recently retired salesman, my dad is perennially reliable. He has smelled like the same mixture of Dial soap and Old Spice aftershave at least as long as I've been alive, is deeply devoted to his two true passions, golf and his flower beds, and is the mild-mannered antithesis to my therapist mother I need right now.

He stops in front of me, holds me away from him. "You good?" he asks.

He's looking at me patiently, like he did when I was younger and knew I wasn't telling him something. Maybe he'd tell me now that losing my job isn't such a big deal, even keep the secret for me. But he's not exactly immune to my mom's interrogations either, and I don't want him to have to lie *for* me. "I'm good," I tell him.

He claps a hand on my shoulder as the Websters' car appears at the top of the road. "Glad to have you back here, kiddo."

After everyone has suitably greeted each other in the front, Ren's sister, Sasha, drags me into the kitchen, settling in at the table and pulling out her laptop.

"Final tally for the bachelor-bachelorette party on Thursday?" she asks. Sasha's a professional event planner and the organizer of this whole week. She once told me that *fun is more fun on a schedule.* I was nine. Sasha was thirteen.

"Us, Leo's brother, the band," I say, leaning against the cool stone of the island. At Sasha's impatient expression, I clarify, "Ten."

"Perfect," she says.

"Oh, we need to add capture the flag to Wednesday too."

"I got your text," Sasha says, eyes on her laptop, everything already rearranged to accommodate Leo's tradition. "I was thinking you and Ren could pick up the kegs Saturday morning."

My hand freezes inside the bag of grapes my mom set on the counter from the cooler she's unloading, my heart stuttering to a halt.

"Ren?" I repeat.

"Yeah?"

I startle at the sound of his voice, eyes finding him as he enters through the mudroom, a box in his arms that seems to be filled with fun-size bags of Skittles, probably from Stevie's car, and a backpack over each shoulder.

"What's up?" he says to the room.

"You and Joni are picking up the kegs on Saturday," Sasha tells him.

Ren's eyes flick back to mine. "Are you okay with that?" he asks me.

It catches me off guard, this open acknowledgment of the state of things between us. I look at him in what I hope is a *what the hell, man* way and he returns it with an exasperated *no taking it back now* expression. But, I remind myself, it's been a long time since Ren and I communicated silently like this, so I could just be misreading him.

"Of course she is," my mom says, the entire upper half of her body hidden inside the fridge as she organizes its contents.

Sasha pats the chair next to her, angling her head at Ren. "Stop moving for a minute," she says. "I haven't seen you in months."

Ren hesitates. He's been carrying everything inside from the cars, pausing to help when my mom noticed one of the blinds on the kitchen windows was loose, crouching down to examine the stairs when his dad stopped him on the front porch within minutes of his arrival and said we should repaint soon. Sasha and Thad are together all the time in LA, but naturally they must not see Ren as often.

He sets the box on the table, slides the backpacks off his shoulders, and sits down next to Sasha. She squeezes his arm, looks up at where I'm standing across from them. Ren follows suit, face inscrutable.

"It's like old times with you two camping out on the screen porch again," Sasha says. Apparently I was the only one not clued in to the sleeping arrangements ahead of time. She picks up her phone, squints at it. "Great opportunity for the two of you to catch up."

I can't help it: I look at Ren again. He and I are united in our deception, after all, and something in this sentiment has me worrying Sasha suspects us, like he's told her. But he just shakes his head imperceptibly.

"Catch up," he says to his sister as I look away and bite down, hard, on a grape. "Of course."

I stare into the bag as I pick through it, tell myself not to read so much into every tiny thing. If I do, we won't last the day.

"Wait, but you two just saw each other this spring." Sasha is still scrolling on her phone, half in this room and half in her well-organized head. "That week Ren was in New York."

My throat tightens. Ren was in New York? Ren was in New York for a whole week and I didn't know? Was it that time in

April when I woke up in the middle of the night convinced I wasn't totally alone in my apartment, or the few days in March I kept glancing over my shoulder, some strange feeling skittering down my spine? *No, Joni,* I tell myself. *Don't attribute cosmic significance to this just to make yourself feel better.*

"Actually," Ren says, looking directly at me. "Joni ended up being on a work trip that week, right?"

It surprises me that I can't respond faster, that making up a lie about being away because of work suddenly seems so much bigger than lying about the fact that I don't actually *have* work anymore.

"Right," I manage as my mom finally extracts herself from the fridge, huffing as she pushes her hair back from her forehead. Because I don't have anything to add to his lie, I just say, "Last-minute thing."

"That's too bad," Sasha says to her phone screen. "When is the last time you saw each other, then?"

"Um," I say, eyes latching on to Ren's again.

"Shit!" Sasha exclaims, slamming her phone onto the table. "I just got an email that the winery is closing tomorrow for the rest of the week for emergency repairs. Something about water damage."

"When are we supposed to pick up the wine?" my mom asks. She's halfway between the cooler and the fridge, a bottle of orange juice in each hand, face stricken.

"Saturday morning. I was going to have you two stop there after you got the kegs." Sasha pushes a hand into her hair, tugs her laptop closer.

"Why don't I just go pick it up now?" Ren says. "My afternoon is free."

Sasha turns to him like he's just defused a bomb. To be fair, to her and my mother, anything that gets in the way of a schedule might very well be on par with an actual bomb. For a moment I feel like my own life's chaos might not actually be that bad. I might not be able to keep my job, but I do think I could manage a minor crisis like a winery being closed.

"That would be so great," Sasha says. Ren starts to get up, and I have to hand it to him. This is the perfect solution. Less time in the house together. Fewer opportunities for us to mess this up. Then she adds: "Joni can go with you. You two can grab a glass of wine while you're there. You're *welcome*."

Ren seems to power down, stuck in a position between standing and sitting. His eyes are on the table, and I think he must feel how I did when I couldn't come up with a good work trip story: brain somehow working both double time and not at all. But then Sasha looks at him and he straightens quickly, lips pressing into a weak smile before he walks over to the front door and grabs his keys from the small pegboard hanging next to it.

"I can stay," I say to Sasha, gesturing at her laptop. "Help with whatever you originally had on the schedule for Ren."

"The next two hours are for organized fun," she says without an ounce of sarcasm in her voice. It's always been like this: Sasha carefully scheduling things to ensure we maximize our time together.

"Don't I need to be here for that?" I ask her.

My mom shuts the door to the fridge and turns to me with a slight frown. I swear, my voice is the dog whistle to her highly attuned ears. "Honey," she says in the same tone she uses when she's trying to weasel something out of her patients. "Is something wrong?"

I've tried too hard to get out of going, I realize. Before, I would have already been halfway to Ren's car, keys in hand. If I protest more, someone will suspect something is up. I smile at her, casually pop another grape into my mouth, prepare myself mentally for an afternoon with my former best friend, who's currently spinning said keys around one finger before he catches them in his fist. But the grape launches straight to the back of my throat, and my mom has to slap my back three times as I cough and spit the whole unchewed thing into my palm.

When I can finally look up again, eyes teary, Ren is watching me from near the front door. "Careful there," he says, trying to suppress a smile. "Wouldn't want to miss the winery."

chapter seven

Thanks to what Sasha thought was kindness, I end up in Ren's passenger seat, one elbow out the window and a song on that I would probably know about if Ren and I were still on speaking terms. To make matters worse, I love the song. Ren didn't get his job out of sheer luck.

The winery is packed when we pull up. We were silent on the ride, letting the music stand in for conversation, and as soon as Ren finds a spot at the far edge of the dirt lot, I lurch out of the car, striding in the direction of the round stone building, the afternoon sun glinting off its windows.

Ren's long legs catch up with me easily in the parking lot. Once inside, we end up in a strange kind of race to the bar, which is fruitless because every available seat and all the spots in between are taken.

We hover at one end, laughter pealing around us, jazzy piano music floating down from mounted speakers. A few doors are open to the patio out back, and a breeze drifts in, picking up the ends of my hair.

"There's a table out back," calls a server as she glides by, tray tucked under an arm, and ducks behind the bar.

Ren leans toward her, carefully avoiding the space of a man who looks like he might be three sheets to the wind. "We're just here to pick up an order," he says over the din of the room.

"Name?" the server asks, eyes on the register.

"Miller."

She taps something on the screen, frowning until her face brightens. "The wedding," she says. "Tony can help you with that. Grab one of the tables out back and I'll bring over something you can celebrate with."

"Oh, we're not—" I say, but she's already sweeping away, walking confidently toward the other end of the bar.

Ren peers down at me, one eyebrow lifting in question. I shrug. Probably better to follow her instructions than try to flag her down again.

I trail him out to the crowded patio, where we sit at a bistro table, paint chipping and a few of the rungs on the back of the matching green chairs missing. When our knees knock together, Ren swings his legs to the side.

We sit in silence again, both of us turning to squint at the water. I can feel the hot metal singeing the backs of my legs and my shoulders reddening in the sun, but I stay ramrod straight, still edgy after the close call in the kitchen. When I glance out of the corner of my eye, Ren seems relaxed, one leg crossed over the other, sunglasses on. I return my attention to the seagulls drifting above the waves.

"For the happy couple!" A hand appears between us, placing two glasses on the table.

My stomach knots. Being mistaken for Ren's fiancée is not on my make-it-through-the-week bingo card. I twist in my seat, gripping the back of it as I look up at the server from earlier, and try to explain again. "We're not—"

If she hears me, she doesn't give any indication. "A gift from the winery. This is our most popular orange." She pours a finger's worth into my glass.

She walks around the table to Ren's side to do the same for him. I shoot him a look, hoping he can still read me enough to know I need his help to get us out of this.

His mouth curves down, lines etching in his forehead. "Thank you," he says to her. "But we—"

The server ignores him too. "I figured you'd probably be having enough champagne this weekend, so this just has a bit of effervescence to it. Not too funky if you're new to orange wine, but enough skin contact that—"

"We're not getting married!" I blurt.

I swear everyone around us stills, all eyes on our tiny, terrible table. The server stands with the bottle still poised toward me, her mouth open as her eyes flit toward Ren for confirmation.

"Maid of honor," he says in a way that makes me think he wishes we could have just pretended to be engaged, waving a hand in my direction before back at himself. "Friend of the family."

"Friend of the groom," I hasten to add. "And the bride. Also, he and the groom work together. Well, maybe not together, but—"

"Anyway, we'll pay for this, but we're just here to pick up the wine order for the wedding," Ren cuts in.

The server glances between us, then shrugs and fills both of our glasses before we can even try the taste she poured. "Their loss," she says. "Wine can be on us since you're the ones who have to check this task off the list, alright? Tony will be out in a few. Enjoy." With a wink, she turns on her heel, weaving back through the tables on the patio.

I stare after her like she's my lifeline on this sinking ship. *Ren* can be, if not cool, at least collected. Somewhere in the realm of normal. Yet here I am, flailing around in what are relatively shallow waters.

I reach for my glass, tap my fingers against the stem. It's just one glass of wine. I should be able to handle this. It's not like Ren is my enemy.

"Were you going to detail both our family trees for her?" he asks.

My gaze darts up from my glass. He's watching me with an amused expression.

"Just back five generations," I say, biting my cheek to hide the smile threatening at my lips. Ren's smiles have always been contagious.

Ren laughs, and the sound produces a familiar warmth in my chest. He raises his eyebrows and lifts his glass in my direction. The moment has me lifting mine too, clinking it against his before we both take a sip.

"So how's Novo?" he asks, suddenly talkative. He uncrosses and then recrosses his legs the other way, his arm muscles shifting beneath the sleeve of his white T-shirt as he rests an elbow on his chair.

I work hard to keep the smile plastered to my face. If there is a worse question Ren could ask right now, I couldn't think of it. "Good."

"Any updates on the movie?"

Okay, maybe there is a worse question. The movie is the thing that got me fired, after all.

"Nope," I say, shaking my head. "No updates."

"Okay."

For a few minutes, we don't say anything else, just sip our wine, whatever tiny step we'd taken toward peace erased by the mention of my job, not that Ren would understand that. I think we might sit in silence until Tony arrives, but eventually Ren sets his glass down, pushes his sunglasses to the top of his head, and leans over the table toward me.

"Listen," he says. "You don't have to tell me everything about your life, but there are probably some basics we should cover."

"Basics," I repeat.

"We were almost caught when Sasha brought up my trip to New York earlier."

I twirl my glass one way, then the other, waiting him out.

Ren's eyes study the movement, then trace their way back up to my face, settling on mine for a beat longer than necessary. "I didn't think you'd want to see me," he says finally.

I don't know if he's just being polite, pretending that he wanted to see me, but I was the obstacle. Or if he genuinely did want to see me, but knew the complications of such a reunion were exactly why it's been easier not to talk at all. What would come after hello? Would we act like things were normal? That nothing had happened between us?

After that New Year's Eve, I'd hoped he'd call. I thought we'd give each other some time, that even after everything, he'd see through me. Or miss me in the way I missed him, which was enough for me to pick up my phone most nights, hover over his contact, but not enough to set aside my fears and hit Call. It wasn't fair, the fact that I wasn't reaching out to him but expected he would reach out to me, but the longer the silence went on, the easier it became to stop scrolling to his name. He didn't want to talk to me. And maybe I didn't want to talk to him either. I didn't really want to talk to anyone about what had happened: not my mom, not Stevie, not my therapist, even when I knew I should go see her again.

He's looking at me now like he's hoping I'll prove him wrong, to confess I did want to see him. But it feels dangerous to undo all my efforts to push the pieces of him from my life, the only way I knew how to soldier on after everything.

When I don't respond, he sits back in his chair, his mouth set in a straight line. "Is there anything everyone else would know that I should too?" he asks. "If some big surprise comes up, it will be obvious we haven't been talking. And you want Stevie's week to be perfect, right?"

I'm still a few steps behind, the disappointed look in Ren's eyes before he sat back burned into my brain. But this question, one with a clear-cut answer, brings me back to the present moment. "Right."

He swoops his arm out as if he expects me to lay my cards down on the table between us. "Then what do I need to know?"

The sad truth of the matter is that there isn't all that much to know. I now do Pilates. I joined and quit a book club. I've kept a variegated rubber plant alive for a whole year, and felt so proud of that minor accomplishment that I named her Dolly. Not exactly the make-or-break items in the crash course Ren is suggesting, other than my lack of job, of course, but Ren and I will be in each other's rear views before that comes to light.

"I don't know." I wave a hand. "I started grinding my teeth in my sleep."

"Mmm," Ren says, like this is important information. "Okay, I don't talk in my sleep anymore."

"You—" I hate the slight shock it sends through me. "What?"

His eyes tick skyward in a half roll. "Apparently, it's not a curable thing, but—I don't know. No more sleep talking."

"A medical marvel," I say.

We watch each other, two wary animals. Ren is as good as a new person in front of me. I'd always thought history between two people was so important, but the fact of him not talking in his sleep anymore is simple proof that time works steadily to erase it, especially if you're not around to pay attention.

"So, what else do I need to know?" I ask. Ren's right. We can't risk slipping up again, not when everyone else thinks our friendship, and all the history that built it, is still very much intact. "How's work for you?"

"Work's good."

I lean my elbows on the table. "Still bartending?"

"When I can." He nods toward me. "Still in the same apartment?"

"Yep." *But not for much longer.* Without a job, I won't be able to continue to afford the tiny studio I found after Stevie relocated back to Portland, and I don't relish the idea of staying in the neighborhood close enough to Novo that I would still run into coworkers at my favorite coffee shop.

I sip my wine, prepare myself to ask the obvious follow-up. If Stevie knows the details of Ren's relationship with Amanda, his gorgeous, whip-smart girlfriend, she's been kind enough not to share them with me. But I have to assume they might have moved in with each other. "You?"

Ren reaches up and rubs the back of his head. "I moved a couple months ago." He doesn't offer any more information than that, and instead glances toward the water.

I follow his gaze, take a healthy gulp of my wine. I'm so busy trying to appear unaffected that I don't notice when he looks back at me.

"Who's your plus-one to the wedding?"

I almost choke and spit out the wine. I know he's asking because it's the kind of thing he might need to know, but the question lands like my mom's hand did on my back earlier, dislodging memories I can't face right now. There was a time Ren might have been my plus-one, but any trace of that is gone now.

"Grapes are really getting to you today, huh?" he asks.

I clear my throat. "What was the question?"

He takes his sunglasses off his head, fiddles with them as he repeats himself. "Who's your plus-one this weekend?"

I had considered bringing someone, but I didn't know who that someone would be. I briefly dated a guy for a few months last year, but it didn't go anywhere, and otherwise, my romantic life has been next to nonexistent. No one has clicked, most dates the romantic equivalent of a Belvita. Not that I've been all that interested in trying to make things work anyway.

"I'm not bringing anyone," I say, squeezing the sides of my glass between my fingers. "What about you?"

Ren shakes his head, his eyes not leaving mine. "Not bringing anyone either."

My grip tightens. *Don't ask, don't ask, don't ask.* "What about Amanda?" It spills out of me.

A muscle tenses in Ren's jaw, and the silence is enough. He's about to tell me that he's the next one to get married, that Amanda's so busy planning their wedding that she can't spare time to attend this one.

"We broke up." He says it flatly, expression gone infuriatingly neutral.

"You— When?" Shame sparks in me that my first response is curiosity. I should be checking to make sure Ren is okay, not demanding details.

"Um. About four months ago." He tugs a hand through his hair. "That's why I came up early."

I sit back. "Ah." The pieces snap into place. Ren wasn't here for purely altruistic reasons. "Not to mow the lawn?"

At this, his mouth ticks up. Not quite a smile, but not the indecipherable expression he was just wearing. "Not to mow the lawn." A couple wanders by, meandering in that slow, lazy way of people newly in love. Ren's eyes track them briefly before he looks back at me. "This is the first big event since we broke up, and my mom isn't happy about it. She thinks I need to settle down. So I thought it might be good to have a day up here before the questions start."

A defensive instinct flickers in me. "Ren, you turned thirty in June. You're not exactly a spinster. What's the male version of a spinster?"

Ren finally cracks a smile, but at the same time, I feel the sting of it, that we haven't been around for each other's birthdays. That there was the usual hoopla in the family group chat, as there is for everyone's birthday, but rather than be an adult and send a perfunctory happy birthday message, like he has on my last three birthdays, I just liked the first celebratory text someone else sent. It was a jerk move, I knew even then, but something about acknowledging the years passing between us in any real way hurt too much.

"A bachelor?" Ren says.

I lean my head back, an exasperated sound rattling out of me. "Why do men get something that they turn into a whole reality franchise, and we get Charlotte Lucas?"

"If I recall correctly, there *is* a bachelorette version of the franchise, and you once told me that you might be okay marrying someone like Mr. Collins if you never had to talk to him."

"You remember that?"

"You made us watch *Pride and Prejudice*, like, a hundred times when you had mono."

"Joni," Ren had said after what I'm sure was our tenth viewing on his computer, angled from his dorm room desk so we could both see it. It was all I really had the energy to do: consume comforting classics in between naps. "Don't get me wrong, I'm all about the Elizabeth and Darcy of it all, but what if we watched something set in a time period where someone wouldn't waste away from what's currently ailing you?"

"What's currently ailing you," I repeated. "Are you trying to *sound* like Darcy?"

On his bed, Ren pressed his hands to his face, groaning. "We've just watched it so many times. Keira Knightley was in my dream last night."

"Okay, that's not because of the movie."

He threw a pillow across the room at me, and I pretended to flail, tossing a hand over my forehead and crying out that I was on my deathbed.

"That must have been the fever talking," I say now, banishing the memory of the month I spent sleeping across the room from him, doing a fair amount of my own NyQuil-induced sleep talking and begrudgingly letting him bring me soup and tea. His roommate was dating my roommate—the source of the mono—and had moved in to take care of her. Because Ren and I weren't the type of friends who made out on occasion, I'd lugged a suitcase over to his dorm and spent my recovery there. "And *Bachelorette* is something entirely different than spinster. It brings to mind visions of feather boas, bride sashes, bedazzled penises."

Ren laughs. I don't fight the warmth that spreads through me.

"I am sorry," I say. "About Amanda."

He lifts a hand as if to brush this away, lets it drop back to the arm of his chair. "Don't be. It was time for us to go our separate ways."

I tilt my glass toward him. "Aren't you well-adjusted."

"To be fair, I did still come up here a day early to mentally prepare for a week with my deeply disappointed mother." He pauses, considers me like he's mulling something over. "Did you really come up early to help get things ready?"

I shake my head, shrug to stall. Lying to Ren has never been easy, but we're not in a place where I can tell him the whole truth. I opt for the most basic answer. "No."

Ren doesn't press. I can feel the words there against the back of my teeth, aching to get out. It strikes me that if there's one person I would want to talk to about this with, it would be Ren. Even after everything.

For a moment, I let myself study him as if the last two and a half years didn't happen, imagine I was here to see the smiles that crinkled his eyes, led to the hint of crow's-feet, to hear how he got that faint scar running up his left thumb that I know wasn't there before. When my eyes latch on to Ren's, there's something vaguely wistful in them, and I wonder if he's observing the same changes in me.

"You must be the unhappy couple!" a voice says cheerfully. We both lurch back and look up at the short, gray-haired man standing next to our table, his arms raised over his head like he's cheering for us.

"Tony," he says. "Let's get you that wine."

chapter eight

We each wheel a dolly stacked with cases of wine to Ren's car, where he puts the seats down and loads them into the trunk. We're quiet again on the drive back to the house, but the air feels warmer between us.

After hauling the wine onto the far end of the screen porch (because it's not only our sleeping quarters, but the place to store every spare thing that has ever come through the door of this house, including a lot of the boxes from the back of Stevie and Leo's car), we join the others down at the beach. We kick our shoes off at the bottom of the path to the sand, and Ren shrugs on the black hoodie he grabbed from the hook. It's cooler here.

A ways down the beach, Thad is helping their dad, Greg, as tall as the rest of the Websters, set up a badminton net. "You and me against Sash and Dad?" he shouts to Ren.

"I'm in!" Ren can never pass up competition, a holdover from his days of playing soccer and running track. He heads off in that direction, his feet leaving imprints in the sand, and I try hard to shake off the feeling that he wants to get away from me, that I misread our conversation at the winery and it was just for the sake of keeping up appearances. But halfway to the net, he turns around, walking backward, his eyes catching mine: something inviting and familiar there. He smiles at me, until Thad tells him to hurry up and he jogs the rest of the way forward.

To one side of the net, my mom and Ren's mom, Hannah, are sitting in beach chairs, laughing with Stevie and Leo, who are on a blanket next to them. But I'm not ready to drive myself into another pothole-riddled discussion, so I join my dad at the water's edge, where he wanders, pant legs rolled up.

"Hey, kiddo," he says, slinging an arm around my shoulders. "Wine crisis averted?"

"Just barely," I joke. "Almost had to reroute to Costco."

My dad, who hates a bulk store, shudders. He toes at something in the sand before bending down to retrieve it. "Look at that. Full sand dollar. Don't see many intact like that."

Sasha lets out a furious cry at losing a point as he hands it to me, and I'm tugged farther into this place. My dad is collecting shells; Hannah and my mom fuss over everyone; we're all on the beach to mark our first afternoon together. This is still the same place it was. Houses like this hold steady, waiting to catch you when you need them most.

It's why I didn't want anyone to know about Ren and me: this house, our families, are a well-balanced ecosystem that thrives on so much of the same. Coming back to the same house, at the same time, doing the same things every year. Any hint of a rift could easily disrupt the balance.

"Your mom's looking forward to catching up with you this week," my dad says, sending a familiar twinge through me.

It's an old routine. In high school, my mother would poke her head into my room every thirty minutes, always just to "check in," and when I didn't give a proper response, she would tell my father that she was worried about me, and he would gently nudge me her way. Then in college, the same thing would play out over the phone.

"Yeah," I say now. "We'll talk." My usual response.

My dad glances over at me, the final step in all this forth-coming. "I know it's a lot for you, her worry," he says. "But it's just because—"

"She loves us all so much," I finish. And yet, it makes me feel like I can't breathe sometimes.

"Richard!" my mom shouts then, waving us over, her other hand clutching her straw sun hat. "Bring Joni back over here!"

My dad raises his eyebrows at me. "We're being summoned." We trudge up the beach. My mom directs me into the spot next to Stevie and thrusts a coconut seltzer my way. "Put on your sunscreen," she says, passing me a tube as she rummages in her truly bottomless bag. "I have another hat in here—do you want a hat?"

"I'm good, Mom," I say as I slather my legs in lotion.

"Sweetie," Hannah says, leaning around my mom from her other side. "Are you and Ren really okay sleeping on the porch?"

"They're fine," my mom says. "They ended up camping out there even after we moved them both inside."

"I know, but they were still kids then."

"They were twenty-three," Stevie says from next to me. She has a pair of round sunglasses on, a finger holding her page in the magazine she's reading. I didn't think she was listening. "What?" she says at the look I throw her, worried she might inadvertently give us away. "You were well into adulthood the last time you slept out there together. That's all I'm saying."

I fiddle with the tab on the seltzer my mom gave me. That was the summer I moved to New York. After that trip, I'd stayed inside with Stevie. Thinking back now, I'm not sure why, what changed, if it was one of many hints of shifting feel-ings that I'd missed or some harbinger of what was to come.

"We'll be fine, Hannah," I say. Putting us on the porch

makes sense, and my former self would have happily gone along with it.

"I just worry we should have added one more bedroom when we did the addition," Hannah says. "Katie might not be the only grandchild. Eventually we'll run out of space."

Katie is Thad's four-year-old daughter, still in Los Angeles with his husband, Gemi, until Saturday. Sasha's husband will fly in in time for the rehearsal dinner on Friday night. Save for Leo, these few days are really the first time it's been just us here in a decade.

I half listen as Hannah and my mom drone on. Best friends since college, they get like this: discussing everything, including all of our lives, like no one else is around. On the sandy badminton court before us, Sasha flings her arm back to serve the birdie. Ren reaches up to hit it back over the net, the hem of his sweatshirt riding up to reveal an inch of muscular abdomen that has me thinking back to the movement of his body when he was mowing the lawn yesterday. The two of them volley back and forth until Sasha misses, cursing to herself, and Thad and Ren bump fists in victory.

A few minutes later, they walk over, arguing.

"What's the score?" my dad asks from a beach chair on Hannah's other side.

"We absolutely beat you," Ren says, pointing at Sasha with his racket.

"That last one you served was out of bounds," she says.

"In what world?"

"This one!"

Ren turns to my dad, lifting a hand in the air in a *who knows* motion. "Sorry, Richard. We don't know the score yet," he says in a smug tone that indicates he absolutely knows who won.

Sasha scoffs.

"Time for everyone to take a break, I think," Hannah says, motioning for them to sit down.

Ren drops onto the sand, leaning his forearms on his bent knees, racket still hanging from one hand.

"Thad, rematch!" Sasha calls, turning to head back toward the net. "If you beat me, I'll buy your matchas at Alfred's for a month!"

"I just don't know how we're going to accommodate everyone," Hannah goes on.

"Speaking of beds," Stevie says. "There are new sheets on ours."

Ren and I pivot our heads toward her at the same time. She's the most observant person I know, which is why I'd had no choice but to tell her about me and Ren. I can't count the number of times growing up I would be talking to my mom in our kitchen at home, only to jump out of my skin when Stevie said something from right behind me, this invisible presence that had been lurking there all along.

"Are there?" our mom asks.

"Yes. I put the striped blue sheets on when we left last month. No one else has been up here since then, right?"

"Not that I know of," my mom says. "Hannah?"

"Not us. Are you sure you put the blue sheets on there?" Hannah asks Stevie.

"I'm positive. I never forget a sheet."

My mouth goes dry, knee starts to bounce. I choose this moment to open the can I've been absently toying with and take a long drink. Leave it to me to blow up this whole week by being polite enough to change the sheets.

"I'm sure it just slipped your mind," my mom says.

"Or," Stevie says, "Maybe someone broke into the house."

"And changed your sheets?" Hannah asks. She smiles over at my mom, says in a low voice, "A thoughtful thief, at the very least."

"I *know* I put the blue sheets on there." Stevie flicks her eyes in my direction. Leo follows her gaze, but there's only happy curiosity on his face, none of the appraising suspicion Stevie wears almost exclusively. I feel a slow burn creeping up my neck. "Joni, did—"

"I changed the sheets," Ren cuts in.

We all turn to him. "You changed the sheets?" she asks. "Why?"

Ren shrugs, tapping the edge of his racket into the sand, the picture of casual. "I forgot to mention that I came up a day early. Sorry."

"You never sleep in that room," Hannah says.

"Why are we so worried about where everyone sleeps all of a sudden?" I ask through a nervous laugh.

"Why did you come up early?" Stevie asks Ren, ignoring my question.

I cast an apologetic look his way, but he's focused on the groove he's digging into the sand with his racket.

"I just wanted to get a few things done," he says, dragging his eyes up to glance around at everyone before he looks at my sister. "Sorry, Stevie."

"Hey, no need to apologize." Leo, who's watched us all volley back and forth with the smile of an audience member at a game show, tucks an arm around Stevie's shoulders. "At least you figured out we don't have a sheet-stealing burglar lurking in the woods, right, babe?"

"Right," Stevie says, her eyes ping-ponging between me and Ren as idle conversation resumes around us.

That night, while Ren is inside getting ready to go to sleep, I sit on the edge of my bed, toes tapping against the floor. Thinking it might be more natural if I was already in bed when he walks back in, I slide under the blankets like I'm trying not to disrupt them, something I've never done in my life. I usually toss and turn well before I fall asleep.

I last all of thirty seconds before the sheets feel like a straitjacket, and I flip onto one side, then the other, kick my legs around until the bedding is comfortable again. I sigh, finally settling on my back and breathing steadily for a minute. When that doesn't work, I scroll mindlessly on my phone.

Ren knocks lightly on the door before he comes in. I set my phone on my chest, glance up in a way that I hope reads somewhere along the lines of *I was just intensely focused on an article about the five movies you need to see this fall and* not *fruitlessly trying to distract myself from the mere act of sleeping in the same space as you again.*

"Hey," he says. We seem to have had the same train of thought about sleeping attire: while I know Ren doesn't usually wear a shirt when he sleeps, he has one on now, and I've put on a pair of shorts, determined to keep yesterday my only pants-less morning here. He points at the light above the door. "You ready?"

"Mmm-hmm." I nod, and he turns it off. It takes my eyes a minute to adjust, but I can still make out his silhouette as he climbs into bed.

I stare up at the place where the moonlight slants in through the gap in the curtains, spreads across the ceiling. The only sound is the ocean rolling in, the wind sweeping through the treetops. Years ago, before the house had central air, I could sometimes hear my dad's snoring or the soft din of the soundscapes Sasha listens to so she can fall asleep. She'd shush us from her window if Ren and I were talking or laughing too loudly. But now, everyone on this side of the house sleeps with their windows closed.

"Ren?" I say after a while. It feels wrong to be out here together without speaking, like the ghosts of our former selves would be disappointed. That, and he did save me earlier, with

Stevie on the beach. I want him to know I noticed, to have his good nature recognized.

"Yeah?"

"Thank you," I say. "For covering for me earlier. About the sheets."

"Anytime."

"Did anyone ask you about it afterward?" I ask, worried he caught some flak for coming up early without telling anyone.

Ren is quiet, mulling his answer. "My mom asked me if I needed to get out of the city because I was disappointed Amanda wouldn't be here this weekend."

I hesitate, still not sure if this is a conversation this version of us should be having. "Are you? Disappointed?"

I can hear Ren's head shift against his pillow. "I don't think *disappointed* is the right word."

I know it's not my place to ask what the right word is, not anymore. I watch the shadows on the ceiling, picking over the day for other topics of conversation so he doesn't feel pressured to answer just to fill the silence. "So you really don't talk in your sleep anymore? Like, at all?" I ask.

"As far as I know," Ren says. "Why?"

"I don't know." Something about the dark, about Ren not being able to see my face when I say it, emboldens me. "I always found it sort of comforting."

"Did you," Ren says.

I lean up on my elbows, looking in the direction of his bed. "I did. It was nice to hear when I couldn't sleep anyway."

Ren's low chuckle is muffled, like he's pressed his hands to his face. "That makes it so much worse," he says. "Not only could you not sleep, but my babbling kept you up longer."

"No," I say. "I was already awake, and it was like... I don't know. It's stupid."

Now it's Ren who's rolling onto one side, pushing up onto

an elbow and twisting himself toward me. "I bet it's not stupid. Tell me."

I'm grateful, again, for the dark. I never told him this even when we were friends. "Okay, so I was already awake, and I would wish you were too, so we could talk. But then, it was kind of like you were talking to me anyway."

"About nonsense, of course."

"Of course." I smile. "But it was mostly just you kind of muttering stuff. And it helped me fall asleep when I couldn't." When he doesn't respond, I worry that I've said too much, offered too much of myself up. That whatever had thawed between us earlier today really was just for show. I consider lying down again, ready to overthink my oversharing until the sun comes up. But somehow moving right now seems worse.

The moonlight coming in just crosses his face, so I can see the moment he smiles back at me. "I can just talk until you fall asleep, if it would help," he says.

I laugh lightly, suppress a yawn like his suggestion already has me tired. "I think we're doing well," I say.

"Well?" he asks.

"You know," I say, without thinking much of it. "Making everyone believe we still like each other."

Ren stills, the smile slipping off his face, a statue cast in shades of gray.

"Do you think we hate each other?" he asks softly.

His question is a punch in the stomach, knocking the wind out of me. *Hate* is never a word I could attribute to Ren.

"No," I say, quickly, wishing I could take back what I said, explain it better, tell him I was joking, that it felt enough like old times for a minute that it seemed like something we were in on together. *Isn't it funny we have to make people believe we're friends? Can you imagine?*

"We just don't like each other," he says.

"I didn't mean it like that," I say. "Just—"

"We're not friends anymore. I get it."

He turns away and lies back down. I stare at the top of his head, trying to will the words out of me. Suddenly, this tenuous civility between us feels like the most important thing in the world, something I need to be gentler with. Ren was always better at that than I was, though, treating things with the reverence they deserved. Slowing down, paying attention.

I lie back myself, quiet until it occurs to me how I might make this better. "Ren?" I say. This time, I don't wait for him to answer. "I would have been happy to see you. When you were in New York."

He's silent for so long I wonder if he's fallen asleep. I try not to take it personally, try not to let it mean anything. *One day doesn't mean you're friends again*, I remind myself. *There might be too much lost time between you for that to even be possible.*

But it felt possible today, laughing at the winery and Ren having my back on the beach. Like some part of me had been unearthed, brushed off.

I'm adjusting my pillow, my cheek finding the cool side, resigning myself to the fact that he's not going to respond when his voice comes out of the dark.

"I would have been happy to see you too."

FIVE YEARS AGO

Lydia and Isaac

Chicago, Illinois

chapter nine

"So," I say, falling onto my bed as I hold up a card. The first rush of April sun streams in through my lone window and catches on the gold leafing around the border. "I have a Save the Date."

"Lydia and Isaac?" Ren asks on his end of the line. "I got that today too. Crazy that our college roommates ended up marrying each other."

It's Sunday afternoon, and Ren and I are on one of our daily phone calls. It's become a habit, working each other in around our otherwise busy schedules. Ren calls me when he's on his way home from the gym most weeknights. I'll call him as soon as he's up on weekends, knowing he usually sleeps later after his bartending shifts on Fridays and Saturdays. Sometimes we talk for hours, through errands and cleaning our apartments, all the way until I'm headed out the door with Stevie or he's off to grab a beer with his old soccer friends.

"Are you free the weekend of July fourteenth?" I ask him.

"I don't know," Ren says, voice going distant, the sounds of a car passing, people strolling by, in the background. "Might have something else going on."

"Okay," I say, trying hard not to reveal my disappointment that our tradition didn't even make it through one year of living apart. "Maybe there will be another wedding. We could—"

Ren's soft laugh cuts me off. "I'm kidding."

"Oh my god," I say, but I'm laughing as my disappointment morphs into relief.

I settle back against my pillows. We hadn't planned on not seeing each other for ten months, had cited my birthday in late October, Thanksgiving, and Christmas, as rewards for our time apart while we were sprawled on the beach at the vacation house last summer. But plane fare is expensive, and time off work is hard to come by, especially when we're each trying to prove our places at our respective companies, and it's turned out that days slip by more easily than either of us anticipated. We'd floated the idea of Ren coming out to New York for my birthday, but in the end, the timing didn't work out. Stevie and I went to Sasha's in Boston for Thanksgiving, where we met her new boyfriend, Alex, and Ren's family went to Los Angeles to spend Christmas with Thad and Gemi.

"Can you FaceTime for a minute?" Ren asks.

"Sure," I say, sitting up on my bed and running a quick hand through my hair. His video request comes in a second later and I let out a confused laugh when it isn't his face but the view from Overlook Park, a spot where you can see a perfect shot of the river and the city skyline behind it, that fills up my screen.

"Just showing off?" I ask as Ren turns the camera back to himself. He's in a denim jacket over a black hoodie, earbuds in, cheeks vaguely rosy from what I know is still crisp morning air. The spring version of himself.

"That's your favorite view in the city," he says. "Thought you could use it right now."

I'd told him that my New York therapist suggested finding small pieces of home to hang on to, to ease the transition of moving, and while I've been settled in here for several months now, I still find reminders of Portland comforting. It's like Ren has some uncanny ability to sniff out when I might be feeling homesick, photos from Sublimity or postcards with the Burnside Bridge coming when I need them most. The fact that we haven't seen each other in so long makes me more homesick than anything.

I sink into my pillows again as we talk through the rest of his walk. Hearing his voice always puts me at ease, but there's something different about seeing him, like the familiar angles of his face, each shift of his expression brings him that tiniest bit closer to me.

"Hey," he says when he's back to his place. "I'll find a hotel for Chicago and book it tonight, okay?"

"I don't know," I say, echoing his comment from earlier. "Might have a work thing that weekend."

He smirks at me before we hang up.

By the time Lydia and Isaac's wedding weekend rolls around, I am deeply immersed in Novo's latest project. A short that features a girl named Antonia and her porcupine sidekick, Paul, who wears a red backpack made from the fabric of one of my own vintage jackets. I have built Paul from the ground up, spending hours twining together each of his individually crafted quills (of which there are three thousand nine hundred and sixty-two per puppet; so far there are nine Pauls), and handpainting each of his tiny, replaceable faces.

The Friday morning I'm supposed to catch my flight, I glance up at the clock above my desk just in time to see that I'm running late. I took the whole day off, but at 6:00 a.m. I remembered I'd left half of one of Paul's faces out to dry at the office and needed to complete his touch-ups. I'd let myself into Novo with my suitcase in tow, sure I'd only need twenty minutes to finish up.

I make it to my gate with minutes to spare.

Once I've shoved my bag under the seat in front of me, I put in my headphones and cue up the playlist Ren sent for the trip. Lorde's "Supercut" plays me through takeoff, kicking off the weekend as if I'm in a movie montage of two long-lost friends returning to each other, which is what I'd told Ren I'd wanted when I texted him to ask if a playlist was forthcoming.

I finally take a breath and let myself turn off the work part of my brain. There's a list in my phone of all the activities I've scheduled for us before the wedding tomorrow, pulled from the recommendations Lydia and Isaac shared to their wedding site. We have so much lost time to make up for, so many moments over the course of the last year when I wished Ren had been there, like when one of his favorite bands was in town, or when no one seemed to make a gin and tonic as much as I liked the one he made me, or when Stevie and I found a vinyl store that had the best collection of rare pressings I'd ever seen and where I'd bought his birthday present this year.

I spend the better part of the flight with my head twisted toward the window, staring at the patchwork world below me like I can watch the miles between Ren and me shrinking. At one point, my seat partner, a middle-aged woman with bottle-orange hair and a heavy dose of something artificially vanilla scented wafting off her, asks if I have a million dollars waiting for me on the other end of this flight.

"Better," I tell her, grinning like a hyena. "My friend."

"Your friend?" she asks.

"My *best* friend," I say.

She frowns. "That's…sweet." She returns to perusing her back-issued *People* magazines.

I'm run-walking as soon as I'm off the plane, hustling past

parents dragging their kids on suitcases and slowing down around groups on the moving walkway.

I'm by baggage claim, Ren's text read as soon as I could check my messages again after landing. We'd coordinated our arrival times as best we could, but he still touched down an hour before me.

Baggage claim seems miles away, but I finally emerge from the swampy halls of the main terminal, bursting through the automatic doors like a plane-sweaty orc free from their primordial ooze. I scan the long line of carousels, searching.

When I spot him waiting by a pillar, sunlight playing in his hair, I break into a full-on run. The sound of my sandals slapping against the tile at full speed gives me away, and the smile that spreads across his face is so much better in person than it is over FaceTime.

He only has to take two long strides before I'm launching myself at him. He catches me and lifts me off the ground, spinning me once around before he sets me down.

"Wow," I breathe as I pull away from him, letting my eyes wander over him. "Look at you. You're perfect."

Ren's cheeks flush, and I decide to lean into it. "A dream," I say. "A sight for the sorest eyes. A work of art."

"Stop," he says, hooking an arm around my neck and tugging me into him.

I burrow deeper into his side, arms around his waist, feeling like I might absorb some of him and subsist on it until the next time I see him. I hadn't realized how much of that I'd already been doing, that it was his voice in my head giving me a pep talk on my first day of work, his T-shirt I put on when I was missing home one night when Stevie was out with her school friends.

"Tell me life is miserable without me," I say when we break away from each other. I loop an arm through his and we walk toward the doors, carry-ons in tow.

"Life is miserable without you," Ren says.

"Tell me how much Portland misses me."

Ren guides us through the doors, a rush of hot air hitting our faces. "Obviously Portland misses you," he says as we hit the pavement and join the queue for cabs.

It's been the kind of summer that makes everywhere uncomfortable, the only place to find any relief a walk-in freezer or a very expensive bar. Even there, the heat seeps in, closing hellish fingers around your neck before you even notice.

I slip my arm out of Ren's and twist my hair up on top of my head. He bends at the same time, so his lips are level with my ear.

"I miss you *more*," he whispers, breath somehow cool against my skin. He's smiling at me like he just told me a secret.

We don't talk much on the ride over to the hotel, on account of the fact that as soon as we climb into the cab we have to stick our heads out our respective windows because the driver is *not* a fan of AC. At one point, I look over at Ren, a bead of sweat rolling between my already sticky boobs, and he shoots me such a miserable glance that the hoot of laughter I let out almost sends the driver careening into the other lane.

"I missed you too!" I shout over at him.

"What?" he shouts back, his head angled toward the inside of the car.

I catch the driver checking on us in his rearview, the wind whipping into his own window sending his hair dancing across his forehead.

"I said I missed you!"

"Oh," Ren calls back. "Sure!"

I laugh and give up for now.

We gasp our way into our hotel and collapse flat onto our beds. Ren rolls his head to the side toward me, and it's just the two of us staring at each other, breathing in the same air again, existing in the same space.

"Hi," I say.

"Hi," Ren says back.

My bangs are stuck to my forehead, and Ren's hair curls at the nape of his neck in the way it does only when he's returning from a run, fresh out of the ocean, when it's July and everywhere is an oven. It always makes him look a little boyish, drawing me back to the adolescent version of him I used to sleep with on the trampoline in his parents' backyard, or teenage Ren, lounging on a chair next to me at the public pool in summer, when it seemed like that part of our lives would never end. All we had was time.

It makes my arms itch in an anxious way, this reminder that this weekend is the exact opposite of days like that. Now, we only have thirty-six hours to fit in all the time we've missed together over the last year.

I push myself up to standing before I can get too comfortable, and extend a hand toward Ren. "Come on."

"Where are we going?" he asks, observing my waggling fingers but not moving an inch.

"Come with me and you'll find out."

For a minute, I worry he won't. That the idea of going back out into the heat is too unbearable, and the list and this weekend will be for naught. That I won't be able to make it all up to him, how inconvenient my move has made a relationship that was once as easy as breathing.

But just as I'm about to try to urge him up again, Ren smiles and grabs my hand.

chapter ten

It turns out my list may have been a little overambitious.

We hurry through the top hits of the Art Institute, ending at the *America Windows*, then hustle through Millenium Park, stop at The Bean and take an obligatory picture in its mirrored surface. I doggedly try to keep us on schedule, checking the time every twenty minutes, while Ren gamely pilots us toward each stop like a dad on vacation, following the blue dot that represents us on his phone screen and turning me toward our next destination when I get so focused on moving quickly that I nearly miss it.

By late afternoon, the next three stops on the list are all bars. "The tiki bar is this way," Ren says once we reach the river.

At the bar, we sit under a speaker that plays a cover of "Kokomo" on repeat that I enjoyed the first three times and is now the auditory equivalent of Baker-Miller Pink, and order Isaac's favorite drink on the menu. They arrive in coconut-shaped cups after fifteen minutes of the thirty I allotted for this place. I gulp half of mine down before my brain freezes from the icy, piña colada–adjacent mix while Ren sips his more carefully. Some of the energy seems to have seeped out of him, and I can't totally blame him. Everything feels sticky here, and we're crammed at a tiny table in between two loud, sweaty groups.

"Let's go," I say, glancing at the time on my phone. Happy hour ends in twenty minutes at the wine bar Lydia suggested, and I can only hope things might be better there. I nod at the unfinished drinks between us, tap mine against his. "Bottom's up." Ren takes one more drink of his, but leaves it mostly unfinished. He's not one for overly sweet things, anyway.

On the walk there, I keep my eyes forward as we pass a beer garden with picnic tables under umbrellas, misters set up around the perimeter. The blazing sun makes every step feel like ten, and my head is starting to spin from all the ground we've covered, but there isn't time for it.

"Let's stop here," Ren says, and I realize he's no longer next to me.

I turn around, observe the border of flower beds surrounding the tables before ambling back over to him. "It's not on the list."

Ren squints toward the tables, the dogs sprawled under them, the people looking a lot happier than we are in direct line of the sun. His eyes stay narrowed as he sucks at one cheek. "Seems like it should be," he says. "Have we considered the possibility that Lydia and Isaac compiled their suggestions in much cooler weather?"

"The entrance isn't even on this side."

He nods at the flower beds, barely knee high. "I think we can manage."

"We can't just climb—" The words aren't even out of my mouth before Ren is wrapping an arm around my waist, pulling me into him as he picks me up easily and steps over the flower bed.

On the other side, he sets me down, my hands finding his shoulders to steady my feet.

"See?" he says, grinning down at me. "Easy."

With the cool water misting down on my bare shoulders

and Ren's arm still around my waist, there is no list, only the yeasty smell of beer wafting out of the building, the soft fabric of Ren's T-shirt against my skin, and the whole evening stretching ahead of us.

But only *one* evening, I remember. I step back, hands dropping to my sides. "This isn't on the list," I remind him again. Tonight is our one night because tomorrow we'll be at the wedding, and on Sunday we'll say goodbye again.

I attempt to leap back over the offending flower beds, but Ren's fingers catch my wrist and tug me back toward him.

"We don't have time for this," I say.

"We do," Ren says. "If we want to have time for this."

"Well, I don't," I say, gesturing toward the picnic tables. "What if this place is terrible?"

Ren smirks. "Yes, because the tiki bar was really a top ten experience."

"It was on the list!"

"Fuck the list," Ren says. I open my mouth to protest, but he continues. "I'm serious." He jerks a thumb over his shoulder. "There are at least twenty dogs here just waiting to be rated." It's another one of our dumb games, picking which dogs are the best on various scales. They're all winners in the end. But it's not what we need to be doing right now.

"The wine bar is, like, fifty feet away." I throw an arm in its direction.

Ren looks down at me with those soft brown eyes. "Joni," he says.

"Ren." I swallow.

He steps up to me so he can take my face in his hands. They're warm on my cheeks, and for the first time since we left the hotel, I feel my thoughts slow down. I lean my face into one of his palms, close my eyes. When I open them, his gaze has gone darker.

"Joni—" he says, a slight edge to his voice. He's going to

offer up another argument for why we should stop, but I'm already convinced.

"*One* beer," I say. Ren's mouth snaps closed, and for a second I see it there: something more he was about to add, something he's not telling me. "Were you going to say something?" I ask. Things often need to be drawn out of Ren, the result of being the youngest of three, with two deeply extroverted siblings, and never wanting to fight for attention.

But Ren just releases my face, a smile spreading as he loops an arm around my shoulders and turns me in the direction of the bar.

"You won't regret it, Miller," he says, pushing me forward.

He scrubs a hand over the top of my head, and I pretend to shove him away. "Yeah, yeah, Webster."

An hour in, Ren is right: I don't regret it.

"I can't believe your dad agreed to go skydiving," he says, grabbing another fry from the basket between us. We're at a table next to a group with three friendly golden retrievers. One named Hopper keeps coming over and resting its chin on Ren's leg, looking up at him with doleful eyes while he scratches behind its ears.

"Believe me, neither could I until I saw the pictures." I dunk a fry into the lake of ketchup I upended into the basket. "I don't think he'd ever do it again. But my mom has made it their personal goal as a couple to *face a fear* once a month this year. Got the idea at some therapist conference she went to. At least she has a hobby and isn't nagging me as much." My phone buzzes against the table then. I pick it up, glance at the screen. "Speak of the devil," I say.

"Do you need to take it?" Ren asks.

I set my phone down again, shake my head. "I'll call her

back. Probably just another one of her interrogations." Ren knows them well from college—my mom calling me every other day to ask how I am, if I went to therapy, if work is overwhelming, so on and so forth. It's always the same questions, and they're never productive.

"Okay, what fear are you facing this month?" Ren asks me, trying to divert attention away from our third guest, I know.

"Answering one of my mom's calls and telling her I'm not sticking to her facing-my-fears plan," I say.

Ren laughs, Hopper raising his head at the sound.

"To facing our fears," Ren says. He lifts his half-empty glass. We cheers.

Now that we've actually been able to sit down, take a breath, we've been working our way through everything there is to catch up on. We might talk every day, but somehow, our phone calls always seem to devolve into arbitrary things like *what's your take on reincarnation* or *how long can we still say we're postgrad* or *let's really dig into that whole glitter conspiracy*. "How's the team?" I ask.

Ren started coaching a youth soccer team in college, something he'd done at summer camps when we were in high school.

"They're good," he says. "We might actually win a game this year. Oh—remember Cameron Velasquez?"

"Star midfielder?"

"And now full-blown teenager," Ren says. "He's my neighbor."

"No way." I swipe another fry into the ketchup. Ren watches the movement before his eyes find mine again as I chew. "Was he already living in the building?"

It feels strange that I haven't seen the apartment Ren moved into a few months after I left for New York. We'd made so many memories in his old place. Evenings out on the balcony, movie marathons on his couch, Wednesday night dinners. But when his roommate, a friend from college, relocated to Washington, Ren decided it was time to find a one-bedroom. I've only seen snippets of it in pictures, or when we FaceTime. It makes me feel one step further removed from his life.

"Moved in a month after me," he says. "He's applying for soccer scholarships."

"That's amazing," I say. "I bet he loves having you as his neighbor."

"He'd love you more. He's super into film stuff. Always wants to talk about Hitchcock."

I pause with another ketchup-laden fry halfway to my mouth. "Ren. You know about Hitchcock."

"I know what *you've* told me about Hitchcock," he says. He leans toward me, hands folded on the table between us. "I hate to break it to you, but I don't really seek out slasher films. Not big on watching people get ripped in half or dipped in wax."

"Hitchcock horror is different than modern-day horror," I say. "I don't want to watch, like, *The Strangers*. That's all Stevie."

"Face your fears, Joni," Ren says.

I smile, let him win this round. "So," I ask. "How are we feeling about the list?"

Ren looks a little wary as he sits back, fingers playing at the sides of his glass. "Honestly?"

"Honestly."

"I say we scrap the list. If we see something we want to do, we can, but I think this last hour has been better than rushing around trying to fit everything in." He flinches as he says it.

"Hey," I say, an uneasy feeling coming over me. "Why are you looking at me like you're scared?"

"Because I don't want to disappoint you," he says, tipping his glass up toward his mouth but not taking a drink. "I get it."

"Get what?"

He gestures with his glass at the sidewalk, where people are still streaming by, at the river beyond. "The list. Trying to fit everything in. I don't want to waste our time together either, but today…"

"Sort of felt like we were wasting it?" I ask.

Ren shrugs. "Yeah."

"Well." I grab a napkin, wipe away a drop of ketchup from my wrist. I wish I'd seen it earlier, wish we hadn't wasted so much of our precious time together before coming to what seems like the now-obvious conclusion. And I don't want to waste a minute more feeling that way. "I agree with you."

"Forget the list?" Ren says, eyes hopeful.

"Forget the list," I say, picking up my glass, extending it in his direction. "From here on out, we do what we want. The whole point is enjoying each other's company."

Ren presses the lip of his glass against mine, keeps it there. "Cheers to that."

Once the sky turns pink, we head back to the hotel, drifting together and apart. The night is finally cooling down.

"Hey," I ask as we wait at a crosswalk. "Did you ever ask your boss about an A&R position?" After enough to drink at the Tiki bar and beer garden, it just falls out of my mouth instead of the more tactful way I'd planned to raise the subject. I haven't brought it up since we talked about it last summer. A&R isn't the type of job Ren's parents envisioned for him—a result of having two overachieving older siblings in more "traditional" fields—law and event planning—and even if he doesn't verbalize it, I know that creates extra pressure for him. But Ren *deserves* to talk about it with someone. He deserves to have a cheerleader, to just be excited about what opportunity might be around the corner.

His eyes scan the street ahead for a minute before he looks down at the sidewalk, back up at me. "I did," he says. "Just a couple weeks after you moved, actually."

"And?" I ask, nudging him. "What'd he say?"

Ren blows out a breath, hands shoved in his pockets. "He said that it's rare a position comes up unless someone retires. Or someone brings him something really great."

"That's good news," I say as we cross the street. When he stays silent, I ask, "Isn't it?"

He tilts his head toward one shoulder, mouth twisting a little to the side. "I don't know. No one there is anywhere near retirement, and what am I going to bring him? I don't even have time to go to shows anymore with my hours there."

"Um, you bring him one of the *amazing* bands you're always sending me that don't have representation," I say, stepping up onto the curb as we reach the opposite side of the street. "You take a weekend off and go to some city where you can catch ten shows in two days, and you bring him the best of the best of the best and you *show* him how much you deserve a job not just as their sound tech, but working for the actual label."

"I think you have a lot more faith in my taste in music than anyone else," Ren says with a small laugh.

I stop him in the middle of the sidewalk, set a hand square on his chest so he'll look at me. He does, throat bobbing as he pastes on a close-lipped smile. "No. I believe in *you*, my best friend, and how perfect you would be for a job in A&R."

Ren is always the one who discovers bands before anyone else knows about them, who drags us to shows in basements or hole-in-the-wall dive bars in Portland and every city we ever visit, who still makes me playlists for every occasion. There's one called "For When Joni Doesn't Want To Put Away Her Laundry But Already Has More Laundry To Do" that I've had on repeat for weeks now, and every single time it's on in the office someone will inevitably stop in their tracks and ask me who's singing, what the name of that song is, why haven't they heard it yet.

Ren reaches up to squeeze my hand, lowers it back to my side, a slight smile on his face. "I know you do," he says.

≈

Back at the hotel, we take turns showering before flopping onto his bed and looking for something to watch. We make it half-way through *Best in Show* before we're both dozing.

Ren is a weird sleeper. First of all, he's out pretty much as soon as he lies down, which has always left me to haul the blankets out from under his dead-to-the-world body when we'd camp out on the trampoline in his backyard as kids. Second, of course, is his sleep talking. For the most part, it's just soft murmurs, but there have been nights I've woken up to him sitting straight up in bed, having conversations with the wall.

I'd thought he was sleeping now, eyes closed and breathing steady next to me, but as I force myself up and into my own bed, I hear him shift, his voice coming out of the half dark.

"Maybe I'll abandon Sublimity altogether," he says. "Move to the East Coast with you."

Something skips in my chest, and I hug my pillow. I give myself half a minute to think about what that would look like. Picking up coffee and going to museums together on the weekends, Ren taking us to shows any night of the week. But the truth of it is, despite how much I want to see him all the time again, make a new home for ourselves, Novo has consumed more and more of my time recently, and images of reinstated Wednesday night dinners and exploring the city together are quickly replaced by my canceling because something came up at work, or not being able to meet him on a Saturday morning because I stayed at the studios too late the night before.

"I think you love Sublimity too much for that," I say carefully.

Ren looks over at me through heavy lids, his cheek pressed to the pillow. Our beds are close enough that I can make out the splash of freckles he gets on his nose in the summer. "Like you love Novo, right?" he asks. The movie is still playing on the TV, Eugene Levy and Catherine O'Hara talking about their dog's *happier-to-know-ya kind of attitude.*

"Right." I love Novo in a bone-deep way. I've learned so much more from colleagues than I could have imagined over the past year. The work makes sense to me in a way other things often haven't in my life: failed classes that seemed to come easily to others, an anxious brain that liked to work against me. Art calms me, makes things go quiet. It's why I wanted to create a career out of it in the first place.

As the moment stretches between us, his eyes flick between mine, like he's mulling something over. Finally, he sits up, grabs the remote off the table between us.

"Done with this?" he asks, pointing it toward the television. I nod, and he turns the movie off.

As he heads into the bathroom to brush his teeth, my mind wanders back to what it would be like to have Ren in New York. To be together like this again all the time. But I tuck it away before I let that daydream settle in and become something real to hope for.

chapter eleven

"There she goes," I say the next afternoon as we float away from the shoreline, the blast of the boat's horn notifying everyone on the banks of Lake Michigan that we are On Our Way.

"Who's *she*?" Ren asks, amusement etched on his face as he leans against the railing next to me, looking out at the still blue water, the Chicago skyline beyond it.

I glance over at him, the cool breeze ruffling his hair. It's bearable out here, not socked in by asphalt and concrete.

"Escape," I say dramatically.

Lydia and Isaac decided to get married on a yacht that won't dock again until nine. It is now three o' clock. Maybe for them six hours on a boat with your friends and entire extended family is considered a recipe for success.

We wind our way to the observation deck with everyone else, pausing to accept flutes of sparkling rosé and say hello to a few familiar faces.

"Priya and Jamie are here together," I say, voice urgent as I grab Ren's wrist. "Six o'clock." He follows my coordinates. "Priya and Jamie from our writing seminar freshman year are here. Together. Priya told me she'd *never* date Jamie," I mutter as Ren steers us toward a table across from where they're standing, his hand on my back.

"Evidently, she changed her mind," Ren says. He nods toward the far side of the deck, at a particularly raucous group shouting over each other in jovial tones. "Remember the parties that house used to throw?"

"Oh, Ren. How could I forget the party there where you declared 'Mr. Brightside' *your song*?"

We were juniors, and one of Ren's friends—a percussion major who always seemed to know about every single party happening—had invited us to the once-impressive Victorian mansion two blocks from campus that housed forty different college students at any given time, with more always spilling out onto the rickety front porch and the unkempt lawn.

It was also the night Ren swore off tequila "for the rest of time, and after that too," a promise that didn't hold up all that long. After too many shots, we were on one side of a beer pong table, feeling overconfident about our skills. In the middle of the game, just as Ren threw, he turned to me, the ball sailing off somewhere into the ether of the crowded basement.

"Joni," he said, gripping above my elbow while I tracked the path of the ball for one drunken second before turning back to him.

"What?" I asked, tipping his direction.

"This is our song." He looked at me like he'd just made a brilliant discovery.

"What are you talking about? This isn't my song," I said, the shitty fluorescent lights reflecting off the red Solo cup in my hand.

"Fine," he said, feigning disappointment. "Then it's *my* song." He slipped his hand into mine and sang the first lines of the chorus, holding his other hand out to me like a microphone.

I snorted, unable to stop myself from grabbing onto his biceps and singing the chorus along with him. His energy was contagious, and soon enough I was bouncing on my feet, and a small crowd had formed, everyone singing along and dancing. After that, anytime "Mr. Brightside" came on, we'd pause whatever we were doing, turn it up and belt the lyrics as loudly as we could, windows down in the car or dancing around the kitchen or at the bar.

I loved when Ren got like that: some of his shell cracking. I'd seen more of that side of him when we were kids, but sometime in high school, this thin layer between the best friend of my childhood and the best friend I know today had taken shape. It didn't make me feel any less close to him, but it did mark some shift between us I didn't feel totally clued into, like Ren had suddenly just grown up faster than me. But it meant that when those parts of him did come out again, I was all the more grateful for them.

"It's not my song," sober Ren says now, taking a serious drink of his wine. "It's America's song."

I shake my head. "Not according to twenty-one-year-old you. As far as he's concerned, that is *Ren's song.*"

Ren grimaces. "Sometimes I really hate our collective memories."

"No, you don't," I say.

His eyes sparkle as he smiles down at me. "No," he says. "I don't."

I lean my elbows on the table. "Is it weird that Lydia and Isaac are getting married?" I say, dropping my volume. "I mean, I still feel like a baby."

"Yeah, me too," Ren says. "But Isaac was a total goner the second you showed up to our room with Lydia move-in weekend. Why wait if you know?"

"Hmm," I mumble against the rim of my glass, eyes skimming the crowd. "What must that be like?"

"Who knows." Ren tips back the rest of his wine, clears his throat and nods toward where Isaac's parents are talking to

Lydia's. "We might be at a totally different wedding if they'd taken their time. Lydia and Jamie."

"It could have been Isaac and Priya," I tack onto this alternate universe. "But I like how things turned out. It was pretty fun getting to play roommate with you half the time."

"It was our duty to foster young love," he says, looking down at me. I roll my eyes, but he cuts in. "I liked it too. Best roommate I've ever had."

I smile, bump my upper arm against his and let it rest there for a minute. Some of my favorite memories from freshman year of college are the ones we spent in his dorm room, talking late into the night like we would on the screen porch. Sometimes I worried it was strange to like Ren as my roommate more than my actual roommate. But when I thought about it, it made sense. The transition to college was scary, and we were familiar, there to center each other if things got hard.

Ren is pulled into a conversation with some of the guys from his college intramural soccer team, and I make my way over to where two girls from my dorm lean against the railing, watching the crowd.

"Joni, hi," one of them—Everly—says. Her white-blond hair is slicked back in a ponytail that tugs at her temples.

The other, Amina, who I also had a few classes with, hugs me hello. We catch up about generic things for a while, work and friends and living situations, before Amina is nodding across the deck.

"*That's* still happening, I see," she says.

I follow her gaze to Ren, always standing a few inches taller than everyone around him.

"What's happening?" I ask.

Amina and Everly exchange a look. "Come on," she says. "When *that*—" here she points with her eyes at Ren, like he is a particularly juicy cut of meat at a grocery store "—showed up to our dorm to walk with you to class like, every single day, we just kind of figured there was something going on between you."

"You know there wasn't," I say, which is true, because they had asked, several times, and I had answered, always the same way. *We grew up together. We're just friends.* It made me uncomfortable when they asked, like they were cheapening our friendship in some way, like we were fuck buddies instead of best friends who had seen each other through our entire lives to date. Like there was no possible way we could love each other just for the sake of it.

"But you two have before, right?" Amina had asked me once, after a similar conversation.

"Have *what*?" I'd asked.

"You know."

I did know, but her question irked me. Yes, maybe sometimes I could come off territorial about Ren, but not in a way that made it hard for me to share him with the rest of the world. Instead, in a way that made me almost angry at other people who didn't love him like I did. *Look at this person!* I would find myself thinking when he and his college girlfriend broke up. *You have the best person in the world in front of you, and you don't even realize it!* No matter how badly I might screw up, I had done one undeniably good, smart thing in my life when I befriended Ren Webster at the ripe old age of three, and it bothered me that people sometimes thought they knew our friendship better than I did.

"Hmm," Everly says now, swirling the wine in her glass. "If you two really aren't dating, do you mind if I take a crack at him?"

"Everly!" Amina whacks her arm at the same time I say, "Take a *crack* at him?"

Everly shrugs a narrow shoulder. "I don't know. It's hard to meet people nowadays. Do you know if he's seeing anybody?"

The question embarrasses me. Or, the fact that I can't answer with a hundred percent confidence does. Why, over the course of the past two days, not to mention the last ten months, have I not thought to ask Ren if he's seeing anybody? Because he would have told me, surely.

But then again, maybe not. When I asked Ren if he'd ever slept with anybody our sophomore year of college, his face went so red that I knew the answer was unequivocally yes and that we also wouldn't be discussing it. He's never been one to share details of his relationships with me, while I throw them around like I'm worried I won't get a chance to voice them before things end, texting him play-by-plays of bad dates and asking for advice.

"You know," I say to Everly now. "I honestly don't know."

"Hmm," she says, the sound grating against me.

Once the boat has stopped, it's time for the ceremony. Ren finds me on the deck, and Everly follows us into a back row and sits on Ren's other side. Behind the happy couple, the water stretches out, sparkling, but all I can focus on is Everly's pinky finger, seeming to strain toward Ren's thigh as Lydia and Isaac recite their vows. If Ren notices, he doesn't give any indication.

We move inside for dinner, to tables draped in white linens and flowers the same shade, a dance floor in one corner and a bar in the other. The dipping sun filters golden through the windows. We're not at the same table as Everly, but by the time dinner is over, she's practically burned a hole through the back of Ren's head from her seat across the room.

"You should dance with Everly," I say, nodding in her direction.

Ren's knee brushes against mine under the table as he turns to look at her. She glances away quickly, waits all of two seconds before her eyes dart his direction again, but he's already turned back to me, one side of his mouth twisting in a confused smirk.

"What are you talking about?" he asks me.

"Everly's into you."

Ren half rolls his eyes as he picks up his glass.

"Ren," I say.

He takes a drink, swallows, sets his glass down again before fixing me with a mock-serious expression. "Joni."

"Dance with her."

"Why?"

"Because she likes you."

"So?"

"So, that's usually how two people *meet*," I say.

"I've already met Everly."

"Ha ha. Why don't you want to dance with her?"

Ren's teeth run over his bottom lip. "Why do you want me to dance with her so badly?"

"I don't know," I say. "I just think it might be good for you."

"*Good* for me."

"Is there a reason you maybe shouldn't dance with her?" I ask. Since Ren doesn't often share this type of information with me, I don't know how else to broach the subject other than this roundabout method. I know he doesn't mean it to come off this way, but the fact that he withholds stuff sometimes makes me feel like he doesn't fully trust me or like I'm giving more of myself to him than he is to me.

Ren raises an eyebrow. "My doctor did tell me not to put weight on my ankle for at least six weeks," he jokes.

"Oh my god," I say, picking up my wineglass. "Never mind."

"No, I'm sorry." He faces me, moving one leg so his knees bracket mine. If Everly didn't believe that nothing was going on between us before, the way we're sitting now might plant another seed of doubt in her mind. I shift away from him slightly. "Why wouldn't I be able to dance with Everly?" he says.

"Are you seeing someone?" I finally ask him.

The half smile Ren has been wearing this entire conversation falters. "No," he says. "I would have told you if there was anyone serious."

"Of course," I say. A strange mix of guilt that I doubted he would tell me and relief that he wasn't withholding something settles over me.

Ren, apparently done with this conversation, nods at my empty glass. "Another?"

"Sure," I say as he stands. "Thank you."

He weaves his way through the crowd, stopping to talk to a few people on the way. He laughs with them, leans in to listen to their stories over the din, nods along at all the right moments. It feels like I'm removed from him, even though he's just across the room, like I'm watching a version of him I don't have access to now that we live so far apart.

The band plays the opening notes to a familiar song, a cheer going up from the dance floor in one corner. Ren is just breaking away from the couple he's been talking to and he turns to me, eyes going wide.

I lift my hands up in a *what are the chances* move. "Your song," I call as he walks backward toward the bar, head bobbing to the rhythm of "Mr. Brightside." I don't know if he can even hear me.

"America's song," he calls back. He pretends to sing into my empty champagne flute, his other hand clutched against his chest.

He grins as people on the dance floor start singing along to the chorus, then sets our glasses on the bar behind him. The bartender is busy, and Ren looks back at me, mouthing the words to the next line before I mouth back the next.

We're about to get to the chorus again when Everly appears behind him, pressing a hand to his back, and he pivots her direction.

A server appears beside me. "Champagne?" he asks, extending a flute.

I accept it and thank him, wrenching my eyes back to Ren and Everly. Ren is holding out his hand with a smile, and

Everly takes it eagerly, the two of them chatting as they snake their way to the dance floor. The song changes to "God Only Knows" just as they reach it.

I sip my champagne as Everly sets her hands on his shoulders, his own hands a polite height on her back. She leans back, says something to him, and he nods, that wide smile still on his face. Her cheek now against his shoulder, he turns his head back toward me. People are singing along, as into it as they were "Mr. Brightside," but Ren's not going along with it this time. He gently sways Everly, but his gaze is locked on mine.

The song is nostalgic in that perfect way, like time is folding in on itself, begging you to notice before it resumes its normal course. We were listening to this song at Ren's parents' house when we were sixteen, his dad's records spread around us on the living room rug, when Ren told me there are certain songs that can burrow so far into your body that it feels like you're hearing them for the first time, and that there's some kind of magic in that that can't be replicated anywhere else in the universe.

For a minute, with the music enveloping us, Ren's soft brown eyes on mine, everything—time, other people, the distance—falls away. My heart presses against my chest, like it's trying to get at something outside of me.

And then the song is ending. People are clapping, and Everly is leaning away from Ren again, and Ren's eyes are back on her.

I pick up my champagne and take a larger sip, the cold bubbles fizzing down my throat as Ren and Everly continue into a second dance. I'm in a room full of people I went to college with, some of whom I'd still call friends, and yet I stay glued to my chair, don't stand up to find any of them.

Amina must notice I'm alone, because she swings by the table and yanks me up and out of my seat. I dance with her and some friends to the next song, a classic Whitney Houston number, eyes on where Ren and Everly have moved to the bar, and remind myself that it's okay. We got our weekend, and if he spends the rest of the night with her, it will be worth it. If he falls in love with her, marries her—

Amina bumps her hip against mine, jostling me back into reality. When I blink back toward the bar, Ren and Everly aren't there. I cast around, suddenly feeling lost in the room without his presence to anchor me.

But then there's a hand slipping into mine. I twist around and smile up at Ren, pulling him into the group. Before long more people have joined, including Everly, who just shrugs in Amina's direction when she gives her a questioning glance. Everyone expands out into a circle, Lydia and Isaac in the middle as we all belt out a Journey song.

"No," I shout later, when "Closing Time" comes over the speakers. "I think *this* is your song!" Ren gives me a quizzical look, our hands clasped between us as we move absentmindedly with the music. "You can just put this on at the bar instead of having to do last call!"

"Oh, god no," he says, a laugh lurching out of me as he suddenly spins me toward him so my back is to his chest, then out again. "Please tell me my bartending days need to be over well before I start doing something like that."

At one point, Lydia sets her arms around our shoulders, brings us in close to her and Isaac. "If you two hadn't been so cool with basically getting kicked out of your rooms freshman year, I don't know if we'd be here," she yells over the music. The skirt of her dress brushes against my legs, a strand of her hair coming loose from her elaborate updo. "Thank you!"

"Seriously, though," Isaac says. "What did you guys do all those times?"

I look at Ren. "Explored Portland?" I offer.

"Studied," Ren adds.

"Sometimes," I say. "I did a lot of art projects in your room."

"Is *that* why our RA thought someone had an illicit soldering iron in the dorm?"

I press a hand over my eyes. "Sorry, Isaac."

"You know what?" he says, pulling Lydia into him and kissing the side of her head. "It's so fine."

After they're dragged away by the wedding party, I turn back to Ren, sliding my hands over his shoulders as the band plays the opening notes of "Your Song," couples around us moving together across the dance floor. "There has to be more than studying and art projects," I say, thinking back to freshman year, when we were trying to branch out, grow beyond our teenage selves, but mostly failed. We still preferred each other's company. "We already knew Portland pretty well. What did we do?"

Ren smiles at me like the answer is obvious.

"What?" I ask.

The hand he has on my waist tightens, fingers spreading up to my ribs, the spot warming under his touch. "It doesn't matter what we did," he says, his voice low enough that I have to lean in to hear it. When I look up at him, his face is close, eyes cast down to mine, that easy smile still lighting up his features. "We were together, Joni."

WEDNESDAY

chapter twelve

Ren is already gone when I wake up. The cool morning air comes in through the screens, and I burrow farther under the blankets. Even though yesterday went as well as it could, I don't feel ready to face the day, to continue on with this charade. But I can hear voices on the other side of the door, and my mom will be in to rouse me if I don't go inside soon, so I force myself out of bed and shrug on a sweatshirt over my pajamas.

"Well, good afternoon!" my mom says when I walk into the kitchen. She's at the table, a newspaper open to the crossword in front of her.

"It's nine," I say. "Hardly afternoon."

"The rest of us have been up for hours," she says. It's a running joke that whoever gets up first has to give everyone else grief, one tradition I don't entirely miss.

"Not true," Stevie mutters as she wanders into the room, also in her pajamas. "You haven't been up for hours."

"Well, good afternoon!" our mom says again. Stevie grunts as she settles herself onto one of the tall chairs at the island.

"Sleep well, sweetie?" Hannah asks when I float over to

where she stands at the counter, an apron tied around her waist and a butter knife in her hand.

Her free arm comes around me easily, and I lean against her shoulder, a yawn stretching out of me. "Sort of," I say.

"Oh, dear, it's those beds, isn't it?" she says. "See?" She glances over her shoulder at my mom. "We just do another addition. We could use the bathroom."

"We're still paying off the air-conditioning," my mom says. "We could put new beds out there, at least. It would be a good spot for grandkids, one day."

"What will we do when they both get married, though?" Hannah asks as the timer on the oven beeps, as if I'm not there. "They'll need better places to sleep."

The front door opens, and Ren comes in wearing shorts and a T-shirt, a bag in one hand.

"Thank you!" Hannah says, rushing over to him and planting her hands on his cheeks. "Can you believe we forgot to bring coffee?" she says to me, like I'm the only one not updated on the situation.

Ren heads over to where the coffeepot sits near the sink, a quick, polite smile passing between us before he reaches up to grab the grinder from the cupboard.

"Are we all ready for capture the flag tonight?" Stevie asks from her spot at the island.

"I think the parents will probably sit this one out," my mom says. "Though Greg's interest was definitely piqued."

In the tradition of possibly every high school in America, Ren's dad was the cool science teacher at ours. He's probably figured out how to make something like capture the flag a class assignment.

"You mean you *don't* want to go skidding down a rocky slope in the dark all in the name of claiming a flag as your own?" I say in mock disbelief.

"Hey," Stevie says. "It'll be *fun*."

"I know," I say. "I'm kidding." I raise my arm in some approximation of a fist pump. "Capture the flag!"

Ren stifles a laugh from across the kitchen. When Stevie shoots him a look, he shrugs. "What? Nothing Joni loves more than competitive sports."

"No one's going to get hurt playing this game, are they?" my mom asks, as if the mere mention of me playing sports is a promise someone will be injured.

"We'll be careful," I tell her.

Hannah pulls a muffin tray out of the oven and bypasses me to deposit it on the island, directly in front of where Stevie is sitting.

"Finally," Stevie says as she plucks one out and swears, shaking the burn off her hand.

"Finally?" I ask. Next to me, Hannah scoops batter into another tray.

"We haven't had these in two summers," Stevie says.

My gaze flicks to Ren. He's focused on a bag of coffee filters, but I can tell he's listening by the set of his shoulders. "Why not?" I ask.

"Because they're *Joni's favorite*," Stevie parrots.

I look at Hannah, hands finding the edge of the counter behind me and curling under as if to support myself. Yesterday, it seemed like it wasn't that big of a deal that I'd been gone, that everything on the beach was part of the normal course of life at the house. I'd even told myself I was being a touch narcissistic to think anyone even cared: life went on, things were the same. My presence or non-presence didn't matter all that much.

But now, the absence of this tiny tradition is proof that it *did* matter. I feel a sudden surge of love for Hannah that she remembered they're my favorite, that she preserved the tradition specially for me.

Hannah must see some of this playing out on my face, because she pats my arm. "I didn't want to make them without you here," she says.

"See what happens when you stay holed up in New York?" Stevie says, raising an eyebrow at me. She's not looking at me with any of her trademark suspicion. Instead, her expression is open, almost questioning, and it has me glancing quickly away. The fact that Stevie has provided me so many opportunities to be honest with her makes keeping things from her hurt all the more.

"Joni's working *hard* in New York." My mom smiles at me from the table. "Right, honey?"

I swallow. "Yeah," I say. "Totally."

The coffee grinder whirs loudly. "Sorry," Ren says, eyes widening just as I catch the small smile slipping off his face. It feels like a hand has reached out to help me over an icy path: even with all the time gone between us, and even though he doesn't know *why*, he can still tell when I'm uncomfortable.

His small effort to redirect things in my favor is thwarted, though, when my mom calls me over to sit down across from her at the kitchen table and slides a hand toward me. "I feel like I've hardly talked to you," she says. "How are you?"

Since I had my first panic attack in high school, when I learned I'd have to retake my second semester of geometry, my therapist mother has been on high alert at any hint of stress from me. Years of therapy have given me the tools to look after myself. Ironically, she never really seems to accept that, so it's become my practice to share as little as possible, and to color what I do tell her the brightest shade.

"I'm great," I say. "So happy we're all together again."

"Yes, but what about *you*," she says, leaning forward like we're friends talking over drinks at a bar. But her questions only ever make me feel examined, picked apart in a way that has me close up more. Stevie, meanwhile, seems to have gained our mom's trust and escaped most of her scrutiny.

"I'm fine, Mom," I tell her, but a slight burn in my chest accompanies the words, some muscle memory unlocked from when I was a teenager. *Don't say too much, don't say too little, don't be too happy, don't be too sad. Neutral, well-adjusted wins the game.*

"Tell us more about work, though," Hannah says from where she's scooping more batter into a muffin tray.

Her statement prods a finger into my spine, sits me up straighter in my chair. "Work?" I ask, like my mom didn't already try to bring it up.

"Yes, I want to hear about work too," my mom says.

"Apparently everyone does," I mutter.

"What?"

Ren runs the grinder again, this time adding one final, seemingly unnecessary second.

I take it as an opportunity to correct course, smile. "Work is so good. Novo's the best." This has been my refrain for so long now that it almost feels like there's a string pulled at my back, rattling the words out of me.

"We all get to come to the premiere, right?" my mom asks, excitedly tapping her hands against the table across from me.

"Oh, we can't ask that," Hannah says.

"I don't know when it is, anyway," I say, lying, again.

"But when you do, you'll let us know," Hannah says. "We're all so proud of you. Tell us about the movie."

"Um," I stammer. "It's been really good…working on such a large shoot." I search for something, anything to say, and land on the last change I made for the movie, an insignificant detail the safest response. "I made some dancing skeletons."

"Tell us about that," Hannah says, nodding, a big smile on her face.

"As if any of us could understand the mechanics of all of it," my mom says, leaning back in her chair. "Joni's *so* good at her job. Can you imagine her doing anything else? Her dream!"

I let out a weak laugh. She's not wrong. It was the dream. All through preproduction, all through the shoots, straight through editing, everything was going well. And then, Ramona Brinkley, founder and CEO of Novo and the person I used to envision myself growing up to be, called me into her office.

I knew what was about to happen, had known it for the past month, since we learned that the project I had fought for as my first film as a lead in the fabrication department three years ago wouldn't be premiering. Ever. The studio heads had taken one look at it—at three *years* of painstaking work on the puppets and sets, figuring out how to make eight sleepaway campers move, how to bring the ghost stories they all told to life with things like cellophane and natural fibers and wire, and, more than once, items from my own home—and said it wouldn't read well with audiences. We wouldn't make up our budget, and so we shouldn't add on to it now.

It happens all the time, they'd said, like that was supposed to be any consolation. *There are movies in our vaults the public never even knew existed. Count yourself lucky critics didn't get their hands on this.*

It doesn't happen all the time to *us*, though, I'd wanted to say. I had been with Novo, albeit as an intern, when it was struggling to make ends meet in its Portland offices: tiny studios, unreliable plumbing, spotty electricity and all. There, no project got off the ground unless it was a sure thing. Sinking millions of dollars and thousands of hours of manpower into a film that would never see the light of day might be a drop in the bucket to the major studio that we were now a part of, but to those of us at Novo, it was a catastrophe.

"Joni," Ramona had said when I walked into her office. "I want you to know that this has nothing to do with how talented I think you are, but—"

"I'm fired," I cut in. I wanted to rip open the wound myself, be in control of my own heartbreak. I had given up everything for this project, had made it my entire personality for years of my life. I might as well see it through to its bitter end.

The rest of the conversation hadn't mattered all that much, in the end. Being fired by someone I'd looked up to for the last decade of my life was about as bad as it could get.

I hadn't had a panic attack in years. Had even, for a while, naively thought they might be gone for good. But after crying so hard on the train home that a woman who had to be pushing a hundred had offered me her seat, all the familiar warning bells went off, and I didn't do anything to stop it.

I received a text shortly after I got home that three other members of the team had been fired as well. A slew of texts came in after that:

Happens all the time, my ass. I bet they're firing us to make up for the money we cost them.

Is this legal? I mean, can they get rid of us at this stage of the game?

Who wants to get drunk and look at job boards?

I felt trapped, untethered. I couldn't fathom discussing it with anyone, that this thing I had given everything to was just over, like that, couldn't even pull it together to commiserate with people because they had full, vibrant lives outside of work to turn to. The only thing that sounded okay was getting out of New York, so I used my miles and dipped into my savings to pay the exorbitant fee to move my flight two days earlier.

"It's the dream," I tell the room now, my eyes stuck on the movement of Ren pouring water into the back of the coffee-pot, as I try to let the natural rhythm of it soothe me. "They're in postproduction, so my role is mostly over." A half lie. I'd had some hand in it the whole way through, if only because I couldn't seem to let it go after preproduction.

Hannah, thankfully, changes the subject. I quickly wish she hadn't. "Are you seeing anyone back in New York?" she asks me.

"No," I say, eyes wrenching away from Ren's hands to where his mom is scooping the last of the batter into the muffin tin. "Not right now."

"All you young people, not wanting to settle down." She bends to slide the tray into the oven, bumps it closed with her hip. She walks over to where Ren is closing the lid to the coffeepot, squeezes his shoulders as he flips the on switch. "This one won't marry the perfect girl when she's right in front of him."

The fact that Ren had considered marrying Amanda shouldn't shut me down. In fact, it was what I'd thought he was about to tell me at the winery, that they were next. But her words are like a rail bridge in front of me that suddenly goes missing, and my train of thought hurtles off. *Marry, perfect girl.*

"And we all know how you feel about that, Mom," Ren says, reaching up to put the grinder back in the cupboard, store the bag of coffee next to it.

Hannah holds up her hands, her attention on her baking paraphernalia. "I'm just saying, I thought *maybe* seeing Stevie and Leo so happy this week might make you reconsider the idea of marrying Amanda."

The pinprick to my spine at the sound of her name, at the reminder of anything even tangentially related to that New Year's Eve night is quick, familiar, so I don't even flinch at it anymore.

"I would like to point out that I am marrying Leo only because I'd like to hang out with him forever," Stevie says, taking a bite of her muffin. "I don't want this week to make anyone feel like they *have* to get married."

The coffeepot sputters.

"It doesn't, sweetie," Hannah says. "It's just that, Ren and Joni are the only ones who won't be married now. Joni, doesn't seeing your little sister preparing for her wedding make you think about it at all?"

I can't get more than a croak out of my throat when she looks at me. I'm thrilled for Stevie, but marriage has always been a vague concept to me, buried under work and working toward a future that no longer exists. I figured it would just sort of happen one day, and so I haven't put the same effort into dating that some of my friends have. And now, with everything in my life so out of control, it's the last thing on my mind.

"Well." Stevie suddenly slaps the island, seeming to understand that this conversation is a dead end. "Sasha told me I need to go down to the lighthouse to see what we need to set up in the cottage." She glances between me and where Ren is watching the coffee brew. "Ren, Joni, could you guys help me?"

"Yes!" I pop up from the table. Ren is already heading in the direction of the door. We just went three rounds—job, Ren getting married, *me* getting married—and I have no interest in finding out what the remaining rounds might entail. "Just let me change."

Stevie trails me onto the screen porch, sitting on the edge of my bed while I root through the dresser.

"Didn't miss feeling like one of Mom's patients again," I say as I grab a T-shirt out of a drawer.

"At least she cares enough to ask," she says. When I look down at her, surprised by her tone, she adds, "Wait until you meet Leo's parents. There's a reason he hangs out with us more than them."

It surprises me. I'd always pictured Leo with parents as exuberant as he is. "Are you worried about Saturday?" I ask as we head back into the house.

"Not at all. And if things get tense, may I remind you it's a pretty steep drop from the lighthouse down to the ocean," she says, face devoid of humor. "Everyone will just have to be on their best behavior."

chapter thirteen

"Sasha says that if we get the tables out today, we won't have to worry about it the rest of the week," Stevie says as she, Ren, and I stand in front of the cobwebbed storage area at the back of the lighthouse keeper's cottage. On Saturday, Stevie and Leo will get married on the lawn that stretches out from the lighthouse and overlooks the ocean, but the reception will be inside and it's up to the wedding party to set it up.

After a spider-ridden, cramped hour—the storage area is little more than a damp closet—Ren and I manage to roll out all the tables into the main room, Stevie providing vague guidance along the way.

"So good to see you two together again," she says as we lean the last of the tables against the far wall, both of us sweating.

"Stevie," I sigh, pushing my bangs off my forehead. While I appreciate her rescuing us from the moms, she has to know that, no matter how badly she wants us to be friends again, it's not so simple for me and Ren.

A few months into the silence, when she casually admitted that she'd asked Ren what happened, it felt like the floor had dropped out from beneath me at the prospect that they might have discussed it. This was a private matter, between me and Ren, and the idea that he might have disclosed it made me question if I ever knew him at all. But Stevie said he'd only told her to ask me, and simply nodded when she asked him if we still weren't talking, and I was relieved that Ren had still been kind enough to keep our secret.

"What? It's been a while," she says now.

"Yes, we *know*."

"What else do we need to get out of storage?" Ren asks, ignoring the conversation.

Stevie shrugs. "The chairs won't be here until Saturday morning, and we'll get the bar and outside ready on Friday, but we should definitely get the tables up now. See how the room looks before we bring anything else in."

Ren starts toward a table, but I narrow my eyes at my sister, suspicious. "Do we *really* need to set this up before Friday?"

"Always good to get a task checked off the list, Joni," she says, like she's echoing something Sasha told her. She tucks her phone, which she used to illuminate our path through the storage space while we hauled out the tables, into the pocket of her shorts.

Ren and I unfold the legs on the only rectangular table and carry it to the head of the room before going back for the circular ones where guests not in the wedding party will sit. He nods at me as he tilts the first one, letting me know when to turn my side, and takes the more difficult, backward path toward where we set up the other table.

Stevie blows out an exaggerated breath, shaking her head. "You know what? I'm the bride. I'll let you wrap up here."

"Don't you want to tell us where they all should go?" I ask after her as she walks to the door, lifting her long, brown hair off her neck like she's the one who's been doing manual labor.

"I trust you!" she calls before she disappears.

"Classic Stevie," I say, turning to the next table and releasing the legs on my side, as Ren does the same opposite me.

"Did you think we'd ever be setting up for her wedding?" Ren asks as we each take a side and flip the table upright.

"I definitely never thought we'd be setting up a wedding like *this* for her." We shuffle the table over next to the other one, arrange it until there's adequate space between them. "I kind of always assumed that if Stevie ever did get married, it would be at, like, a haunted house."

"At the center of a corn maze," Ren says as we walk back across the room.

"If you can find them, you can come to the wedding," I say.

Ren half laughs. "Saturday will be good," he says. "Even if we didn't picture this elegant seaside affair for her."

I watch his face as we tilt another table to its side, his mom's words from the kitchen echoing in my head. "How *does* this week make you feel about all of it?" I ask.

"Hmm?" Ren mumbles. He's crouched down, focused on where one of the legs is stuck.

I stare at the top of his head. "Marriage, settling down, all of it." He bumps the heel of his palm against the hinge. "You weren't lying about your mom being bummed about Amanda."

The hinge gives. Ren pulls the leg open and locks it into place before he straightens and meets my eyes. "You know. It's nothing out of the ordinary."

"Isn't it?" I ask. I know Hannah, like my own mother, can ask a lot of questions, but I don't remember her fussing over Ren's romantic life this much.

"She's just not dealing all that well with the breakup," Ren says, rubbing a hand at the back of his neck.

"Your mom isn't dealing well with *your* breakup?" I ask.

"I think she's worried I won't ever get married," he says, then hastens to add, like he's revealed too much, "or, she's just worried about me settling down. Thad and Sasha are so happy and I'm—" He breaks off, studies the table between us. "She was just really excited when Amanda and I got back together. I think she thought it was a pretty sure thing. And I hate being a disappointment."

The words are hanging right there. *You're not a disappointment.* But before I can say them, he's tipping the table up to standing and nodding at me to take the other side. We may not have spoken in years, but I still know what Ren's face looks like when he doesn't want to talk about something. Flat, drawn-in, inaccessible.

Ren keeps his eyes on the table as we carry it over to the others. But when we set it down, he looks at me across it, considers his next words. "Amanda's amazing."

I nod, trying to keep my expression neutral.

He tilts his head, squinting.

"What?" I say. "Amanda's amazing."

"You never liked Amanda."

"I didn't really *know* Amanda," I point out, which is mostly true. I only met her once, when she and Ren first dated, and then, through vague family updates, witnessed the rekindling of their relationship. It was six months after things between us blew up, and it felt like such an inevitability that I could only feel numb at the news. What I did know about her was enough to tell me that she and I probably wouldn't get along, because she was, in a lot of ways, the opposite of me. Interested in different things, one of those people who might tell a deeply anxious person to just *stop worrying about it!* In a well-meaning, if perhaps somewhat ill-informed way, of course. Ren would never date an unkind person, and I understood what he saw in her. She was self-assured, successful, put-together. "But she made you happy, so I liked her. Fair enough?"

"Sure," Ren says. He shakes his head, reaches under the table to check the legs a last time. "Anyway, she's great. But I just... I couldn't marry her."

He makes his way back across the room, but halfway there, he turns back to me. "What about you?"

"What about me?"

"We're the only two unmarried kids left, Joni," he says with mock seriousness before walking back for the next table. "What are we going to do about it?"

"Know anyone up for a marriage of convenience?" I ask, following him. "I bring a never-ending sense of doom and a total lack of direction to the table."

It's out before the words are even fully formed in my head. It was once safe to say anything to Ren, so much so that my thoughts mostly spilled out unedited. Now, talking to him this way feels precarious.

He pauses, his hand on the table, shoots me a curious look. "Something you want to share?"

"No," I say, waving it off as blood rushes to my ears, and I focus on pulling the legs down. I can't tell Ren what I really mean—that my life is currently the equivalent of a raft floating in the middle of the Pacific, no compass in sight.

Ren is still looking at me, a familiar expression on his face. "Joni," he says. "If you want to talk about anything—"

"I know," I cut in quickly. Then, softening my tone, "Thank you." I've had enough *almost* talking about work today. I try to pivot. "Being back here with everybody has been pretty great."

Ren smiles skeptically. "Even when our mothers won't stop badgering us?"

"Okay, maybe not that part," I admit. The interrogation Ren and I underwent in the kitchen is a great example of why neither of us has told our families, especially our moms, that we're no longer friends. If we told them, they'd force us to sit down in some kind of intervention that would have made it all worse.

"Well," Ren says, picking at the edge of the table with a thumbnail. "That worry is always here for you."

"Maybe," I say. "Maybe I stayed away too long." It's a thought that's plagued me over the years. Everyone was moving on with their lives, after all. There was only so long I could stay away before I would be left behind for good.

I reach down to turn the table over, but Ren stops me, steadying it with his hand so I have to look him in the eye.

"I hope you know you didn't need to do that," he says, a hint of worry lining his forehead. "I could have stayed away, if that would have meant you'd come. I didn't think—"

"No," I say. "It wasn't you."

"It was, though," he says. "If we hadn't—"

"I'm the one who left," I say before we can dance too close to whatever dangerous memory he was about to bring up. Some part of me had just wanted to give him Oregon, keep a country between us so I couldn't mess things up any more than I already had. "I just— I needed to be…"

"On the other side of the country?" Ren supplies.

I exhale a laugh through my nose. "Something like that."

"I'm serious, Joni," Ren goes on. "You're one of us no matter what. Everyone misses you, but no one faults you for not being here." He glances around the room like it represents the house, our families, and I see that mask falling, the best friend I used to know so well starting to show his face. "It's all here for you, whenever you want it."

As we lift another table, Ren's words ringing in my head, I almost forget I have anything to worry about at all.

chapter fourteen

Leo sends a text to everyone to meet in the yard at sunset, and to wear all black.

"Do you think this will work?" I ask, holding up a navy blue tank top I usually wear to Pilates. I brought black leggings, shorts, but somehow, nary a black shirt made it into my suitcase in my haste to pack and get the hell out of New York.

Ren looks up from where he's tying the laces on a pair of black Vans, all in on the dress code. He gestures at his black hoodie hanging on the last hook above the dresser. "You can wear that."

"Thanks," I say, stacking it on top of my folded leggings. "I'll go change."

"I'm done." Ren straightens from the edge of his bed. "I can stand guard?"

I nod. People have a fun habit of using the screen porch as a shortcut from the front yard into the house, often without knocking.

I lock the doors into the mudroom while Ren steps out into the yard. We've already closed the curtains, but I can see his shoulder through a tiny slit as he leans against the door frame.

We used to do this for each other all the time, talking through the door before swapping places.

"When's the last time you played capture the flag?" I call as I slip off my shorts. I kick them over to the dresser, then reconsider, bending down to retrieve them and stuffing them into a drawer instead.

"Maybe sometime in high school?" Ren says. "But I honestly couldn't tell you."

"It's one of those games you're just kind of born knowing how to play, isn't it?" I pull on my leggings. "Did we ever play together?"

"We *were* notorious for joining in on social activities in high school," Ren says.

"*You* were a joiner." I tug his sweatshirt on over my tank top, something sparking in my chest at the familiar smell of it.

"I was on a couple teams," Ren says. "There's a difference."

I grab my sneakers and tap on the door. Ren shifts away and I push out into the cool night air, sit on the steps to put my shoes on. "Okay, but lots of people wanted to be your friend," I say. It's a skill I envied, his ability to make people feel at ease. Ren could navigate any crowd, whereas I tended to stick to people I already knew.

He sits down next to me, arm brushing against mine. "That doesn't mean I liked everyone."

"Doesn't change the fact that everyone liked you," I say, hooking a finger into the heel of my sneaker so I don't have to untie the laces. "You could have been prom king if you didn't spend so much time with grouchy old me."

"Please never suggest that again," Ren says, a smile lifting his cheeks as he looks out at the darkening sky.

"The prom king part?"

He glances back down at me. "All of it."

I bite the inside of my cheek, but it doesn't stop the smile that grows.

Headlights come through the trees, Leo's brother, Oliver, and bandmates arriving for the game.

Ren stands, holds a hand out toward me. His fingers settle against the underside of my wrist as I take it, his eyes locking onto mine at the contact as he pulls me up to standing.

Leo bursts out onto the front porch a few feet away. He catches sight of us, raises his fists in the air and shouts, "Who's ready?" just as his brother leaps out of the car, whooping and carrying on like we really are at a sporting event. Ren grins back at me, something so boyish in it I'm dropped right back into so many similar moments when we were kids up here and he was excited to boogie board with Thad or fly a kite on the beach with Sasha, then he runs over to greet the band. He's the one who signed them to Sublimity, and I know through Stevie's grapevine that he's become good friends with them over the last couple years. It's been a sore spot, the continuation of this world I was no longer a part of. I wanted, more than anything, for Ren to be happy, to get everything he deserved. But now there's a whole world I'm only tangentially connected to, as Stevie's sister.

"Seems like you two made up." I jump, my hand flying to my chest, and turn to find Stevie, who's crept up behind me. She's holding a grocery bag, her eyebrow raised.

"Yeah, we had a lot of time to talk after *someone* left us to set up tables for a hundred wedding guests," I say.

"Sorry about that." She bumps her hip against mine before leaning her head on my shoulder, watching as Ren and Leo laugh with the band, all of them huddled together and bouncing around like a group of overgrown teenagers. I feel the pinch again, of how much I've missed.

"It's just because we all live in Portland," Stevie says, reading my mind.

"Yeah, I know," I say. Location isn't the only thing that matters to a friendship, but I know she's trying to make me feel better. "Hey." I jostle my shoulder. Something has been nagging at me since I learned about Ren and Amanda's breakup. That Stevie, in all likelihood, had to have known, and didn't tell me. But when she looks up at me, eyes the same green as mine, I can't bring myself to ask. Can't open a can of worms that could make her wedding week anything less than perfect.

I loop an arm around her instead, draw her in closer, like if I hang on tight enough, I might prolong all the good of this week. "Never mind."

"The rules are simple," Leo says.

We've all convened around the firepit my dad had installed on the back patio a few years ago. It's unlit, and Leo stands on the concrete edge, hands on his hips. The sun has finally dipped below the horizon, the last stretches of light across the sky making it seem like we're about to embark on some *Goonies*-style adventure where anything is possible.

"I think we've all played capture the flag before," Sasha says. "Can we just choose teams?"

"I want to hear the rules!" I call. Deep down, despite everyone treating me normally, I can still feel myself searching for that opportunity to be part of things like before, to establish myself in this group.

Leo grins and proceeds to explain rules that, yes, we all probably know. But his energy is infectious, and even Sasha is smiling by the time he's done.

"First team to get the other team's flag and make it back to their base camp wins. If you get tagged by someone on the opposite team, you're sent to jail, and have to be tagged out by your own team member. Blue team's camp and jail is here," Leo says, waving a hand at the patio. "Red team's is the old swing set at the top of the yard. Blue's flag is on a tree at the bottom edge of the side yard. Red's is at the top."

Stevie holds out her bag, filled with red and blue bandanas. "You can use the forest for cover," she says as we all reach in to grab one, Leo hopping down from his post to make sure no one tries to choose a specific color. "But no one goes farther than where the path turns toward the lighthouse. We don't want anyone tumbling into the ocean."

"One more thing," Leo says. "Losing team covers the tab at Clyde's tomorrow night." Clyde's is Stevie's favorite bar in town and our last stop on their joint bachelor/bachelorette party.

We split into groups, red heading toward one side of the firepit and blue staying on this one. I bounce on my toes, the sound of the ocean crashing invisibly below racing into my veins. I've never been one for organized competition, hate when people offer me tips for sports I'm already well aware I'm bad at. But something about the fading light, the anticipation emanating off the others, being back in this *place*, has me excited.

Ren wanders over with the concentration he used to display before his soccer games in high school.

"Hey, teammate," I say, holding up my blue bandana as he knots one around his neck.

"No way," Sasha says, tying her red bandana around her arm like she's headed into battle. I stop bouncing as she waves a finger between Ren and me. "These two can't be on a team together."

"Why not?" Leo asks.

"You weren't around for the great charades debacle of 2014," Stevie explains.

"I was not mouthing the answers to Joni," Ren argues. He's always been offended by the suggestion we cheated.

"What about the poker fiasco the summer after they graduated high school?" Thad adds. "You hid cards for each other."

"Or—"

"We get it," I say, knowing this could go on all night. We didn't cheat, but they'll never listen. "Who's trading?"

"I'll be on red," Ren says, reaching up to undo his bandana.

"Hold on," Thad says. "How do we know that isn't already the plan?"

Ren narrows his eyes at his brother. "What *plan*?" he asks.

"I want Joni," Stevie interjects. I throw her a confused look. No one ever picks me for games like this. She rolls her eyes. "Unless you'd like to keep discussing this."

I raise my hands in surrender. "Who am I being traded for?"

The band's bassist takes my bandana, and I head off with the red team, but not before I glance back to see Thad with one hand on Ren's shoulder, strategizing with him in a low voice. It sends a small twinge of disappointment through me. I wouldn't have hated to be on the same team as Ren.

I shake the thought away. We have a game to win.

We all break on Leo's signal, but the first round is a disaster. Ren, who also ran track in high school, puts almost half the red team in jail in minutes, darting around the woods near silently, paving the way for Leo to sail over me where I'm supposed to be standing guard at the swing set to steal our flag. Blue wins.

"Look at them," Sasha says, watching Ren and Leo celebrate after. She squints. "Do they have a secret handshake?"

The second round kicks off, and Stevie and Oliver guard our flag. On offense this time, I run through the forest with Sasha. She stays in front of me, crouched so as not to disturb any of the lower hanging branches and alert someone to our presence. We stick close to the trees, pausing every few seconds to listen for footsteps.

We're about to cross the path when a hand lands on my shoulder, jerking me to a stop.

I whirl to find Ren, who's frowning down at me in a *sorry you had to lose* way, eyes shining at the same time as Sasha howls, "No!" and Thad pops out of the trees above us and lunges toward her. I'd assumed that fatherhood ended his tree-climbing days, but apparently I was wrong.

"Come on," I say as Thad begins to lead us toward jail. "Were you guys just lying in wait?"

Ren jogs backward up the trail, grinning. "Got to keep up!" he calls.

We reconvene at the swing set before the next round, circle close around Sasha.

"You," she says, pointing at the lead guitarist. "You're our jailer this round."

He nods and heads toward the slide, rubbing his hands together in preparation.

"Joni," Sasha says to me. "You run like hell toward the flag."

"She has the shortest legs," Stevie says.

"I am *not* that short," I say, indignant. It is my lot in life to be of average height but surrounded by enough tall people that I seem shorter than I am. I was devastated when I reached my early twenties and had to make peace with the fact that a final growth spurt was never coming for me.

"You are," Sasha says.

"I'll run," Stevie says.

"*I'll* run," I cut in. They both glance skeptically at me. I roll my eyes. "I'm fast."

"Better be," Sasha says as she spots the waving beam of Leo's flashlight, his signal that the round is beginning. Stevie ducks into the trees next to us, ready to keep an eye out for anyone approaching, and Sasha looks at me, eyes going wide. "Go!" she says, thrusting me forward.

"Oh, shit," I say. I take off in a dead sprint across the yard.

My two-second error cost us, though. Just as I'm about to cut through the side yard, Ren steps into my path. I let out a sound that's half scream, half laugh and dart around him, but I'm not fast enough. His arm comes around my middle and he hauls me up against him, my knees bending as I grasp to push him off.

"Oh my *god*," I say once he's set me down. "Are you coming after me on purpose?"

"It's kind of the point of the game. Making sure you can't get the flag."

I throw a hand out, indicating the side yard still stretching out behind us. "I'm yards away from your flag!"

"Be proactive, not reactive, Joni," he says instructively, then lets a wry smile slip.

"Do you say that when you're coaching too?" I ask, taunting him.

"Of course." He hooks a finger under my chin just long enough for me to have to look up at him. "Got to keep an eye on your opponent," he adds quietly.

"Sabotage!"

We both jump at the sound of Thad's voice.

"Stop!" he shouts, cupping his hands around his mouth. "Stop the game! Conspiracy!"

"Thad," Ren says, dragging a hand down his neck, tugging at his bandana. "Come on."

"Nope," Thad says as footsteps come toward us. "You and Joni can't be trusted."

"Kindly step away from our runner," Sasha says as she reaches us, Stevie behind her.

"Your runner?" Ren says. He looks down at me. "Sure you made the right call there?"

"It's not *funny*," Stevie says. "You two are standing out in the open, *conversing*. Whose team are you on?"

"Yours," I say as Leo comes hurtling out of the trees and halts next to her. "Totally yours."

Stevie and Leo turn to Thad and Sasha and they all mutter together. I hear bits of it: *Do we put them in jail? Switch teams?* When I look at Ren to try to parse his reaction, he flashes a suppressed smile at me, shaking his head.

They break apart. "We've decided to give you each *one* more chance," Leo says. He holds up a finger when I start to smile. "But if either of you are found so much as *breathing* in the direction of the other, you're out."

Sasha leads me back toward the swing set, glaring over her shoulder at Ren. "If you could refrain from distracting any more of our team members, that would be excellent!"

"Yes, Captain!" Ren calls back. When I catch his eye, he winks.

Stevie complains that talent is split unevenly between the teams, but we finally win the following round, Sasha racing back to our camp with the blue flag raised in triumph, and we have to call a tie on the next when Stevie and Leo both end up at the middle point with each other's flags at the same moment. He grabs her, tossing her over his shoulder and pretending to carry her in the direction of blue's jail. When he sets her down, she swats at his chest, then kisses him once, quickly, and runs back over to us.

During round six, I follow Stevie into the trees along the side of the yard. The stars are fully out now, any remaining gray in the sky gone, and we make our way down the slight slope, staying well into the woods, the flashlights Oliver handed out aimed at the ground. Since we were accused of sabotage, Ren and I haven't crossed paths again. But just as Stevie and I head toward the place where the woods meet the yard and the firepit comes into view, there's a crunch of leaves underfoot next to us and he pops up out of nowhere, tagging Stevie.

I narrowly skid away, retreating down where the path curves toward the lighthouse.

"Ren!" Stevie growls loudly. "How the hell is someone as tall as you so quiet?" As he drags her toward blue's jail, which is really just one of the wicker chairs around the firepit, she shouts, "Run, Joni! Avenge me!"

It's enough to give me a new burst of energy. I yank the hood of Ren's sweatshirt over my head and dash between the trees, keeping my flashlight tucked up into the too-long sleeve, despite how dark it is. Something about the soft, well-loved hoodie buoys me, like I'm absorbing from it some of whatever confidence Ren's using to slink around so skillfully.

I pick a careful, quiet route deeper into the forest, head uphill again so I might be able to tag Stevie out of jail from behind. I make it back to where I can see the house, the distant orange glow from the windows lighting up the deck and the patio below. At the firepit, Leo is pacing while Stevie sits in one of the chairs, arms crossed.

I shuffle sideways through the trees, crouching low, an eye on the firepit, waiting for the right moment to strike. If I can free Stevie, maybe we can create enough of a distraction that Sasha can swoop in and grab the flag. I haven't heard any commotion, so I assume she hasn't been spotted yet—

A hand wraps around my arm, and I jolt back, colliding with a hard chest. I twist fast, pulse hammering in my ears, to find Ren behind me. I thought I'd been so sneaky, keeping my flashlight off, blending in with the trees. Apparently, Ren is sneakier.

"What the hell," I say. "Why *are* you so quiet?"

He reaches up, plucks the hood off my head. "Don't think it would be a problem if we were on the same team," he whispers, eyes luminous in the dark. He steps back, nods me in the direction of the patio.

But I don't move. "You're not really going to take me to jail, are you?" I say. Maybe if I can keep him here long enough, not alert anyone else to our whereabouts, I might be able to convince him not to give me up to his team.

Something flickers in Ren's eyes, his smile faltering. "That's the game, isn't it?"

"You could break the rules, you know." I take a step closer to him. "This one time."

I fiddle with one of the drawstrings on the hoodie, trying

to ignore how much the smell of it comforts me. Ren notices the movement, looks down at it and back up at me. He's suspicious, but making a run for it would be futile.

There's a rustling near us.

"Ren." Thad's voice rings out.

Ren seems to weigh his options, peering over my head in the direction of Thad's voice and then back down at me. Make us known and win the round, or hide like this longer and risk being caught and accused of conspiring again?

I widen my eyes up at him, attempting to appear innocent, and he grabs my hand, tugging me over to a huge, mossy tree. He leans me up against it, grips my upper arms like he's trying to keep me there, one of his knees just between mine as he stills our bodies.

"He's not as quiet as you," I whisper, and Ren presses a finger to my mouth.

Thad's steps stop. "Ren," he hisses again. "I can hear you."

Ren's eyes dart toward the sound. We wait for a minute, hardly breathing. Seemingly satisfied that I'll be quiet, the hand he has on my mouth slides away and comes to rest where my shoulder curves into my neck, pinning me in place.

There's another rustle from a spot on the other side of the tree, close to where we last heard Thad.

"Did you find him?" a voice asks—the drummer, Dev, I think.

"No," Thad says. "I swear, if he's defecting—"

Ren's eyes fix on mine, questioning. I shake my head.

"I have to," he whispers. "They'll think we're conspiring."

"They'll think we're conspiring if they find out we've been hiding," I whisper back. "And then we won't be able to play anymore."

His gaze drifts over my head, a muscle working in his jaw. He's about to say something when their footsteps shuffle closer.

Anxious not to be caught myself, I fist a hand in Ren's T-shirt and draw him in so we're pressed together, flush against the tree.

Something like surprise passes over his face before his expression goes serious. I feel it like he's run the corner of an ice cube up my spine. His fingers slowly move from my clavicle up my neck, under my hair. I curl mine tighter into his shirt, tilt my chin up as his eyes drop to my lips.

"Blue wins!" Leo's voice rings out, followed by Stevie's wail of disappointment. Thad and Dev's footsteps take off in the direction of the yard.

For the span of two breaths, Ren and I stay pressed together. I've tried not to picture this moment, having him this close to me again. But now that it's here, I realize that even if I've been able to avoid envisioning this fantasy—cool night air, us together, in the dark—that doesn't mean I've figured out how not to want it. His chest rises and falls against mine, and I wonder if we stayed still, locked together like this, if anyone would come looking for us.

It's the fact that I *want* to stay here that has my grip on his shirt loosening and my head ducking to the side. Ren takes the cue, steps away, running a hand through his hair while I remain propped against the tree, heart thrumming in my ears.

It takes him a minute to look at me, but when he does, all the life that was in his eyes earlier is gone. Time comes out of its slow crawl. "We should go," Ren says.

I nod, still adjusting back to the moment. "Right. Don't want them to think we're conspiring."

We walk back to the yard in silence. Sasha narrows her eyes at our late arrival, Stevie in a similar pose next to her, but neither says anything. Thad and Leo are too busy celebrating their victory to clock our presence.

We play two more rounds, but any competitive spark in me is gone. Sasha must notice, because she puts me back on guard at the swing set. When Thad sneaks in to steal our flag, I tag him half-heartedly at the last minute. We win. But it doesn't feel like a victory.

When everything is said and done, blue wins it all, but only by one. Thad and Dev lift Leo onto their shoulders, the bassist bowing down to honor the king. Ren claps from behind them, but his smile is drawn in, the corners of his mouth tight.

"Where were you out there?" Thad asks him as we all trudge toward the house after. "We could have won by more if you didn't totally choke the last two rounds."

Ren pauses to untie the bandana around his neck, and Thad follows suit. As I pass them in the yard, my mind whirring, our eyes meet for a second before we both look down. "Sorry," I hear Ren say, the enthusiasm in his voice forced. He slaps Thad on the back. "At least we won, right?"

I tune out the rest of their conversation.

Everyone cuts through the side yard down to the firepit, but I veer off to the porch and crawl into bed, determined to be asleep by the time Ren returns. I can still feel his hands on my neck, the familiar smell of his sweatshirt, the faint look of surprise on his face as our bodies swept together. I try to push it all away, remind myself it's impossible. But the image of him comes floating back, unstoppable as the tide, again and again and again.

FOUR YEARS AGO

Charlene and Mavis

Navarro, California

chapter fifteen

"Have you seen my black heels?" I call from my bedroom floor. It's midnight, my window unit working double time in the thick July heat, I have an alarm set for four in the morning, and so far, all I've packed is the dress I'll be wearing to my aunt Charlene's wedding this weekend.

"These?" Stevie asks as she wanders in, the heels dangling by the straps from her fingers.

"Thief," I say.

She deposits them into my hands before collapsing onto her stomach on my bed. "Is Collin taking you to the airport?"

"No. He has to work early." Collin, my boyfriend of roughly five months, manages the brunch place where we met. At first, when he'd scrawled his number on my to-go cup, I'd assumed it was his move, what he did to every girl he noticed who came in. But Stevie had stopped me from tossing it, even crafted my first message to him. *It's probably time you try actually dating someone*, she'd said as she tapped out the text for my approval. *You haven't had a boyfriend in years.* She was right. I had been telling myself that when I liked someone enough, I'd make room for them, but there was always something just off enough that

I found a reason not to get too close. Collin was something of an experiment, and so far, to my pleasant surprise, nothing terrible has happened.

"Well," she says. "Enjoy the disgustingly hot subway platform."

I ignore her comment and flash her a puppy-eyed look. "Are you *sure* you don't want to drop everything and come to the wedding?" I ask her. "We could even split *a cab* to the airport."

"I'm sure I'd like to time travel back to March and convince myself not to take summer classes," Stevie says around a yawn. "I'd so much rather drink with you and Mom on a goat farm instead of studying for finals. Besides," she says. "If I go, what will Ren do?"

"We'll miss you," I say.

"Yeah, yeah," she says. "Tell Ren I'll take his thanks for *allowing* him to replace me as your plus-one in the form of student loans payments."

"Totally even trade," I say, tucking the heels into my bag.

Stevie watches as I sort through the pile of folded laundry next to me. "So how do you think Amanda feels about this whole weekend?" she asks me.

I pause, a shirt half-folded over my arm. I've only met Ren's girlfriend once, and briefly, during the holidays, when she and Ren walked into my parents' Christmas Eve party with the Websters looking fresh out of some ad that involved a lot of cross-country skiing and mulled wine by an enormous fire. Stevie and I were stamping out cookies on the kitchen counter and while I'd been excited to meet Amanda, I suddenly felt a little like I'd been banished to the kids' table. Here was Ren, the best friend who I'd once won a flip cup tournament with in college, walking into my childhood home with the air of someone with a mortgage and more than a surface-level understanding of Roth IRAs, a beautiful, tall redhead at his side.

The conversation I had with Amanda—short, polite, nothing profound—was enough to tell me Ren's significant other wouldn't suddenly become my other best friend, like I'd envisioned growing up. Some joint wedding situation, houses next door to each other, things that seem weird to me now but made perfect sense in the mind of a teenager.

"Feels about what?" I fit the shirt and a pair of shorts into a corner of my suitcase.

Stevie scoffs. "About her boyfriend being your plus-one to Aunt Charlene's wedding."

"Stevie, Ren would tell me if it was a problem."

"If you say so."

She doesn't bring it up again, instead passing out across the foot of my bed, which is where she stays the rest of the night. Eventually, I curl up next to her to try to catch a couple hours of sleep, kiss her head goodbye as the sky turns gray out my window.

When the plane touches down in San Francisco, my brain is foggy but wired in an all-nighter kind of way, but I'm sort of used to it now. Because of Novo's production deadlines, I've been staying at work later and later. The schedule is so hectic that I have to miss the week at the beach this year, so this weekend is especially important. Not only for seeing my parents, our promised twice weekly phone calls getting shorter and shorter over the past months, but also for making sure Ren and I take full advantage of our time together, and not in the way we did in Chicago. No lists, just us.

It's three hours until Ren lands, so I pick up our rental car and point it toward the closest coffee shop, where I order a heavily sweetened and extra-large cold brew and slump into a window seat.

My phone dings with a notification from Collin.

Safely there, he sends, no punctuation.

Here! I reply. Grabbing a coffee before I pick up Ren.

He responds with a thumbs-up.

As I sip my coffee, I scroll to the directions Charlene sent about how to get to the venue—Google Maps will lie to you about the turn!—and let my mind wander to the weekend ahead. Tonight is the rehearsal dinner, and my mom wants to go on a hike before the wedding tomorrow, so we can, as she puts it, "test out" the screws she had to have put in her ankle after she broke it mountain biking in the spring. A continuation of the facing-your-fears trend, something she claimed has changed her life and has continued to try to get all of us to participate in, even following the accident. Stevie and I had a shared minor meltdown when my dad sent a text that said only Mom, E.R., call please, in true parent fashion, but my mom has been intrepid about the whole thing.

Ren calls as I'm winding my way back to the airport.

"Shit," I answer. Even without a list to contend with, I don't want to miss a minute with him. "Are you here?"

"Flight landed a little early," he says over the sounds of the terminal, a muffled announcement and conversations building and fading as he walks. "You're stressed."

"I'm late," I say.

"For?"

"You." I crane my neck to see around the line of cars waiting to exit toward the pickup area. "I should have just stayed at the airport."

"Joni, it's good," Ren says. "I'm barely off the plane. I'll hang out. Don't worry."

It's been a long time since I've heard his voice. Between our busy schedules, now we mostly just text, usually mundane things. Grocery store officially has peaches. Faucet is dripping but only in the middle of the night? Neighbor got a cat and it takes naps on the front porch now. All these tiny details shared to prove we're still intertwined.

And yet, I can't deny that there are gaps between us that have grown over the past year. There's his relationship with Amanda.

There are new friends I haven't met. For every *just back from a run* text I get, there is the run itself. For every picture of a dog he sends, there's pausing to talk with its owner, scratch the dog's head. Or maybe there's a crosswalk because he's headed somewhere or a table outside a coffee shop or an errand I know nothing about. I feel it like a constant *tap tap tap* at my skull: here are the pieces you're missing. Here are the things you don't know. I remind myself that even when I lived in Portland, there were moments like these I didn't know about. I can't have all of him. But the physical distance makes it all seem much more important, and these mundane, insignificant details only have me craving more. What else did you get at the grocery store? What color is the cat? Where did you go on a run and what did you see, smell, hear, think about? Let me crawl into your brain and make a home there.

That distance has me feeling even more anxious to get to him now.

By the time I make it to the pickup area, Ren is outside, frowning at his phone. A lump forms in my throat at the sight of him. He's the same: faded blue jeans and a black crewneck, a white T-shirt just poking out underneath, sleeves pushed up his arms. But there's something new about him too, and I can't quite put my finger on it, and I hate that. Hate that it might just be a result of the divide that's formed between us, the one we're not talking about. "Webster!" I shout out the passenger window as I pull up to the curb, startling a tiny, elderly woman with a dog tucked under her arm.

Ren looks up, pockets his phone, and hurries to the car. He throws his stuff in the back seat before crossing to the driver's side and opening my door.

"What are you doing?" I ask, looking up at him.

"Switching with you."

"I'm a good driver, Ren." I set my hands on ten and two to prove it.

"I know you are, Joni, but when have you ever wanted to drive on a road trip like this?"

I roll my eyes, but he's right, and I get out of the driver's seat. As I brush past him, he stops me with a hand on my elbow.

"Hey," he says.

I squint against the sun streaming down behind him, the details of him fuzzy to me until Ren leans in a little closer and they come into focus, the almost teasing look in his eyes, the soft curve of his top lip as he smiles.

"Hey," he says again.

His arms come around me, squeezing, and I feel like I'm home. "Missed you," Ren says.

I fold my arms around his back. "Missed you more."

He pulls away, nodding me toward the passenger seat. I comply, just in time to catch the eye of an older gentleman glaring at us from the front seat of his Toyota Corolla, blinker on, as he waits for our spot.

"So," Ren says once we've gotten past the melee of airport traffic and are headed north. "Predictions for this weekend."

I pout. "I'm so sad I don't get to be at the house this year."

"So we have to milk this weekend for all it's worth," Ren says, turning on his blinker to switch lanes. "I'll go first. Your mom makes some comment about you looking tired within the first thirty minutes."

"Ugh, no thank you," I say and lean back against the headrest.

He taps his elbow against mine on the center console. "Your turn," he says.

"Mmm, I don't know. It's hard to come up with stuff without everyone else there."

"I predict we have a great time," Ren says. He smiles at me in that slow, familiar way, and I find myself sinking into this moment. I reach up, rub the top of his head. He leans into my palm, pulling a laugh out of me.

It's okay that we don't talk every day anymore. We're still us.

We make it to the venue half an hour later than planned due to construction on the road. We were meant to be at the rehearsal dinner fifteen minutes ago, a fact my mom has reminded me of in no fewer than three texts, all sent in five-minute increments.

We swing by the main building to check in before Ren guides the car down a loop dotted with the green-painted luxury yurts where the wedding guests will be staying. They blend in with the trees, and we almost miss number eight even though we're practically crawling, craning our necks to find it.

Ren gets our bags out of the car while I step up onto the tiny front deck, unlock the yurt door, and hustle inside.

Ren changes in the bathroom while I throw on my dress in the main room and paw through the huge welcome gift basket on the bed. It's stuffed with not only what Charlene and Mavis consider wedding essentials, but themed products from the farm too. "Can't Goat You Outta My Head" shampoo and conditioner. "Forgoat Me Not" lotion. Two felted goat key chains, one of which I gleefully attach to my own key ring.

"You have to use the other one," I say when Ren comes out of the bathroom.

After a beat of silence, I glance up to see him hovering by the door, tapping out a message on his phone. He's in a white button-down and charcoal pants, his hunter green tie loose around his neck.

"Sorry," he says, pocketing his phone. "What?"

"For you." I toss him the key chain. "We can match."

He smiles, tucks it into the front pocket of his suitcase.

"I do have one prediction," I say as Ren walks over and zips up the back of my dress without my asking. "Charlene makes everyone sing some song with her at the wedding tomorrow night." I turn around and fix his half-done tie. "Remember my parents' anniversary party a couple years back? She got everyone to sing along to 'Bohemian Rhapsody'?"

"How could I forget." Ren lifts his chin as I straighten his collar, plucks an errant string out of my hair that must have come from my T-shirt when I slipped it over my head.

But he doesn't let go. He brushes my hair back into place, absently rubbing it between his fingers. His eyes lower to mine, lips parting slightly, and my breath hitches as Stevie's words suddenly come back to me. *How do you think Amanda feels about this whole weekend?*

I swallow, jab a thumb toward the door. "Shall we?" I ask.

"Yeah," Ren says, releasing my hair. "Let's go."

But he doesn't move.

"Ren?"

He shakes his head and steps away, holding the door open for me to pass and locking up behind us. As we head down the globe light–lined path, a breeze rustles the trees, the evening sky orange above the mammoth treetops. It feels so similar to Oregon this far north, it could almost be home. I try to focus on this fact, to put the image of Ren's hand in my hair, mine on his collar out of my mind. "This place reminds me of your parents' backyard," I say as we rush down the trail.

"Yeah?"

I look over at him, worried that he's in his head now about zipping up a dress for a girl who isn't Amanda. His eyes are fixed on the ground, hands shoved in his pockets; he's not totally here with me.

"You know," I continue. "A little removed from the rest of the world." It was one of my favorite things about his house growing up: how their backyard abutted the river, so that there were spaces where you couldn't tell we were even in town. It was a good substitute for when we couldn't be at the beach house.

Ren doesn't respond, and I leave him to his thoughts.

As soon as we walk into the barn, I'm swept into a hug, my mom's familiar lilac scent enveloping me. She doesn't ask where we were or mention her texts, but any hint of guilt I feel about assuming she would evaporates when she holds me away from her, inspecting me, and says, "You look tired."

Ren rubs a hand over his mouth to hide his smile before my mom is moving on to him.

"Kiddo," my dad says, drawing me into a one-armed hug. "Good flight?"

"Good flight. Sorry we're late."

He waves a hand. "Cocktail hour has hardly started. You're fine."

The four of us wander past the long tables to the bar. Because so many people are spending the whole weekend here, most of the guests are also at the rehearsal dinner tonight, milling around under the paper lanterns hanging from the beams above us, meandering out to the grassy area in the back. After we grab drinks, we pause to say hello to some distant family members. I wave at Claudia and Clark across the room, their six-month-old sleeping in a carrier on his chest.

After cocktail hour, we sit down to dinner. Ren updates my parents on the adoption agency Thad and his husband are working with, and they discuss Sasha's recent engagement to Alex.

"Did you hear about Stevie's story?" my mom asks us. Stevie has been trying to expand her portfolio before she graduates next year, get more bylines under her belt.

"The site she wrote it for profiles a lot of up-and-coming acts," I explain to Ren. "The piece she wrote was about a group out of Brooklyn." I bump an elbow against his arm. "They've covered a couple Sublimity bands, actually."

He glances over at me and nods. "Right."

"Ren," my mom says, and I watch as he sits up a little straighter, leans forward, face clearing when she addresses him.

"Your mom told me you and Amanda are going to Italy this fall?"

"With her family," he says, as something chilly slides over my shoulders. How does my mom know something about Ren's life that I don't? "For her sister's wedding."

His words push at some sore spot in me. It feels like I'm being shut out of his life the more serious he and Amanda get, and it dawns on me that there might come a time I don't know anything about him at all. I pick up my fork to stop the spiraling.

It's after dinner is cleared and we're at the bar with another round of drinks that my mom focuses her attention on me. "I'm worried about you," she says, seemingly out of nowhere.

I'm mid-sip of Mavis's favorite Napa Valley white and extend it into a chug. "What do you mean, Mom?" I say, pressing my lips together in a tight smile.

Ren and my dad are next to us, discussing an upcoming golf tournament.

My mom frowns as she examines me. "You look exhausted," she says.

"Just what every girl loves to hear," I say, lifting my glass toward her.

"You're still beautiful even when you're tired," she says. "But what's going on? You never answer my calls. Maybe I can help."

"I don't know, how about I flew across the country this morning?" I take another sip, trying hard to pivot in a lighter direction. "And, might I remind you, we are a family prone to dark circles. It's genetic. I look like this whether I'm sleeping or not!" I don't mean it to sound hysterical, but it nearly does, wine sloshing against the sides of my glass as I gesture with it.

My mom peers at me in that therapist way of hers. "Honey. What if you took some time off? Come home for a while."

I set my glass back on the bar, dig my fingers against the base of it. "I don't want to take time off, Mom," I say, choosing my words carefully. If I say too much, she'll find something to latch on to, some way to make this a therapy session. One day I'll think I've demonstrated that I'm fine, through college or my job or my move to New York, and suddenly she'll be here, telling me I should come home because my under-eye circles look bad.

"Did you tell Stevie the same thing?" I ask, picking up my glass again. My mom casts me a confused look. "She's overwhelmed with her summer classes. Did you tell her she should take some time off?"

"Grad school is different," my mom says. "*Stevie* is different."

I take a sip of my wine. Just because Stevie isn't an anxious person, doesn't mean she's somehow more capable of taking care of herself than me. This is why I avoid my mom's calls when I'm feeling stressed. Why I tend not to confide in her. Her worries just multiply mine.

I want to ask her to stop, to just talk to me like she talks to Stevie, but before I can say anything, Charlene is pushing through the crowd, calling my parents' names.

My dad's younger sister, Charlene, has always been one of my favorite relatives. With a booming voice that carries across the room, she's been a river guide, a substitute teacher, drove a Zamboni at an ice rink, and now works at the information desk at a library, arguably her least physically demanding job and yet the one where she somehow managed to break one of the tiny bones in her foot dropping a hefty Sherlock Holmes volume on it, which led to her meeting and falling in love with her podiatrist.

When I reintroduce her to Ren, she hugs him. "As if I could forget that face," she mutters to me after she's let him go and pivoted to me. "Is he still single?"

"Nope," I say, eyeing Ren as he angles away behind her, quickly checking his phone before he pockets it again. "Happily coupled. As am I."

"Pity," Charlene says. My brow creases, but she's moving on to my parents, asking them to come say hi to Mavis's parents.

When I turn back to Ren, he's already looking at me.

"Yes?" I say after he's watched me in silence for a minute. I scrub the back of my hand at the tip of my nose. "Do I have something on my face?"

"No," he says, reaching up to lower my hand. "Just—" He tapers off, head tilting toward one shoulder. "*Are* you tired?"

"Oh my god." I slap both my hands on the bar. "Please. My mother is enough."

"I'm not asking like your mother," he says, bending his way into my line of vision. "You *have* been texting me at one in the morning a lot."

"Why are you up at 1:00 a.m. to be texted?"

"You see, there are these things called time zones?" he says.

I knock his shoulder, roll my eyes as a smile creeps over my face, grateful that he seems to be coming back, engaging with me again.

"I'm also a bartender," he says. "Ten o' clock is when things slow down." He leans in, arm pressing against mine, the warmth of it settling me. "But you *used* to be asleep by that time. At least on weekdays."

I rotate my glass in a circle of condensation. "I'm really okay," I say. "Work's just—" *Never not busy*, I want to say, but other people manage to leave at semireasonable hours. I've just felt like I've had to prove myself since I moved to New York. Like I need to show Ramona and the studio heads that I deserve my spot there, and maybe a better one; like I need to show everyone I can do this, that I'm not some fragile being that's going to break at the smallest thing.

"There's this movie," I say. I lift a hand as if to erase that. It's not actually a movie yet. It's just an idea a few of us have been throwing around, and we need someone who's actually in a management position to pitch it. "I've told you about it."

Ren's brow furrows, like he's trying to remember. I scramble—*have* I told him about the movie? Why I'm working late every night and pushing myself even harder than I usually do? I'm sure I have.

"It's not—" I say, but have to take a sip of wine when my voice comes out hoarse at the prospect that Ren doesn't seem to recall what feels like the biggest thing in my life right now. "It's just this project I'm excited about."

"No, I remember," Ren says, but his vague smile is distracted, far-off. "Just promise me you'll try to get some sleep now and again, okay?"

"I will," I say, but as Ren glances away again, back toward the room, I don't feel better. The terrible thought that this weekend is him fulfilling some kind of obligation runs through my head. That maybe it isn't just work and Amanda. Maybe our friendship really isn't what it was before.

I spend the rest of the evening catching up with various family members, always looking for Ren over my shoulder, but when I can find him, he's either dutifully chatting with my parents and whoever they're with, or standing off to the side, on his phone or just observing the room, lost in thought that I can't chase after.

It's cooled down significantly by the time the rehearsal dinner is over. After saying good-night to my parents at their yurt, we walk back up the path to ours in silence. Ren's shoulders are relaxed, his stride slow, while I'm anxious, crossing and uncrossing my arms, rubbing at my elbows.

Unfortunately, we were so focused on getting to the rehearsal dinner earlier that it's not until Ren is holding the door open for me that I pause to actually take in the room. We both seem to clock it at the same moment, glancing at each other and away quickly when we realize there is a singular bed. Ren's hand in my hair earlier comes back to me, and I hurry into the bathroom, where I change into my pajamas, wash my face, brush my teeth.

When I come out, he's setting up a makeshift bed on the floor with extra blankets and a pillow from the closet. "You take the bed," he says. "I'll sleep on the floor."

"But you'll be in so much pain tomorrow." I grab my water bottle from my backpack and turn on the faucet in the kitchenette, stick my finger under it until it runs ice-cold. Ren doesn't need to sleep on a concrete floor. We're adult enough to share a bed for one night. I sit on the edge of the bed. "Come on. We've slept in the same bed before. It's fine."

Ren, who had been bending over the floor bed, straightens. He's rolled his sleeves above his elbows and plants his hands on his hips as he surveys it. "I won't be in pain," he says, leaning down again and picking up one of the blankets, seemingly just to fold and unfold it again, the tendons in his forearms working.

"Ren—" I say.

"Aren't we a little old for sleepovers?" he asks, the words snapping out of him. The water bottle I was lifting to my lips freezes in the air. He squeezes a hand to his temple. "I'm sorry," he says. He flicks his eyes toward me. "I just— Can we do it this way?"

I screw the cap back onto my water bottle slowly, set it on the floor next to the bed. "Of course," I tell him.

He watches me for a moment before grabbing his things and heading into the bathroom.

I climb under the blankets and stare at the pinprick stars that appear through the skylight above. This is new territory. I've felt it over the last year: the ground beneath me slightly rockier the shorter the texts between us got, but I told myself it was nothing, was consumed enough by work that I could ignore it. But in person this change between us feels different, more pronounced.

I scan through the skylight for the Summer Triangle, the

trio of stars Ren first pointed out to me when we were four-
teen, lying on our backs in the front yard of the beach house.

But I can't find it.

Ren comes back into the room and rummages around in
his backpack, pulls out a charger and plugs in his phone. He
stands over it, tapping at something on the screen, then slides
onto the floor bed, dropping out of my view.

I stare at the stars a moment longer before I'm leaning up
on an elbow, looking down at him, something like determina-
tion firing in my chest. This can't be how this weekend goes.

He has one hand tucked under his head, the other splayed
across his chest.

"Is everything okay?" I ask.

"Of course it is," he says, his voice flat. "Why?"

"Things have just seemed a little…off," I say, nervous that if
I say too much, he'll pull even further into himself. "Between
us. Tonight."

At this, he turns his face up to fully look at me. "I'm sorry.
Everything is really okay."

I let my eyes drift over his features, searching for tension, for
some kind of hint, but they're as unreadable as his voice.

I wait there, hanging over the bed. I want the Ren that pre-
dicted we'd have a great time this weekend.

But he doesn't say anything more.

"Good night, then," I say. I turn off the light and flop back
against the pillows.

chapter sixteen

I wake up the next morning in the same position I fell asleep in, an indication that I actually *slept*. I stretch my arms above my head, then look down to find the floor bed empty.

I locate Ren on the front porch, sink down into one of the chairs next to him as he hands me a mug of coffee.

"I can't get over how beautiful it is here," I say, warming my palms against the ceramic. The sky stretches blue over the trees around us, everything hushed like the world has stopped spinning for a moment so we can take a beat to appreciate it.

But my mind is stuck on Ren, who smiles over at me but doesn't say a word. I'd hoped this morning things might be normal between us again, and a pang flits through me at the thought that I don't know how to fix it.

After a quiet half an hour sipping coffee out front, my parents swing by our yurt on the way to the goat farm, and Ren and I get ready quickly before heading there with them. We meet Donna, owner of the farm and our unofficial tour guide, in that she doesn't actually *give* tours but is easily talked into it upon learning not a one of us knows a single thing about goats.

"And this," she says, holding a brown flop of a thing aloft at the end of her admittedly short tour, "This is Baby Yaya."

"Oh my god," I say when she plops the goat into my arms and it rests its head on my shoulder. After hours of working on puppet animals, cuddling a real, breathing one makes me feel connected to the world again, like I just needed to touch some grass or, in this case, a baby goat. Baby Yaya nuzzles her soft chin against my skin, settling in. "I think this is my peak. It's all downhill from here."

I perch on top of a hay bale while my parents follow Donna to a separate goat pen. "Do you see this?" I say to Ren, who's hovering nearby, as I run a hand over Yaya's head. "I don't think anything has ever been this tiny or perfect. Do you?"

It takes me a minute longer to look up than it should, because I'm still riding the high of quality sleep and this adorable goat in my arms. But when I do, Ren's brow is furrowed as he types out something on his phone.

"Ren," I say.

"What?" His gaze slowly moves up to mine.

I force a smile and proffer Yaya in his direction, hoping she might bring him back to the present.

But he just holds up his phone. "Amanda just asked me to call her. Two seconds?"

"Oh, yeah, of course." I wave him off, watch him shut the pen gate behind him, phone to his ear.

I gingerly set Baby Yaya to the side, pull out my phone and take a picture of her curled up in a ball.

Hey! I send to Collin, and attach the picture of Yaya. This is what you're missing.

When he doesn't respond right away, I set my phone down, tuck my hands under my legs. I glance around the empty goat pen. I'm alone, on a hay bale, wearing shorts overalls over a vintage Bob Dylan T-shirt, Birkenstocked feet swinging. I've never felt less cool than I do right now.

My phone dings with Collin's reply.

Nice. The three dots appear, disappear, and then promptly die as he sends, Goat alive?

Ren walks back in at that moment, eyes glued to his phone.

"Man, really giving our generation a bad name," I say jokingly as he ambles toward me. When he doesn't even look up, I try, "You're giving a whole new meaning to the whole *you hang up first* thing."

"What?" Ren says.

Frustration flares through me. The whole point of this plus-one tradition was to spend time together, not just *exist* in the same place. If I'd known that this was what it would turn into, I would have considered staying in New York with Stevie this weekend, when our parents told us we didn't really have to come. But, on top of loving Charlene, I'd wanted to see Ren, had assumed this tradition still mattered. "I didn't realize you were one of those people whose entire personality would disappear just because you have a girlfriend," I say before I can stop myself.

At this, his head jerks up and he flinches. He pockets his phone. "I'm putting it away," he says as the gate creaks open and my parents come back in.

After my parents take a few photos with Baby Yaya, Donna points us in the direction of the neighboring co-op, and we mosey down a short trail. Ren hangs back with me, hands in his pockets. I feel a little guilty for snapping at him earlier. He's here, after all, honoring our tradition despite having a girlfriend and a whole important life back in Portland. I know my anger is misplaced.

We pass over a small creek, and I stop to watch the clear water gurgle over the rocks, to bring my emotions under control. My parents continue on ahead, while Ren leans next to me.

"I really do remember you telling me about the movie," Ren says suddenly. When I look at him, his eyes are on the creek, forearms dangling over the railing. "The one you want to take to the studio heads, right? Tell me more about it," he says, turning to me, one hand on the railing. "It's what's keeping you up?"

I nod. "It's just something we're doing on the side. We're probably still a year out from being able to pitch it, but Ramona approved the idea, at least."

"Seriously?" Ren asks, eyebrows shooting up. "Why didn't you tell me?"

I shrug a shoulder. "We've both been so busy. It's hard to find as much time to talk," I admit. I've also felt like saying it out loud might jinx it. I'm worried that despite all the work I've put in at Novo, I'm still trying for too much, too fast. "But if I keep working hard, I might be able to slow down. Eventually. Hopefully," I say.

"Can't make a movie if you're exhausted," Ren points out.

"Yeah, yeah," I say. "We've already covered my sleep schedule."

He looks back at the water in front of us, throat bobbing. I stare at him, certain this is the moment he'll tell me what's going on, why he's so off this weekend. If I did something to make it that way. "I know we haven't been able to talk as much this last year," he says. "I'm sorry about that."

"We're both—"

"Busy, I know," he says. "But…" He shakes his head, trailing off.

I wait, wishing for more, but it doesn't come. My heart gives a painful twist.

"You're still—" I say, trying to make small talk. I can't see my parents down the trail anymore, so I nod us back toward it, not wanting to fall too far behind them.

"Trying to get an A&R position, yes," Ren cuts in.

I glance askance at the tension in his voice. "Sorry," I say. "Just doing the annual check-in."

Ren lets out a soft, forced laugh. "Don't apologize. It's just coming up a lot lately."

"Yeah?" I say, kicking at a rock on the trail. "Because you're getting closer, or...?"

"Because I'm not getting closer fast enough," Ren says. He catches the rock with his toe, kicks it along farther. "Because it's not a viable career option."

"Webster," I say, grabbing his arm, half because I want him to know how much I disagree with this and half because he's finally talking to me and I need it to continue. "Who's telling you that?"

"My dad—he says I should go back to school. Try to be a teacher."

"What would you teach?"

"Excellent question. I'll let you know if I ever decide I actually *want* to be a teacher," Ren says, his shoulders set tight. "My mom also doesn't seem to think what I'm doing now is a real job," Ren adds, eyes down the path in front of us. "And—" He breaks off. We've reached the rock where it was kicked. He stops for a minute.

"And?" I say.

When he looks back up at me, the air goes thick, sitting heavy between us. He watches me a beat longer, before he kicks the rock down the trail again. "Nothing. I'm just being dramatic about it."

"You're not," I say as we continue walking. I want him to hear me, believe it. "If everyone in my life was questioning my career, I'd be calling you daily and complaining about it."

"No one could question you," Ren says. His elbow knocks against mine. "Pulling all-nighters just so you can take over the animation world. I'm not working at it as hard as you are."

I know then that I won't get anything more out of him.

His phone chimes from his pocket. He doesn't reach for it,

but I see his shoulders hitch a little higher. I spot the rock and kick it back to him.

"Hey," I say, moving us to an easier topic. "What song do you think Charlene will have everyone sing tonight?" Ren guides the rock down the path, but his heart isn't in it. I can feel him pulling away. His phone chimes again. "I was thinking she might go wedding classic, something like 'Sweet Caroline' or 'L-O-V-E,' or—"

Ren stops dead in his tracks as his phone rings with a call. I look over just in time to see a wince slipping off his face.

"Joni—" He withdraws his phone from his pocket, glances at the screen. "I just need to—"

"Don't," I say, without pausing to think about it. "Don't answer it. Keep talking to me." I realize I sound desperate, that I'm trying to force him into something that might hurt his relationship with Amanda, but I don't know what else to do to save this moment.

His arm goes rigid, and my eyes snag on the single line that wraps around it just below his elbow. I have the same one on my arm, tattoos we got as an ode to our friendship back in college. It was the simplest design we could come up with that still represented the idea of our lives being tied together forever. Back when there wasn't any strain like this between us, when there weren't months that went by without hearing each other's voices. My gaze slides back up to his face, all of it now tense, pained.

His phone goes silent.

"I'm sorry," he says. "Give me two—"

"No," I cut in, waving a hand. "You know what? Do whatever you need to do."

Before he can respond, I turn and hurry down the trail, anxious to get out of earshot before I can hear him say hello.

≈

We hardly talk the rest of the afternoon, awkwardly maneuvering our way around the yurt. I get ready quickly and leave without telling him, rush down the path to meet my parents. The flash of anger I felt earlier is gone, replaced by something hollow, like I've lost some essential piece of me.

The wedding is in the meadow behind the barn, green dotted with golden poppies and purple lupine. We gather there for the cocktail hour. When my mom waves us into various arrangements for photos, I put my dad between Ren and me every time, motion for her phone so I can take a picture of the three of them before she can get a picture of the two of us alone.

We almost hit a record for not speaking to each other. After moving into the barn for the reception, all through dinner, toasts, Charlene and Mavis's first dance. We float in and out of each other's orbits, but never exchange more than a cursory glance.

It feels like I'm looking over my shoulder for someone who isn't there, when I almost cry during the vows and have to stop myself from leaning over to see his reaction; when Mavis's uncle gives a toast that involves a god-awful slideshow, and my mom doesn't seem to find it as funny as I do.

I decide that, if this is how things are going to be between us, I need to start having fun without him. It's a beautiful wedding, my family who I don't get to see all that much is here, and I don't often have opportunities to fully unwind like this.

I spend an hour dancing with a couple of my cousins, even Claudia, to a slew of wedding classics, nineties hits, songs they played at bars when we were in college. All around us, people are celebrating, champagne glasses in hand and the sky going dark. I dance with my dad to ABBA, let my mom tell me I look more well rested today. But there's no one to smirk at her comment with.

By the time an *extremely* drunk Charlene takes control of the playlist and leads everyone in a rousing rendition of "All Too Well," Mavis beaming up at her, the camaraderie around me is too much. I've been putting all my energy into proving I can have fun without Ren, into ignoring what's going on between us, and I'm tired. I wonder, vaguely, as I sing half-heartedly along to the last verse, if it's not just work that's been wearing me out, but my relationship with Ren.

When I leave the dance floor, cheeks rosy, Ren is waiting for me at the table, a glass of champagne in each hand. Selfishly, I don't hate that he looks a little like I feel. But there's some hope too in the way he tilts toward me, offers me one of the flutes.

I take it, still wary, one arm crossed in front of me like a barrier between us.

"Phone's off for the rest of the night," he says.

"Is it?"

"It is." He taps his knuckles against the back of a chair, a nervous tic. His eyes lock onto mine. "I'm sorry. Can we enjoy the rest of the weekend?"

I want him to mean it, more than anything. Ren has never given me any reason not to trust him. But this weekend has shown me that something real has shifted in our relationship, and the idea makes me unsteady. I try to smile. "Of course."

Ren nods toward the open barn doors. "Want to?"

We walk out to a seating area set up between the barn and the goat pens. There are even more stars than the night before, sparkling in the deep blue sky. I angle my head back to look at them.

When I drop my gaze, Ren is staring at me. I let the silence sit between us as we communicate something wordlessly. *I'm sorry* and *Me too.* And maybe *You don't need to be* and *But I do, because I've been doubting our friendship* and there's no way Ren is actually getting all of this, and I've gone and made up some metaphysical connection.

A breeze wafts down from the treetops and I suppress a shiver. Ren sets his glass on a nearby fence post, shrugs off his jacket, and settles it over my shoulders, standing in front of me and tugging at the lapels like he's trying to bring it tighter around me. He takes a breath, then lets go and walks us in another direction.

We drift over to a small circle of chairs, sinking into two next to each other. I kick off my heels and curl my legs under me, burrow deeper into Ren's jacket, which smells like him. We look up at the stars, until the silence begins to last too long. I want us to figure this out, not just silently agree it's over.

I'm tracing the line of the Big Dipper with my eyes when I ask the question I've been holding back. "Does Amanda not trust you?" This has to be why he's been aloof this weekend. Why that moment in the yurt had shut something down in him, why he slept on the ground when he never would have in the past, why he's been glued to his phone.

I can hear Ren shift in his chair. "Yes, she does. Why are you asking me that?"

I glance over at him. "You just seem so stressed about keeping in touch with her, and she should trust you even if you're not checking in 24/7. I don't like seeing you feeling this way."

"It's not like that," Ren says. He leans forward, forearms on his knees, champagne flute dangling between them.

"You've hardly looked up from your phone all weekend."

Ren sits back in his seat again, letting out a sigh. "She just got freaked out," he says. "When I stopped responding for a while."

"So she doesn't trust you," I say, defensiveness on Ren's part flashing through me. *You have the best person in the world*, I'd say to Amanda if she were here now. *You have nothing to worry about.*

"That's not it," Ren says. He thinks for a minute, and my eyes catch on the spot where his teeth sink into his lower lip.

"Her last relationship ended badly. The guy was carrying on a whole other relationship for months before she found out. So I think this weekend is just hard for her."

"Fuck," I say on an exhale, knowing for sure that I'm the asshole, trying to draw Ren back into every moment like he belongs to me. "If I'd known that, I—"

"No," Ren says. "I should have reassured her more before I came. If I had, she wouldn't be calling so much."

"She knows we're just friends, right?" I say.

Ren pauses for a moment, then nods. "She does. And, I honestly didn't think about it until we got here, but—I mean, we're staying in a room with one bed."

"We didn't sleep in it together."

"You're right," Ren says. He goes quiet, then says, "I like Amanda a lot."

"I gathered."

"I think it's reasonable for her to be unsure about this weekend. I mean, what about Collin?"

"What about Collin?"

"How does he feel about this weekend?"

"He doesn't—" A pit forms in my stomach at the reality that I don't even *know* whether Collin is upset about me going with Ren to this wedding instead of him. When Ren told me Amanda was fine with this weekend, however wrong he was, I just assumed Collin was too. I never thought to ask him. I clear my throat. "He doesn't care."

"Why not?" Ren asks, confusion in his voice.

"He just..." I trail off. "He knows we're just friends. We trust each other." But as I say it, I realize how shallow that statement is. I trust that Collin is a good person, that he's not dating other people and that he won't, I don't know, suddenly turn out to be a wanted criminal. I trust that Collin will go out with me on a Saturday night. I don't know that I trust him to take care of me while I have mono, or enough for me to call if I have a panic attack, or to somehow anticipate my emotions before I even know they're coming.

We lapse into silence again. I study Ren's profile as he looks back up at the stars, all these parts of him I've memorized. His thick eyelashes, the strong line of his jaw, the curve of his neck when his head is angled back like this. Even if our relationship is shifting, he's still *him*. My favorite person. The realization softens something in me.

"I really want you to be happy," I say. He lowers his gaze to mine. "And, look, I don't *love* you being so attached to your phone, but if this is you happy, then so be it."

"I promise I'll be more present," Ren says. "Just figuring out a balance."

I settle farther back into my chair, try to open myself up to this new part of his life. Maybe Ren hasn't told me more about his romantic life because I haven't invited him to. But Amanda is different, I can tell. Important. "What do you like so much about her?" I ask.

His mouth lifts at one corner into a half smile. "She doesn't worry too much about anything," he says, then quickly adds, when I shoot him a dubious look, "Outside of this weekend."

"Fair enough," I say. I take a sip of my champagne.

"I don't know. She doesn't second-guess things. I do enough of that for any relationship."

"You're cautious," I say, hackles rising again. "There's nothing wrong with that."

"Maybe," Ren says.

I decide not to press the issue. "What else?"

"She's funny," he says, and for some reason, my stomach twists. He nods in my direction. "Tell me what you like about Collin."

I pretend to think, put my index finger and thumb to my chin, sink into the laugh it prompts out of Ren, triumph racing across my skin. The minute starts to last longer, though, and I still haven't answered. And Ren isn't laughing anymore. He's just watching me, waiting.

"He—" I say, and even though there are a half dozen answers on my tongue, things like *he's a good cook* and *he has cool tattoos* and *his apartment is really close to Novo*, I can't get any of them out, like I've suddenly lost my voice.

"Seems like he has good taste in music," Ren says, saving me.

It's a joke, I know, because I texted him once that Collin had the last playlist he'd sent me on repeat.

"Yeah," I say. "Great taste in music."

I had thought what Collin and I had was good. Fun. Easy. And maybe it is all of those things. But as Ren looks back up at the sky, I realize I never once wanted to call Collin just to talk to him this weekend. He didn't text me just because he missed me, whereas Ren spent most of today on the phone with Amanda just to reassure her. He'll probably send her a good-morning text tomorrow, head to her place right when he gets back to Portland.

The worst part isn't that Collin doesn't do those things. It's that I didn't care enough to notice.

When the clouds roll in across the stars, Ren and I walk back to the party. We take our time, our bodies a few feet apart, the music and sounds of people celebrating wafting toward us. When we reach the sphere of light spilling out from the barn, he steps back, waves me through the doors first.

Ren's question about Collin or, more accurately, my lack of response, follows me inside. I wonder whether I'll ever find someone I want to text or call all the time. The only person I've ever wanted to do that with is Ren. Something about the thought has my hands going numb, nervous energy tingling in my arms. When he looks over at me, I force a smile and give him back his jacket.

≈

Our goodbye the next day is tougher than I expected. I hold on to Ren a little longer at his gate, pay attention to the exact way his arms squeeze around me right before he lets go, like he wants to remind me that we're both still *here*, no matter how far away we may be.

On the plane, I get out the vacation book I packed with full intention of reading during some downtime this weekend, just like I've had every intention of reading it the past few summers at the vacation house. I'm sure there's still sand between the pages from when I dropped it on the beach as Ren pulled me up from my chair and dragged me toward the water, where we splashed in up to our knees and then ran back out because it was so cold.

But it's not sand that falls into my lap when I open it. It's a strip of photos I'd forgotten about since I wedged them in there as a bookmark. In the first Ren is laughing and I'm staring at the camera with my mouth half-open, and both of us are making faces in the second. I can't help but smile as I draw my fingers along the edges, remember Claudia and Clark's wedding just before I left for New York.

As my eyes scan the rest of the pictures, the third photo sends a flutter through my stomach that has me wondering if the bottom of the plane just fell out.

I glance around like I just pulled a nude picture out of my wallet, clutching the evidence against my chest. But everything is normal. The flight attendants are a row up, passing out cans of ginger ale and tiny bags of pretzels. The woman to my right is snoring following the extralarge pill she took as soon as she sat down.

I turn toward the window and hold the strip of photos up to my face again. I remember taking the picture, remember tracing the line of Ren's jaw, the way his eyes fell to my mouth, the way I could feel every place our bodies touched, how it made me a little dizzy.

Deep in my belly, an old feeling bangs against the cage I locked it into years ago, shouts that if the flash hadn't gone off, I might not have pulled away. That some alternate version of us might have stayed in that photo booth.

"Ma'am?"

I startle, jostling the arm of my sleeping seatmate. She doesn't so much as blink. The flight attendant is smiling down at me expectantly.

"Sorry," I say, throat dry. "Just a water, please."

"Coming up."

I shove the pictures back into the spine of the book and slam it closed. Tell myself that if the book was going to catch my attention, it would have by now, that it wasn't work or my moving or anything else that had been getting in my way.

I won't try to read it again.

THURSDAY

chapter seventeen

"Open up!" Fists pound on the doors from the house to the screen porch, stomping feet accompanying them. "Rise and shine!" Sasha shouts.

I bolt upright so fast the blood rushes from my head.

"Wake up!" Stevie calls. "It's my bachelorette today!"

I feel hungover without having had anything to drink the night before, the room slowly coming into focus, brain moving sluggishly. As I stand, Ren is stirring in his bed, the heels of his hands pressed to his eyes, and last night comes flashing back to me.

His hands on my waist.

My back against the tree.

His breath on my neck.

"We're coming in!" Sasha shouts, her final warning.

"I've got it," I say to Ren, who's in the process of swinging his legs over the side of his bed. I just need to do anything but look at him.

"There you are!" Sasha says once I open the door, throwing her arms above her head like she's at the Eras Tour. "It's time to go!"

She and Stevie barge in past me, Stevie walking over to flop across my bed. I glance over my shoulder at Ren. He's sitting on the edge of his bed, hair messy from sleep in a way that makes my pulse hike.

Get it together, Joni.

"You need to get ready too," Sasha says to him, kicking his ankle. "Leo and Thad are in the kitchen."

"Great," Ren says, but he doesn't move. In fact, he seems dazed, like he's still dragging himself out of sleep.

But then his gaze suddenly flicks up to mine, alert, and I realize I've been staring at him. I shift my attention to the dresser, pull a swimsuit and shorts out of the drawer. "Give me five minutes," I say to Stevie and Sasha. "I'll be right there."

"I'll pack the car!" Sasha says, hurrying back inside, Stevie close on her tail.

I'm almost to the doors, going in to change, when Ren says my name. The slight gravel in his voice flutters down my spine.

"Yeah?" I say, turning back. Only a few feet separate us now.

He looks at me for a minute. "Why did you go to bed early last night?" he asks, concern lining his forehead.

"What?" I say, distracted by the shape of his shoulders underneath his T-shirt.

"Everyone went down to the firepit," he says. "And you..." He trails off.

I finally let myself focus on him, on all the planes of his face I couldn't see clearly in the dark last night. It would only take a few steps for me to reach out and touch him. I could brush away that one stubborn wave that falls across his forehead. I could trace a thumb over the line where his eyebrows have creased together. I could press the pads of my fingers to his full bottom lip.

"I have to get ready," I say quickly, pivoting to the door.

Ren grabs my wrist and spins me back toward him.

I look down at where his fingers slide back down against my

palm, breath catching in my throat. He tugged me back to him so easily, like my feet will just go wherever he asks.

"Can we—" he says, my thigh brushing against his knee as I turn to fully face him.

Our hands are still clasped between us. He glances at them, back at me. Doesn't continue.

"Joni!" Stevie's voice has me stepping back, once, then twice, drawing my hand to my side. I hear her come pattering through the mudroom. "Can you bring your Polaroid?"

"Of course!" I say, unable to tear my eyes from Ren.

The sound gets closer, and I shuffle around, hold my clothes up to my chest as if to prove I was, in fact, about to change.

Stevie pokes her head through the door. "Do you have enough film?"

"Yes," I say. "I brought a bunch."

The tension in the room is palpable, especially with Stevie here. I force myself not to look back at Ren.

"Okaaay," she says, slowly. She holds a hand out toward me, wiggling her fingers. "Come on, let's get ready!"

I take her hand and let her pull me out of the room.

Sasha, Stevie, and I drive the twenty minutes into town for coffee and pastries from Stevie's favorite bakery. We head another twenty minutes east to a small lake that connects to the Pacific through a winding four-mile river, their calm waters perfect for kayaking. Stevie's only requests for this week had been to do something outside this morning, and to go to her favorite bar, Clyde's, tonight.

"Look at me," Stevie says as she buckles her life vest on outside the rental shack. "I've gotten so outdoorsy since I moved back to Oregon."

We've kayaked on this river once before, when we were kids.

Stevie spent the entire time exclaiming that *this was her dream* as she languished instead of paddled, letting the current carry her. Today, though, she seems less content to do that and instead hell-bent on proving her kayaking prowess.

"Have you?" I ask, a doubtful laugh slipping out of me as I yank one of the straps on her vest to make sure it's tight enough.

"Yes," she says. "Watch, I'll beat both of you down the river today."

But Stevie hasn't, it seems, become quite the wilderness woman she's touted herself to be, evidenced by the fact that she upends her kayak no fewer than three times just trying to get into it. The guy who we rented them from—a shaggy haired imitation of a Hemsworth, if said Hemsworth smoked a lot of weed and had the air of someone who sleeps in a hammock more often than a bed—looks annoyed when he has to wade into the shallows and help her turn it over *again*. I watch from the shore, one end of my paddle resting against the sand, because when I tried to help, Stevie shrieked that she could do it on her own because she is an *outdoorswoman* so loudly that a flock of birds startled out of the nearest tree.

Sasha, meanwhile, has paddled partway out into the lake and back four times.

I dutifully watch through another two tries before Stevie finally gets into her kayak without turning it over and raises her paddle above her head, her pink bucket hat a fluorescent spot against the gray-blue of the sky.

After I climb into my own kayak, we paddle silently, bob over a tiny, gentle slope at the mouth of the river before we're back in calm water. Sasha, no patience for us amateurs, goes on ahead, pausing every now and again so we can still see her. It's quiet here, the temperate rainforest around us muffling any noise from the road, letting in only bird whistles, the soft dip of our paddles into the water. I stop and close my eyes, breathe in the earthy, damp smell I grew up with, tilt my face toward a spot where the sun filters green down through the layers of mossy limbs.

The sound of Stevie splashing rouses me, and when I open my eyes she's studying me.

"You okay?" she asks.

"Of course." I resume paddling, and she keeps an easy, slow pace next to me. "How are you feeling about Saturday?" I ask as we curve around another bend, Sasha's red life vest already disappearing around the next one.

She lets out a small sigh. "I'm worried for Leo," she says.

I know a bit about his family—that his parents went through a contentious divorce when he and Oliver were kids, that the two of them ended up raising each other, that any sort of family gathering has the potential to get ugly. I wonder if that's part of the reason Leo is the way he is—always sunny, positive, trying to bring people together. Because he had to keep the peace between his parents for so many years.

"If anyone can bring a mood up, I think it's Leo," I say, wanting to comfort her.

"Yeah, but he shouldn't have to," she says. "Especially on *his* wedding day."

"I'll step in," I tell her. I love Leo, and I don't want Stevie to have to worry about running interference on her day either. "You *did* mention the drop-off. Who's going to find a body in those shark-infested waters?"

"That's far too me a comment for you to be making," she says wryly. Then, she shouts at the top of her lungs, "I just want to be married to him already!" She hoists her paddle over her head, words echoing against the trees.

"Words I never thought I'd hear you say."

Stevie shrugs a shoulder as she lowers her arms. "We're malleable creatures. Leo made me soft."

"Yes, the first word that comes to mind when I think of you is *soft*."

"Hey," Stevie says. "I'm plenty soft. I'm romantic, even."

"You're right," I say. "The girl who once told me that 'love is a myth made up by lonely people' is romantic."

"Malleable," Stevie repeats. "I didn't know until I knew."

We paddle for another minute before she asks, "What's up with you and Ren?"

I glance over at her, too abruptly for it to be subtle. Stevie's expression settles into her trademark *I told you so*, and I face quickly forward.

Getting Stevie into her kayak and down the river momentarily may have distracted me, but I've been replaying the feeling of Ren grabbing my wrist all morning. The way he pulled me back to him. My leg pressed against his knee.

"Nothing," I say to Stevie. "We're just— We're good."

"You're good," Stevie repeats. I nod. "And what, exactly, does that mean?"

"It means," I say, peering ahead to make sure Sasha hasn't doubled back. She's still far away. "It means that we're both over whatever happened." Whether that's actually true, I don't know, but I don't want to have this conversation with Stevie before I have it with Ren. If we ever have it.

"Oh, right. I too like to do a lot of staring wordlessly at my estranged friend."

"We're not estranged," I say.

"You *were*," Stevie points out.

She might as well have scooped up cold river water and rained it down over my shoulders. Losing Ren had been like a hole punched clean through me, one I stuffed with work and distance and more work, because if I let myself feel the pain of it, I couldn't breathe.

The memories of those first few weeks after press in on me. I flew back to New York with a throat raw from the perpetual lump in it, like I'd inhaled too much smoke. It was easy enough to throw myself back into my routine at Novo, but every now and again I'd have this shaky feeling run down my arms, the familiar beginnings of a panic attack, the ones I *knew* I should go see a therapist about but was actively ignoring, making it so I had to put down whatever delicate puppet I was working on until it dissipated.

For a while, it was just a matter of feeling the minutes tick by until my heart rate returned to a normal speed, reminding myself that I could go home and crawl into bed and cry or sleep at the end of the day. But work, art, eventually felt good, safe again, even if the rest of the world didn't. I saw him everywhere else, in everyone I passed on the street: dark hair and flannel shirts, brown eyes and strong shoulders. I couldn't listen to music without thinking about him, and so my world became quieter for a while. I wondered about him in every moment I couldn't distract myself, if he hated me, if every time I almost called him he was doing the same, if he'd answer. If he wouldn't. I wondered if he was fine without me, which hurt most of all, even if it was what I'd wanted. It hurt all the time, a physical pain stopping me short, and so I started to diligently shut him out of my brain.

Now Ren and I have been talking to each other again for all of two days, and despite all that, despite how painful I know it is to lose him, here I am, fantasizing about his goddamn *hands.*

I drag in a shaky breath and shove my thoughts as far down as they'll go, smiling over at Stevie. "We're friends for at least this week," I say. "I'm not thinking about what happens after that."

"Why not?" Stevie pushes her paddle off a rock jutting up in the middle of the river, glides around it before she's next to me again.

I know she means Ren, but her question has me seizing up, worrying she knows. About my job, the fact that I don't technically live anywhere anymore, that I have six months of savings, but that six months goes quickly if I don't have an actual plan.

"It's just—" I say, swallow over the achy feeling in my chest. "We don't really know what things look like after this week."

"You could, though."

"What do you mean?"

"I mean," she says, working her paddles in a way that does exactly nothing to propel her forward. "You and Ren have a lot of history. I don't know if your entire relationship is worth throwing away over something that happened over two years ago."

I nod, mostly because I don't want to keep having this conversation. Only danger lies on the other side of it.

"I'll think about it," I tell her.

We catch up with Sasha at the next bend and paddle the end of the river together, until we come around the final curve and the ocean spreads out across a sandbar in front of us, sparkling blue, boats bobbing out of the harbor in town a few miles down, the salty air brushing against my neck now that we're out from under the tree cover.

"Want to go farther out?" Sasha asks, nodding toward the far end of the sandbar.

It's calm here, no rocks or crashing waves to contend with, but it's still the ocean. Hemsworth told us we could paddle a ways out into it if we were brave, which I am certainly not when it comes to aquatic sports beyond, well, the two-inch drop we went over at the onset of this whole adventure.

Luckily, Stevie's outdoorsiness ends here too. "No way," she says. "But I will so happily watch you be adventurous."

"I'll just go for a minute," Sasha says before she heads off.

I turn my kayak to face Stevie and set my paddle across my lap, dip my fingers into the water.

"Hey, remember the bulletin board in the mailroom in our building?" Stevie asks.

"Yeah," I say. "Why?" It was meant to be a spot for tenants to post things like flyers for gigs, sticky notes about a free coffee table, but it more often turned into the apartment message board. *If 4C can* please *start keeping it down between the hours of ten and six, 4B would be* very *appreciative. Blondie with a heart tattoo on your shoulder—u live here? Please stop leaving your dog's shit on the sidewalk, Marcus.* So on and so forth.

"I was just thinking that the kayak rental guy would totally vibe with whoever kept trying to start his pot business on that board," Stevie says, eyes fixed on some far point on the horizon before she swivels them to me, mouth spreading into a wide grin.

I throw my head back, laughter hooting out of me. "Wasn't that Derek?" I ask.

Stevie swats her paddle at the water, hitting me with a splash this time. "You knew who the pot guy was all along?"

"So did you!" I say, gasping with laughter. "He was the one who kept trying to ask you out, but you didn't notice."

"Okay, telling someone you're 'thinking about checking out the new Thai place' does *not* constitute an ask-out. You've got to put some intention behind it."

I frown in solidarity with Derek. "He was nervous."

"He was a drug dealer!"

"He was an *aspiring* drug dealer." This prompts a full-body laugh out of Stevie. She leans back in her kayak, eyes closed as giggles bubble out of her.

"Oh, man," she says when she looks at me again. "Thank god we don't live there anymore."

"What do you mean?" I ask. I dip one end of my paddle into the water to straighten myself out. Our apartment wasn't what either of us dreamed—smaller than we anticipated, a notoriously unreliable landlord—but it was ours, creaky floors, stuck windows, and all. "I loved that apartment."

Stevie's nose wrinkles. Between her hat and her braids, she looks so much like she did as a kid. "Did you?"

"Of course I did," I say. "Did it not seem like I loved it?"

"I don't know," she says. She rolls her paddle across her lap, back and forth. "Sometimes you just didn't seem all that happy in New York."

"I mean—" I say, answers jostling for position in my brain. I go with, "I was a little stressed sometimes, for sure, but..." I shrug.

Stevie keeps an eye on me. "Are you happy now?" she asks.

The words escape me again, so many possible things to tell her right now but none of them seeming exactly true. *I am happy there* would be a lie, especially in the last few years. *I'm lonely* would get me closer to the truth, but it would mean having to dig into all the specifics of that, tell her about the hole I'm worried I've dug myself into.

When I look at my sister, the ready expression on her face, like she knows she's providing an opening for this enormous piece of news, I almost tell her. That Ramona fired me. That I have no clue what I'm doing next. That I've been realizing, lately, that I've been lost for a lot longer than I care to admit. She's not wrong—I haven't always been happy in New York. Stevie seemed to enjoy her time there, but she'd always known it would just be for grad school, hadn't planned on staying beyond that, and she'd stuck to her word.

The loneliness didn't really settle in on me until she left. But even after trying harder, after making an effort to go out with people after work, exploring on my own and creating a haven for myself in my apartment, New York never felt quite like *mine* in the way Portland did. I'd watch other people falling in love with the city while I continued to feel some pull to the West Coast that I couldn't sever. I told myself it wasn't real: that it was just nostalgia. But then I was back, for one brief moment two and a half years ago, and I felt it. Some weight lifted off me, like I was back where I belonged.

As I cycle through the past five years, searching for an answer for Stevie, I realize that there *were* times I wasn't so focused on work, when I let it slip away and my mind cleared again for a minute, and there was almost room to think about a different kind of life, if I'd let myself.

The weddings with Ren.

I twist myself straighter in my seat, the confession dying on my lips.

But I still feel guilty when I shake my head and tell her that yes, of course I'm happy.

"Okay," she says. It's obvious she doesn't totally believe me, and I almost open my mouth to offer up something—what, I don't know, maybe an anecdote about the woman in my building who I am convinced is a lost Olsen triplet—but a cold wash of water goes sailing over my head at that moment, soaking down my back.

I dig my paddle into the water and flip around to see Sasha, eyes wide as she tries to suppress a laugh. "Shit," she says. "I didn't mean—"

The splash from my paddle drenches her hair before she can finish her sentence.

"Oh my god," she says, spluttering. "That's war."

"Stop!" Stevie shouts as Sasha's next splash hits her. "I'm not prepared for this! My hat!"

"Outdoorswoman," I say, swiveling to face Stevie, bangs dripping water down my face. "You've—"

I truly should have known better, but Stevie's look of delight as she gets me square in the chest is the image that will always define this morning for me.

We paddle back to the lake—Hemsworth looking very relieved that we didn't clumsily abscond with his kayaks—and drive back to the house. It's nearing two, and Stevie is singing along to the radio tunelessly in the backseat, hands behind her head as the wind whips strands of her braids loose.

"Okay," Sasha says as we turn off the highway. "Showers, then meet up in Stevie's room to get ready?"

"Do we have stuff for spritzes?" Stevie says, poking her head through the seats.

"Obviously," I say. "It's *your* wedding."

We arrive at the house, and Sasha stops her car in front of the garage. "Stevie, I didn't know Leo was so competitive," she says as we hop out.

I follow her gaze to the beach, where the bachelor party is playing touch football, not a shirt among them. Leo is weaving an impressive line through what I assume is the opposite team, the drummer reaching out and tagging his side.

"Yeah, he fits right in with you Websters," Stevie says, leaning against the hood of the car, shading a hand over her eyes.

"Well, I'm going to shower." Sasha moves toward the house. "I'll meet you upstairs!"

I wave a hand at her before leaning next to Stevie and turning my attention back to the beach. Ren catches the football that Thad hikes to him, runs backward until he brings his arm up, throws it to Leo, cheering when Leo twists and leaps into the air to catch it.

Are you happy now? Stevie had asked me. The broad answer is no. In life, I'm not happy, and it's been that way for a long time, even before the worst happened at my job. But if I were to answer her about right now, I might tell her that yes, everything else aside, here at the house, I'm as close to happy as I've been in a long time.

chapter eighteen

Three hours later, I'm sitting on the floor in Stevie's room, a pot of pink-and-purple glitter gel open next to me.

"Just, hold still for two more seconds," I tell her as I pat it onto her cheekbones over an already impressive streak of multicolored shimmer. Between each round of application, Stevie has squinted in the mirror and turned back to me, asking for more, but now, she's squirming, impatient. I dip my finger into the pot and hold on to her chin to try to keep her still, press it onto her other cheek. "There. I think you're done."

She leans around me to look in the mirror, breaking into a smile when the light catches her skin in a beam that could, frankly, signal a boat at sea. "Your turn!" she says, grabbing the pot of glitter I just set down.

Sasha is lounging on the bed in her pink dress, watching us as she sips her water. *Someone has to wrangle all of you tonight,* she'd told me when she declined a spritz earlier. "That's going to be a bitch to get off when you're drunk later."

"I'm putting it on you too," Stevie says as she swipes a glob of gold glitter over my cheekbone.

Once Stevie is done with me, she coaxes Sasha down to the

floor. Sasha puts on a face of irritation as Stevie picks out a glitter that matches her dress, but even she can't resist smiling at my sister as she pats it on.

"Knock knock!" Our mom's head appears through the half-open door. She pushes into the room with a tote bag straining at the seams. "Here," she says, setting it on the bed. "A care package."

The plan tonight is for dinner and Clyde's and then for everyone to crash at the house Leo's brother and bandmates have rented in town. Nonetheless every parent has stopped by our room to offer to pick us up more than once. More than twice.

"Mom!" Stevie says from the floor as I sit down on the bed and rifle through the bag. "That's so *nice!*"

"That's Stevie's personal prosecco." Sasha nods at the bottle next to my sister's knee that she's been using to top off her glass whenever it runs low.

"Be sure to get some food in her," our mom says as she perches on the bed next to me.

"Oh, I don't think we'll need to worry about that." I pull a bulk box of granola bars out of the bag, unearthing the largest bottle of ibuprofen I've ever laid eyes on. "What do you think we're *doing* tonight?"

"Enjoying yourselves," she says, pulling me into her and rubbing my arm. I burrow closer—maybe a result of the two spritzes I've had, but maybe because she's packed us a bag full of snacks and Gatorade like we're a crew of tipsy toddlers off to soccer practice.

While Stevie finishes up Sasha's glitter, I take the tote bag out to Ren's car, where we've been packing everyone's bags for tonight because it has the most space. I open one of the doors to the back seat, rummaging around for a spot, because apparently we've packed enough to spend an entire week in town. My body is leaned into the car, toes just on the ground, when I feel someone behind me.

"You all good in there?"

My heart jumps into my throat at the sound of Ren's voice. I slide out of the back seat, smooth my hands over my red dress as I straighten. We haven't been alone since this morning.

"Hey," I say.

"Hey." He nods toward where I've left the bag balanced precariously on top of Leo's backpack. "I can put that in the back."

I watch as he reaches inside, heaves the packed bag out, brow creasing as he glances at its contents. "I know," I say. "It's ridiculous." I follow him to the back of the car, prop myself against the bumper as he sets the bag in the trunk, then joins me.

"How was kayaking?" he asks. His arms flex as he crosses them over his chest, my eyes dropping to where his palms rest against his biceps.

All I can think about is his hand in mine this morning, the gentle pressure of it, and how much I want to feel it again.

I try to ignore the way his proximity is impacting me. "Went over some pretty gnarly rapids. Flipped twice." I look back up at him as I say it, eyes on the spot by his mouth where that crease deepens as he laughs. "It was very mellow. Stevie did *technically* flip her kayak three times, but she wasn't actually in it yet."

"Stevie, the outdoorswoman?" Ren asks in jest.

I point a finger at him. "She told you too? I thought she was keeping it on the down-low until the wilderness bureau sent her the commemorative plaque."

"Stevie Miller, Queen of the River," Ren says.

"Stevie Miller, Queen of the Natural World," I amend, forming a marquee with my hands.

"Ceremony forthcoming. Top of Mount Hood."

I laugh, settling farther against the car. "How was football?"

"Football was fine," he says, rubbing at his palm with his thumb like he's trying to find something to do with his hands. Like I'm not the only one thinking about this morning, or last night.

"Ren!" We poke our heads around the car to see Sasha hanging half out the front door of the house. "Do you have Stevie's bag?"

"Leo brought it out!" he calls back.

Sasha lets out a sound that's half exasperation, half relief. "We'll be out in two seconds!" she yells. "Stevie!" I hear her shout as she recedes back into the house. "Your husband took it out there!"

"Her husband," Ren says, voice low. "First time I've heard someone call Leo that."

"Hey," I say, elbowing him. "If you let your friend screw my little sister over..."

Ren's eyebrow arches. "Are we about to have the talk?" he asks, angling toward me.

I laugh. "I wouldn't know how to give the talk."

"Here, practice on me," Ren says. "If I let Leo screw Stevie over, you'll what?"

"I'll—" My eyes catch on his as he comes to stand in front of me, my pulse fluttering. "I'll be so mad."

Ren looks skeptical. "That's all you've got?"

"I don't know." I reach up, pull at the ends of my hair. Ren tracks the movement. "This hypothetical is ridiculous. Leo hurting Stevie? You being fine with it?"

"Humor me," Ren says.

My teeth work at my lip as I think. "I know," I say. "You let your friend screw over my little sister and I'll send *everyone* the video of you singing 'It's All Coming Back to Me Now.'"

Ren's eyes go wide, one corner of his mouth twitching into a disbelieving smile. "You told me you deleted that," he says.

I press my lips together, shake my head. It still exists on my computer, in a folder where I dumped all my pictures and videos even tangentially related to Ren when I couldn't look at them anymore. It freed up a depressing amount of space on my phone.

The video in question is one from my last summer in Portland, when some perfect cocktail of tequila, summer heat, and enough laughter to make us slaphappy had Ren finally relenting when I dragged him into a karaoke bar. Ren will dance with me at weddings. He can play the guitar so well. He can pick out a great musician in seconds. He can*not* carry a tune.

"Had to keep something in case a situation like this ever arose," I say. I'm fighting a smile, even if the video reminds me of saying goodbye to him for the first time all those years ago, of how much time I've spent missing him since. Being this close to Ren is doing a lot to temporarily erase the most fraught parts of our history from my mind.

"Unbelievable," Ren says, edging closer to me. His hand just grazes mine where it rests against the trunk. "And here I deleted all evidence of the Great Senior Year Bleach Debacle."

"Hey." I move to whack his shoulder but he stops me, catches my hand in his. "Half of my hair was blond for *two hours,* and you are the only one who saw it."

I feel myself tilting toward him as he grins, my body drawn toward his like there are magnets at our centers.

"And you pulled it off so well," he says, all the sarcasm lost on me when the low gravel in his voice hits my ears.

The front door slams open again.

"Clyde's! Clyde's! Clyde's!" Stevie chants as she marches down the steps. Leo joins in behind her, Thad and Sasha trailing him.

We drop our things at the house—a huge, sprawling place on the bay—and convene in the open-concept living room and kitchen, where I slip Stevie's *bride* sash over her head, hand Leo's *groom* sash to his brother, Oliver.

I also ordered temporary tattoos of each of their faces and of their initials in the middle of a heart. Putting them on turns out to be a hilarious affair. Because they could only be purchased in quantities of fifty, we have a huge number, and everyone gets creative: Dev, the drummer, spirals a line of Leo's face down his arm; Thad puts tattoos of Stevie's face on both sides of his neck.

I hover between the kitchen and living room, casting around for Sasha or Stevie to help me put one of Leo's face on my shoulder. But Stevie is busy applying tattoos to Leo in the kitchen and Sasha is next to Thad on the couch, lining up one of each on her forearm.

"Here," Ren says, walking over to me from where he's been sorting through the box of tattoos on the coffee table. He motions for me to turn around.

I do as instructed. He slowly brushes my hair to the side like it's muscle memory, even though it's not long enough anymore to get in the way, and sets the tattoo on my shoulder, pressing a cool towel carefully against my skin. After a minute, he removes the towel and peels the paper back, blows gently to make sure it's dry, sending goose bumps radiating out from the spot.

He takes a step back. "There," he says, finally lifting his eyes to mine.

The dark edge to his gaze has me imagining crazy things, like what would have happened if Stevie hadn't come back this morning, if the blue team hadn't won at that moment last night. It's the last thing I need to be thinking about right now, and yet, the longer we stare at each other, I can't help but wonder if Ren is thinking them too. "Okay, your turn," I say, trying to keep my voice light. I flip his arm so his palm is facing up to the ceiling, his skin warm under my fingers.

I grasp one of the initial heart tattoos from the pile and step in closer to him. It's not until I'm gently pushing the tattoo to his biceps that my eyes catch on the single line below his elbow, aligning with the same one on my arm.

"Think this will hurt as much as getting that?" I ask as I hold the damp towel to the tattoo, ignoring the way his muscles subtly move wherever I touch him.

"So far, it's not so bad," he says.

My eyes rise up to meet his again. "Did you ever think about getting rid of it?"

Ren's expression goes tense. "Never," he says, then, mouth softening, "Did you?"

I shake my head. "Never."

"Okay!" Stevie calls from the other side of the room. She has an entire half sleeve of Leo's faces on her left arm. "Let's get this party started!"

Once everyone is finished with tattoos, we traipse down the street to the Mexican restaurant we've been eating at since we were kids. We push two tables together on the patio beneath green and blue globe lights, order pitchers of margaritas. As people swap Stevie and Leo stories and talk about the wedding on Saturday, I snap pictures for them to remember the night by—of Stevie mid-laugh, of Oliver doing an imitation of Leo when he plays guitar onstage—and make a stack of Polaroids in the middle of the table.

When I look up again, Ren is watching me.

Predictions? he mouths from his seat across from me.

I smile as I sink back into my chair, nod at the glass in his hand. *Tequila,* I mouth back. The thing that made some of our best nights possible.

He laughs.

Once we put in our food orders, it's time to begin. "Okay," I say, pulling a sheet of paper out of my bag. "Per Stevie and Leo's request, dinner is for trivia about the happy couple."

"We rule trivia night in Portland," Stevie says from her seat next to me, to the table at large.

"We always come in last, babe." Leo drums his fingers against the back of her hand where it sits on her chair.

"We came in third when they did the decades night," Ren says, gesturing with his glass toward Stevie. He's sitting with an ankle resting on the opposite knee.

"See?" Stevie says, waving a hand in his direction. "Third."

"You'd think a team with a music scout, a culture writer, and a whole *band* would do better," Sasha points out.

Dev, the drummer, raises his hand. "I bring the history knowledge to the team. Majored in it in college."

"Yeah, and when Joni visits, we can finally get all the art history questions," Leo says.

I'm about to interrupt, tell him I remember exactly three facts from my art history classes, when Stevie pipes up. "I think six is the max number of team members," she says almost absentmindedly, as if Leo isn't just being polite and pretending I visit, as if this trip marks the end of my hiatus from Portland and I'll be hamming it up with them at their local bar next month. To be fair, I might be now, and the idea begins to take root inside me. But then again, I could also be living in Nova Scotia next month, for all I know.

"Joni can play for me," Ren says. "I'll just be there for moral support when she's in town." He winks at me, the rim of his glass against his lips, and it's like the prosecco Stevie kept pouring into her glass earlier is fizzing through my body.

"Okay, I *know* I'm good at Stevie and Leo trivia," Oliver says, lacing his fingers and stretching them out in front of him. "Let's play."

When Stevie and Leo asked for this, I leaped at the opportunity, coming up with questions about their relationship, sending them the final draft to get their fully fleshed-out answers, treating it like I did a Novo project. It felt like the least I could do to make up for missing their engagement party. I'd planned to be there, my first trip to Portland in years. But just as I was mustering the courage to purchase my ticket, three puppets randomly went missing and everything went into meltdown—and a small, selfish part of me was relieved to postpone my return. Sitting at this table now, with everyone laughing together, things like they used to be, I don't know what I'd been so afraid of.

"Rules are simple," I say. "You answer correctly first, you win a point. I'm moderator."

We get through only five questions before Stevie turns it into a drinking game that isn't so much a game as it is drink whenever Stevie tells you to, which is sometimes punishment when you get it wrong and sometimes to celebrate if you get it right.

"What song did Leo dedicate to Stevie—at the band's third Sublimity show—that made her admit that she loved him?" I ask.

Dev shouts out "'You're So Vain'!"

Stevie has just taken an enormous bite of one of Leo's fish tacos, but manages to tell Dev to drink, loudly. I fold the paper over so the next question is at the top, read it confidently before I can think about the answer. "Okay, where did Stevie and Leo meet?"

"Sublimity," Ren says to me, and I know that look, have seen it before, have felt the same roller coaster drop as I do now.

"Thanks to Ren and Joni!" Sasha slaps a hand on the table.

"Ren and Joni drink!" Stevie shouts before pointing at us. "Sasha, you too. Drink your water."

I have no choice but to oblige, tilting my glass in Sasha's direction, then Ren's.

"To Stevie and Leo!" Oliver calls out, and now everyone toasts.

"To us!" Stevie coos, leaning her head against Leo's. Everything she says is an exclamation, gaze getting glassier by the minute.

I look at Ren again. His eyes are on mine, his mouth set in a way that I can't read. It's not that it's a bad memory. In fact, the night Stevie and Leo met is a great one, as far as memories go. It's what came directly after that should have the fizzy feeling in my stomach going flat.

But soon enough we're both drawing ourselves out of the

memory of that night. I focus on the way Ren's smile slowly returns, on the laughter around the table, and leave the past to the past.

chapter nineteen

The inside of Clyde's is nothing to write home about, but the
yard out back has always been our happy place on warm summer
nights, at least since we all turned twenty-one and could come
here together. There's a bar in one corner, where locals camp
out in their usual spots, and picnic tables dotted all around,
where tourists sip from plastic cups. A huge tree grows in the
center of it all, lights strung into the branches above. Signs from
old businesses line the walls of the neighboring buildings. Bar-
ry's Boat Rentals boasting its opening in 1979. The Salty Dog
advertising breakfast that hasn't been served in fifteen years.
A faded maroon sign promotes a business called Shear Sisters
that doesn't seem to be a salon but rather a tree-trimming service, maybe the very one that took care of the behemoth that
stretches above our picnic table.

Being here again feels out of time, like I'm a slightly different version of myself that I seemed to have lost and am now
finding my way back to.

From a stage set up at one end of the yard, a twentysomething
guy in striped overalls is crooning out covers on his acoustic

guitar, a drum track behind him, everything from Tom Petty to Taylor Swift.

"Shots!" Stevie shouts to the rest of the red team, who will be footing the bill tonight, her fist in the air. As the lead guitarist and Oliver pop up at the other end of the table and head to the bar to order, she leans toward me. "Is Clyde going to cebelrate—celerate—" She screws up her face, thinking hard.

"Celebrate?" I offer.

She snaps her fingers and points at me. Turns out she was the main participant of her drinking game.

"Is Clyde going to *celebrate* with us?" She pronounces the word with enormous concentration.

"If we can track him down," I say, glancing over my shoulder as if to search for the eponymous—and likely deceased—original owner of the place. We've never met Clyde, but he's something of a legend in town.

Stevie crashes into me, squishing her cheek against my shoulder. "I love you," she coos. Stevie is an affectionate drunk, and this place seems to amplify it in her, the way it makes all of us feel more carefree. "You're my favorite sister."

"You're *mine*." I tuck a lock of brown hair behind her ear as she smiles up at me, this beautiful bride-to-be. She and Leo are perfect for each other, but it hits me now how much I've missed being able to walk into her room and curl up in her bed, or decorating for holidays together, that we may be doing even less of that in the future, and I haven't treated these last vestiges of our childhood with the sacredness they deserve. While Stevie told me she understood when I couldn't make her engagement party, or Leo's shows, I should have tried harder to be there during these important moments in her life.

Oliver returns with a tray of shots the color of Pepto-Bismol. I've been taking it easy tonight, nursing a margarita all through dinner while I emceed the game, so the shot doesn't go down quite as easily as it seems to for everyone else. Except Ren, apparently. At the other end of the table, he grimaces.

"Dance!" Stevie says after she tosses back a second shot, having resorted to communicating in single, easily pronounceable words for the rest of the night. A chorus of cheers goes up around the table.

The line at the outdoor bar is long, so as our table heads toward the dance floor, I weave my way inside to order a beer, desperate to wash away the sickly taste of the shot still on my tongue. On my way back out, the ancient jukebox in the corner catches my eye and I wander over, idly flipping through the records.

"Diet Bob Dylan not doing it for you?"

Ren's presence is so familiar I'm surprised I didn't notice him approach.

I glance up at him, his hair mussed from him dragging a hand through it. He leans an arm on the jukebox as I keep flipping. "Not a G&T girl anymore?"

"No, I am," I say quickly. I squeeze the cool beer bottle tighter, reach out to tap a toe against his. "I've just been waiting for when you can make me one again." In all honesty, it's still my usual order, but Ren will forever make my favorite version.

"Or it's probably not best to mix margaritas *and* gin with whatever's in those pink shots." His knuckles tap against the top of the jukebox.

"No." I shake my head. "Just left my best bartender back in Portland and a gin and tonic has never been the same."

"If you say so," Ren says as I raise the beer to my mouth. He keeps an eye on the bottle, like one Modelo is so damning.

"I haven't changed *that* much in two years," I say.

"Two and a half," Ren says.

My hand stills as I'm raising the bottle to my lips again. I'd said it casually, tossed out in the name of seeming like the six extra months aren't *that* important, when really, they're scratched on the inside of my brain like tally marks. "What?"

"Two and a half years," Ren says, eyes suddenly, deeply focused on me. "Or, if you want to be *really* specific, thirty-one months, one week, five days, and roughly—what, twenty-one hours?"

For a second, I feel a little off-balance, like I'm back in the kayak.

"I've missed you, Joni," he says quietly.

On the list of things I've wanted to hear from Ren, this is near the top. Some acknowledgment that the time we spent without each other was worse than however complicated it would have been to remain in each other's lives. His admission buoys and scares me in equal measure, the implications too much to think through in this setting, and with his body so close to mine. *I've missed you too,* I want to say. My brain is repeating it, but the words don't come out. *Say it, say it, say it,* I think, but I'm stuck on the way Ren's mouth moved around the words.

I look up at him, warmth thrumming between us as his expression shifts into something almost hopeful. "I've missed you," I tell him, even as I think that maybe I should lead us out of this territory into something less dangerous, where we aren't making tipsy confessions, where the years lost between us aren't laid bare.

"Hey!" We both turn at the voice shouting from the now-open back door. Sasha leans inside, glaring at us. "What the hell are you two doing in here? Get your asses onto the dance floor!"

Ren looks back at me once she's disappeared. He holds out his hand. "Shall we?"

I wish I could say I weigh my options, but the pressure of his palm against mine again is too tempting. I lace my fingers through his, and he leads me outside to where the guy is now covering a blink-182 song but with a folksy, acoustic bent that doesn't altogether work.

We wind our way onto the dance floor. I take a long drink of beer to steady myself and extend the bottle toward Ren. He takes a sip and hands it back like it's the most natural thing in the world, and I remind myself that some things can just be here and now, normal, not heavy with meaning. Not everything has to be so wrapped up in history.

Bob Dylan Lite transitions into Big Star's "Thirteen." Everyone around us moves together, arms looping around necks and faces pressing against chests. Ren is still holding my hand, and a small laugh spills out of me as he spins me, once, before pulling me into him, our bodies fitting together in one easy line. I rest my wrist against his shoulder, bottle dangling behind him.

"I love this song."

"I know you do," Ren says.

I swallow, suddenly aware of all the places our bodies are touching. I bring the bottle back around and offer it to him, watch as he takes a drink, his eyes not leaving mine. I drain the rest, cast around for a place to set it. Ren lifts it from my hand and stretches over to a high top.

"Tell me about your new place," I say because I have to say something. I'm afraid that if we don't, I'll inch even closer into him with no point of return.

Ren hesitates.

"What?" I say.

"It's—" He breaks off. "It's the house with the crescent moon window in the front door."

I slow, still swaying, but now the world is swaying around me too.

Ren and I used to walk by that house all the time. A bungalow off Mississippi—near Sublimity—that we both loved for its quirkiness. There was a sunroom on one side where we would sometimes see a dog napping, a front porch that reminded us of the vacation house, the crescent-moon-shaped window in the front door. When we were in our early twenties, it was one of our favorite games to pretend which houses we'd buy if we could afford them.

"Did you—" I say, the reality of the discrepancies between my life and Ren's dawning on me. "Do you—"

"I bought it," Ren says. "A couple months ago."

"In this economy?" I murmur, like we're talking about something secret, like someone might overhear us.

Ren laughs softly, the lines at the corners of his mouth showing up and making my heart swell. "There's actually a lot of work that needs to be done. The outside is better than the inside."

"But still," I say, gazing over his shoulder as images of Ren doing things like sanding, standing over a table saw, ripping out floorboards, whatever it is you do when you renovate an old house, flood through me. "You're a homeowner."

"I guess so."

"So grown-up," I say.

Ren rolls his eyes. "Please."

"Please what?" I say, drawing my head back. "You have your dream job, in your dream city, living in your dream—"

Ren's grip on me tightens. "I don't have everything," he says, and something in the way he's looking at me has my head going dizzy again.

There's a squeal from the stage, and a familiar voice rings out. "This next song," Stevie says, not entirely upright, the microphone clutched in her hand. "Is for—" She hiccups, loudly, the sound echoing into the microphone and around the yard. Leo whoops. "Okay," she says. "This next song is for my family, who's here tonight." She waves a hand in the general vicinity of the dance floor, as if everyone at this bar is her family for the night, before turning back to Bob Dylan. "Take us away, Bernie!"

"Bernie," Ren says, just as Thad appears over his shoulder. We step apart, and let him in between us.

"Name's not Bernie," Thad says, extending one of the pink shots toward each of us. "It's Hank or Bob or something like that."

"Please let it be Bob," I say, eyes flashing to Ren's.

He's smiling, but it's a little weak at the sight of the dreaded shot glasses suspended between us.

"I really hate these shots," I say.

"To Stevie?" he asks.

I let out a small groan of protest, but tap mine against his anyway. "To Stevie."

We both throw our shots back. Diet Bob Dylan launches into an enthusiastic cover of Hilary Duff's "Why Not." We listen for a second before Ren asks the all-important question, "Does this song mean anything to any of us?"

"It matters to Stevie, I guess."

She ballerina leaps around the dance floor, Leo applauding her from the sidelines.

"This isn't a slow song," I point out, her moves not exactly matching the music.

"It's not," Ren confirms. He takes my plastic shot glass from me and stacks it in his, sets it on a table before he offers me his hand.

I take it, and he pulls me onto the dance floor toward them. I don't know what comes next, but I let myself enjoy it, a snapshot memory I'll hold on to forever.

After another hour at Clyde's, we make it back to the rental house. On one side of the living room, Leo starts up a rousing round of charades that Ren and I are not allowed to play because of our prior alleged but totally false cheating scandals, while Sasha curls up on the couch to spectate, eyes sleepy.

Stevie drags me into the kitchen, where she busies herself making what she's calling a "blended Long Island daiquiri." I force her to drink two glasses of water and eat a piece of toast as she chatters on.

"It's going well, don't you think it's going well?" she says, all in one mad rush, as she dumps another shot glass of lemonade into the blender. She sniffs it, thinks for a minute, and then adds a glug of Midori Sour that I think she found in one of the rental's cupboards.

"It's going well," I say. "Are you having fun?"

"I'm having *fun*," she says, before she pouts out her lower lip. "I'm sad, though."

Worry courses through me, warning bells going off and lights flashing. Affectionate Stevie is one thing. Sad drunk Stevie cannot come out at her bachelorette party.

"Why are you sad?" I ask, wary that by merely *asking* the question I'll inadvertently unlock the floodgates, but not quite sure how to proceed without having more information.

"I'm sad that the guy back at the bar didn't know any One Direction!" She half shouts it.

"Was *that* the song you wanted to dedicate to all of us?"

"Yes," she says, gripping my wrist with both her hands. "I wanted everyone to dance to the sounds of our youth."

"Stevie, I hate to break it to you, but I think *we* were the only two who loved One Direction."

"That's not true. Sasha saw Harry Styles in Paris!"

"She did?" I ask, whipping my head to look toward the living room at the same time Stevie shouts, "Fire in the hole!" and turns on the blender without the lid on.

I make another, less offensive, drink for Stevie and turn on One Direction on the Bluetooth speaker. She calls for more games, and we all gather around the dining room table to play Trivial Pursuit, which is missing most of its cards.

By the time we've made our way through two albums and the game has disintegrated into reading questions out loud to the group, giving points to whoever can answer, Stevie is yawning.

"I need a nap," she says.

"Let's head to bed." Leo's hand plays at the top of her head.

"No, just a nap," she protests, even as her eyelids are fluttering. "I'll be ready to go after that."

"Come on, babe," Leo says, helping her up from her chair.

I head back into the kitchen to tidy things up. Through the small window into the living room, I watch Ren set up two air mattresses, the pump whirring, then make them neatly with the blankets we both brought and found here.

"I can do that," Sasha says, wandering in behind me. She leans in the doorway while I scrub some of Stevie's blender mess off a cupboard. Sasha has planned the whole wedding, organized this week down to the second, but no matter how good at it she is, it seems like tonight has finally worn her down.

"Maid of honor duty," I say, turning back to her. "You should go to bed."

She yawns. "I think we did a pretty good job today."

"We did a *great* job today. Thank you, Sasha, seriously. I couldn't have planned any of this by myself. The wedding is going to be incredible."

"Oh, sure you could have," she says, waving a hand before drawing me in to a quick hug. "You head to bed soon too, okay?"

"Oh, I'm just waiting for everyone to rally. We're heading back to Clyde's, right?"

She laughs as she leaves the kitchen. I wring the rag I've been using into the sink, looking up only when I hear the door to the back deck opening and see Ren slip outside alone.

I focus on the glasses that need to be loaded into the dishwasher, the rest of the kitchen cleanup. By the time I'm done, Sasha is in the bathroom, Thad sprawled across the couch, everyone else in their respective bedrooms.

I grab a sweatshirt from my bag, shrug it on over my dress, then slide the door to the deck open. Ren's standing at the top of the stairs that lead down to the beach, and he looks back at me just as he puts his phone into the back pocket of his jeans.

"I promised the parents I'd check in with them," he says.

"They're still awake?" I cross my arms against the slight chill of the night, watch the way the gentle breeze sifts through his hair.

"Seems like they had their own party back at the house. But they're headed to bed now.

"Tired?" Ren asks after a moment of silence.

"No," I say. "You?"

"No." He tips his head in the direction of the beach. "Want to walk?"

I smile. "I'd love that."

Ren gets a flashlight and his own sweatshirt from inside, a gray one I used to steal when we were in college. There are worn spots at the cuffs where I would jab my thumbs against the inside, hook them there to pull the sleeves down over my hands.

The beam of Ren's flashlight lights up a path along the beach in front of us, and we gravitate together and apart over the cool sand, arms brushing together and then away and then finding each other again.

"Can I tell you something awful?" I say as the lights of the house fade behind us. We're one of the few homes still awake on this stretch of beach, the rest of them just shadowy shapes above us.

"I'd love to hear something awful," he says, voice low even though it doesn't need to be.

"I'm sure you did such an excellent job setting up those air mattresses," I say, moderating my own volume to meet his. "But I would kill to sleep on the screen porch tonight."

Ren's shoulder jostles mine as he lets out a chuckle. "Can I tell you something awful?" He leans in so his lips are closer to my ear, his hand cupped around them. "Me too."

"Stevie would be livid if we didn't participate in the slumber party," I say.

"Interesting slumber party," Ren says. "Do most people go off to separate rooms and pass out because they danced too hard to Hilary Duff?"

"She'd just *know* if we left."

"She would. I think we'll do okay on the air mattresses."

I kick at the sand as the light catches on the edge of a sand dollar. It's only a half one. "We do have to be well rested for tomorrow," I say. "Lots of setup to do."

"I've heard hungover is the best way to get anything done."

"Hey, not us." I flip around and walk backward. I want to see his face. "We haven't had anything since those pink shots. What do you think was in those?"

"We make something pretty similar at Sublimity," Ren says, nose wrinkling. "I think I'm going to shield you from that one until there's a little more space between us and them."

"Get a lot of bachelorettes at Sublimity?" I'm still walking backward, and Ren's eyes drop to my ankles, skim back up my legs.

"We do, shockingly." He aims his flashlight between us, but I keep my eyes trained on his face. His brow is furrowed, one hand extended my direction, like he's ready to catch me if I fall.

"Really?" I ask, something about the dark or the pink shots or the week in general making my tongue loose. "The indie music venue with the hot bartender is a real bachelorette destination?"

The heel of my sandal scoops up more sand than I expected.

I hardly stumble, but Ren grabs me, tugging me to him with an arm around my waist.

"I'd feel a lot better if we could both face forward while we're walking on the beach in the pitch dark, Joni," he says into my shoulder. "This flashlight's not that strong."

"Okay, Webster, I'll face forward. Just for you." His arm slowly slides from my waist as I spin around, and we continue on in silence.

When we reach a salt-beaten log, we finally stop and sit in the sand, our backs against it.

"Look," I say, pointing up at the sky above us. "The Summer Triangle."

Ren follows my finger to the trio of stars. I've searched for them every summer since he first showed them to me. Living in New York these past years, where you can't see the stars, it often felt like a reminder of what we'd lost, like Ren and I were no longer under the same sky.

"Joni," Ren says.

I look over at him, watch the way his throat bobs, his face only inches from mine. "Last night—" he says, but I don't want to talk, not about last night or this morning or what happened or anything that exists outside of right now.

I shake my head, and he quiets as I reach up to trace the curve of his jaw, down into the hollow beneath, unable to stop myself from touching him any longer. He closes his eyes for what might only be a second, but I feel it like time has stopped and handed me this precious moment.

I let my fingertips come to rest on his neck until he opens his eyes again.

"I missed you too," I say, because I worry that we moved on too quickly earlier and it didn't land, and I need it to have landed. "Of course I did."

He takes my cheek in his palm, then leans forward and kisses my forehead, leaving his lips there for a minute before pulling back. He examines his hand, a confused smile flitting across his face, and looks up at me.

"What?" I ask, my heart picking up.

"I think I messed up your glitter, Joni," he whispers.

I smile, and so does he.

Something silent passes between us then, *are you sures* and *yes* and *it's us* and *it's this*, and I know that I'm not making it up this time. When he finally kisses me, it's steady, certain.

It's supposed to be impossible, being with Ren like this. We are just friends again, and I should be afraid of what this will do, should consider the fact that this is the time of night when bad decisions are made. But none of that strikes me as very important when I twist my body toward his and his hand falls to my hip, hoisting me up and onto his lap.

I melt into him, my hand sliding up his chest, then pausing at all the important spots: over his heart, the pulse point in his neck, the back of his hair. My knees rest on either side of him, and I press down slightly, eliciting a quiet groan from him that sends a line sinking through me, tying my center to his lips, his tongue, to the hands that skim the outsides of my thighs, the fingers just reaching under the hem of my dress.

Suddenly, he pulls away again.

"What?" I ask, frozen, worried that he's changed his mind.

His grip tightens on my hips, keeping me in place. "I promise this isn't what I meant by *walk*," he says.

I kiss him again, smile against his lips. "Well, for future reference, this might be the best walk I've ever been on."

THREE YEARS AGO

Willow and Martin

Boston, Massachusetts

chapter twenty

I spot Ren before he spots me. He's leaning against a wall near the departure board, arms folded across his chest as he scans the crowds, and I swear I can already smell his faded, sage green T-shirt. When I'm halfway to him, his eyes find me, brightening, his tall figure stepping easily around a family, each of their five kids on one of those ridable suitcases, all of them coordinated in neon shirts, The Baileys Take Bahston! emblazoned across the backs.

When we reach each other, he hugs me to him. "There you are," he says softly.

Ren was on a work trip during the week at the beach house this year, and even that extra month made our time apart feel longer. So much of our friendship has been defined by these types of moments the last few years: transitional spaces filled with hustle and bustle, the hopeful, excited hello when our time together stretches ahead of us and the comedown on the goodbye.

I squint at the scruff on his cheeks. "Are you growing a beard?" I ask.

Ren rubs his knuckles over his jaw. "Just didn't have time to shave before my flight this morning."

"I bet you could totally rock a beard," I say, holding my hands just away from his face like I'm styling him. "Or a mustache?" I straighten my index finger above his lip. "Love a mustache moment."

He lowers my hand. "I'm shaving as soon as we get back to the hotel."

We drop our things at the hotel, where Ren does indeed shave, and I change out of the wrap dress I wore to a pitch meeting this morning and into a black, denim overalls dress. We bought tickets for a music festival weeks ago when we realized it coincided with the wedding of a friend from the art school.

"A bummer Sasha and Alex don't live here anymore," I say as we wait in a line for beers. The heat of the late August day is just creeping out, replaced by a hint of crisp evening air. "How are they settling in in LA?" They moved there three months ago, when Sasha's company decided to open a West Coast branch, to be closer to family, including the adorable baby girl Thad and Gemi adopted.

"Great, as far as I know," Ren says, hands in the front pockets of his jeans. "Busy planning the wedding."

"A New Year's Eve wedding." We inch forward in line. "How very Sasha."

After Charlene's wedding, I worried our friendship was forever changed. It had nagged at me intermittently growing up—that at some point, there was the possibility he and I wouldn't be the same *us* we'd always been—but the idea never really stuck until it happened. I had built a life of my own in New York, knew that I could be okay without Ren by my side, and yet, I didn't *want* that. Life was better with him in it.

We still texted each other, but I'd begun to accept the distance between us for what it was. Growing up, maybe.

But then late one night, Ren called me out of the blue. He

had texted a few weeks before to tell me he and Amanda had broken up, and he was fine, and we had continued on with our scattered texting, tiptoeing around the subject.

I'd been making boxed and mac and cheese when my phone rang.

"I see you're still burning the candle at both ends," he said, his voice filling in spots in my body I hadn't realized were empty.

"Actually," I'd said, turning off the burner, heart swelling at the sound of his voice. "I'm just getting home from an event."

"An event?" Ren had said, like it was something I'd forgotten to tell him. Like we'd talked two days ago. "Wait," he continued. "I didn't say hi."

A smile pricked my cheeks. "Hi."

"Hi," he said. I felt it down to my toes. "Tell me about this event."

He called me the next night too, slightly earlier, and then we talked every night after that. Even when we were busy. Even when we were tired. On more than one occasion, when he could tell I was struggling to stay awake, he'd tell me stories from our lives, his perspective making them new for me, and I fell asleep with his voice in my ear.

A few months couldn't erase a lifetime.

I head to one of the stages to claim a spot, respond to a text from my mom that yes, I am here safely, and another from Ramona about the meeting this morning about a new movie proposal.

Ren joins me, handing me a cup of beer. "Here," he says, then reveals a baseball cap with the classic Red Sox *B* on it from under his arm. He works the brim before putting it on my head, settling a hand on top as if to make sure it's on correctly.

"Where's yours?" I ask. "It can't be a trip souvenir if we're not—"

He produces another from under his other arm, puts it on.

"—matching," I finish, smile spreading. I reach up and flip his hat around so it sits backward. Some of his dark waves stick out, curling near his ears. "There you go," I say. "Have to show off that handsome face of yours."

He tugs the brim of my own hat down in response.

As the sound check continues and people fill in around us, I ask him the question I've been holding off on for the past eight months. Ren is always harder to read over FaceTime, so it felt like something that needed to be addressed in person, where I could try to gauge his real feelings, comfort him accordingly.

"Ren," I say.

He turns to me, mimics my serious expression, drops his voice. *"Joni."*

"How are you doing?"

He side-eyes me, a confused smile on his face. "Aren't we a couple hours too late to be asking that?"

I wave away his question. "I mean Amanda. How are you doing?"

"Ah." He studies the stage, nodding once. "How *am* I."

"So?" I ask, after he's been silent for what must be a full minute.

He looks at me like he already answered the question and I just missed it. "I'm fine."

"You're *fine*?"

"It was eight months ago," he says, eyes fixed on the stage again. "I've moved on."

"It's okay if you haven't," I say. I know he might not tell me if he was still hurting, but I want to make sure he knows that he *can*.

"You've moved on from Collin, right?"

"Yes," I say, feeling a little guilty at how quickly I answer. I broke up with Collin not long after Charlene's wedding, my conversation with Ren about his relationship with Amanda shamefully in my head the entire time. I didn't care about

Collin like I should. I try with Ren one last time. "What happened?" I ask him. "You still haven't really told me."

At this, the fingers Ren has been drumming against his cup still. He looks over at me, something unreadable on his face. "I just wasn't the boyfriend she needed me to be."

It's an answer that doesn't compute. I scoff, wave a hand in his direction.

"What?" he says.

I don't know how to explain to him without sounding crazy that I don't believe for a second there's a single world in which he isn't the best boyfriend, so I just say, "You have to be a great boyfriend. You're perfect."

One corner of Ren's mouth twitches, tongue just slipping between his lips before he leans down to me, breath against my ear. "How do you know that, Joni? I've never been *your* boyfriend," he says. He pulls away, but not very far, our faces inches apart. For a minute, I can't hear the cheers around us. But I can see every shade of brown in Ren's eyes: chocolate and almost black and hints of amber where the light hits them.

The slight smirk on his mouth as he straightens away from me has me shifting away too, bringing my cup to my lips. "Fair enough," I say, before I take a long drink.

After an hour, Ren leads us in the direction of a gate. We weave our way through tour busses and vans, past a white catering tent where Ren grabs two water bottles and hands me one. Technically, he's also here with Sublimity, who asked him to keep an eye out for new talent, and our VIP passes get us past security.

While Ren heads back to the artist hospitality area to meet with a couple acts, I make my way over to the main stage to catch a singer I used to listen to in college, all poppy beats and dreamy guitar. Stevie got a job writing for a culture publication in Portland as soon as she finished her degree last December, and I know she would kill to be here for this. I've missed her since she moved.

I'm near the outskirts of the crowd when he finds me again.

"How'd it go?" I shout over the music. "Did you close the deal?"

Ren chuckles. "No deal to be closed, yet. But there are a couple acts I think they'll set up meetings with back in Portland." He nods toward one side of the stage. "There's one more band I need to check out."

He takes my hand and snakes us through the crowds over to one of the side stages, glancing over his shoulder every now and then to make sure he still has me. Backstage, he navigates us around groups of people to a small space at one edge. He positions me in front of him, my shoulders warming where they meet his chest.

"She's good," I say, craning my neck back up at him when the singer is halfway into her next song. There's something vaguely familiar about her feathery vocals, the indie-pop synth, and I wonder if Ren has included her music in one of the playlists he began sending me again the past few months. I'd missed them; another line of communication between us that had been cut.

As the crowd cheers at the end of a song, the sun dips toward the horizon, the world becoming golden. "There's a friend of mine here tonight who's a big part of the reason I get to play to a crowd like you," the singer says into her mic. "He convinced some people he works with to give me another go, and I told him if he ever needed a favor to call me. If phoning it in for a Joni Mitchell cover is his big favor, then I think he got the short end of that stick. So I can sing it, but—" she unslings her guitar from around her neck "—I need someone else to play it for me."

She casts around like someone might volunteer until her eyes land on us and her face lights up. I look up at Ren, confused.

His lips are parted and he's staring out at the stage, communicating something to the singer I can't follow.

"I'll be right back, okay?" he says, at last.

I nod, but I'm still lost as he steps around me and the singer extends her acoustic guitar toward him. He reaches the stage and loops the strap over his head, the crowd cheering as he adds a capo and tunes it. The singer is talking again, but I'm too mesmerized by the sight of Ren up on that stage to hear what she's saying.

I've seen Ren play many times, but always in casual settings: when he first learned how to play when we were kids; when I would lie on the floor of his bedroom in high school and college and he'd mess around with some chords; when he helped with sound check at Sublimity.

This is something different. He plays the opening notes of "Cactus Tree," my favorite Joni Mitchell song, and the pieces click into place. As the song continues to build, Ren smiles over at the singer, a layer of boyish joy underneath it.

I feel his quiet confidence square in the chest. My eyes get stuck on the way his fingers glide over the frets, how his body moves with the music. The way his shoulders shift under the arms of his T-shirt, how he watches the singer then looks back down at the guitar. Everything that isn't him goes blurry, but he's clearer to me than ever.

Having Ren more firmly in my life again these past months has slowed me down in a way I hadn't realized I'd needed, made me appreciate each day. I leave work at a more reasonable hour, wake up excited to greet the day, and for him to wake up on the West Coast too so he can tell me how his night was. Our conversations have brought some part of me back to life, reminded me I'm a person outside of Novo. He inquires after my cranky neighbor, wants to know what books I'm reading, has more than once sent me locations for shows he thought I'd like. I've gone to a few, but it's not the same without him next to me.

Talking to him every day again has brightened the colors that had faded for me, and I swear to myself now that I will never let it get that way again.

Onstage, the singer is finishing out the song, pausing so the crowd can sing along with the last verse. Ren turns toward me for the final notes, soft smile never leaving his face, and my heart starts doing something that feels vaguely familiar, but new, like I've finally pulled it off its shelf and blown off the dust, cracked its spine again, and opened it up to my favorite page, the one I thought I had memorized, only to discover there are so many things I may have missed.

chapter twenty-one

Ren rests an arm on the window, his other hand on the steering wheel as we wind our way to the coast the next morning. It feels like summer back in Oregon, salt air whipping through the open windows while music from the festival yesterday plays through the speakers, Ren occasionally nodding along to a song.

We arrive at the sandstone mansion where Willow and Martin will get married tonight, check into the hotel just adjacent to it, what Willow referred to as a "terrible eyesore" when she called to tell me she was so excited I'd be coming to the wedding.

The "terrible eyesore" is actually a half estate itself, sprawling and historic, with ocean views on one side and sweeping garden vistas on the other. Ren and I luck into a corner room with a balcony that overlooks the water.

Once we've hung up our wedding attire, I spot a fluffy white bathrobe and shrug it on over my clothes, hold my arms aloft, twist my hips side to side. "Is this the fanciest place we've ever stayed?" I ask. "Should I wear this to the wedding?"

"The hat really ties it all together," Ren says from where he's lounged on his bed, one hand behind his head, nodding at the

Red Sox baseball cap I put on this morning. "You've really got a handle on the whole black-tie thing."

I laugh and lie on my stomach next to him, feet kicked up behind me. He untucks his hand and reaches down to tweak the brim of my hat.

"Far cry from the screen porch," I say, glancing over at the open balcony door, a sea breeze coming through, bringing with it the sound of waves rolling in, seagulls swooping for dinner.

Ren follows my gaze. "I think I prefer our view on the West Coast."

As the afternoon wears toward evening, we take a short path through a garden to the mansion, joined on the way by other people in ground-sweeping dresses, suits, laughter bubbling around us that sounds very old money.

We enter the candlelit space, everything done up in cream tones, roses lining every surface, and pluck cocktails off a passing tray—an elderflower martini and an old-fashioned, only the first signature drinks of the evening—and wander over to where three banks of doors are thrown open to a huge stone balcony overlooking the ocean. We find a spot to one side near a pillar.

Ren squints at the glass in his hand. "Pretty sure this bourbon would be in high school by now," he says. He hands it to me and I take a sip.

"I'm getting notes of whiskey," I say. Ren's eyes crinkle with laughter, and I smile over the rim of the glass, test another drink before handing it back to him. "Since when are you up on your bourbon game?" I ask.

"I'm not," he says. I raise an eyebrow, and he relents, sinking one side against the pillar. "Amanda's dad was big into whiskey. Tried to study up to impress him."

"Ah. Well, you impressed me." I take a long drink from my own glass, let the sweet of it wash away the bite of the old-fashioned, the mention of Amanda, the smell of Ren's woodsy hotel shaving cream.

We sit through the elegant, if over-the-top ceremony, drink wine at dinner with some people from art school who I only vaguely recognize. When the plates are cleared, desperate to escape the small talk, we excuse ourselves and observe the room from the bar: the ornate gilding on the ceiling, the crowded dance floor, Willow and Martin floating through it all like they were made for the spotlight.

"That guy," Ren says, leaning down so our faces are level. I follow his nod toward a man in a deep blue tux, the flop of blond hair on top of his head obviously fake. "He's the richest guy in the room."

"Look at his tux," I say. "You think that's old money?"

"I never said old money. I said richest in the room."

I face him as he stands to his full height. "You make a habit of knowing what tells rich people have?"

Ren laughs as I reach up to tweak his tie, some invisible force drawing my hand there. His eyes lift across the room again. "Obviously," he says. "You have to know who to bump into at the right moment. Who else is going to invest in all my million-dollar ideas?"

"Name one million-dollar idea you've had," I say.

Ren pretends to think. "Quick-freezing ice."

I snort. "Okay, Webster, you go wow Mr. Toupee over there with your idea for *quick-freezing ice.*"

"Fine, I admit it," Ren says. "I have no ideas. I want him to invest in a high-speed, cross-country railway so it's easier for us to see each other."

"You think a high-speed railway would be faster than flying?"

"Joni," he says, almost incredulous, eyes sparkling as they focus intently on me. *"Yes."*

When Willow is in her third dress of the night, the classier, early-evening band is replaced by a DJ, the music *loud,* and it occurs to me that Martin might know how to throw a party as well as Willow knows how to attend one. Their playlist is mostly comprised of songs that played in frat house basements in college, and bottles of something that costs as much as my student loan payment are being passed around.

"Hey," Ren says as we sway on the dance floor. "What if I came to visit you in New York this fall?"

"This fall?" I say, as he draws me closer, something about the sight of his hips moving in time with mine making it hard to think beyond this room. "If you want to," I tell him.

He brushes the hair from my shoulder, thumb smoothing absently back and forth along the strap of my dress, straightening what doesn't need to be straightened. He's watching the movement, his face serious.

"I do want to," he finally says.

He's looking at me in a way that has every late-night phone call, every moment in our lives I found myself wanting to move just a little closer to him crashing over me, tugging me under like a rough wave. *I've never been* your *boyfriend* plays in a loop in my head, and suddenly I want to ask why not. Suddenly, all I can think about is yesterday, Ren so casually cool onstage, his fingers sliding over the guitar strings.

"I need some air," I announce.

Ren's answering nod is quick, a crease appearing between his brows. "Of course. Let's—"

"No, you stay." I smile, but it's difficult. I wonder if I had more to drink than I thought, but I know I didn't. "I'll be back in a minute."

I don't give Ren a chance to respond and instead push through the crowd of bodies until I'm on the other side of it. I step out onto the balcony, but it's nearly as loud out here as it is on the dance floor, so I clomp back inside and over to a table of coupes filled with champagne, grab one and toss it back.

I bring a hand to my forehead. Am I losing my mind? I feel

like I can't hang on to any one thought, palms gone clammy, a constant fluttering in my stomach since the night started.

But it's not long before my eyes scan the room, searching for him. I crane up on my toes, step to the side, and there he is, standing by the bar, attentively talking to a couple we sat next to at dinner. He laughs at something they just said and smiles, and it's at that moment that it flits across my brain, filling my heart up until I think it might burst.

There you are.

The room tilts, or maybe it's the earth under me, its axis re-organizing itself after a molecular shift.

I've felt like this before. Of course I have. Or I've felt some version of it. I stare at the cut of his profile, and realize I've felt this way before about *Ren*.

History is rewriting itself in real time as I think back over the weddings, over our college years, our entire lives: Ren in a photo booth, hand on my thigh; Ren on the beach, skin glistening under the July sun; Ren at the bar, singing along to the Killers while I laugh; Ren's soft breathing on the screen porch, a rhythm I could fall asleep to; us on the phone for hours; the smell of his old Sublimity shirt I never gave back; Ren's eyes and arms and mouth and shoulders and chest and hips and—

How didn't I know? Or did I? Again, my mind is stumbling over itself, every memory something new, a before and an after.

That's when Ren looks at me. I've been staring at him for who knows how long, eyes stuck on his face. The polite set of his mouth disappears into a concerned frown, cheeks that he shaved again this morning hollowing.

I know what I must look like. My lips are parted and I think my expression must be somewhere in the realm of someone who's just received reality-altering news. *Ma'am, welcome to the multiverse. A meteor is headed for the city. The aliens have landed.* The news hasn't quite hit yet, but I'm stunned, even awed, at its magnitude.

His gaze latches on to mine and the room goes still, music quiets. An image suddenly flashes through me, of Ren under a streetlight at twenty-one, head leaned back as he laughed at something I said. There's a week-old tattoo on his arm, proof that we are a part of each other forever, and I want to reach into that moment, pause it, pluck us out so I can examine the evidence that's been there all along.

My heart turns over in my chest at the way his eyes travel across my face now. But then he tilts his head toward me in an *are you okay?* move, and I'm yanked back to the pounding bass and raucous celebration of the room. *Get it together, Joni.*

But I can't get it together. I bob my head yes and dart away, ducking behind a large potted plant where I can be alone to sit with the way that the world has just changed.

chapter twenty-two

The first thing I do is hurry down the nearest hallway and call Stevie. But after two rings, I end the call, holding the cool phone to my chest. Do I even want to tell Stevie? Do I want to drag her into this when I don't even know what *this* is yet?

I lean against the wall, stare up at the ornate ceiling. Being here, in a ballroom full of people I don't know, and feeling this way might be one of the most out-of-body experiences I've ever had. It's like someone has opened me up, ripped out my most important parts, filled them up with new ones before shoving them back inside.

I can't be in love with Ren, and yet, it's overwhelmingly clear that I am, that I've always been. I think about the Joni Mitchell song again, the pad of his thumb smoothing lazily along the strap of my dress when we were dancing, summers on the screen porch, every single playlist he's ever carefully made for me, and have to squeeze my eyes shut.

"Joni." I jump at the sound of his voice, turn my head against the wall to look at him as he strides toward me. Suddenly, Ren isn't *Ren*, and instead some romantic lead, all dark eyes and tousled hair, like someone should put a light and a fan on him, set him up for a cover shot.

Think, I tell myself. *Think of times you didn't want him.* But I come up alarmingly short. Can a brain really rewire itself in so little time? There has to be something. But all I can think of is a particularly bad hangover, his head in my lap as he opened his brilliant brown eyes to look up at me and my breath caught in my chest.

"Ren," I say. Maybe I'm dreaming. Maybe it doesn't matter if I reach out and fist a hand around the lapel of his jacket, press my knuckles over his heart. There are no consequences in dreams. In a dream, I can do anything I want.

"Are you okay?" he asks as he stops in front of me.

"I'm great," I say, settling for a brief tug on his jacket. "Are you okay?"

"I'm—" Ren says, his eyes drifting down my body and back up to my face, like he's checking for damage. He lays a tentative, gentle hand on my waist, but the contact just sends a new tremor through me. "Are you sure?"

I swallow, straightening at the hint of worry on his perfect face. "Yes," I say. "Sorry."

Maybe it's just the wedding, I tell myself. Maybe it's this weekend and this bizarre playing at a kind of adult we'll never be in the ballroom of a ridiculous estate. Maybe it's his suit and my dress and just missing him.

Maybe.

He looks at me, and the air between us draws taut. I think for one crazy moment that I might die if he steps away from me.

But that thought disappears as his hand subtly slips from my waist to the small of my back and he beckons me closer. He lowers his head, his eyes hooded with something unspoken, and our lips brush, once, before we both pull away.

"Are we drunk?" he asks, his hand inching up my side, curving over my ribs.

I manage to shake my head, whisper, "I'm not drunk. Are you?"

"No," he says, dark gaze settling over my skin. "I'm not drunk."

The next thing I know, our mouths are meeting again, more forcefully this time, bodies arching toward each other. I'm too focused on how we fit together, on learning the feel and taste of him, to pay much attention to how we get from the wedding venue to our hotel room door. It's not a long walk, but we stop along the way, to kiss by a hedge, then again at the fountain that marks the halfway point, until we're both breathless and one of us has to draw away, urge the other down the path again. I wouldn't be surprised if I opened my eyes and we were back in Boston, getting ready to say goodbye, having made our way back without ever breaking away from each other.

Outside our hotel room, I tug Ren closer by his tie and he pushes me up against the door. I try to force the key card into the slot behind me, moving blindly as Ren's teeth catch on my lower lip.

Someone clears their throat behind us.

We separate just enough so we can turn our heads. Another wedding guest—Willow's uncle, or Martin's cousin?—is standing in the hallway, arms crossed.

"I don't think you'll have much luck," he says, nodding at the key card in my hand, which is now jammed into the blinking red reader on the door. "Seeing as this is my room."

Ren and I look at the number on the door—211—then over to the door next to us: 213.

"We're so sorry," I say as Ren steps away from me, holds his fist over his mouth.

As we shuffle clumsily, guiltily away, the man nods once, then enters his room.

Once his door is safely shut, Ren slips the key from my hand

and pulls me toward our room. We stumble inside, palms to each other's mouths to control our laughter.

Ren kicks the door closed behind us, and I stretch up onto my toes to kiss him, forcing his jacket off, working at his tie. He sets one hand over my hip, the other at the nape of my neck. But then suddenly he's straightening, arm loosening from my waist so my heels drop to the ground.

"What?" I say. His hand comes to rest at the base of my neck, his thumb grazing over my collarbone. It's so similar to what he did in the ballroom earlier and I find myself making a humming sound, my eyes almost fluttering shut.

"What are we doing?" he asks.

"Like, in life?" I ask. It still feels like I'm in a dream, tantalizing and slow moving.

Ren lets out a soft huff of a laugh, catching my elbows and putting a measured distance between us. "Joni," he says. "I need to know that you want this."

For years, our entire lives, really, I'd assumed friendship was like this: some skip in your heart when they called, overwhelming affection when they picked you up before class or lay next to you under the stars. You were *supposed* to want to talk to your best friend more than anyone else. And maybe that's all true. But something about the thrill that went through me that first night Ren called—I hadn't let myself think about it for too long. And now I understand why.

I could kiss him to answer his question, but when I look at him, there's something in his expression—concerned, wary, hopeful—that has me nodding seriously. Even just scratching the surface of our lives, I think I might have always wanted this. "Yes. I want this. Do you want this?"

Ren pauses for a moment, then dips his head to mine again, kissing me once before he draws us back together so his hips are pressed just above mine, and I feel exactly how much he wants this. "I want this," he says.

And it's settled.

He lifts me onto the table in the entryway, my legs around his waist. Standing between my thighs, he slowly slips off one of my dress straps, mouth grazing the spot where it sat, the small mark it's left on my skin. He does the same to the other side as I pull off his tie and undo the top buttons on his shirt. Then he ducks his head to my neck, lips skating across the column of my throat, and our bodies rock together, my head falling back, his palm catching it like he knew it would. We move impatiently together, chasing friction, trying to get at more, more, more.

"Why is it this good?" I ask breathlessly, locking my ankles tighter behind his back. "This never feels this good." I rake my teeth against his collarbone, smile as the sound that releases from his chest vibrates against my mouth.

"Because it's us," he murmurs, easing down my zipper, sliding my dress off as he picks me up off the table.

He slowly lowers me onto his bed and crawls over me, trailing his teeth and tongue and lips over my ankle, my calf, my knee, taking so much delicious time that I grow restless and reach down, play at his hair until he looks up, the dark, almost hazy cast to his eyes overwhelming every part of me.

A breeze floats in through the window, waves crashing in far below, as he makes his way up my body, then hovers over me, propped on one arm. I try to finish unbuttoning his shirt, but only get halfway down before I'm pulling at it greedily. Ren stills my hands, lips curving into a smile against mine, and undoes the buttons I've missed, sits up to kneel between my legs so he can shuck off his shirt. I follow the movement, lean up to run my fingers over his taut stomach, lower until they catch on the waistband of his pants.

Our eyes meet, and whatever sense I abandoned earlier comes rushing back to me. I'm overeager, too excited, an embarrassing, obvious level of enthusiasm coming off me. I flop back against the bed and hide my face in my hands.

Ren shifts from between my legs and lies down on his side next to me. "Hey," he says, cradling the back of my neck. "Talk to me." The way his fingers, which were kneading at my hips not moments ago, now entangle themselves in my hair raises goose bumps up and down my arms, and in the most appalling show of self-betrayal my body has ever committed, I shudder.

Ren's touch skims to my shoulder in a barely there way, then falls away from me.

I roll onto my side, grab his waist to anchor him next to me. "Don't. Please don't leave."

"I'm not going anywhere," he says. "I just want to give you some space."

I think I can pick out every singular thing I've ever loved about him on his face, but they all read differently to me now, like my powers of observation had only been operating at 50 percent before. The way his eyes are constantly working, shuttering and opening and darkening is a whole new line of communication unlocked. The faint freckles across his nose, only visible to me this close and only ever out in the summer, even the white sliver of his teeth behind his parted lips light up previously undiscovered pathways in my brain. I thought I knew his face better than my own. But with him looking at me like this, everything is new.

"I don't need space," I say. I don't, but I can't explain what I feel. That I want him, but I need to catch up with myself. "I don't want space."

"Okay," he says, but I can tell by the tone of his voice and the tension in his body that he doesn't fully trust it. He places a hand on my waist, but it's light, hardly there.

"I don't want space," I repeat. "I want you."

"Okay," he says again. His hair is messy from where I'd been running my fingers through it, and something about the sight, seeing him undone, only makes me want him more.

"Ren, I want this. I just..." My cheeks heat. I've never had to talk to him about something like this before. Not when it's us. I've never really had reason to feel like this around Ren. "I'm embarrassed."

Ren's brow lifts. "Embarrassed?" he asks in a rough whisper. "Why?"

"Because I feel like I'm too excited about this. And you're…" I gesture at him, like I might encompass his whole person, everything he means to me and that we mean to each other. I can't tell if Ren is as shocked by this turn of events as I am. "Perfect, basically."

Ren leans back. "Joni," he says. When I don't answer, he readjusts, propping himself up on one elbow and taking one of my hands in his. "Joni."

"Ren," I say in a low voice, copying his joke from yesterday. It's a poor attempt at levity, but a thrill speeds through me when his lips twitch into a smile.

"Okay, I'm going to tell you something," he says. His mouth flattens, his eyes go serious. "The amount of time I spend thinking about you like this is actually embarrassing. I have to actively put it out of my head more than I'd care to admit to you. I want this to such an uncool degree. And…maybe that's something we need to talk about, but you wanting this?" He shakes his head, reaches up to brush my hair behind my ear. "Not embarrassing in any world, and the best thing to ever happen to me."

I smile, a small thing that grows. "You've thought about this?"

Ren nods sheepishly. "So much. In excruciating detail. Where we'd be," he says, his eyes dropping to my mouth. "What you'd taste like."

I curve closer to him. "And?"

He parts my lips with the pad of his thumb. "Amazing."

My heart starts to race at the picture of Ren wanting this. "What else did you think about?" I can't help but ask him.

Ren's smile is slow now. He slips his hand from my lips to my jaw, my neck, over my shoulder. "What you'd feel like," he says, as his fingers trace across my chest. "All the sounds you'd make."

"Good?" I ask, my chest rising toward his hand.

"So good," he murmurs at my neck. My breathing hitches at the contact, and I can feel him smile against me. His fingers sweep my side, then higher, higher, until they brush against my breast. "Everything we'd do."

The soft moan that comes out of me sets off something in both of us. Ren's hands slide behind me, unclasping my bra. He casts it aside, dips his mouth to my breast, lips parting and tongue circling. My fingers thread into his hair as he moves down my body, his breath hot against me as he hooks his fingers into the waist of my underwear and pulls them down my legs. He resettles between my knees, kisses the crease of my hip, trails his mouth lower and lower, until it's closing over me.

I grasp at the sheets. There's no coming back from this now.

He holds my body to him with one hand, the other working in tandem with his mouth in patient, deliberate movements. His name rushes out of me as I shudder against him, vision going spotty as something coils low, spreading down my thighs. "Ren," I gasp as my spine curves.

He positions himself over me again as I blink back into reality, my skin flushed and limbs heavy. I cup his cheek and he turns his face into it, lips warm, before he looks down at me again and kisses me, unhurried, slowly rocking his body against mine.

I reach down to unbutton his pants, his abdomen drawing tight when I wrap a hand around him. We've never been bare in front of each other, and for all my disbelief I also feel the weight of it, the distinction of this moment.

Everything off, I push gently at his chest until he rolls onto his back. I swing a leg over him and straddle him, the sound that emanates from deep in his chest sending a new wave of heat through my center. His hands tighten on my hips as he sits up, our bodies fitted together.

"I'm on birth control," I say. "And there isn't anyone else, but everything's clear too, according to my doctor, at least, but if you—"

Ren silences me with a quick kiss. "Me too," he murmurs. "But I have a condom, if you'd rather."

I laugh, settling my arms on his shoulders. "Why did you bring condoms, Ren? Were you planning to get lucky this weekend?"

He chuckles, eyelashes fluttering. "It's been in there for a while." He pulls me in closer, eliminating all space between us, and I can feel the rough spots on his fingers from years of playing guitar, love how they lightly scrape against me. "I didn't dream I'd ever get this lucky," he says.

I press my palm to his chest, count the fast beats of his heart in my head to tie myself to this moment. *One, two, three, Ren smiling at you over the bar at Sublimity, four, five, six, the feel of his chest under your cheek when you hug him goodbye, seven, eight, nine, ten, this, right here, right now.*

Before I can slide my hand between us again, he grabs my hips and flips me onto my back, reaching down to hitch my leg up against him. Then he eases into me, his thumb moving in circles, my hips arching toward it until Ren crushes his body to mine, dipping his forehead to the pillow, rocking just slightly. When he moves, it's achingly slow, emptying me and filling me up again.

I would have thought I'd feel nervous. Heart pounding, mind racing, contemplating all the ways this could mess everything up. But as Ren looks at me with those brown eyes, I feel like everything might have led us to this moment. Like it was always supposed to happen. Like our friendship was one long precursor to this. Like ours is a love story.

As our movements quicken, he scoops my hips up to him. My legs tighten around his waist as he sinks fully into me, his forehead against mine, stars bursting behind my eyelids. I can tell he's still holding back, waiting for me, so I wrap a hand around the back of his neck, kiss him, and then I surrender to every sensation coursing through me. With a final push inside me he does too, breath against my neck as we're pulled under together.

Afterward, I lie with my head on his chest as he traces slow lines up and down my back, the sheet tossed on top of us. His heart beats steadily beneath my ear, the same one I counted earlier, the same one that's carried him through so much life by my side.

I doze intermittently, ocean air cooling my skin until I startle awake, smiling lazily up at him when I remember where we are, burying my nose against his neck. I could smell Ren for days and never grow tired of it. Here is the scent I know so well, and here is the sweat dried on his skin and here is the soap he used earlier and here is something deeper, something new that makes me move against him again, smiling at the sound it draws out of him.

"Joni," he says against my hair, fingers dancing up my spine. "Should we—"

"Tomorrow," I whisper, angling my head so I can kiss him.

I wait for him to respond, to tell me we *should* pause and talk, but instead, the hand he's had on my back floats up to my head, fingers weaving into my hair as he tugs me toward him.

If we were anywhere near hesitant before, gentle because of how fragile this is, now everything is just shy of bruising, fingers pressing and mouths dragging across skin, and I know, with a deep, yawning ache inside of me, that things will never be the same again.

FRIDAY

chapter twenty-three

When I wake up in the rental house the next morning, Ren is lying next to me, his palm over mine. We're both on our sides facing each other, the same position we fell asleep in after we walked back into the house to discover Thad spread-eagled on the air mattress he was supposed to share with Ren, and Sasha sound asleep on the sofa. We'd settled onto the remaining air mattress.

Ren smiles at me, warm and slow, like he's still waking up. There's a healthy distance between our bodies, but his fingers slip from mine and trace down them in slow, featherlight circles that have me almost curling closer to him, my own fingers folding down to capture his.

Morning, I mouth, not sure who else is awake in the house yet.

"Good morning!" Stevie calls from the kitchen before the sound of a coffee grinder whirs loudly.

Our hands release as I sit up on one elbow, and Ren rolls onto his back. Stevie watches us from the little window into the living room, her hair shoved up on one side of her head and dark shadows beneath her eyes. She looks, nonetheless, incredibly smug.

"Coffee's almost on," she says as she lets go of the button on the grinder. "I need Fern's." At that, she picks up the grinder and carries it deeper into the kitchen toward the coffeepot.

Ren rubs at his eyes, then tucks his hands behind his head, tanned arms flexing. He looks up at me, another smile passing between us.

He considers me, a wordless *come here* and *I can't* and *let's go somewhere* passing between us until Thad is stirring on his air mattress, a groan emanating from him, our silent conversation dissipating with it. "Pink shots," he grumbles. "Pink *shots*."

Ren and I brush our teeth at the kitchen sink while everyone else cycles in and out of the bathrooms. We lean against opposite counters, his mouth never far from a smile and his gaze climbing around inside me.

As planned, we herd the crew—those we can actually coax out of bed, at least, leaving the band's guitarist and bass player and Oliver behind—down the street to the diner, Sasha pausing to lean over a flowerpot with her hand at her stomach, one finger held aloft behind her in a *don't come any closer* gesture until she recovers and, thankfully, doesn't puke into the peonies.

"Are you okay?" I hear Ren ask her.

"I had a rough night," she says, patting his shoulder. "But thanks, little brother."

At Fern's, a classic diner if there ever was one, we pile into a corner booth with its familiar green-vinyl seats cracking in places. Ren and I slide in next to each other, and because we're all crammed in, I can feel every small shift of his body, his forearm against mine when we both reach for our waters, the thigh of his jeans when Thad moves on his other side to grab sugar for his coffee or when Leo leans across us to talk to Dev. At one point, Ren stretches his arm along the back of the booth, his fingers lightly tapping the part right above my shoulder, and I have to work hard not to relax into it.

"Ready to go over the plan for today?" Leo asks.

Sasha doesn't respond. Her sunglasses are on, and she looks something of a strung-out Kennedy as she sips her coffee, all dark hair and stained lips, a crisp white button-down casually listing off one shoulder.

"Don't ask about a *plan* for at least another hour," Thad says.

"You knew today was about wedding setup." Sasha seems to come alive again, but there isn't much conviction behind it. "No one forced the pink shots on you."

"*Please* stop saying pink shots," Thad says.

"See, when the pink shots taste like that, you try not to take so many of them," I say. A loud thump rattles the salt and pepper shakers. "Sorry, Thad." His head is in his hands, elbows on the table.

When the server comes by, redirecting everyone's attention, the hand Ren has stretched behind me just falls against my shoulder. It's innocuous enough that nobody would notice unless they were looking closely. Under the table, our legs press tighter together and the conversation fades to a dull buzz and—

Someone clears their throat, shocking me back into the present. I swivel my head toward the source of the noise. Stevie is staring at me. When our eyes lock, she starts shoving fries into her mouth one by one like a ravenous hamster, making the whole thing scary. I reach forward and pick up my coffee, Ren's hand flat against the back of the booth again.

On the way out, Stevie grabs my arm, dragging me back under the awning in front of the restaurant and tucking us in next to a newspaper rack.

"Do you want to tell me where you and Ren went last night?" she asks. "Or why you were holding hands this morning?"

Thad and Leo are at the candy dispensers that sit at the opposite end of the patio, holding cupped palms underneath as Thad puts a quarter in and a rush of years-old Chiclets falls out.

"I don't know, Stevie." I glance toward where Ren is leaned

against a building post near the vending machines, sunglasses on and hands shoved in the pockets of his faded blue jeans as he listens to Dev animatedly tell a story, the cool shape of him sending a pleasant flutter through me even from a distance.

"Joni," Stevie says.

I look back at her. "It just happened while we were asleep," I say, which is still technically the truth.

"You're lying to me." She sinks her weight onto one foot, fixing me with a small pout. "I just can't figure out why."

"It's nothing, Stevie," I assure her, then offer another small kernel of the truth as penance for lying to her at all. "We talked last night."

"About what?"

"About being friends again," I say. We did have that conversation, just not last night.

She squints at me, half because of the blinding sun streaming down and half because she's trying to figure something out, I know.

At that moment, Thad lets out a shout, startling a group of passersby who jump back into the street.

"Look!" he calls, rushing toward us and raising something iridescent above his head. "Look what Leo just got!"

"No fucking way," Stevie says as Ren and Dev stride over, all of us gathering around while Thad holds out his prize triumphantly.

"You did not get Fratty Chicken," I say.

"I thought it was a myth," Stevie says. "False advertising to make us keep putting quarters into that stupid machine."

Thad holds between us a sparkling sticker on which is emblazoned, inexplicably, a chicken on a surfboard, wearing a backward hat, sunglasses, and clutching what we have long assumed to be a six pack of PBR under one wing, though the illustration is fuzzy. Fratty Chicken, as we named him, is a storied figure in town, imposed on the side of the vending machine next to the candy dispensers with all of the other sticker options: ice cream cones and cats and the occasional cowboy hat–wearing dolphin. But no chicken sticker has ever come out of the machine. Until now.

"There's no way that's just been in there all these years," Ren says.

Leo, always wanting to be helpful, runs back over to the machine, digging into his pocket for more quarters.

We were just kids when we first tried for Fratty Chicken. Fern's for breakfast was tradition on the last Saturday of the trip, all of us piling into cars and driving into town, the parents at one table and us kids at another. Stevie would insist on sitting between me and Ren, claiming that we whispered too much when we were next to each other, and because he would play tic-tac-toe with her on a napkin, letting her win every time.

We'd finish our food quickly, our parents lingering over coffee and the view of the harbor, and we'd pool all our change for the vending machine. When we realized no one ever got Fratty Chicken, it became our exclusive goal, never with any luck. Ren and I would grow tired of trying, and he would buy Skittles from one of the candy machines and the two of us would sit with our legs stretched out, him pouring the candy into his hand for us to negotiate over the best colors, while Sasha and Thad continued at the machine, Stevie watchful between them. I still find stickers floating around sometimes, as bookmarks or tucked into coat pockets. I have a popsicle sticker that's lost its shimmer on an old water bottle.

"You guys!" Leo hollers from the bank of vending machines, and we all look at him at once like we're a single collective body. He raises a fist above his head. "Machine's empty!"

"No fucking *way*," Stevie repeats. "Fratty Chicken was the last sticker *ever* in there?"

"You know what this means," Thad says. We all look at him. "We said we'd do it."

The rest of us are silent.

"Come *on*," Thad says, stomping his foot. "We promised we'd get Fratty Chicken tattoos if we ever got him!"

He turns to Ren, like he might convince him. "You and Joni are the only ones who have matching tattoos among us."

"Not true," Stevie says. Leo hands her a gumball and she pops it into her mouth, pushes it into her cheek. "Joni and I got tattoos together when we moved to New York."

"The sun and moon on your ribs?" Ren asks me about the tiny symbols, reminders that Stevie and I are each other's better halves. He's standing behind me, voice low, but Stevie hears the question, her eyes flying to us. I dig my elbow into his stomach, and he coughs to cover up the small *oof* he let out.

"None of us are getting Fratty Chicken tattoos," Sasha's voice startles us from a few feet down the sidewalk, her face stony underneath her sunglasses. "We're not twelve. You're a parent now, Thad. Grow up."

Debate over, we head in the direction of the house, Ren falling back a step to walk next to me.

"I just can't believe this part of our lives is over," Thad says ahead of us. "I thought Fratty Chicken would never end."

"Ten dollars Sasha tries to steal it by the end of the night," Ren says, sliding down his sunglasses and leaning in toward me. "According to Thad she's always stealing his stuff in LA."

"Oh, I'll put fifty on Stevie having it by the end of the weekend," I say.

"You don't want it?" Ren asks.

"I'm not brave enough to put up that fight."

"Mmm-hmm," he mumbles. We're smiling into each other, angled together as we walk, his fingers lifting to trace the tattoo we share below my elbow, then down to my palm, applying the slightest bit of pressure.

I look up just in time to see Stevie's sharp-eyed gaze slipping away from us.

chapter twenty-four

"If I never have to see a twinkle light again, it'll be too soon," Thad says across from me as he rips another shepherd's hook stake out of the ground, looping the strand of lights already hanging there over his arm.

We're all scattered around at various sites, checking items off Sasha's list while Leo and Stevie are in town with his family, who arrived last night. In the kitchen before they left, Leo was quiet and tense in a way I'd never seen him before, and I worried that his family's presence could be what sends everything off the rails. But then I clocked Stevie's fingers lacing through his, and I knew they would get through the day together.

"I thought the lights at your wedding were gorgeous," I tell Thad. We're halfway down the path to the lighthouse, and I'm sweating through my tank top as I mimic his actions, ripping what we had thought, for the third time, was a perfectly placed stake out of the ground, only for Sasha to inform us that they needed to seem like they were part of the tree line, then that they didn't start soon enough at the top of the path, and now that we're short string lights and instead need to use these to line the lawn that stretches from the old lighthouse keeper's cottage to the end of the headland. To, you know, make sure no one plunges to their death during toasts and dancing at the wedding tomorrow.

"They *were* gorgeous," Thad says. I can just glimpse the ocean through the trees behind him as he pauses, takes in a deep breath. "Because someone else put them up."

I snort, yanking on a particularly stubborn stake that comes free abruptly, sending me reeling backward. My heel catches on a rock, and I trip to the ground, hands flying back to brace my fall at the last minute.

"Are you okay?" Thad says, dropping his meticulously looped lights in a heap and lurching toward me, slipping easily into parent mode. Except in this case, I'm the child.

"I'm fine," I say, something like delirious laughter bubbling out of me as I brush my hands together, take his waiting one.

He pulls me up to standing, rubs a hand down his face.

"Thad." I knock my elbow against his arm. "What's up? Fratty Chicken got you down?"

He meets my gaze almost reluctantly, the same brown eyes as his mom and Ren. "I love Katie so much," he says. "Being away from her this week feels like there's this whole part of me missing."

"I'm sure it does," I say, waiting out the rest of whatever he's going to say. Thad is like an older brother to me, and while he's always been playful, his earlier comment about that part of our lives being over has me wondering if he's struggling with something deeper.

"I don't know," he says. "It's just—trying to balance lawyer life and fatherhood hasn't left a lot of time for anything else. I haven't hated having a break to just feel like myself again." He exhales, squints at me. "Sorry if I went overboard last night."

"You mean sorry if you had too many of the shots Stevie was showering on everybody?" I ask, hating that he thought we felt that way. "I think you're allowed to have a break sometimes. It doesn't mean you're not an excellent father."

Thad sighs. "Thanks, Joni," he says. "Anything you want to divulge?"

"Oh, plenty," I say, stepping toward the edge of the path again. "But we have a job to do."

"These fucking lights," Thad says.

"These fucking lights," I repeat.

"*These* fucking lights—" Sasha's voice echoes from behind us, as she marches up through the trees from the direction of the lighthouse, clearly back to her normal self "—can stay on the path. We found the ones we need for the lawn."

"Are you kidding?" Thad throws an arm out toward the work we've just undone. "Sasha—"

"Sometimes it takes a few tries to get it right," she says, mirroring his gesture. "Rome wasn't built in a day."

Thad tips his head back, letting out something close to a growl. "Good thing we're stringing shitty lights for a wedding and not building an empire, then," he says.

"Exactly," Sasha says. "So you can— Joni, you're bleeding."

I look down at where she's pointing. "Look at that," I say. Blood trickles from a short cut on my ankle, heading toward my sandal that Sasha, to be fair, did warn me was not appropriate light-stringing attire as we left the house earlier. "It's fine." I wave her away.

"It's not fine if you get gangrene and can't be in your sister's wedding tomorrow," she says. "Come on."

"I don't think that's how you get gangrene!" Thad calls after us as she hauls me away. "I'll get these lights, don't worry!"

"I'll send her back in five!" Sasha shouts back to him, like the drill sergeant she absolutely could be. She guides me down the path toward the lighthouse, one hand on my arm like my minor scrape might send me off-balance at any moment, crashing through the trees to the rocky bluff and down into the ocean.

She leads me past where my dad and Greg are mapping out the placement of the chairs that will be delivered tomorrow for the ceremony on the lawn, and up the steps into the cottage. The long bays of doors are thrown open on either side of the room where Ren and I set up the tables the other day.

"I have a first aid kit somewhere," Sasha says, shoving me into the lone chair in here, next to the bar where Ren is unloading boxes. "Hang on."

"Are you okay?" he asks as Sasha ducks behind the bar and rummages around with the air of someone who thinks the time it will take to grab a Band-Aid is what will derail the wedding.

"It's a tiny scratch," I say, rolling my eyes. "She's—"

"Sasha!" We both turn to see my mom hurrying in, eyes near rabid.

"What?" Sasha barks, popping up like a gopher out of its hole, first aid kit in hand.

"The trucks are here," my mom says.

"What trucks?" Sasha's voice reaches a decibel that bounces around the room.

"The chairs, the dance floor, the tent," my mom says.

"They're not supposed to deliver any of those until *tomorrow*. Today is for minor setup only!"

Ren widens his eyes at me from the bar and I have to stifle a laugh behind my hand.

"Ren," Sasha says, slamming the first aid kit against his chest. "I need you to handle this emergency. Carol—" She nods at the door and the two of them take off at a dead sprint, both straight-backed and clear-eyed.

"Does she seem bossier than usual?" Ren asks as he drags a footstool out from behind the bar and next to me. He pulls my leg onto his lap, fingers soothing against my skin.

"A little," I agree. "Weddings can do that to people. It's probably also the hangover."

He's focused on my ankle, gently rotating it so he can see the cut. I watch him as he cleans it, puts a Band-Aid over it.

"What do you think?" I ask. "Will I live?"

"Prognosis looks good," he says. He keeps a hand on my leg, lifts his eyes to look at me. "Hi."

"Hi," I say, unable to help the smile that threatens at my cheeks. "How's it going down here?"

"Oh, you know," Ren says. "Sasha thinks getting the bar set up is a life-or-death situation."

"Well, she chose the right man for the job." I glance at the bar behind us. "Thad and I are on our fourth go-round with the lights."

"So I heard." Ren's fingers slide a little higher, over my knee. "I can ask Thad if he wants to trade."

"Mmm," I say as his fingers continue their path until they're just reaching under the hem of my shorts, toying with a loose string. "Do you *want* to get all scratched up threading lights through a bunch of underbrush?"

"If you're there, absolutely." He grabs the leg of my chair and yanks me closer to him, his other hand still on my thigh.

I slide my leg around his hip and smile against his lips as he kisses me. "This is exactly what we're not supposed to be doing," I say.

"What, kissing you isn't on Sasha's list?"

"Hey," I say between kisses. "Good work bringing up my tattoo earlier."

"I've seen you in a swimsuit since you got it," he protests, smiling as his grip tightens on my back.

"Something my sister, who is deeply suspicious of us, doesn't care about at all."

"So we should probably stop this, then," he says, nodding as I do.

But we don't stop. He roams under my tank top, fingers

coming to rest against the tattoo in question, and swallows at the sound that escapes me.

Ren's phone vibrates in his pocket.

"Mmm-hmm," he answers over Sasha's shrill orders on the other end of the line. "No…Didn't you—" He stops, sighs, extends his phone toward me. "She'd like to speak with you."

"Hi, Sash," I say. Ren's attention returns to my leg, still slung across his lap. He tucks his fingers in, then slowly releases them over my knee like he did when we were younger. I'd laugh about it then, kick him away, but now it's shooting up to my center in a way that has my toes curling.

"We don't have enough lights," Sasha says.

Ren trails his lips over my shoulder and I have to work to keep my breathing even. "Didn't you *just* say—"

"Yes," she says. "But that was *before* they fucked up the delivery schedule and *didn't* bring the lights for the cottage and—" she says something to someone else on the other end of the phone that I would distinctly not like to be on the receiving end of "—I need you and Ren to run into town and buy every twinkle light you can find."

I hang up, look at Ren as his head lifts, his eyes soft and open, waiting to hear Sasha's decree. I wish, very much, I could lean forward and kiss him right now, wrap us up in this moment instead of going on an errand to make this wedding visible from space. I sigh, comb my fingers into his hair. "Sounds like you and I are going into town, Webster."

As it turns out, being in Ren's car is a welcome respite from the chaos of the house. On the drive, I admire how he manages to make a plain white T-shirt look so good, return the face he makes at me when I've been staring at him for several long minutes. I think I could swallow this moment, let it nourish me, survive on times like this, alone with Ren.

At the hardware store, I lean against him as he walks us down the narrow aisles. He's wearing a pair of camel-colored shorts, and I never thought a bare knee against the back of my thigh could send such a decided spark shooting through me.

We find what we're looking for in a back corner full of long-forgotten party supplies: inflatable flamingo pool floats marked at 50 percent off, their boxes dented or torn open, Fourth of July tablecloths that will be full priced again next year, and in the middle, what will hopefully be enough twinkle lights to satisfy Sasha.

"Should we do a box of two fifty-foot twinkle lights, or a box of the single hundred-foot strand?" I ask. The arm Ren isn't using to hold the shopping basket is wrapped around my hips, fingertips skimming under the hem of my shirt as he towers over me, his nose brushing against my neck.

"Hmm," he murmurs, voice vibrating through me. I fold both my arms over the one he has around my waist, trapping it there and letting its warmth sink into me. "We need to think long and hard about this, Joni."

"Don't you think Sasha will want us back at the house soon?" I ask, my head dizzy.

"I couldn't care less what my sister wants right now," he breathes into my ear.

"We could drive somewhere," I say, tipping my head back against his shoulder.

He squeezes my waist. "Joni," he says, voice gravelly. "Should we talk about this?"

Embarrassment flashes through me that Ren had to be the one to call out how obviously we've been avoiding reality. "Of course," I say. "But not now? We have the rehearsal dinner tonight, the wedding tomorrow. We can wait until we're back in Portland."

Ren's brow creases at the same moment I realize what I've said. I stay stock-still like prey spotted. Maybe if I don't move, he won't catch it.

I'm not sure why I said it. I know I'll have to move out of my place in New York sooner rather than later, but I haven't been thinking about it this week, have assumed it's an issue I'll deal with—it hits me with stomach-dropping clarity—the day after tomorrow. Sunday. When I'll be getting on a plane to head back to a life that doesn't exist anymore, and here I am, making out with Ren in the aisle of a hardware store like horny teenagers, like the past and future don't concern us.

"I mean," I say, twisting to face him. "When we're... I don't know. When we're in the same place again."

He looks at me like he used to, like he can see straight into my brain. I wait for him to question me, but instead he just pulls me into his chest, all the spots our bodies touch working to erase the anxiety clawing through me. I think it might solve all my problems if he never lets go. He reaches up, tugs lightly at the ends of my hair. "I like this new haircut," he says. "Don't get me wrong, I love your long hair too, but this feels like you."

"It does, doesn't it?" I say, wrinkling my nose. Ren smiles thoughtfully at me, and I'm transported to a world in which we didn't fall apart, in which maybe I didn't need to cut my hair, or maybe I did anyway and he was there much sooner to tell me that it looked like me. "I'm so annoyed by that."

"Why's that?" he asks.

I shrug weakly. "Sometimes I just don't think I know what I want until the universe gets fed up and hits me in the face with it."

Ren laughs. "The universe hit you in the face with a new haircut?"

I rest my chin against his chest, look up at him. "Something like that."

I don't tell him what I really mean. That three years ago, my feelings for him dawned on me so suddenly I felt like I'd been flipped upside down and shaken out, and that I don't think I was turned upright again until now.

chapter twenty-five

We spend a rushed rest of the afternoon restringing the twinkle lights and putting up the new ones, Ren continuing with bar setup while my mom places the centerpieces just so on the tables, everyone else spread around wherever Sasha positions them.

I barely make it to the last ten minutes of my shower slot before the rehearsal dinner, washing my hair and shaving my legs in record time. I dry my hair in front of the mirror in Stevie and Leo's room, change into my cowl neck, terracotta slip dress, then nearly run into someone in the hall.

"Hey!" Sasha's husband, Alex, has just arrived, bag over one shoulder. "Long time, no see!"

I hug him hello, start to ask how his flight was, when Sasha sticks her head out of their room, looking as close to frazzled as I've ever seen her, color rising in her cheeks and wavy hair wild. It's not the first time she's seemed overwhelmed this weekend, and it strikes me as odd. Sasha is usually so cool under pressure.

"Are you okay—" I ask, but she interrupts.

"You have twenty minutes to get ready!" she shouts, whether

at Alex or me, I don't know. We give each other a knowing look and head in our opposite directions.

When I step out onto the screen porch, Ren is just finishing buttoning up his shirt, the top two still undone. I can smell the vaguely citrusy soap our moms always stock the house with from here, his hair slightly damp from his own shower. There's music playing from his phone, a Nick Drake song. I shut the door behind me and drop my dirty clothes on my bed, turn to him.

"How's your ankle?" he asks as I run my fingers over his collar.

I lift my foot, glance down at the new Band-Aid I put on. "Basically healed," I say. I look back at him. "I had a *very* good doctor."

He reaches into his back pocket. "I got you something."

"You got me something?" I ask, trying to peer around him to see what it is. "Are we going to prom together?"

Ren rolls his eyes and smiles. "We *did* go to prom together."

"Yeah, and you broke the heart of every eligible girl in the twelfth grade by going with your *friend*," I say. It had seemed so obvious at the time; of course we'd go together. Now it's just another item on the list of signs I might have missed. There were plenty of other girls Ren could have gone to prom with, and I could have probably mustered the courage to ask the guy who sat next to me in Government. We've always chosen each other.

"Am I not your friend now?" he asks, hand still tucked behind his back.

Of course you are, I want to say, but it's more complicated than that. No matter how easy, natural, it's felt this week, Ren hasn't been just my friend for years now. I settle on, "I think you're a little more than my friend."

"I think so too," he says, and my heart gives a light flutter. "Okay, close your eyes. Hold out your hand."

"You're not going to put a bug in my hand, are you?" I say, shutting my lids.

"Do you think I've just been carrying a grasshopper around in my back pocket, Joni?" he says, drawing a finger back and forth along the underside of my wrist.

"I don't know." I shift between my feet. "Despite all your innumerable amazing qualities, you're still just a boy."

"I promise you here and now that I will never put a bug in your hand, eyes open or closed." He slips what feels like a small piece of paper into my palm, folding my fingers around it and placing his hand firmly over mine. "Ready?" he asks.

I open my eyes, smiling up at him before looking back down at the sticker in my hand. "You got me Fratty Chicken?"

"He's yours to do with what you will," Ren says.

It's just a sticker, but it means much more: a reminder of a simpler, past version of us, a reminder that I'm still a part of this place, these traditions, even though I've stayed away these past few years. Ren understood how much I needed this.

I study the sticker again, transported back to the past, to me and Ren and Sasha and Thad and Stevie inserting our coins into that machine. There are a lot of people who feel similarly attached to this chicken. "How did you even get this?" I imagine him slinking into Thad's room, stealing it while he was in the shower.

Ren looks a little chastened, teeth sinking into his lower lip before he admits, "I paid Thad a hundred bucks."

"Ren, you spent a hundred dollars on a vending machine sticker for me?" I ask, not sure if I should be grateful or alarmed that he'd spend that much money on something like this.

Ren shrugs, mouth quirking toward a smile, and reaches for the sticker. "I can get you something better."

"No," I say, snatching it away and holding it behind my back. "You can't have it. I love this sticker."

"It's okay if you don't like it, Joni." He grasps around me for it, tickling my sides, but I manage to sidestep him and thrust a hand out to keep him away.

"Tell me you know this is the perfect present," I say. Suddenly, it seems like the most important thing in the world that he knows how much the gesture means to me.

"It's just something dumb," he says, head bowing slightly so that a lock of hair dances free. "Something to remember this week by."

The mention that this week will end at all sends a small shock wave through me. I'm not ready to accept what that will mean, for my life or for me and Ren, for whatever we've just gotten back.

A smile plays across his face, his gaze drawing me into the past, to when things were so briefly good. I swear I can smell it, that last time I was at Sublimity: beer and a faint hit of cold Pacific Northwest air as I walked through the door; the shoulder of Ren's flannel under my nose, something woodsy and clean and so buried in my senses I could only ever identify it as *home*.

"I'm not coming back over there until you tell me it's perfect," I say now.

"It's a perfect present," he says quietly, like it's important to him to say it too.

I walk back over, and he locks his arms around me. He knits his fingers into my hair, brushes his nose along the side of my nose, lips just hovering above my lips.

In that moment, I think I could tell him. That maybe I don't want to talk about it later. Maybe I want to talk about it *now*. That I've spent two and a half years learning to be without him and realizing that I don't want to be.

Maybe I could be that person, someone who can open up her mouth and confess all of that, rather than fantasizing about it. But everything is so fragile, and Ren deserves someone who knows what the next day looks like, and I can't risk holding on to this thing between us any tighter than I am right now.

I just got him back, and no number of kisses on the beach or hundred-dollar stickers can make this moment last longer than I wish it would.

≈

"To Stevie and Leo!" my dad says, extending his wineglass toward the two long tables of guests.

We all echo my dad's sentiment. The sun is just setting, sky a gray-blue above us as strung lights wink on. I'm seated next to Stevie, who seems happy, cheeks rosy above her short, white dress with lacy bell sleeves that looks like something she plucked directly out of Penny Lane's closet. On her other side, Leo has been intently focused on our dad, guffawing at the bad jokes he sprinkled into his speech. He cheers louder than anyone else before pulling Stevie into him, her face breaking into a huge smile before he kisses her.

After our dad has taken a seat again, Stevie turns to me, leaning in close. Leo's arm is still around her, fingers playing absently at her hair, which hangs in waves down her back.

"I know something," she tells me.

My brow knits together. "What something?"

"Something you're not telling me," she says, jabbing a finger against my shoulder. She has to mean Ren. We've tried to be subtle, but she was already acting suspicious before anything happened between us. I almost smile at the ridiculousness of her perception, but then she leans in closer. "Something life-changing. Something you wouldn't want anyone to know."

My heart seizes at that last line, *you wouldn't want anyone to know.* I grab her hand to stop her. "Can I talk to you for a minute?" I say through a forced smile.

I pull her up from the table and guide her to the bar, smiling and nodding at Leo's grandmother as we pass.

"Two reds, please," I say to the bartender, just to have something to do with my hands.

Stevie gives me a smug look, arms crossed over her chest.

"Stevie," I say. "What, exactly, do you think you know?"

She pouts. "I *do* know," she says. "You just won't tell me because you don't really talk to me anymore."

"Stevie," I say, even though she's right. After the rift opened between me and Ren, I became well-versed in only sharing surface level things, with Stevie, with my parents, retreating further into work and myself until ignoring what happened became second nature.

"No," she says on a wobble. I can't tell if it's because she's tipsy or about to cry, and my immediate reaction is to do anything to stop the latter, tell her anything she wants to know. But she continues first. "Ever since Sasha's wedding, you're not talking to me like you used to." She sinks a hip against the bar. "I know you're not happy, Joni. I can tell. And I know it was you who changed the sheets."

I squint at her. "How—"

"Because you came up early," she says. "You don't listen to soundscapes. You *should* have been at work. It was the middle of the day on a Monday. Why—"

I grasp her wrist to angle her toward the bar so the people at the tables can't hear her rapidly rising voice, contemplate all the ways she could have figured it out. Maybe I left my phone open to an email from Ramona. Maybe I somehow caught Ren's sleep-talking and she overheard me. Maybe Stevie is *just that good* of a journalist. My eyes dart down the table to our mom, who's laughing at something Hannah just said.

"Stevie, I'm really sorry. I should have told you, but—" The bartender returns with our wine and I thank him, give one to Stevie, try to keep the shaking in my hands to a minimum. "I just didn't think your wedding week was the time to tell you."

"Why not?" she asks, that same hurt splashing across her face.

I falter, confused. Even Stevie, queen of not really caring, should be able to suss out why I wouldn't want to tell her about the dissolution of my life right before she gets married. "I mean, I just didn't want it to get in the way of things."

Her brow furrows. "How would that get in the way of anything? I'm not going to tell anyone."

I soften. "I appreciate that," I say. "But me getting fired isn't really what we need to talk about during your wedding week."

I know I've made a mistake as soon as Stevie's expression morphs into one of pure shock, her grip on her glass tightens. "Joni," she says. "That's not—"

"You got *fired*?"

We both whirl at my mom's high-pitched voice, all the color drained from her face where she stands behind us. She's said it loudly enough that all other conversation slowly dies, until the entire deck of wedding guests is staring at us. It feels like Stevie and I are spotlighted against the flowered bar, each of us holding a glass of red, each of us frozen.

My eyes go to his immediately, the only person I know will center me right now. He's at the table closest to us, between Sasha and Oliver, that sliver of chest I was finding so distracting during dinner now rising as he takes in a breath through his nose. He looks at me like he's just a little confused, like I've shared some anecdote he's not totally familiar with, and for some reason it hurts more than if he'd shouted at me and stormed out. Not that Ren would ever do that.

"I—" I stammer, every sip of my previous glass of wine seeming to suddenly make their way to my brain as the earth rocks beneath me. I swallow, try to steady myself. I knew this would happen eventually, that I would have to tell my mom. I just didn't think it would be at Stevie and Leo's rehearsal dinner, in front of so many people I love and others I just met for the first time who have no context for the situation and are here to celebrate, not listen to my sob story. I thought, at minimum, it would be on my own terms.

"You were fired?" my mom asks again, still speaking at a volume that carries across the deck, all eyes still on us.

"Mom," I grind out. "Can we not have this conversation right now? It's Stevie and Leo's rehearsal dinner."

"That's not going to stop her," Stevie mutters.

"Sweetie," my mom says to me, shifting into therapist mode and completely ignoring Stevie's comment. "Why didn't you tell us? Are you alright?"

"I'm fine, Mom," I say, but it isn't true. That same quaking unsteadiness I felt when I walked out of Novo a week ago is vibrating around my knees. Only a week ago, really? It's like I took a step off the edge of my old life and plunged into an alternate one I deluded myself into thinking could be real, and now I'm waking up, scrambling to climb back into it, but can't get a strong enough hold.

"Sweetie, do you need to talk about—"

"I'm *fine,*" I whisper harshly, shoulders hitching up as I try to quiet the buzzing in my ears. I don't want to be someone who was just fired, who people will pity. I want to crawl back into some moment three years or five years or ten years ago and make a different choice. Don't move to New York. Or, if you do, look around at your life once in a while. Don't put everything you have into your career. Don't pitch the idea for a movie that everyone will hate. Don't, don't, don't.

If there were crickets around, they'd be sounding right now. Instead, someone drives by blaring Justin Bieber, and I see Leo's lips twitch before he tries, hard, not to smile. And suddenly I can't help it either. A laugh stutters out of me. At the music. At the absurdity of the situation. About what a terrible job I've done keeping secrets.

When I look at my mom, I know it was the absolute wrong thing to do. "What else aren't you telling me?" she asks. There's hurt in her eyes, and the fact that I can't undo it is a weight bearing down on me.

"Nothing," I lie, attempting to bring my voice to neutral. The car is moving on now, and the musical soundtrack isn't so funny anymore. My eyes drift back to Ren's over her shoulder. His mouth is open, like he might jump in, but it wouldn't be fair to ask him to help me through this, because I kept this from him too. "It's just— Can we please talk about this another time?"

"No, I think we can talk about it now."

"Mom," Stevie says. "Don't force it on her."

"No, I'd like to know what else we're all keeping from each other," my mom says. I knew there would be questions, but I didn't expect this reaction, the sudden color in her cheeks, the anger in her voice. My mom can be overbearing, but she's rarely mad.

"I only have four toes on my right foot!" Leo calls from the table. We all look in his direction. "Biking accident when I was eight."

"No, sweetie, that's not the kind of thing she's talking about," Stevie tells him, and it hits me that Leo is trying to put a stop to the drama that *I'm* causing, even though our family is supposed to be a safe place for him.

"There aren't any more secrets, Mom," I lie as she stares back at me. The only remaining secret isn't one that's just mine. There's a reason Ren and I tacitly agreed all these years not to share what happened between us with anyone. If our families know we imploded, we erase years of the status quo. Would it hurt my mom's relationship with Hannah? Would our dads still be the same kind of *want to grab a beer* best friends they've become? Would Sasha and Thad hate me for what I did to their brother? We've both been trying to maintain some semblance of normalcy for the people around us. I'd be betraying him if I said anything.

My mom and I keep staring at each other. The silence expands around us until someone has to break it. Greg steps in.

"I hate golf," he pipes up, shooting a guilt-ridden look at my dad. "I'm so sorry, Richard."

"It's okay," my dad says. "I sort of knew. Surfing sounds miserable to me."

"I understand," Greg says.

"I hate wine!" Dev calls from the far end of one table.

"Good thing that you don't drink then, man," Leo says.

"Oh," Dev says. "Right."

I feel like I'm getting whiplash.

"I hate that we feel so much pressure to make the week here together work," Sasha says from her place next to Ren. All eyes swivel toward her.

"Rich coming from the event planner that tells us when we can *shower*," Thad mutters.

Alex covers her hand with his, but Sasha rears back. "Apologies for trying to organize some *fun* for everyone if we're all going to make such a big deal about everyone being here at the same time every year!"

"Sasha, since when do you have a problem being here?" Thad asks. "And last time I checked, *organized* is not everyone's definition of *fun*!"

"Well sure, when you just get a week off dad duty, I guess you get to act however you want," she snaps.

"Oh my god, Sasha, I'm still a *person*, with or without my daughter!"

At this, Sasha shrinks, mouth in a thin line.

"You'd think everyone would behave better at the rehearsal dinner." All eyes now swivel to where Leo's mother is leaning toward him.

I've never seen Leo angry, didn't know he was capable of it, but at this comment, all of the good nature I'm used to from him vanishes. "Mom," he says. "Are you seriously going to talk about families arguing right now?"

And that's it. The patio erupts into chaos. Suddenly, Hannah is jumping in to settle Thad down, Leo's father says something to his mother that upsets her and in turn gets Oliver going, Dev and the guitarist, for some reason, start shouting. Everyone is talking over each other, voices rising, accusations hurling.

I stand at the bar, my eyes finding Ren's again. My mom steps closer to me, saying something about how I'm the reason we'll remember the rehearsal dinner this way, that if I'd just been *honest* this wouldn't have happened, but I only see Ren. He gives me a sad smile from his spot at the table, the only thing that's still in the movement around him, shoulders straight and gaze clear, the eye in the middle of my hurricane.

Everything quiets. The world, the deck, my mind. He looks at me, and I know, beyond a shadow of a doubt, that I can't lose him again. That I can't risk anything like being in love with him if it means I can't have *this*. Ren, in my life again, the point of gravity around which my personal galaxy revolves. For the last two and a half years, I've drifted off into space, meandering alone, existing but not in the way I really want to, telling myself it was fine, that I didn't really *need* anybody. But this week, as I zipped back into orbit again, finding that center to spin around, I've realized how foolish that is. Needing someone isn't some weakness. In fact, it might be the whole point.

I return his smile, but it's a little hard to keep on my face. I want Ren, but I need him, the best friend who so much of me is built around, the most important person in my life even when we weren't speaking, more.

And then, Stevie steps forward.

"Joni and Ren are sleeping together!" she shouts at the top of her impressive lungs.

This time, it's not a slow fade as much as a bomb dropped, the sound of the impact ringing in everyone's ears.

"Stevie," I hiss. She throws a hand over her mouth, eyes going dinner-plate round. "What the fuck?"

"I'm so sorry," she says. "I think I might be drunk."

Everyone's attention is ping-ponging between me and Ren, waiting for one of us to say something.

"We're not—" Ren stares straight at me, brow knitting. "We're not sleeping together…"

"Anymore," I finish for him, without thinking. Then, as if it matters, as if anyone out here needs to be privy to the twisted timeline of our relationship, "Yet?"

Next to Ren, I see Sasha muttering something before Thad hands her a folded bill. When her eyes snag on mine, she shrugs. "Sorry," she says, looking between me and Ren. "It's just…it's not *surprising*, is it?"

And that's when the anger hits me, drowning out everything else. "Are you—" I say, heat flaring in my chest. "Are you taking *bets* on us?"

"Joni," Ren says, voice rough. He stands up, strides around the table toward me and sets his hands on my shoulders, probably trying to put an end to this pathetic scene.

"No," I say, leaning around him to peer at the others. Hannah looks stunned, Greg's mouth is turned down in a way that suggests he's not that surprised either. My dad, beyond him, is intently studying his water glass. "Is it all just some joke? Ren and Joni will eventually get together?" Ren kneads at one of my shoulders, trying to calm me, but I can't keep it in now, not when I've withheld it from them all these years for *their* sakes, neglecting how that would impact me. "Well, who had three years ago?" I say, voice high. I swear I see Leo's hand twitch upward, and I want to throw my glass of wine in his direction. "Because I hate to break it to all of you, but that's when it actually happened. This week was just a victory lap!"

"Three years ago?" my mom says next to us. Apparently she, at least, wasn't in on this betting pool.

"Is that why you haven't been here the last two summers?" Sasha asks.

"No," my mom says, shaking her head. "Of course not. Joni's been working." She seems to reconsider this, adds, "At the job she's been fired from, I suppose."

"No, let's get it all out in the open," I say to her. Ren has dropped his hands and stepped to the side of me, opening the scene up to the deck again, my protective layer gone. "Isn't that what you wanted? Yes, Sasha, great guess. Did you have any money on that one?"

"Hey, I'm the one who defended you not being here," she says, holding up her palms. "And it was because of *Ren*?" She gestures toward where he's standing next to me, his eyes stuck on some spot on the ground.

"It wasn't his fault," I say.

"So you two just slept together and then you *happened* to stay on the East Coast for two and a half years."

I scramble, my anger suddenly muddled, like I can't find my footing. "Yes. But not like that." I look up at Ren, but his posture is rigid, drawn in. I've gone too far, and I can see the slight wince sweeping off his face, there and gone and replaced with a forced, small smile before he thinks I can notice his hurt at every stupid, desperate thing I just said to try to explain this away. "I'm not saying what I mean."

My mom's voice, softer than before, startles me. "What do you mean, then?" she asks.

"I mean…" I trail off again, cupping my elbows. Everything is spilling out, and I can't contain it.

"Joni?" my mom says. She's eyeing me like she used to when I had a panic attack in high school, questions brimming behind her teeth.

"I didn't come back because I knew that if we saw each other again, we'd ruin each other's lives," I blurt. It's why I left, after all, what I told myself every time I almost called him, almost flew home, almost took back everything I'd done. That this was how it had to be.

The confession lands on the deck with the rest of me, for everyone to see. Everything goes silent.

Ren shifts, suddenly another inch farther from me, and when I look up at him this time, he's staring straight ahead, frowning. We haven't had a conversation about what happened between us. There's still so much for us to say.

"I'm still confused," my mom says. "So you two haven't seen each other."

I hesitate, still watching Ren. I've shared enough, and it's not just me at the center of this anymore. It's both of us.

At my mom's question, he seems to come to. He shakes his head. "Until this week, Joni and I hadn't spoken since Sasha's wedding."

Someone blows out a sigh at the table.

"But you two talked about each other like you were," my mom says. "Didn't you?"

Whenever my mom asked how Ren was over the past couple of years, I'd lie. Say he seemed good, but never elaborated beyond that. It was part of why I'd pared back on my already slim communication with my mom, because I knew that if we talked too much, I might trip up, and she might drag the truth out of me, especially on one of my bad days, when I missed Ren so much I could feel it in my veins. Ren must have lied to Hannah too.

"I guess the two of you seemed so fixed that we all just assumed…" She looks over my head at Ren as if for confirmation, but he's gone still.

"Are you two okay?" This comes from Stevie, who I'd almost forgotten was there.

There's something like an apology in her eyes, her hands hovering like she might lunge over and hug me, and for some reason, it's the thing that does me in. I clench my jaw, try to think of ways to reabsorb tears as the selfish truth I've been burying shoots to the surface: I haven't told Stevie what happened between me and Ren because I'm ashamed. Of how I ran. Of how I couldn't bring myself to fix it.

"I'm—" I feel it in my head, everything tilting around me like it has before, in a way that feels like the end of something.

"Honey," my mom says, reaching toward my shoulder.

I slide her arm away. "I'm okay," I say, my eyes on Ren. All I want is to extract him, the pieces of him I got back this week, from this mess, and run off with them into the night. But I can't get him to look at me. "We'll talk about it later," I tell him. We have to. He doesn't even know all the details of why I left him the night of Sasha's wedding.

But later, it turns out, doesn't come. The whole ugly argument effectively ends the night, and we make our way back to the cars, all the seats in Ren's already taken. At the house, people go to their separate rooms or sit around the firepit, conversation gradually returning to the realm of celebration.

I go inside and check Thad's room, thinking Ren might have gone to talk with his brother, but it's empty. In the kitchen, Hannah is putting a kettle on the stove. As I round into the hallway I almost collide with Alex again. Everywhere, there's someone else, but Ren isn't among them.

When I check the living room one last time, my dad is sitting on the couch with his phone.

"Slow down a minute," he says as I walk past him.

I pause, turn to him. "Have you seen Ren?"

He sits forward, sets his phone on the coffee table, pats the cushion next to him. I perch on the edge and he reaches over, stills my hands as I wring them in front of me. I glance down, the lump in my throat twisting ever tighter.

"You know who's a great person to talk to about this kind of thing?" he asks. I shoot him a beleaguered look. I know what he's going to say. "Your mom."

"Mom doesn't want to talk to me right now," I say.

"She always wants to talk to you, sweetie."

But there's only one person *I* want to talk to right now, and the only way I know how to handle a crisis like this is one anxious step at a time. My mom is an issue for a later date. My dad seems to recognize this, hand sliding off mine.

"He's somewhere," he says. "Give him some time."

But Ren and I don't have time, we only have one day. I keep searching, checking and rechecking every spot, always getting some approximation of the same reaction from everyone I run into: an expression somewhere between avoidance and pity. No one knows what to say, and no matter what corner I turn, I still can't find him.

Eventually, I go back to the screen porch to wait for him. I sit at the foot of my bed in my dress, teeth working at my lower lip until it hurts.

I wait until the house is silent, and the breeze coming in through the windows is cold. Until my mind goes from blank to frantic to blank again.

Ren doesn't come back.

TWO AND A HALF
YEARS AGO

Sasha and Alex

Portland, Oregon

chapter twenty-six

"Sister's back in Portland!" Stevie shrieks from the window of her car when I walk out of PDX, bags in tow.

I race toward her, the hood of my down coat jostling off my head. She pops her trunk and I throw my things in before diving into her passenger seat, leaning across the console to hug her to me.

"Welcome back to Oregon!" she says as she pulls out of the pickup area, reaching forward to crank up the music so loud we have to shout over it.

Ren would have picked me up at the airport, but Stevie insisted she be the one to get me, and *I* insisted to Ren that we don't let on that anything is happening between us until we see each other in person again, so we couldn't push back too much. Some part of me is still scared of the enormity of this, still reeling from realizing my feelings for Ren existed at all, from how all-consuming they'd become, how quickly I'd been willing to put our history, our entire friendship at risk to satisfy my own curiosity. Not only *our* friendship, but our families'. What ties us all together began long before Ren or me. What if we told everyone, and then Ren changed his mind about us?

What if he woke up and decided he *did* love Amanda? Where would that leave our families? The house? Would things be able to just go back to normal?

My knee starts to bounce the closer we get to Sublimity. For the past four months it's felt like we've been inching toward some kind of finish line that kept moving ever farther away. First, Ren was going to come to New York in September, but then his dad had a minor health scare, and he had to cancel last minute. Greg was fine, he assured me every time we talked, but it had still frightened us, made me feel even more distant from everyone. My parents, Stevie, and I spent Thanksgiving with Charlene and Mavis, assuming we would all be in Oregon for Christmas, but then I got promoted to lead fabricator and the movie was approved in early December, so I stayed in the city with a coworker to get ahead on the principal characters.

But now, Sasha's New Year's Eve wedding the day after tomorrow, that finish line is in sight. I try to grab on to it, this moment I've been anticipating for so many months, but by the time we're parking on Mississippi, my knee's movement is almost violent, knocking against the car door. I trail Stevie inside, my heart feeling like it might rattle my teeth right out of my jaw at the prospect of seeing Ren. We had to say goodbye so quickly after Willow and Martin's wedding that I'm not sure what this looks like: us, together, more than friends.

The band is still setting up, but Ren's preshow playlist is playing over the speakers, people already bobbing their heads at the high tops and up by the stage. Sublimity seems almost new to me, a reminder of how long it's been since I've been here.

Stevie is saying something to me about Mom, when she and Dad will arrive ahead of the rehearsal dinner tomorrow. I hear only half of it as I scan the room, neck craning, searching, nerves tingling up and down my arms.

When I spot him through the crowd, on the opposite side of the room, I fully tune her out. He's behind the bar, angled away from me as he talks to tonight's bartender. His arms are folded in front of him, hands on his biceps, a worn flannel I want to take off him and burrow into every night rolled up to reveal his forearms.

He laughs, throwing his head back, and then sees me out of the corner of his eyes. He's already smiling, but now his whole face lights up, and *how didn't I see it before*. I want to reach into the past and shake myself—*He's right there! Look up for two seconds!* It's like my blood flows faster as I take stock of the tiny ways he's changed in the last four months. The messy wave of his hair, the sharp line of his jaw. Maybe none of it is actually new. Maybe each time I've seen him again, he's been this perfect.

He rounds the corner of the bar and weaves through the crowd toward me. Stevie keeps gabbing, and all of a sudden I'm finding it hard to move.

Ren is a few feet away now, and he's real, and then he's scooping me up into his arms, and I'm nestling my face just below his shoulder, inhaling, every synapse in me firing. Relief like I've never felt before, that I didn't even know I needed, washes through me.

"Hi," he says, low, in my ear.

"Hi," I say over a tightness in my throat at how good it is to be wrapped up in him, at every feeling I've been sorting through since Boston. "I can't believe it's you."

He leans just his head back, smiling down at me, our bodies still pressed together. I risk hanging on to him a second longer.

Stevie coughs.

We both whip our heads around. I'm the first to let go, Ren's hands dropping from me as I turn to her.

"I need a drink," she says.

Ren nods us in the direction of the bar, ducking behind it while we stand at one end. He's not bartending tonight, but he makes us our drinks before sidling back out.

"Hey," I say, motioning up at the stage where a lanky,

golden-haired guy is fiddling with a mic stand while another sets up a drum kit, the name *Bearcat* on the kick drum. "Weren't they in Boston?" I remember them—an indie rock group we saw at the festival.

"Yeah," he says. "We just signed them."

"Seriously? And they still didn't give you an A&R position?" Indignation flashes through me.

"It's fine," he says. Something in his face wavers for a second, but then he's smiling down at me in a way that has me wanting to sink back into him. *One thing at a time*, I tell myself. *Try to enjoy being back together before you start overanalyzing every tiny thing, Joni.*

We walk over to the stage, where he jumps up to assist with setup. He holds a hand out to help me up, then reaches down for Stevie.

"Hey, Leo," he calls to the lead singer as he unravels a cord. "This is Joni."

I shake Leo's hand. "This is—" I turn, but Stevie is squatted down at the front of the stage, brow furrowed as she reads over their setlist.

"Is 'Kiss on My List' just a cover, or do you have your own song called that?" she asks no one in particular as she straightens. "Because I think you'd be better off with a different Hall and Oates song. 'Private Eyes,' maybe?"

She pivots toward us, and her gaze locks on to Leo. She lifts her glass to her mouth but misses her straw, tongue searching for it.

"Stevie, this is Leo," I say slowly. My eyes flick to Ren's across from me. He's grabbed a guitar, pick between his teeth, and he matches my expression at the way Stevie's acting. "Leo, St—"

"Stevie," he cuts in, bypassing me and walking over to my sister. "I'll sing 'Private Eyes' tonight if you want."

Stevie shrugs a shoulder, straw finally in her mouth. "If you want to," she says casually, but I can see the way she fiddles with her skirt.

I watch the two of them talk in ever-shortening sentences, bantering back and forth as their bodies drift closer. Ren steps around them to me, twisting the tuning pegs of the guitar as he plucks at the strings.

"Are they—" he says, glancing between Stevie and Leo.

"I *know*," I say, fascinated by whatever strange mating ritual is unfolding in front of us. Stevie is usually a hi-and-goodbye type of person, sure that they'll find her if they want her. But now, she's smiling, fiddling with her hair, giving no indication of leaving.

The two of us study them in awe. Ren eventually leans over and sets the guitar on its stand, and I'm drawn away from the conversation and back to his movements, the flex of the tendons in his forearms, the height difference between us when he straightens again. "Hey," he says, grazing a hand against me that feels as good as if he'd slid it under my clothes. "Want to put your coat in the back room?"

I'd hardly realized I was still wearing it. I shuck it off, begin to fold it over my arm before Ren grabs it from me and tosses it over his shoulder.

"Come on," he says, jerking his head in the direction of a door marked Employees Only at the side of the stage.

We let our fingers intertwine as he leads me to it, knowing Stevie is too busy flirting—or not flirting, I'm not totally sure what is happening there—to notice.

The door closes behind us and we walk down a hallway and into a small room I've been in before. It houses an ancient pool table that one too many people have set their beers on, its slight slant favorable or disastrous depending on where you're shooting from.

"Can't believe Bessie's still around," I say as Ren sets my

coat on a chair by the door. I rest my back against the edge of the table.

"You haven't been gone that long," he says as he comes over, runs his hands down my sides to my hips, thumbs just tucking into the waistband of my jeans. "She's still got some life left in her."

I raise an eyebrow as he lifts me in one quick move onto the table, steps between my legs. I hook two fingers in the belt loops of his dark jeans. "I don't know about that, with what you have in mind."

"I can't imagine what you're talking about," Ren says, lips curving against where he's dropped them to my neck. "I'm just saying hi to an old friend."

"You greet all your friends like this?" I ask, the same ache I've felt so many times over the last four months settling deep in me when he tilts my hips closer to him.

He shakes his head, pulls away to look at me. "Just you," he says. "Only ever you."

I tip my face up to his, smile just before he kisses me.

By the time the sounds of a guitar drift through the walls, Ren's flannel is pushed off his shoulders, the hem of his T-shirt raised up so I can explore the contours of his abdomen. His hands are warm under my sweater, one at my waist, the other working over the lacy fabric of my bra until I can't breathe, something in me arching me closer, seeking more friction, more pressure, more him.

"Mmm," he hums against my mouth as a drumbeat kicks in. "I've got to do sound check."

"We're not at Sublimity," I say as he slowly drags himself away from me. I'm not ready for this to stop. It's been months of waiting, of talking on the phone late into the night, always dancing around the topic of what we mean to each other now. "We're somewhere far away, just the two of us, no responsibilities."

"I'd love to take that trip with you," Ren says as he turns to adjust himself, then shrugs his flannel back on, his palms coming to rest on my thighs. I fold his collar down. "Maybe whatever wedding we go to next."

But my only real fantasy at the moment is being alone with him. "No. No weddings. Just you and me and nothing to do but each other."

Ren's eyes sparkle as his hands slide up and settle on my waist. "Are you saying you won't be my plus-one anymore? Is our tradition dead?"

I pretend to think, squinting over his shoulder. "I could be talked into it," I say. "No one's a better dancer than you."

"It is what I'm known for," Ren says.

I kiss him one more time, long and hard, before hopping off the table. "Come on, slacker," I say, tugging my sweater back down. "You've got a job to do."

In the open booth at the back of the room, Ren performs sound check, adjusting volume levels while I sit on a stool next to him.

"Bass is good," he says from his own stool, nodding toward the stage. I flash a thumbs-up at Leo, my small contribution so I can continue being close to Ren. I can't seem to leave his side. "Mic two." I hold up two fingers and Leo shifts over onstage. "You're a natural," Ren says, bumping his shoulder against mine.

Eventually, Stevie wanders over from the bar, eyes stuck on the stage.

"Hey," she calls over the repeated *tap tap tap* of the drums. "Any chance Joni could crash with you tonight, Ren?"

Ren doesn't look away from the stage, just swivels on his stool the tiniest bit so his knee nudges mine, something silent passing between us. My chest lifts at an excuse to spend more time with him. The schedule is packed with wedding prep and family time starting tomorrow.

"Of course she can," he says, his knee pressing closer in the booth, out of Stevie's line of sight.

"Why do I need to stay with Ren tonight, Stevie?" I ask, smirking.

She rolls her eyes skyward in a *you know why* move. "You can get your things out of my car if you need to."

"Oh, I'm sure I can just borrow one of Ren's T-shirts to sleep in," I say. I turn back to him, pat his shoulder as I sit up straight. "Can't I, friend?"

His cheeks have gone a little pink, jaw flickering like he's trying to suppress a smile. He scrubs a hand over the top of my head. "Of course you can, Joni."

I grin at Stevie. "You and Leo have a great night."

She straightens her skirt, smooths her tights, and walks back to the stage.

"Smooth," Ren says. "She'll have no idea now."

"Please," I say, watching as my sister leans up against the stage toward Leo. "She's not thinking about anything else tonight."

When I look back at Ren, he's smiling at me, distracted from the job in front of him. "What?" I ask.

"Nothing," he says. "Just happy you're here."

chapter twenty-seven

Any other time, I'd have asked for the grand tour of Ren's apartment, spent time poring over how he organized his records (the same meticulous way he did at his old place, I'm sure—by genre, then artist and album in release order), observing all the things that make it his and not just another box in this building. Is his guitar still propped in one corner of his living room? Does he still keep a Chemex sitting on his stove? Did he ever get rid of that hideous lamp we found in a thrift store in college?

But as soon as the door closes behind us, Ren is hoisting me up against it, kissing me greedily.

We move together easily, barely making it to his kitchen before I'm unbuttoning his pants and he's pulling my sweater over my head, dropping to his knees in front of me to kiss a line across my abdomen and tug my jeans down.

We stumble into his bedroom, and he sheds the rest of his clothes. On the bed, I sink down onto him, Ren swearing, a low groan stretching out of him, his hands coming up to my hips to guide me. For a while I'm nothing more than a body, chasing after every sensation until I fall against his chest, his fingers scraping up my spine to hold me to him. I'd worried we might not be able to replicate the magic of that night outside Boston, had to tell myself every time we confessed we were missing each other in that way, up on the phone late into the night, that it was us that had made it wonderful and not the hotel on the coast, the over-the-top wedding, the vacation mindset we were in.

But I didn't need to. This is something almost better: a familiarity that lets me anticipate how we'll touch each other, the push and pull of it all.

After, I lie on top of him, my cheek resting on his sternum. He dances the pads of his fingers over my arm, across my shoulders, down the other arm.

I think I could live with Ren like this forever, but that's half the problem: we don't have forever.

"What are you thinking?" he asks me.

I roll off him, onto my side, haul his oatmeal-colored sheet over me. Over his shoulder, I can see three framed vintage concert tour posters, one that I recognize and two that I don't. His Red Sox cap sits on a shelf underneath them, a stack of books next to it. He tucks the comforter up over us before he lies on his side too, one hand coming up to rest at my waist.

"Nothing," I say. I don't want to drag Ren down into my swirling anxiety, because it's rarely right: I'm just overthinking, worrying needlessly. I don't want him to think I don't want this. "I'm just— I'm so happy."

A soft smile plays at his mouth as he exhales what's almost a laugh. "I don't think people usually say *I'm so happy* in that tone."

"I am," I say, curling closer to him, but still keeping a notable distance between our bodies. I want to close it, want to pull him into me again, because that seems to be the one time I can get my brain to quiet. But I know this will still be waiting on the other side. I've been trying to ignore it, but being here with him, in his apartment, in his bed has forced it all to the forefront of my mind, cast a spotlight on it. I don't know when we'll see each other again after this week. What if we can't see each other until the summer? It's been hard enough being long-distance best friends for the last four years. But every time we've tiptoed toward this discussion of us, a future, a *plan*, over the months, we've veered the other way, both of us hesitant to mention anything, I think, that could screw this up. Both of us, I know deep down, without a real solution.

Like he can sense my anxiety hiking, Ren draws me against him. He asks me to tell him about the movie, and I do, and I ask him for his predictions for Sasha's wedding, and we agree Stevie might have just met her person. I say things I know will make him laugh, storing the sound somewhere deep in me. We talk about everything but us, and for now, I tell myself, that's okay.

I try to believe it.

In the morning, Ren drives me to Stevie's apartment. She's already outside, car keys in hand and her face burrowed into her coat. There isn't any snow on the ground, but it's cold, the tip of her nose visibly red as she comes over to the window, resting her elbows on it once I roll it down.

"How was Ren's couch?" she asks.

"Come on, Stevie," Ren says in mock disappointment. "You know I'd never let Joni sleep on the couch."

"Chivalry isn't dead, then." He smirks at her comment, and she sticks out her tongue at him, then taps the window's edge. "Come on. We're due at brunch in thirty minutes. Sasha will hate it if we're late."

I push the door open and dislodge Stevie from her post. My hair is still damp from the shower Ren and I took together, Ren behind me like it was something we'd practiced. I turn back to him, hope Stevie won't notice that his hair isn't totally dry either, that I smell like his soap. "See you at the rehearsal dinner?" I say, ignoring the slightly hollow feeling that developed in my stomach on the ride here at the way this weekend already was no longer ours.

He nods, eyes drifting over my face.

Stevie has walked back over to the front door of her building and is shifting between her feet, rubbing her arms. "Come on!" she calls, antsy.

"Okay," I say, gaze finally dropping from Ren's as I hop out of the car.

"Joni," he calls through the window as I start across the sidewalk. Stevie grumbles in protest when I pivot, walk back to his car and lean into the passenger window.

Ren has one arm draped over the steering wheel as he angles toward me, mouth in a straight line.

"We'll talk about it," he says. "We'll figure this out. Okay?"

Something on Ren's face tells me he might have spent the night worrying about this too.

"Joni!" Stevie shouts, impatient as ever.

Ren's mouth twitches into a smile, and my heart gives a hopeful beat.

"Okay," I say, smiling back at him.

"I am freezing my *ass* off for you," Stevie calls.

I roll my eyes at Ren, and he laughs as I hustle across the sidewalk toward my sister.

"Sorry, Stevie!" he shouts.

"Yeah, yeah," Stevie says. She doesn't sound all that irritated when she adds, "You two are so annoying," opening her door and ushering me inside.

I turn and wave at Ren one more time before the door closes behind us.

≈

After Sasha's bridesmaid brunch, we head back to Stevie's apartment and curl up under the extra-fluffy duvet on her bed, both of us sleepy after mimosas.

"Remember how freezing it was in our apartment that one winter in New York?" I ask as I tuck the blanket farther under my chin. "Your place feels like that."

"Yeah, but that was because our landlord was an asshole and took a lifetime to fix our radiator," she says, her hair fanning out on the pillow. "I'm just being economical."

I tap my icy toes against her shin. "Did Leo think your place was freezing?" The corners of Stevie's mouth pinch as she tries to hide a smile. "You *like* him, don't you?"

"Clearly," she says, nodding over my shoulder. "That's his sweatshirt."

I twist my head to look at the green crewneck hanging over the back of her desk chair. "Stevie Miller," I say. "You did not let a *boy* leave his clothes in your apartment."

She buries her face into her pillow, letting out a groan that doesn't sound altogether bad. "I *know*."

We nap, talk until it's time to get ready for the rehearsal dinner. We'll meet our parents at the restaurant, and while I'm excited to see everyone, something inside me buzzes as the seconds tick down until I get to see Ren again. I feel a little like I'm losing my mind, giddy anticipation coursing through me as I fix my hair, apply mascara in Stevie's bathroom mirror, and it occurs to me that this secret might not be so easy to keep.

When we arrive, he's standing with Thad and Gemi in the back room of the trendy cocktail bar in a pale blue button-down and navy blazer.

"About time you got here," Thad says, throwing an arm around my shoulders. I've only flown into Portland since moving to New York, always headed to the coast or south to see my parents, and haven't been here when Thad or Sasha have come up from LA.

I hug Gemi before I turn to Ren.

"Joni," he says, like we're in on some joke, like a hummingbird isn't fluttering against my rib cage, like he wasn't just biting his cheek to keep himself focused.

"Ren. Long time no see."

"Ages," he says, cheek hollowing.

I push down the impulse to throw all caution to the wind and kiss him right here.

True to Sasha's form, the rehearsal dinner is immaculate down to the tiniest details, a carefully curated menu based on the places she and Alex have traveled together, everyone's place card done in careful calligraphy with the flowers of each guest's birth month twining around their names. Seated next to each other as usual, Ren and I spend most of dinner with our legs tangled together under the table, his hand sneaking every so often to my thigh or my hip, pulling mine over to his leg so he can flip it palm side up and trace lines across it.

When Hannah asks how I am, I tell her I've never been better.

When my mom says I seem good, healthy, happy, where it once would have grated against me—*what did I seem like before, Mom?*—now it just lifts me higher off the ground, that she can see how well I can take care of myself.

At the end of the night, while everyone is saying goodbye, milling between tables and chairs and raving about the food, Alex's best man corralling everyone who's going out with them tonight, Ren and I duck down a side hall that I think might technically be staff-only, a velvet curtain falling closed behind us.

"Is it insane that I missed you today?" I ask as he kisses me, his leg coming between mine.

"No," he rasps, thumbs pressing into my hip bones. "I missed you too."

"You know," I say, something reckless riding up in me, from a night of touching under the table, or Stevie's confession about Leo, or just *Ren*, I don't know. "You could just tell Alex you can't come tonight. Take me home instead."

Ren pulls his head away, body still flush against mine as he smirks. "You don't think that would be too obvious? Stevie wouldn't care you spent another night at my place?"

I pout, getting a laugh out of him. "Fair enough," I say. I pat a hand to his chest. "You go out and have your fun."

"Trust me," he says, grip tightening as he leans down to kiss me again. "This is the most fun I've ever had."

chapter twenty-eight

"I have to hand it to her," Stevie says, elbows on the table as we watch Sasha and Alex on the dance floor, the chandelier light above casting a glow on the sheer sleeves of her dress, the last chorus of the song wrapping up. "This might be the only New Year's Eve I've actually enjoyed." She draws her fingers through the rose gold confetti scattered over the white tablecloths. Everything is sparkly, strands of tiny paper stars dripping down from the white- and champagne-colored balloons floating against the coffered ceiling. "She knows how to plan a wedding."

"Maybe she can plan yours," I say. "You are going to marry Leo, right?" She's been on her phone again all night, was still on it last night when I woke up randomly to grab water.

She glowers at me, but before I can tease her more, there's a hand on my shoulder, warm lips hovering close to my ear. "Will you dance with me?" Ren asks.

I look to where couples are rising from their tables as the first dance applause dies down, a Lord Huron song now coming through the speakers.

"Careful," Stevie says wryly as I stand, my hand in Ren's. "Everyone will think you're dating."

"Call Leo," I say. "Sasha told you to invite him earlier." As soon as Sasha heard Stevie was vaguely interested in anyone, even someone she'd met a mere forty-eight hours prior, she'd insisted he come to the wedding. It was a testament to how happy Sasha was this weekend that she would complicate her meticulous plans, even in this minor way.

"I don't know who you're talking about," Stevie says, getting up and brushing her hair over her shoulder. "I'm going to the bar."

On the dance floor, I settle my wrists over Ren's shoulders, his hands falling lower on my waist than usual.

"Careful," I say, glancing around.

He slides his hands half an inch up. "What if I don't want to *be* careful, Joni," he whispers, sending goose bumps along with it.

Our hips sway together, and I bite my lip as he again inches up.

"How about now?" he asks suggestively.

I slit my eyes at him, but can't keep a straight face when his palms suddenly fly up to my shoulder blades, full middle-school dance height.

"Point made," I say.

He lowers them to a respectable spot on my waist, leaves them there.

"So how do you propose we spend midnight?" I ask.

"Stairs, hallway, duck under a table," he says, nodding his head in the direction of each. He smiles at my laugh. "Tell everyone we're just so sad we don't have anyone else to kiss that we decided to kiss each other as friends. Make it our origin story."

"A man with a plan."

"I just got you," he says. "You think we're going to miss our first New Year's together because our families don't know yet?"

His words expand in my chest.

Twenty minutes before midnight, I leave Ren with Thad and Gemi and run to the bathroom. My cheeks are flushed, limbs loose. I feel it—a contentedness flooding through me that would have unnerved me before, some worry that being so happy meant it could be taken away. But it's a beautiful wedding, I'm surrounded by the people I love, and Ren and I are going to figure this out.

In the bathroom, a woman with bleached blond hair is sitting on the counter, scrubbing at one side of her mouth. "Fucking *lip liner*," she slurs as I wash my hands.

I offer her an apologetic look and head back in the direction of the stairs, fifteen minutes to go, dodging the line that's grown longer at coat check, people preparing to walk out to the balcony or the sidewalk to watch the fireworks. As I'm about to round the corner to the stairs, a familiar voice drifts toward me with the snippets of music floating out of the ballroom.

"We're so *proud* of you," Hannah is saying. I can just make out her left elbow, her back to me, but I can't see who else she's talking to. Something about her voice, the way it's slightly hushed, stops me in my tracks. "You've worked so hard for this."

"Sure." This is Ren, his voice my favorite sound in the world, like the type of song he once described to me: one that's made a home in you, but also feels new every time.

Greg chimes in. "So what exactly does an A&R manager *do* at a record label?" he asks.

My heart gives an overjoyed leap. Ren got the job. Ren got the job he's wanted for so long, the one he almost gave up on.

I'm ready to round the corner, too excited to care that I've been eavesdropping, eager to celebrate, but I falter when I hear Hannah's voice again.

"Have you told Amanda yet?" she asks. My palms go clammy.

"No," Ren says evenly. "Because Amanda and I aren't together anymore, Mom."

"But she was so nice," she coos, the sound abrasive. "I know I'm a broken record, but she was just such a good *fit* for you, honey. And with this job offer…" She trails off.

For the first time, I worry how Hannah would feel about Ren and me as more than friends. If I would be the partner she'd want for him, or if she wanted someone who didn't need to be calmed, who was more self-assured. But while I don't know the specifics of their breakup, Ren did allude to Amanda not thinking his job was serious enough. Someone who feels that way can't be the right fit for him.

I'm about to leave them to the rest of their conversation, find another way back into the ballroom when she says, "So you're really not going to take it?"

I freeze.

"There are record labels on the East Coast, Mom," Ren says.

"I just don't know why you're suddenly running off," Hannah says. "You finally get this job you've worked so hard for and now you're, what? Deciding you don't want it? Sweetie, this is your moment. You can't be a bartender forever."

"I'm not—" Ren starts, but I'll never know what he was going to say.

"If you're moving for Joni—" Hannah says, breaking off. "You can't base your whole life around your best friend."

I've heard enough. I spin away, hurry down the hall, and slam my way back into the bathroom. The same woman from earlier is still in the midst of reapplying her lip liner. It looks like she's wiped it off and tried again several times. She eyes me in the reflection, one razor-thin eyebrow raised. "You good?" she asks.

I'm wringing my hands and pacing, so clearly *not* good that her question prompts a small bark of laughter out of me. "Yep," I say, before locking myself into a stall.

Ren. Ren is giving up his dream job. For me.

I think back to Sublimity the other night, when he said he wasn't offered the position even after successfully scouting a band in Boston. I think about the strange expression that moved across his face.

I stand, clenching my fists at my sides, trying to breathe in a steady rhythm. I can't let him do this. This is his whole life, everything he's worked for. Earlier I was desperate to talk about the future, how things would work. But now I'm only wondering if he would have even told me about the job or just given it up without mentioning it at all, just told me he needed a change of scenery and was ready to move to New York. I think, for a minute, that maybe Hannah is right. Ren deserves a relationship with someone in the same place, a house and weekends together and a future, instead of phone calls and cross-country flights and missed connections and time lost and no end in sight.

I hold one clammy palm to my equally clammy chest, where I can feel my pulse skipping erratically. The bathroom door swings open and closed, the sound of heels tapping against the tile. For some inexplicable reason, I hold my breath.

"Joni?" Stevie says.

I stiffen. It's almost midnight by now, and Ren is probably searching for me, wondering what happened. People will be heading outside to watch fireworks, arms around each other, and I'm supposed to be there with him, in some place where we can keep this whole thing secret.

"I can see your feet," Stevie says. "Why are you just standing in a stall?" She exchanges a low murmur with the woman at the sink before she raps on the door. "Joni, come out."

I almost don't open the door. Maybe I can sit in this stall forever. But when Stevie knocks again, I unlock it, let it swing pathetically open, because I know she won't just give up and go away.

I don't know exactly what my face looks like, but when Stevie sees it, her eyebrows slant with worry. "What is it?" she asks.

I just shake my head.

"Come here," she says, leading me out of the stall and sitting me down on the couch across from the mirrors. I no longer care that five feet away from us there's a drunk woman applying lip liner like she's a baboon and someone dropped the pencil into her enclosure. "Tell me," Stevie says, her knees angled toward mine, hand squeezing my limp one.

"I—" It's all I can get out, blood rushing to my ears. "I can't."

"Are you sick?" she asks. "Did something happen?"

I let out a small burst of a laugh. Everything happened. I fell in love with my best friend and didn't recognize it until our time was already running out. I wasn't smart enough to stop it before everything imploded. "I can't do this," I say.

"Can't do what?" Stevie asks gently. I look at her a moment, willing her to know, to read my mind. She leans back like she does, or at least suspects. We haven't been that careful these past few days, after all. "Joni, no," she says.

"No, it's good," I say quickly, because if I don't, I will break down into a mess on her lap. If I don't, I will convince myself that this is okay, that Ren can give everything up for me and that he won't resent me for it in two months, six months, a year, and that I won't resent him for the pressure it places on me. I will convince myself that we won't break up because he chose me over everything. That we aren't headed for a grossly inevitable cliff. "It's good because Ren can be happy this way," I say, my cheeks hurting as I try to smile.

"What are you talking about?" Stevie says, and I swear her eyes go shiny too. "He's so in love with you, Joni."

I should ask her how she knows, how *long* she's known. But my hands are growing numb, the ringing in my ears getting louder with each second, and her words hardly mean anything to me.

"Stevie," I say in a strangled voice, reaching out to grip her wrist. "Please don't ask me why. I just— I have to go." As I rise, I can feel the woman at the mirror watching us.

Stevie's expression shifts to one of, if not understanding,

acceptance, as she stands up with me. "Okay," she says. "I'll come with you."

"No. You stay. Have fun. Call Leo."

"I don't care about Leo right now. I'm coming with you." She tucks her hand into the crook of my elbow.

"Stevie, *no*," I snap, shaking her off and whirling on her. "I'm going alone."

She falls back a step, stunned.

"I'm sorry," I say. "I'm just— I'm going to go back to your apartment, and I'll see you when you get home, okay?"

I can tell she wants to protest. "Okay," she says instead.

I force a small smile even as I feel my heart caving in. "I just— I need to go. Can you make an excuse for me?"

"Of course," she says.

I start to leave, turn back to her at the last minute. "Please don't tell Mom."

Stevie gives me an odd look, lips pursing like she's almost disappointed. But she nods, finally, and I go.

In line at the coat check, I grip my elbows, toe tapping against the floor, glancing over my shoulder every few seconds. I have to get my things and get out of here before my mother, Thad, *Ren* comes down the stairs. I check the time on my phone. Eight minutes to midnight.

As I step out the doors, the cold air hits me like it's trying to shove me back inside. I draw my coat tighter around me and duck my head against the icy breeze. There's a dusting of snow on the ground, flakes drifting down lazily. When we arrived earlier, I thought the facade of the historic hotel was romantic, all brick and white detailing, but now it just seems imposing, stark against the modern buildings around it. I pull out my phone and order a car that's close before checking to see if I can get on a flight out tomorrow morning.

I tell myself I'm doing the right thing. That this is what loving someone is: putting their happiness before yours. That this is an opportunity for me to prove to Ren exactly how much I love him.

But I never expected loving someone would hurt so much.

"Joni?"

At first I'm surprised when I hear his voice. But the sound of it quickly settles over me. Of course he'd find me.

I turn, shove my phone back into my pocket.

"Let me take you home," Ren says. He stops just short of me on the sidewalk, no coat, just his suit jacket, snow already in his hair. "Stevie said you're not feeling well."

"No." I shake my head. Panic is creeping in like it hasn't in months, years, maybe. Raw and sharp with a life of its own. "I already requested a car. You should stay."

"I don't care about staying," he says. "Let me take care of you."

"Ren," I say, voice pleading, my arms wrapped around my middle. "Please go back inside."

I watch as his brow furrows, his mouth flattens. "Where are you going?" he asks.

I swallow. "Back to Stevie's," I say.

"Joni," Ren says, and it's in that moment that I drop a veil between what I'm feeling and how I have to act. I can't let Ren know how much this is killing me, leaving him. Leaving *this*. Us. I channel every time I've ever seen *him* do exactly this, shut down any flicker of emotion on his face.

"Will you talk to me?" he asks, stepping in closer, his hand lifting toward my arm.

I retreat, twist slightly out of his reach.

I look up at him, heart thudding painfully in my chest as his lips part, body goes remarkably still.

"Ren," I say. "This won't—" The words catch. I try again, my voice small. "This was a mistake."

He doesn't move. "What was a mistake?"

"All of it."

He stares at me quietly for a minute, eyes locked on to mine. His mouth tightens like he's trying to work something out. I stare back, work as hard as I can not to betray anything.

"You don't mean that," he says finally. He's looking at me like he doesn't believe it, like what I just said doesn't add up, short breaths lightly fogging the air in front of him.

This will be my memory of tonight, I realize. Ren in his suit and tie on a freezing city street.

I lower my gaze to the sidewalk between us. "I do," I say. "August shouldn't have happened. We—we rushed into things."

"What about the past few days?" Ren asks, voice just breaking on the last word.

It makes me look up at him, which is a mistake. I've never imagined what hurting Ren would look like, would feel like, but it's a stab at my side, a knife hollowing me out.

"I'm sorry," I say. "I should have said something sooner. But we can't do this, Ren, it's too—it's too much."

"Okay." Ren nods, rubbing at one temple. "Then we pretend it didn't happen," he says, a desperation in his voice.

I want to take the last four months back, but it's out there now, the truth of how I feel about him, and I know our friendship won't be able to recover, not fully. If I tell him I can pretend, I know I'll stumble sooner rather than later, and I'll let him move for me, let him give up his dream job, the whole life he's built here, just because I want him. Maybe a year from now I won't feel this way. Maybe I'll wake up in a month and decide I was too rash. But right now I'm having trouble thinking beyond my next breath, and I have to get out of here, and explaining any of that to Ren will just land us back in this same impossible place.

"I don't know if I can," I say.

Ren takes a step toward me and says, hoarse, "You're my best friend. What—what am I supposed to do without you?"

I can hear the same fear that I feel in his voice: I can't picture a world without him in it either. It seems impossible.

"We messed it up, Ren," I say, and swipe an angry hand at my cheeks when I realize they're wet. "We crossed a line we said we wouldn't and now we can't go back to how things were before."

"When did we say we wouldn't cross that line?" Ren asks.

My gaze floats back up to his. "What?"

"When did we ever say we wouldn't cross that line?" His voice is firm, like he's found some point to keep me here.

"We didn't," I admit. "But—"

"Then what's the problem?" Ren presses. "So we crossed it, so you don't want this anymore. I—"

"Best friends don't *do* that, Ren."

"Well, we did," he says. He takes another step toward me. "We wanted it."

I shut my eyes, squeeze them closed like it might make all of this easier. But nothing will make this easier. The only thing that will make him accept this is if I lie, if I say something I don't believe but that cuts to some vital part of him.

"I don't think you know what you want," I say, and Ren falls back a step.

"I don't know what I want," he repeats to himself.

"Your job," I say, willing him to understand that I *know*, that I can't tell him I know because if I do, he'll be able to talk me out of it. That I'm doing this because I know, in the end, it will be what makes him happiest. I add, for good measure, "Amanda. She was good for you."

"I want *you*, Joni," he says, eyes pleading.

These are, at once, exactly the words I want to hear and exactly the words I can't hear. I scramble, picking lines out of books and movies that I think might work to push us apart, protect us from the damage we might do to each other. "I think you want some version of me," I say. It's wildly unfair, but I don't know how else to convince him. "You've only had this vacation version of me for the last few years anyway. This is only romantic when our time is limited. You want this tradition." I wave a hand toward the building. "The weddings."

"That's not true." He scans my face like he might find some proof that I'm making this all up.

"It *is* true," I say, the words coming hard and fast now. "We were never going to be real, Ren. It was always going to be a fantasy."

He goes quiet at this, my last blow landing. But something else seems to occur to him then, his gaze darkening. "Were you just going to leave?" he asks.

"I—" I break off, put a hand to my stomach. I have the distinct feeling that whatever stitches hold me together are rapidly unraveling, like one of my carefully constructed Novo characters destroyed. "No, I—" Standing here, the wreckage of us at my feet, I lower my head. "I would have called."

Vaguely, somewhere above us, voices are counting down. Both of us glance up. We should be part of that crowd, ringing in another year. We might have been up there in another life, and maybe this one can still be it. We could erase this, make it work. *I just got you.*

But then his eyes are back on me, expression flat.

"Called." He nods. I want to reach for him, want to tell him that I love him, that I take it all back.

"Ren—" I say, as a cheer rises above us and the first firework launches into the sky.

"No," he says. "It's okay." He looks back down at me, and I feel like something has been stolen from me. He's backing away, gold shimmering behind him, one hand in his pocket, the other rubbing at his jaw. He drops his hand. Nods at me. "Good luck with your movie, Joni."

Just like that, he's gone.

SATURDAY

chapter twenty-nine

I fell asleep without closing the curtains last night, so I wake up earlier than usual, jerking upright in the direction of Ren's bed.

But his blankets are undisturbed.

As I change into a pair of jean shorts and a crewneck sweatshirt, shove my feet into my Birkenstocks, I try to comfort myself with the fact that at least life was beautiful again for one brief, shining moment.

The house is still quiet as I cut through the kitchen and out the back door, walk the short path down to the beach. The tide is out, seagulls circling in the gray morning. I gaze down the long stretch of coast that comes to a point far in the distance, then back toward the lighthouse, my heart stuttering when I see him, walking toward me from where the sand runs into the rocks, still in his clothes from last night. His hands are in the pockets of his dark gray chinos, a hunter green fleece that I think belongs to Thad—one he wouldn't have had to grab from the porch, at least—pulled over his white button-down.

"Hi," he says when he gets to me. He's barefoot, the hems of his pants just rolled to avoid the wet sand. There's stubble on his chin, faint lines under his eyes. I'm sure I don't look much better. "Did you sleep?" he asks me, his toes kicking the sand.

"Not really." I ask it plainly, no pretenses left between us. "Where were you?"

Ren squints up at the house. "I just needed a little time to think," he says.

I look away too, but in the other direction, toward the water, trying to match my breathing to the steady in and out of the waves. Though I know where things are heading, it doesn't make it hurt any less.

"I understand," I tell him.

"Joni." He reaches for me, slips his fingers into my hair. I shiver at the contact, and how much I don't want it to end. "Will you walk with me?"

I nod. Kick off my sandals and set them near his shoes, the ones I missed, at the base of the path. We start walking down the beach that seems like it stretches on forever.

"So," he says, sooner than I expected. Diving right in. Ren usually takes his time with his words. "You got fired."

"I got fired," I say through a shaky breath.

I can feel him looking at me, and I glance up at him. His mouth is turned down. On anyone else, I might call it pity, but I know Ren better than that. He's pensive, ready to help if I need it. "What happened?"

"Um," I say, not quite sure how to sum everything up now that I'm finally saying it out loud. "The studio didn't want the movie. We screened it for them and they said it wouldn't read well with audiences, and—and it cost a lot of money, so Ramona had to fire someone. The team I worked with to pitch it—a bunch of us were fired."

Ren is quiet, his lips pursed. "There wasn't any point during production that someone could have told you it wasn't working?"

"No, I know," I say, before we can go too far down that

road. It's crossed my mind too, that Ramona, at any point in the last three years, could have told me it wasn't shaping up how it should be. That some studio head who wandered through to "see how things were coming along" could have thought to themselves that the movie wasn't going to read well with young audiences. I should have trusted the few times I felt things weren't working, like when the lead character didn't read right on camera, or our shooting schedule was always behind because sets and puppets were getting too complicated. I was so desperate to use work as the thing to keep me afloat, that I ignored how my desperation was hurting the work itself. "But they took a risk on us. I wanted to prove we could pull it off."

Ren's head tilts, a ghost of a disbelieving smile playing at one side of his mouth. "You're always defending Novo," he says.

"What?"

He shakes his head. "Just—no part of you is a little mad? All the time you put into that company, and this one mistake—"

"A million-dollar mistake," I cut in.

"Okay," Ren says. "Fine, a million-dollar mistake. But there were a lot of people who approved your idea, who worked on it too. Ramona just let you pour all of yourself into it and then take the fall?"

"It makes sense that they fired me."

"Maybe," Ren says. The sand scratches against my ankles as we walk. "But Novo isn't perfect. I know you've put everything into that company. Your whole life. But this situation isn't all your fault."

His words hit me square in the chest. *Your whole life.*

I had been ignoring the signs, was so determined to prove myself there, to prove to everyone by doing well there that my anxiety didn't rule me anymore, that I didn't see what this singlemindedness was doing to me, not until Ren helped me see it, brought me back to myself. But then when I lost him, it only got worse again, like now I also had to prove it to *myself.*

I thought that if I worked harder, happiness would magically be there waiting on the other side. But it wasn't. Because happiness was never going to come from tying my self-worth to my job. It couldn't come from any one thing. I had to build it, and I hadn't. Life continued on without me.

There have been glimmers this week, small glimpses of some version of me that exists outside of Novo. I thought the week would be one painful lie, but it hasn't been. In a lot of ways, it feels like I'm looking up at my life for the first time in years, that maybe, some cosmic force intervened once it realized I might never do that unless I was forced to. That it happened now, because this place—the house, the beach, the people, Ren—was always going to be what would bring me back to the parts of myself that had gone missing.

It hurts, though. Giving Novo up. Letting it go.

I look over at Ren. His eyes are focused on the sand in front of us. "I just— I had it, you know? This job that I worked so hard for. That I loved, even if it exhausted me. And now I'm almost thirty and what do I have to show for it? This isn't where I'm supposed to be right now."

"You'll have it again. Besides, I think *supposed to be* is highly subjective," Ren says with a knowing smile. When his career path wasn't the same as his siblings', his parents worried, and then when he did find professional success, his mom shifted her sights to marriage. Always the next thing. Always concern that came from a loving place, but piled up to feel like disappointment. But it's always easier to apply that kind of thinking to someone else's life than your own.

"I don't mean to discount how hard it is, though," Ren says, nudging my shoulder. "I wish I could have been there for you." We walk in silence for a minute, our only other company the breeze and soft hush of the waves rolling in. I can feel him glance over at me before he asks it. "Why didn't you tell me?"

I suck in a breath, let it out. "I just got you back," I say, something about last night cracking the remainder of any delicate shell around us. "It felt fragile. And selfishly, I wanted to be happy for a minute."

"I understand," Ren says, jaw working as he nods, his eyes on the ground again. "But I don't think we're all that fragile. Two and a half years didn't do us in."

"Can we sit?" I ask, suddenly exhausted. From waiting so long to have this conversation, from missing him, from trying so hard to figure out how to say what I mean.

Ren follows me toward drier sand, dropping down next to me, his forearms resting on his bent knees, hands dangling between them. I want, more than anything, to lean into him, let his arm come around me, but I know it can't be that simple.

"I'm sorry," I say, tone half-joking. Ren looks quizzically over at me. "I just couldn't not kiss you."

He chuckles, gazes out at the gray ocean. "Joni," he says softly. "I think I'm always going to be waiting for just five minutes of you loving me like I love you."

I turn my head toward him. We've never said things like "I love you" beyond friendship.

Ren's mouth tilts down. "I've never…liked talking to you about other women, relationships, whatever it is. And look, for a while it was just because I thought I liked you in a way that would eventually go away." He lifts a hand, rakes it through his hair once. "But I realized it's because I was comparing all of them to you. Trying to find someone who made me feel like you do. But no one is you."

Hannah's words from Sasha's wedding night echo through me. *Such a good fit for you.* "What about Amanda?" I ask.

Ren nods, looks down at the sand between his legs. "After what happened between us, I thought maybe it could be her. I hoped it could be, because if it couldn't, then I had to be pathetic, right? I'm just someone who's been in love with my best friend since forever and can't get over it."

The revelation races over my skin before settling somewhere deep in me. "Since forever?" I ask.

He looks up at me. "I started to feel it sometime in high school."

I remember how overwhelming it was when my feelings dawned on me at Willow and Martin's wedding. The thought that Ren had been carrying that alone for so much of our lives makes my chest hurt.

"But, Joni," he says, "I knew you didn't feel the same way, and yes, I'm still in love with you, I have been for so long, and I thought about telling you more than once. Before you moved to New York, in Chicago before Lydia and Isaac's wedding. I should have told you in Boston. But I also love you. Care about you more than anyone else. And I don't want you to think our friendship was just some act."

I love him too, still, I know. I never stopped. I don't think any amount of space or time could stop me from loving him. "I don't think that," I say emphatically. "I don't think our friend-ship ever *could* be an act."

"Amanda deserves someone who feels about her the way I feel about you," he continues, eyes on the water. "I decided I would propose to her, back in March. It made sense. I went to look at rings and I just—I saw you everywhere." He sighs, rubs a hand down his face before he drops them both between his knees again. "I tried to shut you out for so long. I told myself that I'd been wrong about us, that we weren't something out of the ordinary, that maybe I just loved you that way because we've been so much a part of each other for so long. But as soon as this other, possible future with someone else actually started to happen, as soon as I decided on it, I couldn't get you out of my head again, and I…" He pauses, gathers his thoughts. "You're it for me, Joni, and maybe there's some day down the line where that isn't true, but it hasn't come yet. No matter how hard I've tried to will it. And the truth of it is that I'd rather be alone than with someone else. Maybe there's something sad in that."

I don't want it to come, I want to say, should say, but Ren isn't done yet.

"I was so scared to see you this week," he says. "After I broke up with Amanda, it was like I was right back to where we started, years ago. Except this time we weren't even friends. It felt like losing you all over again.

"I was so angry with you after you left," he says, and it slices through me, this acknowledgment of what I did to us. "I mean, at first, I was just numb. I couldn't see any way forward. But after a while, I think being mad was the only way to deal with it? I just couldn't comprehend that you didn't even care about our friendship."

"I did care," I say, digging my fingers into the sand.

"I think I knew that. Or I hoped. But it was what I told myself to get out of the hole I was in."

I have to look away, over my shoulder in the direction of the lighthouse. I want to reach into the past, find him where he was after I left, hold him through it. I want to tell him I was in that same hole, always digging deeper down but never any closer to his.

I glance back over at him once I've composed myself. "You didn't seem mad when you got here this week."

Ren's smile is soft, barely there. "I haven't been mad at you for a long time," he says. "I spent a lot of time trying not to think about you, but I wasn't angry anymore. I hoped we might talk this week, I hoped—" He breaks off. "You were right," he says. There's something like regret on his face. "It was too much back then. I'd had years to sit with how I felt, so when we got together, I just assumed it was forever. But it was new for you, and I put too much pressure on you. I expected so much, and I couldn't see that you didn't want it in the same way." His lips press together, then part as he looks at me like he's asking for forgiveness. "I'm so sorry, Joni."

"I wanted it," I say, and Ren's eyes narrow in confusion.

It breaks my heart that he didn't know, that this whole time, he truly believed me when I said it was a mistake. That there wasn't some small part of him that suspected I was lying when I left him, taking what I know now was the easy way out.

The truth finally hurtles out of me. "I heard you talking to your parents that night. About your job offer." I watch his face shift, eyes beginning to clear as he works it out, as that night reorders itself in his head. I offer up the remaining pieces I have. "You were going to give up everything you'd worked for. And you're right, I had just figured out how I felt about you, and it terrified me. It felt so enormous, and I didn't know how to protect it. You. I needed you to be happy, and I knew if I left any door open between us, I'd slip through. I was so close to taking it all back on the sidewalk that night. I *wanted* to be with you, but it just seemed…safer. To cut you out."

It all sounds so foolish now. In my mind, I'd been doing the right thing for both of us. The pain of that night washes over me again, like it did for months after I went back to New York, until it lessened to a subtle, constant ache, like some old wound I carried around that had never healed properly.

Ren's jaw works as he looks out at the water, the sun breaking through the clouds to paint it golden. I want to ask him what he's thinking, but I keep my mouth shut. Give him the same space he's always reserved for me.

"Joni, you've always believed in me," he says. "More than anyone else. About my job, about everything. I might have stopped trying a long time ago if you weren't my best friend, but—" He rubs a hand at his neck. "I would have been fine in New York. Happy, even. My work isn't everything."

I think about that night, how my brain started working against me again. I loved him so much that I let it cloud my judgment. "I'm sorry that I tried to make that decision for you. That I was projecting all my own anxiety onto you," I tell him. "I just… I couldn't think of anything but the worst what-ifs. If you moved and hated me for it. If I hated you for it." I let out a sad laugh. "But the worst possible thing *is* what happened. We didn't speak for—"

"Two and a half years," Ren finishes for me.

If the last few days have shown me anything, it's that time has done nothing to dull my feelings for him. I want what I never gave us an opportunity to have. But I keep coming up against the fact that my life is in free fall right now. I'm unemployed, all my things are in an apartment on the other side of the country, I haven't *actually* dealt with any of the mental fallout of getting fired, what the absence of that work, art will do to me. If Ren and I are going to be together, it has to be different this time.

I look over at him, some tempered kind of hope in my throat. "My life is a mess right now," I say. His face tells me he disagrees, but I continue. "But I don't want this thing between us to be a mess. I know it's a lot to ask, but maybe if we just pause for a little while. Maybe if we're friends again first, and then after I've sorted everything out we can…" It's unfair, I know, to ask him to wait, but I'm worried if I don't at least try, this will be it, the end of our love story.

Ren takes a long time to answer. He stares out at the tide as it slowly begins to make its way back in for so long that I almost know his answer before he says it.

"I thought I'd do anything to be with you," he says, "and I'm sure I'll hate myself for saying this, but I don't know if I can be with you and be worried that every time things get complicated, you might leave again." He pauses, takes a deep breath. "Loving you…it's like my heart exists outside my body, and that just hurts, sometimes. And losing you once… I got this glimpse of a person I didn't want to be. And I'm so afraid of that, Joni. Surviving it once was hard enough. I can't risk losing you again."

I have to bite the inside of my cheek, urge myself to stay steady for him like he always has for me. I love him so much, and I want to give him what he's asking for. "I don't want it to hurt," I say. "For either of us."

He holds his hand out toward me then. I cover his palm with mine, fingers sliding between his. He squeezes, once. "You're still my best friend. And I'm not interested in a life without you in it," he says.

"Neither am I," I say, my heart turning over in my chest like it's trying to beat for the first time. I meet his eyes, the same warm brown eyes I've looked for all my life. In the halls at school, across crowded rooms, on busy sidewalks in a city he wasn't even in.

"I'm sorry—" he says, but I raise a finger to his lips, silencing him.

"I think we've apologized enough." Part of me wants to say more, get to some core we haven't reached yet. But I need to trust what he's telling me, not force a decision on him again. Appreciate the dream this week has been. "We still have today," I say, wanting to preserve it longer. "And I still want you."

He smiles, a laugh exhaling through his nose. "I still want you too."

"Then we enjoy the time we have left," I say, trying to sound cheerful. "And the rest..." I flick a hand toward the vast Pacific in a *que sera, sera* movement. Ren smiles.

His arm comes around my shoulders, and I curl against him, head tucked under his chin, eyes closing.

I want this to be a new start. I want to sort out my mess. Find Ren when I have a clear path forward. I want to have mornings and nights and a *life* with him.

I want this to be a love story.

But there's also this. A quiet moment worth the kind of attention I've been reserving for work. An opportunity to let my thoughts settle. To feel Ren's strong arm around me, to let everything we've just told each other sink in.

I don't know how much time has passed, but soon Sasha is calling Ren on his phone, demanding to know where we are, and we have to move on to the reason we're all here: Stevie and Leo's big day.

We stand slowly, brushing the sand off our pants, stretching our legs. As we amble back in the direction of the house, the sun warming our shoulders, our hands find each other's, holding on tight.

chapter thirty

Sasha's efforts have, once again, paid off. When we get back to the house, everything is running smoothly, if quickly. Thad and Alex are down at the lighthouse, setting up the last of what was delivered yesterday. Hannah and Greg are in town picking up the flowers. My parents are tidying up the house, readying it for relatives planning to stop by before the wedding.

As we enter the kitchen, Sasha gives Ren his car keys and me a steaming mug of coffee. "Kegs are under your name at Clyde's," she says to him as she ushers me out of the room. "Photographer will be here in an hour to take pictures of us getting ready, so you better depuff those eyes," she says to me. "Did you sleep at *all* last night?"

Ren smiles a little wistfully at me before Sasha turns me away.

She herds me upstairs to my parents' room, the one with the best light streaming in through the picture window. As soon as I walk through the door, arms are coming around me with so much force they knock me off-balance. Some of the coffee sloshes out of my mug, and Sasha takes it from me and sets it aside.

"I'm so sorry," Stevie says when she releases me. Her face is all screwed up, nose red. "I didn't mean to tell everyone, it just came out."

Sometimes, Stevie will surprise me with something that fits the classic younger sister stereotype. For the most part, she's just my friend, our age gap small enough that it doesn't make that much of a difference. She's never needed all that much taking care of, for instance. In fact, oftentimes, she's the one who's had to take care of me. But there are moments, like last night, when our birth order comes starkly into view. Case in point: her declaring for the whole world that I'm sleeping with Ren, and her explanation that she *didn't mean to*.

"You could have talked to me about it first," I say as the door closes quietly behind us—Sasha leaving.

Stevie sighs, flops onto the edge of our parents' bed.

"Stevie, you *know* Ren and I being together is a big deal. Exactly the kind of thing Mom would freak out about. I'm not sure it was the *best* moment to bring it up."

"Yes, because she cares so much about you," she says, twirling her engagement ring around on her finger. "Our whole lives, it's always been you Mom worries about."

"Stevie. You don't want Mom to want to be your therapist."

"Maybe sometimes I do," she says, mouth twisting. "Maybe sometimes I do want her to worry about me, just a bit."

I don't answer right away. The picture she's painting is completely at odds with what I've spent so much of my life believing: I needed to escape our mom's worry so I could just *live*, prove to her I was steady enough for her not to read into every detail of my life like I was one of her patients. But Stevie never had this impulse because our mom doesn't ask after her in the same way. If Stevie has a problem, is stressed out, overwhelmed, Stevie just goes to her. I always assumed the difference was because she trusted Stevie to handle things on her own, to speak up if she needed help. But maybe it would begin to feel like my mom cared a little less if she *didn't* ask me so many questions.

"Mom worries about you too," I say. When Stevie protests, I cut in with, "She does. You two have a special bond, so maybe it doesn't always come off that way. But she trusts you in a way she doesn't trust me."

"Well, I am sorry I gave her so much to worry about," Stevie says.

"I get what you mean, though," I tell her, even if I'm still wrapping my head around it. "At least you have the perfect supporter in Leo. I see how well he looks after you."

"Yes, like last night when he asked why I thought our rehearsal dinner was the time to share your secret with everyone. In a very gentle way, of course."

I roll my eyes good-naturedly. "It's okay," I say. "It's not like you made something up."

"Wait, so you and Ren *are* sleeping together?" she asks sarcastically.

"Stevie," I say. "You obviously figured it out."

"Maybe, but you didn't actually tell me any details."

"It's messy," I sigh.

"I have time," Stevie says.

"You literally don't."

"So I look a little tired in my wedding pictures. So what?" I laugh, pull my legs up onto the bed.

Her face softens. "Are you in love with him?" she asks.

I force a smile, my eyes starting to burn. As soon as I saw him in the kitchen that first morning, lit golden, I knew. I tried to convince myself it was just some trick of nostalgia. But the feelings hadn't gone away. As soon as I knew I loved him, they were never going to. "Of course I am," I admit, nervous to be sharing this with Stevie. It makes the fact of me having wasted so much time, of us still not actually being together too real.

When Stevie came home after Sasha's wedding, crawled into

bed next to me and hugged me silently while I cried, or when she called me every day for months after I flew back to New York, always asking if I was okay and not pushing in her usual fashion, I felt like I was letting her down by not being able to share any of what happened with her. More than that, I was ashamed of what I'd done, how I'd handled things with Ren and everyone. And telling her this now makes it something to discuss, dissect, brings to light all the ways I could have been better. It means my conversation on the beach with Ren is confirmed, final.

"Took you a while," she says. She leans back, mouth twisting to one side as she thinks. "I guess I just thought that when you and Ren finally got together, it would be forever."

"Yeah," I say softly. "Turns out it's all a little more complicated than that."

"Why?"

I shrug a shoulder, looking at my sister. For all of her idiosyncrasies, she always knows what she wants. To go to school in New York. To move back to Oregon. To marry Leo. "I don't know what my life looks like anymore," I say, though I'm not totally sure how true that is now. There's something murky beginning to take shape in my mind. I just can't distinguish its parts yet.

"Are you okay?" she asks. "Novo was everything to you."

"Not everything," I point out, because it's true, even if it seemed like it. Even if I let it be, there were still so many other things that mattered. I just shut them out to make room for the thing that I felt like I had the most control over. "I'll be okay. I just don't think I can jump into something with the way my life is going right now. And I might have caused too much damage when I left last time. I don't think he trusts me in the same way." I glance down at my hands, back up at Stevie. "Maybe friends is all we're supposed to be."

Stevie rolls her eyes, not like she's exasperated, but like she's rolling them at what she's about to reveal. She steels her shoulders, takes my hand in hers. "Listen," she says. "I'm only going to say this once because I feel like I've doled out more affection than my weekly quota allows—you have something that's kind of a miracle." Her eyes are going watery now, and I need her to stop. If Stevie cries, I'll cry, and then we'll really be on Sasha's shit list. "I've grown up watching you and Ren be this example of the kind of love I always wanted. You two are each other's center in this way that doesn't just happen. And look, I know someone might say it makes sense, you grew up together, but I don't know if it's just that. A lot of people spend their lives together without ever really knowing each other or ever really loving each other, but you two are this thing entirely your own.

"Neither of you have been yourselves since Sasha's wedding. And I've felt like I needed to be neutral—not tell you when he moved in with Amanda, not tell him when you tried dating again—but you're just half of yourselves without each other. You can still be happy like that, I know, but after seeing you two together, it's like you just shut down when things fell apart. And I know I don't know exactly what happened, why it fell apart. But I love you both so much, and all I've wanted for so much of my life is for you two to be together." She sniffles, almost laughs. "I think that might be why I did what I did last night. I thought that maybe, deep down, I was helping."

"I mean," I say. I'm going to be a puddle soon, no longer a body, just raw emotion. Stevie's announcement was abrupt, but it might have been the thing Ren and I needed to get everything out in the open instead of ignoring it until it blew up in our faces. "It did force us to talk."

"I know that I'm getting married today, so I'm really into this love stuff, but I just think you should try, if you can. People spend their whole lives looking for something that comes close to it."

I'm searching for a response to this when a light knock on the door saves me. It swings partially open, our mom poking her head in. "Can I join you?" she asks, and Stevie waves her over to the bed.

"Are you talking about—" she asks, and at Stevie's nod, she quiets, reaching out to cup a hand under my chin.

I shrug her off, suddenly tense now that she's here. "It's Stevie's wedding day. We don't need to talk about me anymore."

"Sweetie," my mom says. "Why don't you want to talk to me?"

There's a reason I haven't tried to have a conversation about our relationship with her. How do you tell someone their well-meaning worry is stifling you, pushing you farther away? If I didn't give her anything to analyze, there was a chance she could just be my mom.

"I want to talk to you, Mom," I tell her. "It's just— Sometimes I want to be able to tell you things without you worrying it means I'm spiraling. I can handle my life, truly. And I appreciate your worry, I do, but sometimes it makes me feel like you don't always trust what I'm telling you."

There's a glimmer of recognition in her eyes that thaws some of the distance between us. She smooths a hand over my head, grabs Stevie's free one. "I love my girls," she says. "I think that sometimes I worry I'm not doing enough."

"Mom," I say. "You're *always* doing more than enough."

She gives me a watery smile. "I just wanted to help you," she says. "When things first got bad. And when I couldn't—I think I doubled down. I felt helpless."

"You're a great mom," I tell her. "You do help me. But maybe we can all stop worrying about being the best version of ourselves and just, I don't know. Talk to each other."

My mom nods, then, almost sheepishly, asks, "Can I just ask one question?"

"Mom," Stevie says.

"No, it's okay." I put a hand on Stevie's knee. She's right. I don't let our mom in like she does. I've never given her all of me. And maybe I never will be able to, maybe that's the point: that everyone is going to get some version of you, except for the person who gets everything, if you're lucky. But I've been assuming so much on the part of the people who love me that I've held them at arm's length. Even when everything fell apart. Even when I needed them most. I want my mom to ask me questions, just not question me. I want to answer them, but I also want to tell her when it's too much.

"Do you know what you're going to do?" she says.

If there was ever a question to open with, I guess it might be that. The elephant in the room. *Joni's life just fell apart.*

"Um," I say, wobbling. "Well—"

"You can move in with Leo and me!" Stevie bursts in, clutching my hand. "Oh my god, we'll be gone for three months, and you can get all settled into the office—it's tiny, but you can totally fit a twin bed in there—and then when we get back, we could be *roommates*, and—"

"Stevie," our mom cuts in, eyes staying on my face. "Maybe Joni wants some time to figure it out for herself."

This is part of what's wonderful and terrible about this place: it lets you forget about things for a while, regroup when something has gone wrong, but it spits you out on the other side having not faced it. "That's so scary, though," I say, tears brimming.

"Maybe," she says, swiping a thumb across my cheekbone. "But I think you're going to be just fine."

We curl closer together, and I let them wrap their arms around me. When I apologize for this mess, they both shush me.

Eventually, I'm sitting up straighter, eyes cleared, smiling.

"Now, when were you going to tell me you'd finally realized you were in love with Ren?" my mom asks.

"Did everyone know?" I groan, laughter bubbling out of me when they both smile. "Someone could have *told* me."

"You wouldn't have believed us if we tried," my mom says. The door flies open.

"The photographer will be here in fifteen minutes!" Sasha shouts. When her eyes land on me, she throws her hands up in the air, stalks toward us. "Oh, for heaven's sake," she says, crouching down on the floor at the foot of the bed to join our huddle.

We fold around each other again and, after a while, I feel Sasha settle her cheek on my knee. When she finally leans away, she has to swipe a hand over wet cheeks.

"Sash," I say, grabbing her hand. I don't know if I've ever actually seen her cry. "What's going on?"

"Oh, you know," she sniffs from her spot on the floor. "Weddings always bring out the emotions in everyone." But when her gaze meets my mom's, her face falls again. "Do you and my mom tell each other everything?" she asks.

"This family loves secrets," my mom says.

Sasha's hand is still in mine, and I feel her palm tense before she looks almost apologetically at Stevie. "I wasn't going to tell anyone else for a while. It's still so early, so there's a lot that could go wrong," she says. "But I'm pregnant."

Stevie shrieks, sliding off the end of the bed to pull Sasha into a hug. I feel like I did when we first found out about Katie: some sort of awe at the fact there would be a whole new human in our family, that time keeps diligently passing and bringing so many changes with it.

I move to the floor to hug her too, then realize she's still crying. She looks at me and waves a hand. "I'm fine," she says, then, at some expression my mom shoots her, "I am. I'm just— I had this whole plan. I was going to get pregnant when we owned a bigger place and I could take more time off work and none of that will happen for at least another two years, and you're supposed to be so excited that you're having a baby, but

I'm freaking out and—" She breaks off, pressing her face into her hands. "We aren't supposed to be talking about this during your wedding, Stevie."

"Have you seen what's going on around here?" Stevie asks. "Please, let it out. If anyone has anything else they want to share, I'm all ears. Besides, you've done a remarkable job hiding it."

"Really?" Sasha asks, lifting her face and looking at my sister. "I feel like I've been a huge bitch. I wanted everything to go as planned this week, but that also meant I didn't let myself absorb what was happening to me. It'd only been a week since I found out, and I was trying to act fine. And then I felt sick the next morning at Fern's, and it all just hit me." I remember, suddenly, Sasha almost throwing up in the flower beds on the way to breakfast. I'd been so distracted that morning that I'd forgotten she hadn't been drinking the night before, that she couldn't be hungover.

"You mean when you told Thad he's a terrible father?"

"Stevie," I say.

"Sorry."

"It's okay, she's right," Sasha says. She nestles against my side, leans back against my mom's knees. "I talked to Thad. We're good. It wasn't fair of me to take it out on him."

"I bet he's so excited," I say. "You'll all be in LA together."

Sasha almost rolls her eyes. "I think he's almost as excited to be Uncle Thad as he was to be a father."

"You're going to be a great mom, Sash," Stevie says, snuggling against her. "You'll have the most badass baby."

Sasha slouches further, so I can put my chin on top of her head. And then, her voice muffled, makes us all descend into much-needed laughter: "Joni, I'm really sorry I bet on you and my brother, but I'm not sorry that I was right."

≈

Stevie and Leo say "I do" as the sun lowers behind them and casts them in a golden glow. Leo's face is tear streaked, because of course he was always going to be the crier between the two of them. Stevie beams at him, the white flowers embroidered on the overlay of her dress picking up the fading light.

I catch Ren's eye behind Leo. He's already watching me, like he's cataloging my response to the ceremony, understanding his own reaction in relation to mine, the same way, I realize, that I often did with him. His gaze races through me, searing into my heart, and then Leo is dipping Stevie for a kiss, and we're all cheering and laughing, and another tiny moment I want to hang on to is gone.

The night is perfect in all the ways it should be. It's like I've sloughed off some skin and am feeling everything *more*. Like I've wandered back into some room I'd left only to find everyone I love is still there, waiting for me. I'm laughing, tearing up, flat out crying at how wonderful it all is. Sasha leans into Alex, content; Ren holds Katie and makes her shriek with laughter; Thad and Gemi talk happily with Oliver; my dad and Greg stand at the edge of the bluff like they're keeping watch over the ocean; Hannah and my mom meander through it all, arms around each other; Stevie and Leo don't let go of each other for more than a second.

Once dancing has gotten underway, all of us—our families, even Leo's, the band—dance in a huge circle to "Come On Eileen," cheers echoing into the night and onto the waves below, floating out along the surface of the ocean. Ours is just a small, bright spot on the edge of the continent, on the earth, but to me, it contains everything.

When a slow song comes on, Ren finds me at the edge of

the dance floor. Wordlessly, he pulls me to the middle of it and moves my body into his until I give in, relaxing against him.

I tip my head back to smile up at him, cup the back of his neck. "Don't they play this song at every wedding?" I ask as "I Will Follow You into the Dark" rolls out of the speakers above us.

"For good reason," Ren says with a shrug. "Says what a lot of people can't."

His words lodge into my heart. I think about all the ways he's sound-tracked my life, tried to tell me things I didn't know to look for in his meticulous playlists. If I study our lives, gather up all the moments I thought Ren wasn't sharing all of himself with me, I realize I was just missing all the ways he was trying to.

Music for every fleeting feeling, even the ones I didn't know were coming yet.

Keeping our plus-one tradition alive.

An *I love you* in a photo booth.

"You seem happy," he murmurs, brushing behind my ear a strand of hair that's come loose from the many bobby pins Sasha stabbed into it earlier.

"I am," I say. "I'm so happy right now."

I lay my head against his chest and he holds me to him until the song ends, then through the next one too. A part of me hopes this moment might stretch on forever, our life one never-ending playlist. But it's gone too soon, just like every part of today, and before we know it, we're doing the send-off—ceremonial, because Stevie and Leo are staying at the house tonight—and grabbing sparklers from a table for them to run under.

Later, after we've all danced again until our feet hurt and sat at the swiftly emptying tables sipping champagne, we all wander back up the path to the house. Arms are slung around shoulders and eyes are tired. Greg points out the sky already turning gray behind the house and we let out a collective groan at how little sleep we'll get. But no one sounds that unhappy about it. My mom hugs me good-night at the door, and I don't let go when she starts to pull away, hold on to her for a minute longer.

On the screen porch, Ren has already taken off his suit jacket. I leave my heels by the door as I step into the room, and he looks up with those soft brown eyes, and I wonder if there's still any chance we'll ever get to be that miracle Stevie said we were, or if this moment is all that's left of that part of us, and we'll continue on loving each other as we always have. In a different, but no less important way.

I don't know what the future will bring, but I know what I want right now. I walk over to him, slowly unbutton his shirt. I've never loved someone like I love Ren. Like every time we come back together, we're discovering each other anew again.

I slip his shirt off his shoulders, and he goes still, something silent working behind his eyes. I don't chase it, let him think through it on his own. And then his face changes, and he reaches around me and unzips my dress, draws his knuckles down my spine.

When all of our clothes are gone, cast to the floor, he picks me up, lays me down on his bed, and everything is hushed. Ren's lips are on my sternum and then mine on his hip and then all the parts of each other our bodies know like they've touched this way a thousand times.

SUNDAY

chapter thirty-one

Everything moves quickly. Ren and I probably only sleep for an hour or two, and by the time we blink awake there's already commotion in the house. We scramble to get dressed, shoving things into suitcases, going where we're needed to help clean up, gather gifts, get the house in order. Stevie and Leo are off to a four-day honeymoon on San Juan Island before the tour starts. Sasha and Alex have to be back in Portland to catch their flight by five; Thad, Gemi, and Katie are spending a few days with Hannah and Greg at their house. Ren is helping to drive some of Stevie and Leo's presents back to their apartment this afternoon.

My flight leaves at two, so after stuffing the last of the twinkle lights into my parents' car, I grab my bags and head back to the rental car from hell. Everyone is out front, in various states of hungover, ready to hug goodbye and send me off.

"You could live here for a while, if you needed to," Hannah says after she's let me go. "Get things settled."

"Thank you," I say, hesitant, not sure she liked what she heard at the rehearsal dinner.

"Joni," she says, sensing it. "You do what makes you happy."

My eyes drift over her shoulder to where Ren is talking to Thad on the porch. Hannah turns to follow my gaze, then back to me. "I hope that what Stevie meant is that he finally got it together and told you how he feels. I didn't bet on you, but I've been hoping."

My forehead creases in confusion, and Hannah's mouth curves into a chastened smile. "Amanda's wonderful," she says. "But she's not you. And I wanted him to find some way to be happy, if the two of you weren't going to be together."

I don't have the heart to tell her that we're not. Together. Instead, I hug her one last time before I move on to my dad, my mom, everyone else heading back inside to get things together.

Ren is the last one, standing near my bumper. He'd come down the porch stairs when I was saying goodbye to my dad, leaned against my car in a pair of faded jeans and the same gray T-shirt he arrived in, a classic Ren outfit if I've ever seen one.

"I'll call you," I say in his ear as I hug him. He holds me tighter, and I breathe him in, squeeze my eyes shut when they begin to burn.

"I could drive you," he says once we pull apart. There's something conflicted on his face, like he doesn't want to say goodbye either. "We could talk. We—"

"We will," I say, stopping him. "We'll talk. I'm not just leaving again." Even as I say it, it feels like I am.

I watch him in the rearview as I drive away, until the break in the trees closes. Until he disappears from sight.

Every mile that stretches between us aches, and about halfway to Portland I can't hold the tears back any longer. For Ren, sure, but also for me. For all the mistakes I've made. For how long I've spent ignoring my life in favor of giving everything to a job that was never going to love me back. For every time I've ignored a phone call from my mom when I should have picked up, because I didn't want to answer any of her questions. For not confiding in Stevie sooner. For all the time I've wasted not paying close enough attention to the things that matter most. I've thought for so long that proving I could do it on my own was the most important thing, but in the end, it's letting myself need people that's started to bring me back to myself. That's going to carry me forward from here.

I wipe my eyes and return the rental car, check my bag before heading through security. I'm in leggings and, I realize too late, Ren's black hoodie. He'd put it on me at four in the morning, half-asleep, scooping me up into his chest when I shivered against him.

At the security line, the TSA agent asks if I'm wearing anything underneath it, and I have to strip down to my tank top, hold my arms up in the machine. I watch the bin with Ren's sweatshirt like a hawk as it goes through the scanner, lunge for it as soon as I can and slip it back over my head.

I wander toward my gate, grab a coffee on the way. I find a seat, tuck my knees to my chest, and pull the hood of his sweatshirt on, and with it comes an onslaught of every memory from this week. Ren in the kitchen, seeing him again for the first time. Ren at the winery across from me, sunglasses shielding his expression. Ren's voice coming out of the dark, and his body against mine during capture the flag, his hands on my hips that night on the beach. His arm around me yesterday morning, everything laid bare between us.

It strikes me as ridiculous, suddenly, that I asked him to wait. That as soon as he said he was worried I'd run if things got hard, I didn't tell him he is the only thing I want right now, or ever, no matter how messy or undecided my life is.

I catch sight of a couple sitting near the windows, where planes are taxiing and people are getting ready to depart, to carry on with their lives. They're laughing, leaning into one another, their faces together.

I've been wasting so much time worrying about what could go wrong that I never paused to consider everything that could go right. Every way life could continue to be beautiful, with Ren. There will always be something complicated, but that's the point: I want to face those things *with* him.

I pull my phone from my bag, dial Ren's number, but it goes straight to voicemail, my heart dropping. I've still never told him I love him. He said it yesterday, on the beach, and I didn't say it back. I guess I assumed it was obvious, the way it was to everyone else.

"Hi," I say to his voicemail, just as the gate attendant announces our boarding, loudly. I raise my voice over it, avoiding the stares of the travelers around me. "I know you're probably on the road. Or maybe you're like, halfway to somewhere else, taking a second for yourself." It all comes out quickly then. "I didn't handle things like I should have before. I shouldn't have run from you. From us. I know I can't change what I did, but I can say I'm sorry for not trying to fix it sooner. And I'm never going to leave you like that again, but I did forget to tell you that I love you. That I'm in love with you too. And I'm sorry I didn't tell you sooner.

"But I want you to know that, even when I didn't know, it doesn't mean I didn't love you that way. It's always been us. It just took me a while longer to figure it out. I think that maybe you've always been the smarter of the two of us. Anyway," I say, as another announcement rattles out overhead. "I'm getting on a plane, and I love you, and I already miss you so much. Like, there was just a guy in line at bag check with a sock stuck to his pants and I was going to tell him but then he was such a dick to the airline agent and—this isn't important. I just wanted you to be there. I wanted you to witness it with me and I want to witness everything with you. And I know I messed it up before, but I don't want to waste any more time. I want you, and I want to figure everything out together, no matter how messy. So, that's all, okay—I better go before I tell you another stupid story or the voicemail cuts off, so bye. Bye."

I hang up, a ringing in my ears.

That's it, I tell myself. That's all I can do.

It's what I tell myself as I cue up the playlist Ren shared with me for my flight, the first one he's made me in years, "Mr. Brightside" the opening song.

What I tell myself through my entire flight.

When I check my phone after landing, and I still don't have anything from him.

On the car ride back to my apartment.

When I fall asleep that night with my phone next to my face, just in case.

MONDAY

chapter thirty-two

The next morning, back in New York, I trudge out for groceries to last me through a day of packing. Ren still hasn't called or texted, but instead of obsessing, I've made a game plan. I'm moving back to Portland.

I could feel my body missing Oregon as soon as I got on the plane yesterday, like the West Coast was calling me back to it. I'll sublet for the rest of my apartment lease here and live in Stevie and Leo's shoebox office until I get my feet under me. I'm determined that will happen within three months, so I don't bother them when they get back from Leo's tour. I'm going to find a job in the city that made me fall in love with stop-motion in the first place: where my commitment to Novo was formed and where I took the first steps to make art not just the thing that calms my mind, but my career. If it means making coffee while I freelance, working the front desk of an art gallery, calling up some of the Novo people who stayed behind when the Portland office closed and seeing if they know of anyone's friend of a friend of a friend who needs help with some unpaid project, I'll do it. I'll make it work.

But I'll also look up. I'll take advantage of living in a place that feels so much like mine. I'll spend time with the people I love. I'll carve out space in my brain that I don't need to immediately fill, give myself time to discover new things to care about, to take up those empty spots.

I'll find my way back to Ren, whatever that looks like. Even if it means swallowing past the way his eyes make my heart work overtime, getting used to only having him in my dreams. It's what he had to do for so long, after all. Maybe friends is all we were ever really meant to be. Maybe timing really is such a bitch.

But the love that comes with our friendship won't go away. Ren was right: it survived two and a half hurt, shoved-down years, and a lifetime of twisting and bending and reshaping before that. It's spanned miles and other relationships and missed opportunities. It was never going to be something I could control, but we can keep choosing it, promise each other that no matter what, we won't turn our backs on it again.

It's this, the knowledge that he'll still be my friend, that I'm stuck on when I walk home, hit the first step to my apartment door, digging my keys out of my tote bag. I look up to avoid tripping, and my heart skips a beat as eyes—red-rimmed and exhausted—meet mine.

"What are you—" I say, breath catching in my throat at the sight of Ren sitting on my front stoop. Did he get my voicemail? I never thought about what I would actually say if he returned my call, just hoped that he would.

He stands, towering over me as he always has. "I tried to catch you in Portland," he says. "I got in the car to go after you, but didn't realize I hadn't charged my phone last night, so I couldn't call you, and you were already gone by the time I got to the airport, and I couldn't get on a flight until the evening and it had this terrible overnight layover in Chicago and by then I realized I'd left my charger at the beach house and some lady with this truly heinous kid finally let me borrow hers for a minute so I got your voicemail but then the plane was taking off and it died again somewhere over Ohio, and—"

"Ren," I say, something blooming in the center of my chest at how he's rambling, so unlike him.

"I'm sorry," he says. "The rehearsal dinner, Joni, just the way everything that happened between us was suddenly out in the open—it felt like that night at Sasha's wedding all over again. We had this wonderful thing and then it was all falling apart.

"But watching you drive away yesterday also reminded me of that night. It felt like maybe you would just be gone again. Like I was saying goodbye to the most important thing in my life."

His shoulders tense beneath his T-shirt, like he thinks there's a chance I might deny it when he says, "You love me."

"I do," I say, the confession coming easily because it's the truth. "I love you so much, Ren. And I'm sorry I didn't tell you sooner. You said it's like your heart exists outside of you, and I get that. I understand how scary it is. But it's you, Ren, of course it is, and I don't need to get my life in order, I don't need to wait until everything's perfect. I was just afraid, of what all this mess I'm still dealing with might do to us. But—" I break off, worried I've said too much. He's still watching me, face betraying nothing, and maybe I got it wrong. Maybe it doesn't matter if I say it out loud. There are still so many things that could go awry, after all. All those years ago I still made a decision that hurt us, even if it was the best I could do at the time. "But we can just be friends," I say. "I just… I needed to tell you. I never told you."

Ren takes a careful step toward me. He draws in a breath like he's readying himself. "I'll be your friend, if that's what you want. If something's changed since you left me that voice-mail. I'm not going anywhere," he says, taking another step closer, sliding one cautious hand into mine. "But if you meant what you said, if you want this, I'm here for all of the mess. Whatever that looks like. I'll fly here every weekend. Or I'll help you pack up your apartment and ship it across the country and hold your hand on the flight back. Or pack it all into a U-Haul and take two weeks to drive it back to Oregon and stop wherever we want along the way. Or, if you don't know yet, if you want to move to Omaha or Idaho or Spain, then I'll spend everything I have on plane tickets or invent teleportation, break the laws of physics just so I can fall asleep with you every night. Whatever you want, Joni, because honestly, I'm just so fucking tired of not being with you."

It feels, at first, like something has burst inside me, the walls of some vital organ giving out, and I worry for a split second that there isn't enough room not just in my body but in the whole world for loving Ren.

I thought that maybe I wasn't *supposed* to love him, that by doing so I would be risking something fundamental to both of us. But now, with Ren here, standing in my life, the one I know for certain doesn't fit me anymore, I see our story for what it is: cool nights and warm hands and soft brown eyes and arcade games and laughter and *memory, memory, memory* with every rapidly increasing beat of my heart.

I don't waste any more time now. I step forward, press the tips of my fingers to the tattoo we share, twin lines tying us together. "I love you," I tell him again. "And I'm so fucking tired of not being with you too. So what do you say?"

Ren's mouth twitches into that skeptical half grin of his, but there's something more to it right now. Something soft and vulnerable and full of hope. "To what, Joni?"

I smile. "To us."

His arms come around me, and I can feel the thrum of his pulse against my chest, can count every shade of brown in his eyes.

He dips his face close to mine, like he's about to kiss me, but pauses. "I decided on us a long time ago, Miller," he says.

He kisses me then, my heart lighting up as we take the first step into the next part of our story. Every memory that came before this one and all the ones yet to be made stretch out around us, but the most important moment is here. Now.

ONE YEAR LATER

"Finally!" I cheer, clapping a hand on the side of Ms. Pac-Man as *High Score!* slides across the screen. I toggle to our letters, the top slots all RAJ again. "Can't *believe* you didn't defend our good name while I was away," I say.

"Had a few other things on my mind," Ren says, smiling shyly. He slides a hand under my freshly trimmed hair and rubs at the back of my neck. I melt into it, his thumb working over a sore spot. "We're getting you a better work chair this weekend."

"I *have* a work chair," I say.

"A kitchen stool is not a work chair, Joni," he says.

Nine months ago, after weeks of getting in touch with people, trying to promote myself in a way I was painfully unfamiliar with, I got my first freelance job. It was for a travel company in Portland that wanted to do an ad highlighting all of the best tourist spots in Oregon. Four little stop-motion animals, outfitted with backpacks and hats, tiny maps, made their way around a tiny stop-motion city. It was more work than I'd ever done on my own before, but over the course of the project, I made sure to put the work down and do all the things it takes to build a life. I grabbed drinks with old friends, and flew to

Los Angeles with Ren to visit his siblings. I joined the trivia team with the band, Stevie, and Ren (Stevie was wrong about the maximum number), and started to sometimes, occasionally, not-actually-all-that-often, go with Ren on his runs in the mornings. I picked up and finished books, explored new corners of Portland. I let myself lean on the people in my life when I needed them.

Because my job is freelance and not always steady, I also spend three mornings a week working at a coffee shop/gallery/ (as luck would have it) twinkle light retailer down the street from the house Ren finished most of the major renovations on last December. The one I moved into after bouncing between there and Stevie and Leo's apartment, viewing and applying for and being denied or priced out of place after place, where on New Year's Day, Ren and I opened a bottle of champagne on our living room floor, toasting to a new chapter.

Our house, he reminded me.

"I like this neck," Ren says now in the darkness of the arcade, kissing the side of it. "I kind of want you to keep it."

"I'll look at chairs," I tell him, sinking into him.

He sets two more quarters on the machine. "One more game?" he asks, looking at me with an inviting angle to his head.

"Just one?" I turn around, press up onto my toes to let him kiss me against the machine. "How about five?"

Ren laughs softly, fingers scraping up my neck to knit into my hair. Something I've discovered about Ren over the last year: he's always finding ways to touch me, whether it's the edge of his hand against mine, or a kiss brushed against my shoulder, or a palm splayed across my stomach. Something I've discovered about myself in the last year is that I'm always chasing after it, leaning against him in grocery store aisles and cupping his knee on car rides home, folding my arms around his waist while he cooks, closing my eyes at the rise and fall of his breath.

There's still a lot I don't know. For instance, I don't know when or if I'll be able to quit the coffee shop and focus on what I love. I don't know when Stevie and Leo will move out of their apartment, or how my relationship with my mom will continue to change.

If we'll all be able to get to the beach house again at the same time.

I also don't know that, after two more games, Ren will pull out not a quarter, but a ring from his pocket, and set it on the machine in front of me, and that I'll cry, a *lot*, in the middle of this, frankly, kind of shitty bar.

What I do know is that I have all the love in me that I ever needed. I knew that my and Ren's love story would be different than our friendship, but I hadn't anticipated just how many new corners of my heart I would uncover, like a house remodeled, just waiting for us to fill it. All the nights we spend lying on the floor, listening to music but also to each other's hearts beating. All the events we go to together as real plus-ones. All the times I remind myself that, yes, life is still *life*, there are hard days and challenges and we will always be works in progress, but we'll do it together. That this stretch I feel in my chest all the time isn't scary, but wonderful, my body making room for all the people and places and jobs and experiences I'll love in my lifetime.

The first on that list, of course, is the man standing next to me, who has known me through it all, every iteration, every ugly, beautiful thing.

★ ★ ★ ★ ★

acknowledgments

When people say it takes a village to get a book out into the world, they *mean* it, and I have some of the very best people to thank.

An enormous, never-ending thank-you to the agent of my dreams, Kristy Hunter, for all of your kindness, support, and excitement about everything, and for loving and believing in Ren and Joni. This book wouldn't exist if you hadn't fought for it the way you did, which included convincing me not to shelve it when it looked like it might not find its home—no small thing. I can't tell you how grateful I am that these are the characters I'm debuting with. You made my whole big dream come true.

The biggest thank-you to the editor, also of my dreams, Melanie Fried, who saw what this book was and tirelessly, patiently, skillfully turned it into the best version of itself. You made this story so much bigger than I ever thought it could be. Thank you for talking on the phone for hours on end, for just trying so many things to see if they worked and being okay rerouting if/when they didn't, for loving and understanding these characters and this story the way you do. You've made me a better writer. I can't thank you enough for that, and I'm honestly just thrilled every day I get to work with you.

Thank you to everyone at Canary Street, including but not limited to Lindsey Reeder, Alexandra McCabe, Leah Morse, Riffat Ali, Amy Wetton, and Gina Macedo. A huge thank-you to everyone else on the marketing, sales, subrights, publishing, and production teams who worked behind the scenes, as well as everyone on the Knight Agency team. I'm overwhelmed by and in awe of everything that goes into making a book and all the work you do.

Thank you to Sandra Chiu for creating the most perfect cover. I truly couldn't believe it when I found out you would be the one bringing Ren and Joni to life. I want to look at this cover all the time. I do look at it all the time. You are so ridiculously talented!

I wouldn't be able to write about *any* kind of friendship without having personally won the friendship lottery. You're all such cool, smart, funny, kind, generally amazing humans and I don't know what I did to deserve you.

Michelle and Aline, two of my favorite New Yorkers, sisters, influencers, general humans, thank you for your endless, enthusiastic support—I'm going to listen to the voice memo you sent when you saw the cover every day for the rest of my life. I can't wait to cheer on every amazing thing you both do in the same way you've cheered on this book: inexhaustibly and louder than anyone.

Shelby, if you hadn't knocked the entirety of *Hot Fuss* back and forth on our shared dorm room wall with me, helped me research Massachusetts senate races (even if that book will never see the light of day), or sat through my literal hundreds of "I'm writing another book!" Snaps, Ren and Joni might not exist outside my computer. I know I promised you a dedication—I hope this can be a placeholder until that day.

Ciera, you're my constant reminder that if you feel like you'd be best friends with someone, you should probably chase that. Thank you for listening to me in my worst moments and being there for the best. Thank you for picking up the phone every time our queen and savior Taylor Swift does literally anything.

Georgie, our origin story makes me believe the universe pays attention sometimes. Thank you for so many things, but right now, for being patient with me while I edited this book and talked endlessly about it all the way from California to Montana (and on FaceTime before and after that too), for agreeing Seth Cohen is the blueprint, really, just for existing. I love you forever, petunia peach.

To Mom, Dad, Anna, and Beth, thank you for seeing me through everything it took to get to this point. Beth, thank you for letting me copy you my whole life and for staying home on Saturday nights with me and for introducing me to Guy Patterson, who is also the blueprint. Anna, thank you for whispering *The Voyage of The Dawn Treader* to me in hotel rooms and for sharing your sense of humor with me. I hope Joni does justice to the older sister shoes I've never had to fill. Mom and Dad, thank you for supporting your three daughters exploring so many different things, even when you probably wanted us to just pick one thing. Also, I'm sorry, but Levi and I love hanging out with you. You can't change it! Let's go to London! There's a book to celebrate! Really, though, I couldn't write the wonderful parts of a family without coming from what I firmly believe is the best one. I'm the luckiest to be one of you.

Finally, thank you to Levi for making every moment something worth writing about. I know this is short, but there's too much to say, and I'll tell you later anyway. I'll leave it at this: you are, above all, my best friend.

friends to lovers: the playlist

"Walk"—Griff
"Don't You (Forget About Me)"—Simple Minds
"Supercut"—Lorde
"You're Gonna Go Far"—Noah Kahan
"Thirteen"—Big Star
"That's Where I Am"—Maggie Rogers
"Always, Joni"—Trousdale
"Where do we go now?"—Gracie Abrams
"It's Nice To Have A Friend"—Taylor Swift
"Love You Like That"—Dagny
"True Love"—Hovvdy
"Mr. Brightside"—The Killers

https://bit.ly/FriendstoLoversPlaylist